Sissy!

Book One of the Jessica Radford Trilogy

by

Tom Mach

D0556333

Lawrence, Kansas

SISSY!
Book One of the Jessica Radford Trilogy

Published by:

Hill Song Press
P. O. Box 486
Lawrence, KS 66044
www.hillsongpress.com

Library of Congress Control Number: 2003097633

Publisher's Cataloging-in-Publication

Mach, Tom.
    Sissy! : book one of the Jessica Radford trilogy / by Tom Mach
    p. cm. – (The Jessica Radford trilogy: book 1)
    ISBN 0-9745159-2-2

1. Kansas—History—Civil War, 1861-1865—Fiction
2. United States—History—Civil War, 1861-1865.
3. Women pioneers—Fiction.
4. Historical fiction

I. Title

PS3613.A224S57 2004   813'.6
                             QB133-1633

First printing: November, 2003
Second printing: July, 2004
Third printing: November, 2006

The cover for *SISSY!* is from
a painting done by renowned
Kansas artist Ernst Ulmer

Acknowledgments

There are many people to whom I am indebted for *Sissy!*. I greatly appreciate Ernst Ulmer, the famous Kansas artist, for doing the painting represented on my cover. I would also like to thank Karen Sells Brown in Topeka for carefully editing my work as well as making her keen suggestions. I could not have written this book without the encouragement of my fellow writers in the Kansas Authors Club and helpful writers I have met in various critique groups. I thank the fine people in the Kenneth Spencer Research Library, the Lawrence Public Library, the Douglas County Historical Museum, and the Kansas State Historical Society for their invaluable insight into historical events in Kansas in the 1860s. Above all, I would like to thank my dear wife Virginia for her wonderful encouragement throughout my writing career.

"No place in the broad Union has had so conspicuous a history in the progress of slavery emancipation and the events of the war as Lawrence, the county seat of Douglas County. In early days it was by general consent called the 'City of Freedom,' and was really, during the slavery agitation of 1854-5-6, the only place in the territory where it was safe to speak against the institution of slavery. Its thrilling history of suffering, preceding and during the war, has given it the significant appellation of the 'Historic City.'"

Kansas State Board of Agriculture
First Biennial Report

Foreword

It was the bitter turmoil in Kansas—and not the firing at South Carolina's Fort Sumter—that precipitated the Civil War. After passage of the Kansas-Nebraska Act of 1854, people from the North and South settled in Kansas Territory, and strong, ideological differences about slavery resulted in violence—giving true meaning to the term "Bleeding Kansas." John Brown, a controversial figure in the late 1850s, inflamed the public mind about the evils of slavery and led groups of men to fight against proslavery factions. While controversy reigned over whether Kansas Territory should join the Union as a free state, the Free State Hotel was built in Lawrence, Kansas, as temporary quarters for settlers from Massachusetts and other eastern states. But in 1856, the Free State Hotel was burned to the ground by proslavery forces led by the infamous Sheriff Sam Jones. It was rebuilt by Colonel Shalor Eldridge, who added another floor to the newly named Eldridge Hotel, vowing to add another floor each time this hotel was destroyed.

During this time, the Underground Railroad, a movement involved in transporting thousands of slaves to freedom, was active. In *Sissy!*, a fictional Topeka, Kansas, man named Otto Heller is typical of the people in the Underground Railroad who risked their own lives to shepherd slaves to freedom.

Antislavery publishers did their part in forming public opinion. John Speer, for example, started the *Kansas Pioneer*, the first antislavery newspaper distributed in Lawrence, Kansas. He went on later to edit the *Kansas Weekly Tribune* in Lawrence. Thanks to Speer as well as other abolitionist leaders, Kansas became a free state in 1861, abutting proslavery Missouri to the east. As a result, border wars intensified. Jayhawkers from Kansas embarked on freeing slaves from their rebel masters while confiscating rebel property for use by the Union. One of the more prominent leaders of the jayhawkers was James Lane, a senator from Kansas who had been ordered by President

Lincoln to raise troops to protect Kansas from invasion. (Although Lane reportedly thought of himself as holding the rank of brigadier general while forming volunteer regiments, he did not really serve the Union as a true general since it would have cost him his senate seat.)

The proslavery counterparts of the jayhawkers were Missouri bushwhackers. These included such notorious men as William Quantrill and Bill Anderson, who were not recognized by the Confederate States of America (CSA) as belonging to any CSA fighting unit. Quantrill raided several Kansas towns, such as Shawnee and Olathe, but his most devastating attack was at Lawrence.

When the Civil War erupted in 1861, many people believed that slavery was not the primary issue. For the North, it was the preservation of the Union, and for the South, the formation of an independent Confederate States of America. As a result, in 1861 and through a portion of 1862, President Lincoln, concerned about driving border states into the Confederacy, did not want either slaves or free blacks to serve in the war. While Congress gave Lincoln the right to employ former slaves in the service of the Union, these slaves were only allowed to do chores, rather than to carry weapons and fight. However, in 1862 James Lane organized a Kansas unit that included slaves and free blacks, known as the First Kansas Colored Infantry. These black soldiers would shortly be the first to see battle and die in action. *Sissy!* describes two fictional former slaves, Tinker and Lazarus, who initially join the Eighth Kansas Volunteer Infantry as workers. But when they learn about the First Kansas Colored Infantry, they receive permission to transfer to that unit. At Island Mound, Missouri, Tinker joins other brave black soldiers in a successful skirmish with the Confederates. What is particularly significant about Island Mound is that here black soldiers fought for the Union *before* the enactment of the Emancipation Proclamation.

Native Americans were also discriminated against during the Civil War, particularly the Cherokee Nation. The Cherokees had divided loyalties that arose from a treaty requiring them to leave Georgia for the Oklahoma Territory. Matt Lightfoot, a fictitious part-Cherokee lieutenant, witnesses as a young boy the torment Cherokees endured in their forced move from their own lands and describes it as a "trail of tears." In this novel, Lightfoot endures the prejudice of one of his fellow officers.

Two major battles in *Sissy!* are those that occurred in Perryville, Kentucky, and Murfreesboro, Tennessee. Perryville was a decisive battle fought in October, 1862, between the Federals under Major General Buell and the Confederates under General Bragg. More than 7,600 soldiers lost their lives over that small piece of real estate, including Colonel Webster and two generals—William Terrill and James Jackson. The three officers discussed at a campfire on the eve of battle near Perryville whether they would survive. In the Battle of Murfreesboro in Tennessee, twenty-year-old Jessica Radford, disguised as a male soldier, fights bravely—until she encounters the man she is certain killed her parents.

Incidentally, during the Civil War a few women, like Jessica, masqueraded as men and fought along with the soldiers. While historians disagree on whether their number ranged in the dozens or in the hundreds, such incidents occurred on both sides of the conflict. One of these was a soldier named Alfred Luther, who had enlisted as a corporal in the First Kansas Infantry Regiment. After her death, it was discovered that Luther was actually a woman in her twenties. Very limited information on this woman exists, and even her real name is unknown.

Equally significant was the heroism that the women of Lawrence, Kansas, displayed on the day their town was invaded by William Quantrill and his 448 marauders. About 180 men and boys, mostly innocent civilians, lay dead in the wake of all this destruction. Yet during this nineteenth-century act of terrorism, women again showed remarkable bravery in protecting their husbands and sons from danger. Women mentioned in this novel—Amelia Read, Mary Lane, Mrs. Jennings, Elizabeth Fisher, and an unknown Lawrence woman who saved fleeing men by hiding them in a secret underground cellar—actually existed and exhibited the incredible courage described in *Sissy!*.

This novel, then, is a tribute to these brave ladies who never received the recognition they should have for their remarkable contribution to freedom and justice.

Prologue

A high-pitched scream sent a chill through Otto Heller's body. He quickly doused his campfire and stared through the snow drifting across the night. Could that be someone from the search party? Maybe one of the slavers had spotted his fire and signaled the others.

Otto crawled on his belly, bringing himself closer to the bank of the great Missouri. The grand river ate the snowflakes that alit on its glassy surface as it lumbered on. An owl hooted, and Otto instinctively pushed the butt of his Springfield against his shoulder. There was another sound, not an owl's call. A scream!

Another scream. Otto froze. His eyes searched the bank and stopped at the sight of something wriggling, something in a blue blanket, moving, hands flailing. He got up, steadying the rifle in front of him, his heart banging against his chest.

"Sissy!" a young girl's voice screamed. "Help me!"

Otto, confused, charged toward the source of the commotion. *A child?* He was right. It was a girl. A young Negro girl about ten or eleven wriggling out of her blanket, like a caterpillar emerging from her cocoon.

"Sissy!" she screamed again when she saw him approach. Her legs were caked with mud and her arms shook as she attempted to cover herself with her filthy blanket. Her eyes were wide with fright, and Otto dropped his rifle on the ground and offered her his coat, to show her he was her friend.

"I won't hurt you, child. You have no reason to be afraid of me."

She looked at him with suspicion as he draped his coat over her bony shoulders.

"You called for Sissy before. Is Sissy your mama?" he asked as he buttoned the coat.

She shook her head. "Sissy's my friend. My momma done leave me here, but she be back." Her eyes filled with tears. "She be back. White man take her, but she say she be back."

Otto's heart sank. This girl's slave mother would never have a chance to come back for her. Happened more often than he wanted to think. Last year he picked up a nine-year-old boy whose mother had abandoned him in a barn near Wellington and he had taken the boy over to Fort Riley, along with two adult slaves. It was mind-numbing to think a woman would have to do that just to protect her child. But his wife Helga, if she were a Negro slave, might have done the same.

He put the girl on his horse and sat in his saddle behind her. Her body shook as he held onto her waist with one hand and the reins with the other. "I wish I could take you back with me to Topeka," Otto said, not caring whether or not the girl understood him, "but I can't. Slavers like the ones who took your mama are after me. They don't cater to white folks like me who take their runaways and bring them up north."

He had to think fast. Obviously, he couldn't leave the girl here alone to either die or be taken captive. If her mama was a slave, she most likely was long gone by now, maybe headed back to her owner. What a way to spend Christmas Eve, he thought. He surveyed the hills, rows of leafless trees silhouetted against the ashen sky, and a bridge… a small bridge crossing a stream… there… a house… yes, a farmhouse, windows lit, smoke curling from the chimney. Maybe the folks who lived there could… *Don't be a fool, Otto, what if they're slavers? You're in Missouri, not exactly a state friendly to folks from the Underground Railroad, like yourself.*

He dismounted and lifted her to the ground. "Tell you what. See that place over there? Well, I'm going to ask you to hide while I knock on the door and see what kind of people live there."

She stared at him as if not comprehending, then said, "My name's Nellie. What's your name?"

He smiled at the girl, who looked strangely cute with the way his coat covered her small frame like a gown. "Mine's Otto. Where's your friend Sissy?"

"She's standing next to you," she said, her teeth chattering from the cold. She likes you."

Otto looked around. There wasn't a soul in sight. "Oh, I understand, Nellie. She's an invisible friend of yours."

"She's an angel. She always looks after me when I'm in trouble."

Otto widened his grin as he tied up his horse. "I see. Well, maybe you ought to ask Sissy to help me find you a place to stay tonight."

He finally made it to the door of the farmhouse and looked behind him to see Nellie hidden in a grove of trees, crouching behind the stump of an oak. He hoped his plan would work. He didn't know what he'd do if it didn't.

Otto watched the snow float to the ground as he waited for someone to answer the door. *Come on, folks, there's a girl freezing outside, a girl whose mama may be going back in chains. I don't care if you're slavers or not. It's Christmas Eve and you are human beings and there's such a thing as love, isn't there?*

The door opened.

1862

"…sure as Life holds all parts together…"
--Walt Whitman, *Leaves of Grass*

Chapter 1

June, 1862
Lawrence, Kansas

"Thank you, but I'm not helpless," nineteen-year-old Jessica Radford said when the stagecoach driver offered her his hand after she opened her door.

The man narrowed his eyes in surprise as he dropped his hand. "Sorry, ma'am, I was only askin'."

Jessica hoped she didn't sound rude, but men shouldn't assume all ladies were helpless. After all, she used to plow Pa's field and chop wood at home, didn't she?

She whisked away strands of her blond hair before lifting her two bags, one containing her college textbooks. A ragtag band played "The Battle Hymn of the Republic" outside the four-story, eighty-room Eldridge House. The magnificent red brick hotel, displaying a great deal of red, white, and blue bunting, together with that hypnotic Glory-Glory-Hallelujah refrain, reminded her of this insane war. When would it finally be over? Six years earlier, border ruffians had burned this same building to the ground when it was called the Free State Hotel, and Kansas bled long before the first shot was ever fired at Fort Sumter. However, war was now being raged not only over here in Kansas but everywhere.

The red summer sky was yet another reminder of this senseless massacre. At Carlotta College, a private woman's college she attended this year, the War between the North and South was practically all the students talked about. Some of the young ladies even engaged in heated arguments over it.

Could she escape from it here, at home? After all, the major battles were being fought east and south of Kansas. Still, there were those awful stories about civilians... residents at Shiloh, Tennessee, killed by Union forces... a child hit by musket fire at Fort Pulaski, Georgia... an innocent bystander slain while he observed a battle in Yorktown, Virginia....

How was her family doing here in Kansas? She hadn't heard from them in weeks. Could something have happened?

Those awful stories about civilians. No. That dream she had last night could have meant nothing. Maybe she was just tired. The three-day steamboat ride on the Missouri from St. Louis to Westover, combined with the six-hour journey over bouncing corduroy roads to Lawrence had plumb wore her out.

Jessica waved off a stranger who offered to carry her bags and looked around at the throng of people on Massachusetts Street—once a road so wide there was room to spare even with three wagons driven alongside. Today, all she saw was a street crowded mostly with Federals on horseback and women in their Sunday best waving goodbye to their men.

Everything looked the same as she remembered it...the cabinet shop at the northwest corner of Winthrop and Massachusetts, Allen Farm Implement and Hardware to the northeast, and the Simpson Bank directly across from the Eldridge House. But no sense wasting time looking, Jessica thought. Picking up her bags, she forced her way down Winthrop Street. She tried not to think about a young pregnant woman in tears whom she had just passed. It was indeed possible that woman's baby would never see her father return. All this pageantry and hoopla about uniforms and military balls and such, and no thought whatsoever about being killed...and guns made it all so easy....

It was an accident, Claire.

She shivered, ordering herself not to think about that again. It happened three years ago, and she'd best forget it. She headed for the Eldridge Stables on Vermont Street a block away. Once there, she dropped her bags and leaned against a hitching post. The odor of hay on the stable floor wafted through the still air. A black stallion neighed. A squirrel climbed up a locust post across the street, jerking its head back and forth in search of enemies.

Where was Pa? He said he'd be here, unless...the nightmare that had jerked her awake last night returned... *"They're all dead, rebels got 'em"...* Jessica yanked the memory from her consciousness.

"Jessica!" a familiar voice called out to her.

Jessica turned, relieved to see her father, a man with bushy eyebrows and long beard, sitting in the shay and waving to her. He wore a black derby, light brown satin waistcoat,

7

and dark brown trousers. He ought to dress up more often, Jessica thought as she smiled and moved toward him.

"Pa!" Jessica exclaimed, hugging him tighter than she ever had before. "I was so worried about you and Mom and Nellie, with the war'n all."

"Pshaw! Nothing to be concerned about, Jessica. C'mon. We'll talk on the ride back to the farm."

But Henry Radford said nothing even after he took the reins and drove his shay down Massachusetts Street, past familiar places—the *Kansas Tribune*, Duncan & Allison Dry Goods Store, Ward Meats, Danvers Ice Cream Parlor, Brechtelbrauer's Saloon. He turned west on Henry Street, passing a few more shops and a tree-lined ravine, until only small farms surrounded them.

When Pa headed north toward a grassy field fronting the Kansas River, Jessica decided to break the silence. "How's Ma?"

"Oh fine, and fit as a fiddle. She's helpin' out tryin' to raise money for gettin' uniforms and supplies and such. She's also doin' all she can for her church, with bake sales and helpin' out in the sacristy and things like that."

"I assumed both you and Mom would be here today."

"Foolish woman," Pa grunted. "She plumb thinks she'll go to hell if she misses Sunday Mass. That's why she ain't here."

Jessica stared down at her hands, fighting her disappointment. Nellie wasn't here either. Didn't that girl know how much she missed her? Maybe it was Ma's fault that Pa didn't bring Nellie with him to the station. Didn't Ma say, more than once, that Nellie was an embarrassment at times? It wasn't that the girl was so terribly uneducated. It was that Nellie was a Negro girl, three years younger than herself, and people would always ask the same question about Nellie—is she slave or free?

Jessica shifted in her wooden seat. Truth was, Nellie was a slave child whom a courageous white man named Otto Heller had discovered on the bank of the Missouri River five years ago on Christmas Eve. "You have to take her as your own," Otto had pleaded with Pa. "She's crying her eyes out for her mama, and her mama can't hear her cries. She's been taken by the slavers. If you don't take the child in, she'll surely die."

8

But why didn't Nellie come to the Eldridge House with Pa to meet her today?

As if reading Jessica's mind, Pa added, "Ma took Nellie with her to church. Wants that poor child to be a papist like herself."

His abrupt comment stopped Jessica from going further with this line of questioning. Her parents had never agreed about religion. Ma would always be a fervent Catholic, and Pa'd always be an occasional Methodist. Sometimes Jessica wondered if they believed in the same God.

"Any news about Uncle Adam, Pa?"

His face fell a little, but he kept his eyes on his horse. "Didn't yuh get our letter?"

"No."

"Well, maybe it got lost or something."

"But what about Uncle Adam?" she asked, not hiding her impatience.

"I got the news 'bout three weeks ago. Still can't believe it…" His voice trailed off.

Jessica put her hand to her mouth. "Oh no, Pa!"

He turned his head for a moment. There was a tear on his rough cheek. "He was at Shiloh with the Eleventh Indiana Volunteers. Gave up runnin' his medicine and drug company so's he could fight them rebels. Killed at close range with a shotgun. Died right quick they say, but your ma didn't take no comfort in that."

Jessica closed her eyes for a moment, agonizing over her uncle's death and wondering why people made killing so easy. It happened three years ago, but her hysteria after the gun went off still haunted her….*Please, Claire. Please, please, wake up!* But Claire Silas, her seven-year-old cousin, had never recovered.

"Y'know," Pa continued, "how your uncle was always wantin' to help others? By thunder, that's why he even gave Ma enough money to put you through college for this year."

Yes, she thought, and Uncle Adam had intended to have her manage the firm he owned, the Silas Drug Company, after she graduated. He was the only man she knew who believed women could hold an equal position with men in business. She often wished Pa were like that.

9

Pa ran his hand over his beard. "Shot a deer yesterday. Right from my bedroom window I did. Eight-point buck. Used a handgun, too, by golly."

Jessica visualized Pa pointing his pistol at the animal. It was different than the Colt .31 caliber pocket revolver hidden in her luggage. Uncle Adam made her promise she'd keep this weapon, the one that a kind stranger insisted she take after saving her from Sam Toby three years ago....

She'd never forget that stranger's face. It was broken with lines of worry. But his stern jawbone and eyes of steel spoke volumes of his determination to face danger without fear. He offered her the Colt revolver. "This here's Sam Toby's weapon. Picked it up from the ground in the cornfield after he took off. Nice small revolver. It's yours now, young lady."

"It's not mine," she had said. "I don't want it."

He ran his bony finger down his long white beard. "For your own protection, ma'am, you ought to have it. We're livin' in a dangerous world." He forced the gun into her reluctant palm and glanced down at Nellie. "Want me to see to it that this here slave girl gets further north? I can get her over to Illinois."

"It won't be necessary. My family already took her in as one of our own."

Uncle Adam...how could he be dead? She took a handkerchief from her dress pocket and dabbed her eyes. Dead? No, it couldn't be. He was the only man she knew who understood her love for literature, even though he was also a shrewd businessman. She still cherished the book of poems he had given her, poems penned by an obscure writer named Walt Whitman. But he also gave her something she never wanted—shells for her Colt revolver....

"No use just having an empty pistol," Uncle Adam had said. "You need these, too. You never know when you might come face-to-face with a rebel."

"But I don't want these shells," she answered. "I don't even want this gun."

"You may need it someday. Promise you'll always have it

with you."

How could she tell him who had shot his daughter Claire with this revolver? That the one responsible for Claire's death wasn't Sam Toby, but it was—"

He grabbed her hand. "Promise?"

"Yes," she said, struggling with her awful secret.

As she listened to the rapid klip-klop-klip-klop pace of the horse pulling the shay, Jessica brought her attention back to the news about Uncle Adam's death. "Pa," she asked, "how did Ma take the news about her brother?"

"Pretty hard. Before he left for Shiloh, he gave Rachel a chest full of his valuables. 'Jest in case something happens to me,' he said. She didn't open that there chest yet. And she didn't get her brother's body back home so she could bury him proper. Yuh know what I mean? The whole thing has busted her up pretty bad." He turned to Jessica for a moment. "Yuh know, of course, this means no more money for college."

Jessica felt a twinge of guilt as she inwardly admitted it was true. She had hoped to graduate some day. Maybe then she'd manage her uncle's firm. Better still, she'd write important books. Now those dreams were shattered. And... and... Uncle Adam was dead. She felt awful about that, and she knew if she let herself cry, she would. "I don't care about the money," Jessica lied. "How's Nellie been?" she asked, changing the subject.

"Oh, Nellie's same as always. Sometimes slow 'bout some things, like her mind's asleep or something."

Yes, Jessica thought, an uneducated sixteen-year-old girl who still played silly little girl games. That's at least how Uncle George described Nellie in his last letter. But the Radfords loved the little Negro child they had taken from Otto on that cold Christmas Eve in Missouri. "I will try to be a real mother to her," Ma had said when she brought Nellie to their new home in Kansas. But as far as Jessica was concerned, Nellie was sweet, even though she still acted like a child most of the time.

"Does Nellie understand what this war's all about?" asked Jessica.

He smiled for the first time. "I reckon so. But she's not afraid of it. Y'know, that there girl's got more spunk than all of us put t'gether. Yeah, she's not afraid of nothin'. Believes God will take care of everything. Y'just have to believe in Jesus, she thinks. Keeps tellin' me the stranger who saved you' n her from Sam Toby surely must be in heaven now for all the good he'd done."

In a flash, Jessica recalled her last conversation with the stranger....

"I appreciate your kindness, sir," she had said, "and I want to thank you for your help. But I don't even know your name."

The man paused, his face as solemn as a cemetery. "Ma'am, perhaps you've heard about me and the Underground Railroad," he said calmly. "My name's John Brown."

Jessica pressed her fingers around her neck. What good had come out of John Brown's hanging? People still owned slaves.

Pa stroked his beard and glanced at Jessica. "Collar too tight?"

"No," she said, dropping her hand to her lap.

"Say, I'm sure glad yer back—I guess for good now. Sorry Ma and I can't 'ford to send yuh back now that Adam's gone."

"I'm not concerned about that, Pa." There was no use telling him her hope for a better life and Ma's dream for her were both shattered. "I guess I could work, but I don't know if anyone here would want to hire a woman for anything except cooking and cleaning."

"Well," Pa said, "yuh kin help us out with the chores. By golly, yer the best field hand I ever had, with the way yuh can shoe a horse or drive a mule. Hope that college of yers didn' make yuh afraid to use your muscles."

"I'd like to use my brain muscles for a change."

"What's that?"

"Never mind."

"Yuh know," Pa said, "in the fall, yuh kin even do some teachin'. Don't need no diploma to do that, I reckon. Why, yuh kin even get one of them certificates if yuh kin jest read and write."

"I know that, Pa."

"Heck, most girls your age never even seen the inside of a college."

"Ma almost did," Jessica said, recalling how Ma used to tell her how wonderful it had been meeting Mary Lyon, the founder of the first woman's college. Back then, Ma wanted to earn a degree and teach college in Massachusetts. Instead, she became Pa's mail-order bride.

"If your Ma would've got college learnin'," Pa said, "she wouldn'a met me. And then where would yuh be?"

"But Pa, if I had a diploma, I could do a lot more things. Maybe run a business like Uncle Adam wanted me to. Or maybe even become a famous writer. Just think, my book would be in libraries, next to such names as Longfellow, Shakespeare, Bacon, and—"

"I like my bacon with eggs," Pa laughed, slapping his free hand against his knee.

Jessica let it go. Good thing Ma had pressured him to let her attend Carlotta College in St. Louis. Pa thought education was a waste on women.

By the time they arrived at the Radford homestead, the rim of the sun nestled itself on the roofline of the barn. Cows stood like statues in the field, while Haley, the Radford's collie chased a jackrabbit toward the creek. Jessica swept her eyes over the homestead, inhaling the memories of her childhood. She and Nellie had helped out in the field while Pa and his farm helpers plowed the ground or harvested the fruit of their labors. Other times they'd rest, enjoying the sunflowers, making mind sculptures out of cloud formations. But one day Sam Toby, a former trusted field hand, had cornered Nellie, Claire, and Jessica in the cornfield when Pa wasn't around....

Sam Toby slapped Nellie when she started to recite the "Our Father."

"What's wrong with yah, slave child? Let's see what yah got under there." He undid her petticoat. It dropped to the ground, leaving her standing in her white cotton drawers.

He turned next to Claire, crying, her head in her lap. "Stand up, girl'n watch. Yah might learn somethin'."

"Stop it!" Jessica screamed. "Just stop it! Leave them alone."

13

Sam waved his gun at her. "You're right. Maybe I oughta take a good look at yah first 'stead of that little slave bitch. Let's see what yah look like, Jessica. Take them clothes off. All of 'em. Your dress'n everything."

Jessica's face wrinkled into a mask of tearful dignity as she pleaded with him. "Let go of us. Let us go, or I'll—"

"You'll do what, little girl? What will yah do to me?"

No, Jessica promised herself she wouldn't think about that. Pretend it was all just a bad dream, Ma had said. After all, John Brown had chased that devil away, hadn't he?

"Hey," Pa said, removing her bags from the shay, "yer staring at this here place kinda funny like. Yuh scared 'bout something? Yuh all right?"

"I'm all right," Jessica answered, trudging toward the porch of the log farmhouse. Forget about that awful summer. Think instead about this house. Pa was rightly proud of this six-room house and that porch overlooking the field. Had a right to be. Built it after they all moved here from Missouri when she was fourteen. He and Ma took with them a frightened eleven-year-old Negro girl named Nellie, a slave rescued by Otto Heller. Now Nellie was like family living here in this big house.

Happy place this was indeed. Listening to Pa tell his tall tales about being a close friend of Lincoln or "knowing" where to find gold dust in the Kansas River...watching Ma start a flower garden...teaching Nellie how to add and subtract...playing poker with Pa, which Ma thought was sinful because only gamblers in taverns played poker.

Jessica inhaled deeply when she got to the porch. Stew. It could be Ma was making venison stew.

"What d'yuh got in that bag?" Pa asked when he finally caught up with her. "Looks mighty full."

"Oh, clothes and things." Jessica couldn't tell him she was carrying the Colt revolver that Adam urged her to keep. Pa probably wouldn't like the idea of her carrying it. Told her once guns were dangerous and only men who knew something about them ought to use them. Pa was right. She never intended to use it. *Not after Claire got killed with it.*

Unexpectedly, Haley barked, and Jessica took a sudden step back.

Pa laughed. "Why are yuh so jumpy, Jessica? Look at the way he's waggin' his tail. By thunder, see how glad he is to see yuh?"

Pa opened the door and Haley raced in ahead of Jessica. Nellie, even though now sixteen, had her black hair in braids and tied with pink ribbons. She wore a brown and pink cotton dress and was putting plates on the table, while Rachel ordered her to take the kettle off the stove. The dullness in Nellie's large brown eyes transformed into a sparkle of excitement as she beamed back at Jessica. A huge smile hugged Nellie's round face, and she almost dropped a plate in her excitement.

"You're back home!" Nellie shrieked. "I'm mighty happy." She wasted no time in giving Jessica a bear hug of a welcome. "I been achin' to see you at the station. I wanted to, but Ma said no. She says I gotta go to church."

"Hush, Nellie," Rachel said, wiping her hands on her apron. "You know Mass is important." She smiled slightly at Jessica. "Good to see you, Jessica. You hungry?"

Jessica nodded. She knew she should be used to Ma not showing any affection, not coming to her and hugging her like Nellie did. But today there was an awful sadness in Ma's eyes.

During dinner, Pa droned on about the war, then shifted his focus to Uncle George's ex-wife. "Heard Aunt Penelope sold her small bottlin' plant in Toledo. Now she's wantin' to buy another company somewhere. Imagine, a woman wanting to run a business instead of lookin' for a husband and raisin' children. Gonna end up being like Josiah Miller, but in a dress." He laughed at his own joke.

"I'm happy for Aunt Penelope," Jessica said. How come, she thought, it was fine for a man like Josiah Miller to be a shrewd business person, but not a woman like Penelope Phillips? Penelope was a twenty-nine-year-old mulatto whom George Radford had divorced after three years of marriage. She was always a thorn in his side. George could not tolerate her stubborn insistence on doing things her own way. But single now for five years, she had found unusual success in her many business ventures—and Jessica admired her for it.

"Bah," Pa said, "that woman oughta get married again. Not right for her to be livin' alone like that. No husband, no family."

"Marriage isn't for everyone, Pa." Jessica said.

15

Henry grunted in disagreement. "By the way, I got a letter from that fella from Topeka. The one workin' with the Underground Railroad."

"You mean Otto Heller?" Jessica asked. "What did he say?"

"Oh, his wife Helga don't want him makin' another dangerous trip to rescue slaves. His business is doin' good, and he appreciated yuh sending him that piece in the St. Louis paper about that literary society in Topeka. He hoped yuh were doin' fine in school. Yuh gotta tell him you're not goin' back."

Jessica hung her head for a second. "I'll tell him, Pa."

Pa cleared his throat. "He also asked about Nellie."

Nellie stood up, excited. "He did?"

"Of course he did. Wants to know how yuh are doin'." He shifted his gaze to Jessica. "By the way, did Uncle George write to yuh?"

"He did, Pa. I got one letter from him from Shenandoah where he's been fighting. He says he heard that other Confederate regiments will soon be pushing into eastern Kansas."

"Ain't true!" Pa exclaimed. "We had a few skirmishes with the slavers. They still think we're hidin' escaped slaves here. And the Redlegs'n bushwhackers are always at each other's throats, killin' each other. But other than that, I ain't seen much action in these parts. Yuh worry too much, Jessica."

"But I hear talk," Nellie interrupted, "I hear bad people around here. Bad people who kill Yankees. They's all around these parts."

Ma leaned forward. "I think she's referring to the news in the paper about Confederate renegades being spotted just east of Lecompton."

"Yuh can't believe everything you read," Pa said.

"Maybe it's true," Jessica added. "I had an awful dream last night about you and Ma."

"Dreams don't mean nothin'," Pa said, adding more venison stew to his plate. "Besides, if them rats are loose in this area, someone is bound to catch 'em. Everyone here hates them rebels. I'd string 'em up myself if I caught 'em."

"Henry!" Rachel shouted. "You're supposed to be a Christian. How can you talk like that in front of the girls?"

"Pshaw!" he answered, with a wave of his coarse hand. "It's about time they learn how to deal with murderin' rats."

16

Ma rose from her chair in a huff. "Henry, watch your tongue! I hate when you talk about killing folks. Adam's dead 'cause of all this killing going on."

Ma put a handkerchief to her eye. Pa reached over to touch her, but she moved her arm away. "I'm fine. Just got something in my eye, that's all."

The room was quiet except for the sound of knives and forks hitting tin plates as they ate. Ma looked around the table and focused on Pa. "Henry, have you forgotten what happened to Adam's little girl? Poor Claire got shot by a rebel slaver."

Jessica took a quick look at Nellie and saw her eyeing her back, sharing a common secret. Jessica swallowed hard.

Pa slammed his hand on the table. "Claire got herself killed 'cause she done run away from that bastard Toby."

"No matter," Ma said, glaring back at him. "Why even Reverend Lightfoot, that Indian preacher man you and George like so much—I bet he wouldn't agree with how you'd love to kill scoundrels."

Pa filled his cup with milk from the pitcher, his face getting a tinge red. "Just 'cause the preacher and me like to go fishin' and huntin' and drinkin' together don't mean nothing as far as what I believe. He don't go 'round killin' people. Besides, he ain't Indian jest 'cause his daddy come from the Cherokee Nation."

Ma clenched her jaw and her narrow green eyes burned with anger. "I don't care. Killing is wrong, no matter who does it. You ought to read the Ten Commandments if you call yourself a Methodist."

Jessica, sensing the beginning of another eruption over religion, spoke up quickly. "How's Reverend Lightfoot doing these days?"

"He's been asking about you," Ma said, frowning. "Makes me wonder what his intentions are."

Jessica felt her face turn warm from embarrassment. "Really? He asked about me? What'd he say?"

"He says you'll make a fine writer someday," Ma said. "He liked that school essay you wrote on justice. He wants your permission to use it in his homily."

17

Pa laughed. "That man's sweet on yuh, Jessica. But Ma don't like it none 'cause she thinks yuh oughta only go out with Catlicks. I take a likin' to the preacher man and so does my brother George. And it don't matter to me if'n he's got any Indian blood in him, but maybe it matters to your ma here."

Ma glared at him. "I just don't want her keeping company with Matt Lightfoot any more. I don't care if he likes the way she writes. And it doesn't matter to me if he's got Indian blood. He's still a bad influence. Thinks it's fine to own slaves. Says the Bible agrees with him."

"Maybe so, but you don't like him 'cause he's not a Catlick," Pa interjected.

"What's wrong with that?" Ma countered. "Catholics and Protestants shouldn't hang around together."

"You're all messed up about religion," Pa shouted. "You made a darn fool of yourself that time you didn't want us to eat meat on Friday. You're crazy, woman!"

When words started flying between Ma and Pa, Jessica asked to be excused from the table. After promising to help out later with dishes, she headed out for the corral. Checking to be sure that her pistol was buried in the deep pocket of her dress, she saddled her horse Leroy. It would start getting dark in about a half hour. That'd give her enough time to figure things about what to do, now that she wasn't returning to college.

"Wait for me," Nellie called out.

Jessica turned to see Nellie tying the strings of her purple bonnet as she ran toward her. "Jessica, please let me go with you."

"I'm just going to trot around the field and get away from all of this," Jessica said, turning Leroy to face her.

"Let me go with you," Nellie pleaded as she saddled up a two-year-old chestnut horse named Blister.

Jessica shook her head. "Ma lets you ride Blister?"

"Sure thing. I rode Blister with Ma to church this mornin'."

Jessica drew back in surprise. "You used to always call Ma 'Rachel.'"

"I know she not my real momma. My real momma—" Tears welled up in her eyes as she paused. "My real ma may

18

still be 'round somewheres. She plumb gotta be 'round somewheres."

Jessica quickly changed the subject.. "So Ma let you ride her favorite horse?"

Nellie shook her head and gave Jessica a forced smile. "But she don't like it none if'n I go by myself. She still thinks I'm a little kid or something."

"I don't think that's it. I think she doesn't want people thinking we're harboring a slave. Might be some Yankee folk who don't cater to the notion of our letting a slave girl ride a horse around here."

Nellie squinted. "Listen here, I got papers that say I ain't a slave no more."

Forged papers, Jessica thought. It was nice of Otto Heller to do this for Pa. And now that Kansas was a free state, maybe papers weren't all that important anyway.

Jessica smiled back at her. "Well, I guess it'll be fine if you ride with me. I plan to just go down yonder to the creek. Just want to get away from things." Jessica nudged her horse toward the distant hills that began to hide the setting sun.

"Never rode this late before," Nellie said, keeping pace alongside Jessica. "Fact is, Ma don't like me bein' out by myself around sunset. She got mad at me once. I been playin' hide'n seek with Sissy. It got real dark. Got lost comin' back home."

Jessica had almost forgotten about Sissy, Nellie's invisible friend. Ma and Pa had tried to tell Nellie she was a young woman now and that Sissy didn't exist. "Yeah, she's real," Nellie would say, with eyes as white and wide as two full moons. "She say she an angel, but she don't have no wings, like that angel statue in church has."

Angels? Jessica shook her head. At times, she wished she were like Nellie when it came to understanding the supernatural. Nellie accepted angels, God, and everything at face value. And Jessica envied the spirited way Nellie sang at church, pouring out her soul.

But what was church? Jessica remembered Ralph Waldo Emerson saying that he liked "the silent church before the service begins, better than any preaching." Being quiet and being still was her "church" so she could let her soul feel free and wonderful. Church was a grassy field stretching out forever...

19

a twilight resembling the gradual dimming of a candle... a breeze rippling through the cedars... the sound of a coyote in the distance... and, yes, even the steady beat of horse hooves evolving into a hypnotic rhythm in the evening air. God wasn't only in some wooden building. He was everywhere.

Jessica glanced at Nellie. "Where's Sissy now?"

"I dunno. I didn't see her today."

"Maybe," Jessica laughed, "you didn't need her anymore when I showed up."

Nellie frowned. "I don't know what you mean."

"Never mind. I hear Pa's been going to church now more often than before."

"How d'ya know that?"

"Oh, Reverend Lightfoot tells me a lot in his letters. He told me you want to be baptized a Methodist, but you're afraid to tell Ma."

"The reverend writes to you a lot, don't he? Y'know, I bet he's sweet on you, just like your Pa said. Is it true? D'you like him?"

"He's a nice man. Need to know him better, that's all. He wants me to write some stories he can use in his homily. Maybe I ought to do it. Only thing that bothers me is he's thinking about joining up with the Yankees as a chaplain."

Nellie's eyes lit up. "Would you go with him, Jessica? I mean, to the war?"

Jessica felt an empty ache in her soul when she thought about all the killing she had read about. "No, I don't think I can do that. Don't believe in war."

"What about that nice man, Otto—the one who done find me by the river. Does he believe in war?"

"I don't think so. He believes in saving lives, not taking them away."

"I wish I could see him again. I like sleepin' with his coat."

"That old thing?"

"He wrapped me with it once 'cause he loved me. Too bad he never come by again."

"He's pretty busy with his business and all, Nellie." Jessica stopped her horse when she came to a tall cedar. "Say, I remember climbing that tree long time ago. I would've made it to the top if Pa hadn't spoiled it." She dismounted and led her horse toward the creek.

"I remember," Nellie said, getting off Blister. "I told Henry—I mean, Pa—I told him I dared you to do it. But he said I didn' have no brains and you should know better."

Jessica instantly recalled how Ma and Pa used to tell her Nellie would always be a child. It didn't seem to bother her any, Jessica thought. Maybe she was afraid to leave the new world she had discovered here in Kansas. A safe world. A world where she didn't have to worry about some cruel slave owner.

"I've always liked this spot," Jessica said, getting off her horse. "Gives me peace of mind just listening to the water rippling down the stream."

Nellie joined her at the bank. "We used t'go fishin' here, you'n me. You remember? Done never catch nothing."

Jessica nodded. "Pa told me later there were no fish there. Made me think there were bass and pike and all kinds of fish in that creek."

Nellie returned a guarded smile. "You mean your Pa tol' yah a lie?"

"I wouldn't call it a lie. He just wanted us to believe in things."

"Henry says I gotta believe in some things. Like this here pretty medallion he gave me last year." Nellie removed from around her neck a silver chain that held a round reddish-brown metal object. She showed it to Jessica. "Pa says it's his favorite Psalm."

Jessica held the heavy bronze object in her hand. It was plain except for something which was engraved on it. There was just enough light from the setting sun for her to make out the words:

For He has given His angels charge concerning thee, to keep thee in all thy ways.

Jessica was about to return it when Nellie asked her to look at the back of it.

On the other side of the half-dollar-sized object was inscribed the name "Nellie Radford." "Looks like Pa wants to think of you as his own daughter," Jessica said, smiling as she gave her back the medal. "I guess this makes you an official member of the Radford family."

Nellie put the chain back on her neck. "He tol' me that this will keep me from harm. Is believin' in this a lie, too?"

Jessica gave her a reassuring pat on her leg. "No, we all have to believe in something."

"Like Jesus? Do you believe like your Ma that if'n we try real hard to be good, He'll take us to heaven?"

"I don't know. Pa thinks all we got to do is believe we're saved and that's it."

Nellie smiled at her. "What d'you believe, Jessica? You don't talk much about God. D'you believe in Him?"

Jessica didn't have the heart to tell her she didn't know what she believed in. Maybe Reverend Lightfoot was right. If she read more of the Bible, maybe she'd know for sure. "Well, you know, Nellie, I'm real glad you believe in Jesus. At college, I learned we sometimes have to believe in things we can't see firsthand, things like beauty and love. We can't see them, but we know they exist."

Nellie moved her hand over her braids and cocked her head. "Yer so smart, Jessica, goin' to college and book learnin' and everythin'."

"You don't have to go to college to be smart. Look at Aunt Penelope. She's sold her own business in Toledo and is looking for an opportunity to buy another. I don't feel as smart as that, although I did learn a lot about literature and history."

"What's history?"

"History is the story of all of us, going way back. Sometimes, they get it wrong, though. Like I think the students got it all wrong about John Brown. They say he was a murderer and an outlaw. But he saw Negroes as human beings with souls and not as animals that can be sold for money."

Nellie leaned toward her. "If someone wanted to hurt me, would you kill'im with your gun?"

"That's a foolish question," Jessica said. She got up and walked toward her horse. "C'mon. We'd best be going. Getting late. It's already dark."

Nellie mounted Blister about the same time Jessica got on Leroy. Blister neighed, and Nellie petted his mane. "Y'know,"

Nellie said, "you're an awful lot like your Ma. She reads a lot. She hates guns like you do."

Jessica moved her horse closer to Nellie. "I know. Ma made me promise something when she got real sick that time. Remember when the doctor said she might have pneumonia and die? Well, she made me swear that if she passed on, I would never kill anyone because killing is a big sin and we have no right to take a life that God gave. No right at all."

"But you tol' me that John Brown gave you Sam Toby's gun. You aim to keep it?"

"I don't know." She pulled out the Colt revolver from the pocket of her dress. "I still got this with me because maybe I'll need to use it some day. But I don't want to use it. Not ever. I'm scared even holding it like this." She put the gun back in her pocket. "Besides, maybe Ma's right. I don't want to be responsible for another person dying on my account."

Oh, dear Claire! I've killed you!

Jessica choked. "You're the only one, Nellie, who knows what really happened that day. You're the only one. I made you promise not to tell."

Nellie squinted. Her carefree, pudgy face became serious. "I done keep my promise. But you didn't mean to kill Claire. You made a mistake."

"It was an accident," Jessica corrected. "I know that. Still, I don't ever want to use this revolver. Ever."

"I shore appreciate Sissy savin' me from Mastah Toby."

"Nellie! You're only three years younger than me, and you act like a child. Sissy's not real!"

Nellie still wore her frightened mask and looked as if she were going to cry. "But she *is* real. She *is*! She was there when he had my dress off and she—"

Jessica turned Leroy around. "No good talking about this, Nellie. Happened long ago, anyway. It's over, and I want to forget it."

Nellie moved Blister alongside Jessica's horse. "Jessica, are you mad at me?"

"No, course not. I'm just mad about the way things turn out sometimes. I think we ought to be getting back, though. I don't want Ma and Pa to think we ran away."

Nellie laughed. "Yeah, but might be fun if we did."

They came to a narrow trail and Jessica let Nellie ride ahead of her. Tomorrow, Jessica thought, she'd have to figure out what to do with her life now that she wasn't going back to school. Pa was right about being able to get a job teaching. Didn't pay much, but it'd be something. Maybe it'd also give her ideas for writing stories.

She thought she heard men shouting in the distance. Maybe they were jayhawkers making their way to the border, or maybe they were celebrating something. Whatever it was, it needn't concern her.

A shot rang out, and Blister reared from fright. "Oh, no!" Nellie screamed, kicking the animal with her boots. Blister moved at full gallop, Nellie yelling at the horse to stop. He ran like a runaway train, with Nellie hunched forward, holding the reins.

Jessica raced to catch up, screaming at Nellie to stop. Another shot sliced through the night air.

The nightmare exploded in her mind again, and this time she couldn't shake it off—

"They're all dead, rebels got 'em"....

Chapter 2

Blister veered to the left, running away from the direction of the farm, crossing a road, leaping over a low hedge. A few locust trees fronted a gently sloping hill, where Nellie, screaming for help, had disappeared. Gone. It was as if the earth had swallowed her whole.

Jessica's heart raced, hoping that the incline of the hill would slow Blister enough so Leroy could catch up. Another shot rang out, this time coming from where Nellie had vanished. Jessica reached the thick cluster of trees at the base of the hill and stopped when she thought she heard something.

What was that? Men's voices?

With beads of sweat forming on her forehead, Jessica nudged Leroy forward, as slow and as cautious as a raccoon hunting for prey. Walnut trees towered over her like threatening giants. In the distance to her left was the Kansas River, its peaceful glass surface illuminated by a bright moon. She moved her head to the right and left, searching for any sign of movement. A faint yellow glow crowned the top of the hill. It wasn't the moonlight, Jessica thought. A campfire perhaps?

Jessica cupped her hands near her mouth. "Nellie! Do you hear me? Nellie!"

Nothing. Maybe Nellie had ridden clear through to the other side of the hill. But the gunshot.

What about the gunshot?

A shadow scampered ten yards in front of her. Jessica, breathing heavily, reached into her pocket for her Colt revolver. It might have been some small animal, she thought as she felt her hands shaking. She was about to call out again but stopped herself when she heard the distant sound of voices. The damp smell of wet leaves irritated her nostrils as she moved up through the wildflowers and prairie grass. Her hand quivering, she slid the gun back into her pocket, afraid she was going to accidentally pull the trigger.

She dismounted and began the rest of the ascent on foot, leading Leroy. Nellie was so careless! Why did she insist on riding with her tonight? And why did Nellie show her that huge worthless medal she wore around her neck? It didn't have magical powers like Nellie believed it did. All that nonsense about angels! Too bad Sissy wasn't a real angel who'd protect Nellie from harm.

As Jessica approached the top of the hill, a horse neighed. *Blister?*

Terrified at what might lie ahead, she paused before reaching the ridge. A shadow moved off to one side. Jessica's heart beat like a hummingbird's wing. The shadow moved closer. Jessica was about to run when she saw Blister pacing toward her, his head moving up and down as if nodding in recognition.

Jessica tied Leroy to the nearest tree and climbed to the crest of the hill. Men's voices sliced through the silence. One was a menacing voice, angry, snapping and cursing. Jessica's nerves crackled throughout her body. She felt like she had that time, three years ago, when she had fought with Sam Toby for the gun....

Sam had taken off after the pistol discharged, with John Brown in hot pursuit of him. Jessica focused in horror on the large, growing bloodstain on Claire's pale blue dress. Claire's young eyes had rolled back in her sockets. Her mouth was frozen in a cry of pain. And that gun was still in Jessica's hand. That horrible gun.

Jessica's thoughts were shattered by a scream. A terrifying scream. *Could it be Nellie?*

She made it to the clearing at the summit and froze. Ice pumped through her veins. There, some twenty yards away, the light from a campfire flickered as a Confederate trooper in a gray frock coat and trousers tied a dirty cloth over Nellie's mouth. The girl's hands were tied behind her back, but she stomped her boots on the soft ground as the man waved a bowie knife inches from her face.

"She's a wild one, she is," the man shouted, laughing and cursing. He glanced at three soldiers who warmed themselves around the campfire. "Like a jungle savage!"

"You sure like to burn them houses, Sam," one of them, obviously drunk, yelled back. "Didja find any loot?"

"No time," Sam replied, holding the struggling girl by her waist. "They was too poor. The old lady kept callin' for help, and the old man he done shot at me. So I got 'em both."

"Whatcha gonna do with that there slave girl, Sam?"

Sam roared with laughter. "What I'd like to do with all them slave whores."

Jessica shut her eyes. This could not be happening. Maybe this was a horrifying nightmare.

Nellie's brown and pink cotton dress was ripped. Her white cotton petticoat was blackened by dirt. Her face was cut, her eyes wide with horror. Her purple bonnet, also torn, still clung stubbornly to her quivering head.

Jessica reached for her Colt. She held it up in his general direction. Her hand shook so much she had to steady it with the other.

Nellie kicked the heel of her boot against the man's shin, but he only laughed harder.

"Hey," he bellowed, "I'm not gonna put up with yah movin' aroun' like a bobcat. Do what I say, and I'm not gonna hurt yah."

Jessica caught her breath as she aimed the gun at his head. His coarse face, the way his bushy eyebrows arched, his prominent nose, the rudeness in his low voice…it all came back. *This was Sam Toby.* His coarse brown hair hugging his large head like a crown. His face, rough like gravel. His eyes dark as the devil himself, penetrating her soul.

"Hey, Sam," one of the men called out, "maybe you oughta leave her alone and get yourself one of them full-grown white ladies in town. This one's jest nigger trash anyways."

Sam Toby shook his head. "Nah, I think I know this one. Face looks sorta familiar." Moving his crude fingers toward her throat, he grabbed her bronze medallion. "Well, lookee here at this big thing hangin' round her neck." He yanked the chain off her with a force that made Nellie moan through her gag. He squinted as he held it near the fire. "This here thing's got a name on the back of it," he said, bringing the large medal close to his eye. "Says here her name's Nellie Radford. Well, I'll be a pig's uncle!" Toby roared with laughter. "So you're the little slave girl staying at the Radford farm. They even gave yah

27

their family name. Ain't that nice? Well, one thing's for sure, that crazy ol' white man's not gonna stop me from havin' my way with yah now. He done gone for good. They hung him at Harper's Ferry."

Jessica held the gun steady, telling herself she had to pull the trigger.

Sam Toby planted his rough hand on Nellie's bosom. "Oh yeh," he said, laughing, "I can see y'all a lot more grown up now."

Toby sneered the same way he had three years ago when he cornered Jessica, Nellie, and Claire in the cornfield....

Nellie had disrobed when Sam threatened to kill her.

"I want y'all to watch," Sam said, waving the gun at Jessica and Claire. Nellie, sobbing, started to pull down her cotton drawers. Just then, the distant voice of John Brown thundered, "Get out of that cornfield, mister!"

Jessica jumped at Sam, wrestling him for the gun. Her fingers trying to force his grip on the trigger. Then the explosion. A soul-piercing shriek from Claire. A gush of blood. Jessica froze in horror. She had just killed her seven-year-old cousin.

Jessica cussed at herself for not being able to fire her weapon. Her mind raced. Maybe she could just go out there and scare them off. But there were four of them. She'd never get away with it.

"Sissy!" Nellie screamed through the night air.

"Who are you callin' a sissy?" Toby laughed. "I ain't no sissy. That's for sure!"

Jessica's mind raced. Pa. If only she could get to Pa. He'd surely blow his fool head off.

She raced downhill, praying and pleading for God to help her. The men's voices grew louder as she untied and mounted Leroy. Her heart felt as if it were in her mouth, her mind spinning.

"Hey, I reckon someone's been spyin' on us," one man shouted behind her. It could have been Toby, but Jessica didn't dare turn around. A bullet whizzed by, inches from her ear. She grabbed the reins. Giving Leroy a swift kick, she rode faster than ever before. Wind rippled through her hair. Her heart beat against her chest.

"Blister is such a stupid horse," she said aloud, choking on her tears. "It's all his fault." This couldn't be happening, she thought. The world had gone insane.

Leroy's hooves pounded the ground, and Jessica prodded it to go faster. Home, she thought, would be just over that ridge. Then she'd get Pa to help rescue Nellie. She hoped it wouldn't be too late.

The smell of burning wood assaulted her senses. At first, she assumed it to be the remnants of a campfire. But bright flames leapt into the night sky. As she approached the fire, the horror of what was happening hit her....

The Radford house was in flames. Torrents of sparks darted through the sky and plummeted to the ground through red clouds of smoke. Crackling sounds drew voices to her head, voices once alive, now dead....

"Why are you so jumpy, Jessica?"

"Henry, watch your tongue! I hate talk 'bout killin.'"

The voices disappeared into the crackling and hissing of flames. Dead. Gone...Forever.

"No!" Jessica cried, racing closer to the blazing inferno. "No, please God, no!"

Two days later
Oak Hill Cemetery, Kansas

Reverend Matt Lightfoot noticed how detached Jessica looked, sitting in her coach seat of the carriage. When she lifted her veil, he saw how her eyes were glazed in a frozen stare. How joyless she appeared. He wished he could hold her in his arms and tell her he'd gladly bear the pain for her if only he could.

It was almost noon when the carriage made it to the gate of the cemetery. Matt turned his head and tried to think of something to say to Jessica. But what? That it was God who willed this to happen? That it was time for her parents to leave this earth? He didn't believe it himself. Besides, God didn't control our destinies. Look what happened to the Indian nations when the white man came to this country. Did God will that?

No, just like God didn't will the murder of the Radfords. But the way Jessica grieved now, no amount of talking would help. Best be silent. She'd come around.

After the other three carriages stopped behind him, Matt got out and helped Jessica down. He approached the gathering crowd. The grave, open like a dark wound in the earth, lay some ten yards away. Skipp Forester, the town blacksmith, stood between two pine coffins. He had helped Matt cart the charred bodies back to town. Skipp's hands were folded in front of him, his eyes downcast, although he did look up for a moment when Matt approached. "I hear they got three of 'em yesterday," Skipp said in a matter-of-fact monotone.

"Rebels?" Matt asked.

"Yup. But there's one still loose. Name's Sam Toby."

Jessica stepped forward and clenched her hands into fists. "I hope God sends him straight to hell!" she said, with a vulgarity that made Matthew cringe. He put his muscular arm on her shoulder, but she moved away from him. "I don't want to be here, Matthew. Told you that before, but you made me be here. We should be out looking for Nellie instead."

"Believe me, I'm doing my best to find her, Jessica," Reverend Lightfoot said, tapping his tattered Bible with his long fingers. If only Jessica knew how very special she was to him. He'd ride all day and night in search of Nellie—if only he knew where to look. "I've been praying to the Lord about this," he added.

Jessica dropped her arm on the smaller of the two caskets. "Ma," she whispered, "I know you wanted me to be somebody. And I will, someday."

She moved over to the other casket and touched its pine surface. "Pa," she said, lifting her veil as she surveyed the cemetery, "I'll get Toby for this, if it's the last thing I ever do."

Jessica's eyes were moist, but her face was molded into a mask of anger. Matt again put his arm on her shoulder, but this time she didn't resist. He wondered if Sam Toby and the rebels might have kidnapped Nellie, or perhaps she had run away from them. Matt and a group of men had spent all day searching the area where Jessica reported she had last seen her. There was no sign of a body anywhere. The three men who were captured weren't talking either. Why should they? They knew they faced certain hanging.

Reverend Lightfoot, in the center of a circle of mourners, began reading from the Bible. Jessica, sobbing, rocked slowly forward and back. Turning toward her, Uncle George reached for her gloved hand, but she jerked it away and made a fist.

Matt finished reading and held his Bible by his side. He glanced at the friends, neighbors, and relatives of the Radfords, but his eyes focused for a long moment on Jessica. Raising his head high, he sang:

> *"Amazing grace, how sweet the sound*
> *that saved a wretch like me!*
> *I once was lost but now am found,*
> *was blind but now I see.*
> *'Twas grace that taught my heart to fear,*
> *and grace my fears relieved...."*

"Sam Toby!" Jessica shouted.

Reverend Lightfoot stopped. "What?"

"Sam Toby," she repeated, both her hands now tightly clenched. "He's the wretch I'm going to send straight to hell."

Amelia Read, with a sympathetic smile, greeted Jessica after the funeral service. "We've lost touch with each other ever since high school. You were my best student then," Amelia said, her warm eyes searching Jessica's face as if to recapture those earlier moments. Jessica had always thought of Amelia, now twenty-six, as a good friend, despite their age difference.

"School never did succeed in making me a Unitarian though," Jessica answered, reflecting on her dreary high school days in the damp basement of the Unitarian Church where she learned the finer points of grammar, composition, art, mathematics, and the Bible.

"I suppose not," Amelia said, "but I used to notice how well you did in composition. I think your mother was right in saying you'd be a great writer some day."

The well-intentioned comment only deepened Jessica's grief over her loss. After a brief silence, Amelia hugged Jessica goodbye and wished her well. As Jessica walked away from the crowd, Mary Delaney caught up with her. "Mind if I walk with you, Jessica?"

"No, I'm glad you're here."

"I'll always be here for you," Mary said, pressing Jessica's hand in support. "I'm your best friend."

"I know," Jessica said, her voice sounding hollow. "I truly appreciate you and your friends making it possible for me to have these clothes and loaning me money for food and lodging."

"You would have done the same for me, Jessica."

"Nevertheless, I'm touched by your generosity, and I—" Tears flooded her eyes, and she was glad her veil hid them.

Mary surveyed the landscape, apparently searching for the right words. "Remember, Jessica, when you'd be the first one to disagree with the teacher when something didn't sound right to you."

"I've never been known to be a silent lamb."

"I wish I were more like you, Jessica. I tend to give in more. Maybe I feel sorry for them, I don't know. Like the time Jamie, sitting across from me, stole my apple. I let him have it because he was skinny and poor. Besides, I knew the next day I'd be visiting at your farm and could pick some more. I guess I liked apples a lot. Even baked apple pies just about every month after graduation. In fact, you used to call me 'Apple Mary.' Remember?"

"I remember, but now it's time to forget. My folks are dead now. Memories hurt."

Mary's claret-colored hair, woven into a chignon, barely stirred in the sudden breeze. Her warm green eyes were moist with tears. "I know how you feel, Jessica. In times like these, no words of comfort are possible. But if there is anything you need, just ask."

"What I want you don't have."

Mary turned briefly to look at her friend. She seemed surprised but said nothing.

Jessica stopped in front of a cluster of wildflowers. "Remember that book of poems Uncle Adam gave me last Christmas? The one I showed you?"

"*Leaves of Grass?*"

Jessica nodded. "In that book, Mr. Whitman said that 'sure as life holds all parts together, death holds all parts together.' I don't understand that, do you?"

"No, but in the Bible, God tells us that we—"

"Toby won't get away with this," Jessica whimpered.

"Most assuredly he won't," Mary said. "Remember though, that 'vengeance is mine, saith the Lord.'"

Jessica pulled away from her friend and looked out at the vast stretches of meadow before her. A formation of birds circled the sky. White, puffy clouds hung like cotton from the blue mantle. Farm fields, in small, neat, rectangular groupings, hugged the earth. But the beauty of the day mocked her growing guilt.

"You don't rightly know what I'm dealing with," Jessica said, sensing Mary's uneasiness over the long silence.

"It's a heavy burden, Jessica. Hard to figure out why God lets these things happen."

Jessica felt the anger boiling inside of her. As she lifted her veil, she reminded herself not to blame Mary for misinterpreting her. "That's not it at all, Mary." She stared long and hard at her friend. "When Sam was messing around with Nellie, I could've sent him straight to hell. My Colt was pointed right at his head, but I couldn't pull the trigger. I just couldn't do it! I'm so afraid of that thing."

Mary looked away, staring at the countryside in silence. Jessica was thankful Mary didn't sermonize her about the evil of killing. If it was so evil, Jessica thought, why did God permit Toby to kill her parents, maybe even Nellie?

Jessica trudged back to the waiting carriage, with Mary walking alongside, her hands clasped in front of her. About thirty yards to their right, a Union Cavalry officer and four soldiers trotted on horseback down the road toward the river. Jessica stopped to gaze at them. The men looked mighty sharp in their blue kerseys, dark blue forage caps, and short jackets. A bearded officer wearing a saber in his belt was in the lead. The soldier tailing the group carried a snare drum and looked terribly young.

"Heavens," Jessica gasped, "that soldier looks like a boy."

"I wouldn't be surprised," Mary said. "Seems the Yankees are letting some of them lie about their age so they can enlist. They need all the help they can get."

"So why don't they take women?"

Mary smiled. "Women don't belong in the army, Jessica. Besides, the fightin' men need women back home to take care of children and tend house. Anyway, I can't picture any self-respectin' woman shootin' a man."

Maybe Mary was right, Jessica thought. When she had Toby in her sights, she couldn't pull the trigger. Not sure if it was her promise to Ma or Matt Lightfoot's bad feelings about using guns on people...but she just couldn't pull the trigger. But if she had, maybe she'd at least have Nellie with her here at the funeral.

That afternoon
Ft. Pillow, Tennessee

Sam Toby stared through the cracked dirty window of the gunboat as it rippled through the massive Mississippi toward the port in the distance. A clock ticked heavily in the small room, crowded with charts, maps, ledgers, a half-empty whisky bottle, and a large wooden chest.

He congratulated himself on his successful escape from the law. A Federal marshal and his deputies had him cornered after he docked in Paducah to get supplies. He was sure he was done for until he spotted a small band of ragtag Confederates who started shootin' at the approachin' Federals, and Sam made a quick getaway down the river.

This war was makin' it tough for folks like him in the slave trade, Sam thought. Next time, he'd raise his fee 'cause of all the trouble he had. He leaned forward in his creaky chair and studied the daguerreotypes of each of the ten slaves he held in a cabin in the bottom of the boat. The big man with arms like a wrestler would likely fetch a good sum. But that man looked mean, the way his jaws clenched and those big eyes that glared with hatred. The next four were older men, maybe not fit for more than being house servants. The next two were young boys, one probably ten, the other maybe twelve, not useful for much right now. Two additional slaves were women, one in her twenties and sickly, the other probably fifty and not too useful since her teeth were bad and she walked with a limp. The next one was a loud-mouthed middle-aged Negro woman named Phoebe who sang a lot of stupid Christian hymns and could take the whip several times without breaking down. A good field hand, but might be a problem for her owner.

It was the last slave, though, that interested him: a sixteen-year-old slave girl who claimed her name was "Nellie" and that she was free. She certainly was a beautiful Negro girl, with an attractive face and smooth figure. He figured he'd get a good price for her, but he decided he'd own her himself. Although he told the trade company he had caught nine slaves, he didn't tell them about the tenth one.

"Cap'n Toby," one of the men yelled from the deck, "we're a-comin' into port now, and we better chain the niggers."

Sam opened the door to his cabin. "Don't chain that there young girl with the others."

"Why not, Cap'n?"

"Got my reasons. Jest do as I say!"

Sam Toby hastened to the rear of the boat and watched as each of the slaves, bound by yard-long leg and arm chains, climbed slowly up the steps to the deck. Phoebe, the woman at the end of the line scowled at Sam and went on singing:

> *"We gone in a chariot, Jesus, to our cross must we go*
> *We done leave an angel crying*
> *Cause she must go all alone, all alone.*
> *But we be one body and we cry for her return*
> *We will help her find her true way home*
> *Dear Jesus, show us how, show us how."*

Sam lunged at the woman. "Can't yah keep you mouth shut, nigger? I'm gettin' might tired of yah moanin' to yer Jesus."

Phoebe stopped singing immediately, but her lips formed a tiny smile of rebellion.

A gunboat mate tugged at Sam's sleeve. "Could be she's singin' some sort of message. I hear that these niggers will do that."

"Well," Sam said, slapping Phoebe across her mouth with the back of his hand, "one way to stop that is to keep their mouths from movin'."

After the slaves left the deck, Sam went down below to check on Nellie. He held his nose because of the stench of urine, vomit, and feces. Nellie was sitting in the back of the cabin with her head between her legs. "C'mon," he ordered, "I gotta hide yah."

She raised her head and looked at him with vacant gray eyes. "I wish you'd just kill me, Mistuh Toby."

"Kill yah? Yah gotta be crazy, girl! Yah worth more'n all those other slaves together. C'mon, get up."

"I can't."

"Then I'll carry yah." He grunted when he picked her up and carried her to his cabin. She fought as he stuffed her into the wooden chest, but he managed to get her in and lock the cover. "Now you're all mine," he said and left the ship so he could collect his bounty for the other nine slaves.

Chapter 3

"We've always given him what he wants," James Fowler told his wife Teresa. "Wanted to learn music when he was twelve, and we let him. Right?"

"Yeah."

"And he didn't want us to give him our last name, and we didn't. Am I not right?"

"Can't argue," Teresa said. "You're right about that."

Sitting in the far corner of the kitchen, Lazarus felt like telling the Negro couple to shut up. He tapped his forefinger and thumb sharply against the arm of the rocker, in cadence with the faint drum beat coming through the open window. Some soldiers at the military fort, a half-mile away were beating a tune to "Battle Hymn of the Republic."

"Teresa," James continued, "he didn't even want to go to church with us no more, and we didn't make him. Now with the war'n all, I guess he was bound to want to join up."

"But he's only fifteen," Teresa said. "He still got things to learn. War's for grown men."

Lazarus jumped up. "You both talkin' 'bout me like I ain't here," he growled. "I got somethin' to say about all o' this. You ain't my real parents. You only knowed me for six years. I still dream a lot about my momma back in Tennessee see'n how she still slavin' for her mastah."

Teresa gave him a sympathetic smile. "I know how you must feel. That's why when we saw you in Lawrence, we wanted very much for you to have a home. A real home—here, in Fort Riley."

Lazarus remembered how he'd hidden in a smokehouse, in a ravine, in barns with other slaves, until the Underground Railroad got him over to Lawrence, Kansas. When he saw Mr. Fowler with his arms stretched out in welcome, Lazarus had thought it was a trick to get him sent back to Tennessee. He'd

37

heard about Negroes who were also slave owners, and they were just as mean as white slavers. But the Fowlers were nice to him. Still'n all....

The chime of the pendulum clock in the next room broke his thoughts. Teresa approached Lazarus with a plate of scrambled eggs. "Hungry?"

Lazarus nodded.

Teresa brought her chair closer to him. "Mr. Fowler be right, you know," she said. "You a young'un yet. Why someday you'll meet a fine woman'n get married'n have chillun."

How could she talk about him marryin' some day? He didn't know much about women. Like how men helped women get babies. Too embarrassed to ask the Fowlers, he once asked another boy in school. The boy laughed at him, told Lazarus he was stupid if he didn't know by now. Lazarus felt like telling him he wasn't stupid...that he did once see a woman's body—a slave woman's swollen breast—when he was nine. He had been weak and hungry. He barely recalled what she looked like when she had him drink milk from her breasts. Her milk tasted a bit sour. She stroked his head, sang to him. Although she wasn't his momma, he remembered her love. Were women always that giving?

"Lazarus, I'm talkin' to you."

Lazarus blinked back at Teresa. "Sorry. I weren't listenin'."

"You been happy with us these past six years, haven't you, Lazarus?"

Lazarus shrugged. Not as happy as he'd like to be. The Fowlers were nice people, but sometimes they protected him too much. He had to get out now. The war'd be over by the time they'd let him fight.

"Are you sure we can't change your mind about enlisting?" James asked him.

"No, you can't change my mind. I won't rest till I do somethin' about freein' my momma. I gotta score to settle with them slavers. I can't just sit here at home'n do nothin'. Gotta get her free."

"But what can one person possibly do to change all that?" James asked. "After all—"

Teresa quickly interrupted him. "I understand what you're sayin', Lazarus, and if that is what you must do, then my prayers are with you."

Lazarus entered the recruiting station at Fort Riley, trying to ignore the eyes of others, who all seemed older than he was. All sorts of men had crowded the room, waiting for their turn to be called. Some were young men, probably in their early twenties, while others were older types with gray beards and long white mustaches. They all seemed to be talkin' about this here war, 'specially them battles at Shiloh and Manassas, where thousands of Union men got themselves killed.

"We gotta teach them Southern boys a lesson," one man shouted. "Yeah," the other replied, "and when I get them rebels, I'm gonna shoot 'em up so bad, they all gonna be full of holes." Laughter followed, with backslapping and name-calling.

"Hey, boy," a man dressed in a blue artilleryman's shell jacket and forage cap called out to Lazarus. "Are ye lost or something? This here place is for recruitin' men for the Yankee army."

Lazarus traded stares with a man sitting behind a desk who seemed more like he was chewing his cigar than smoking it. His forehead was furrowed like a field ready for planting, and his lips were cracked.

Lazarus bristled at the word "boy." That's what his master had always called him....

"Hey, boy," the slave owner had said to him, "you don't know how t'pick peaches, do ya? Ya grab the best ones'n ya put 'em in this pail. But no stems or leaves, y'hear?"

"I be plumb tired. Been here all day already. Gotta go see how my momma doin'"

The slave owner, looking at Lazarus up in the tree, sneered. "Ya wanna see how yer momma's doin'? That right? Well, lookee down there."

"Where?"

"Over there, you moron," he said, pointing his long finger toward a post near the large stone house. A slave woman's wrists were being lashed to a post. A white man ripped off the

39

top part of her dress, exposing her bare back to the hot afternoon sun.

"She done get five lashes for talking back to a white man. Now you watch, boy. Watch what we gonna do to yer momma 'cause of that."

"I'm talkin' to ye, boy," the man at the desk repeated.

"Sorry," Lazarus said, leaning forward, fighting the urge to return the stares of the other men in the room. "I'm here 'cause I wanna join the Yankees. Wanna fight is what I wanna do."

The man leaned back in his chair and roared with laughter. "Ye want to do what? Fight? Ye niggers don't know how to fight."

Lazarus clenched his fist. It would have been so easy to draw back and bash him in the mouth. He restrained himself, convinced they might hang him for that. "But I be strong," Lazarus said, "and I know how to load a gun'n all. Not 'fraid to use it none either."

"Izzat so? How old are ye, boy?"

Lazarus thought quickly. Teresa once told him he looked older than he was. "Sixteen," he lied.

"I don't think I can let ye handle a gun, boy. Can ye play music?"

"Music? Yeah, some. But I wanna fight, suh."

The man shook his head and leaned forward on his desk. "I hear niggers have good rhythm. It's in their blood since they're sorta wild, like animals. So maybe we can use ye as a drummer boy if ye can play the snare drum."

Lazarus closed his eyes. Another remark like that and he knew he wouldn't be able to restrain himself. "I can play the drum, sir. But what good is that in this war?"

"Plenty. The soldiers who carry the colors and play the bugle or the drum can inspire the fightin' men. And that's important."

Lazarus swallowed. This wasn't what he wanted. But he'd be out there in the war, and maybe, just maybe, he'd get a chance to do somethin' for momma.

Jessica was glad her house on Indiana Street was only a thirty-minute walk from the Kansas River. Uncle Adam had included her name on the deed to this second home of his after his wife had died. "I don't want this place to go into a trustee sale should I die," he had told her. "I'd rather you have it." Before she had left for college, he gave her a key to this house, telling her she could use it whenever he was back in his other home in Ohio.

Uncle Adam had taken advantage of the fact that Penelope lived only a block away on Mississippi Street. She had moved to Lawrence after her divorce, and Adam had her watch four-year-old Claire as often as twice a month. "Penelope's good with children," Adam would say. "She's very creative the way she makes learning fun for them. That lady will go places."

The sturdy Amish-built rocker sat empty in her dining room, where Penelope used to sit with Claire on her lap. There, she'd read the child stories or play guessing games with her.

"I didn't mean to shoot you, Claire. Please wake up!"

Jessica wondered what Penelope would think of her if she knew what happened back in the cornfield on Pa's farm. No sense worrying about it, Jessica thought, shaking her head as if she could shake herself loose from that horrible memory.

She always liked her uncle's house. Now that it was hers, she'd be able to truly enjoy it. She appreciated the fact that it was closer to the Kansas River than when she lived on the farm. A wade along the river's edge was something she could now look forward to. She found the August heat a little more tolerable with the cool splash of the water on her bare feet. It also helped her forget her concern over reports of war casualties, particularly in Kentucky, where Uncle George was serving with the cavalry.

As usual, Levee Road bustled with the activity of merchants unloading their wagons of foodstuffs and wares at the ferry. She looked out over the river. Toward her left, the concrete supports for a new bridge stood like silent monuments.

An eagle, with its massive wings, graced the cloud-spotted morning sky as it floated toward the Delaware Indian reservation on the other side of the Kansas River. But on her side of the river, a man stood on the grassy bank, fishing pole in hand.

Jessica stopped. It was Matthew Lightfoot. He recognized her with a nod, then took a puff from his long-stemmed pipe. His high forehead, broad face, and long black hair tied in the back stamped his part-Cherokee heritage. But dressed in blue denims and a torn blue shirt, his face scraggly from not having shaven, he also looked more like a young farmer than a preacher-man.

She wondered why she was flattered by all the attention he had shown her. He wasn't rugged or particularly handsome. But he had a way with words and a sincere demeanor when talking about something in which he truly believed. There was a magical quality about his singing voice, too. Its deep baritone made a song special.

Lightfoot dropped his pole on the grass, brushed himself off, and ran over to meet her.

"Beggin' your pardon, ma'am, I figured you might be comin' by this way," he said, out of breath, "so I waited for you."

"Catch anything?"

He inhaled the smoke from his pipe and cocked his head as he looked back at her. "No. Shucks, Miss Radford, I don't enjoy it now as much as I did when Henry and I would—" He stopped and pursed his lips as if trying to form the right apology.

"It's all right. I've come to accept my parents' deaths by now." It wasn't true that she had accepted their murder. She'd never accept it. She still dreamed about Ma and Pa—and about Nellie—almost every night, and then she'd wake up with the same sour realization that they were gone. All because of that bastard—Sam Toby. The sheriff had posted wanted notices in town for Sam. Jessica took one of those notices with Sam's daguerreotype image on it and kept it with her belongings. It was a face she'd never forget. As far as she was concerned, he was the devil himself.

Lightfoot took her hand and held it with a featherlike touch. "Miss Radford, I've missed seeing you on Sundays at the Methodist church," he said. "Thought maybe you're now goin' to St. John's instead. His eyes waited for her reply.

She looked away for a second. "I'm not going to that Catholic church either. Not going to any church, matter of fact."

He forced a smile while letting go of her hand. "Hope at least you're readin' your Bible. Probably more important now than ever that you do."

"Why's that?" Jessica asked. Please, Matthew, she thought, don't sermonize on how the inspired word of God would bring me comfort in my time of sorrow. The only thing that'd bring her comfort would be seeing Sam Toby dead and buried.

Lightfoot took another drag from his pipe and steadied his gaze on her. "Because a Union victory in this here war will help prepare the way for the Kingdom of God on earth. It's all in the twentieth chapter of Revelation. You ought to read it, Miss Radford."

"Why are you telling me this? I don't much care for this idiotic war anyway. I see men dressed up in their smart uniforms getting attention from the ladies. But they don't seem to know they can get killed."

He returned a nervous smile. "Shucks, the only lady I aim to get attention from in my new uniform, Miss Radford, is you."

Jessica frowned and put her fingers to her lips. "What? You mean you're—"

"Yup. Enlisted with Colonel Henry Wessells's regiment. Had a hard time gettin' in, though. Seems some men have a tough time acceptin' a man with Cherokee blood in him. But thanks to Major Radford's help, they took me in. I'm puttin' my service in for a year. By August next year, I plan to be back here in Lawrence preachin' again."

Two weeks later

Although every day men were getting killed, fighting somewhere in the country, Jessica tried not to worry about Uncle George. He had written earlier that he was headed for

43

southern Kentucky. He saw Matt Lightfoot the other day. "Fine man," Uncle George told her. "Lightfoot really wants to do all he can for the cause, but he really misses being away from you." He added, "you might not recognize Matt when you see him. He got rid of his long hair and changed his appearance so he'd look more like one of us."

Uncle George gave scant mention of his ex-wife. All he said was that even though Penelope was now living in Ohio, she still owned their house on Mississippi Street in Lawrence and had been renting it out all these years. "Fool woman," he said, "all she thinks about is money and herself." Then he wrote about Adam Silas and said he had Uncle Adam's chest with him and had come across some daguerreotypes of her Ma and Pa, and of Nellie, too. Told her he'd bring them along when he returned. But when would that be? Two weeks had already slipped by.

She'd never get over the nightmare of losing her family to the rebels. Not even witnessing the hanging of the three men the Federals caught helped her get over it. In fact, it was just last month when she sat in a chair with the others, fifty feet from the gallows....

The sergeant placed a noose around the necks of all three men charged with the murder of Henry and Rachel Radford. One of the condemned men spat at the sergeant when offered a blindfold. "I don't need that," he said, cursing. "I want to look at that there Radford girl. I want to tell her that I'm glad we did it. At least we got two Yankees."

Jessica stood up, stabbing her finger into the air. "What about Nellie?" she shouted. "You got Nellie too, didn't you? Where did you bury her?"

"I'm not tellin' what happened to your little slave girl."

"Don't do this to me!" Jessica screamed. "Is she dead?" She ignored the imploring tug on her sleeve from Matt Lightfoot and clenched her fists. "I'm talking to you! Is she dead?"

"Yer gonna hafta ask Sam," he shrieked as a Union officer raised his sword. The trap doors opened and all three men swung like bags of flour.

The execution seemed so long ago, although it was only last month. The public hanging didn't bring her the satisfaction she had hoped. Fact was, Sam Toby was still alive, maybe even fighting the Yankees somewhere. There was no word of his whereabouts, or Nellie's for that matter. Sam must have murdered Nellie, she thought. But if only she could find her body she'd know for sure. Ma and Pa had a decent burial, but not Nellie. She deserved better. Too bad Sissy didn't protect Nellie from harm.

"Listen to me, Nellie—Sissy doesn't exist. No such thing as an invisible angel."

"But Sissy loves me, Jessica. She does!"

You are such a child, Jessica thought. If Sissy were real and if she truly loved you, she wouldn't have let Sam Toby do this to you. Didn't Reverend Lightfoot preach that God is far from the wicked, but the prayers of the just He hears? So where are You, God? Why did You let Sam get away?

Thinking about all of this again simply made her furious. It'd be best, she realized, if she could just forget it. She'd take her daily walk along the river's edge, cook a meal, and spend her evening knitting or reading. Wasn't much else to do. Lucky she got to spend her most of her daylight hours watching the Sullivan twins and the three Lawson girls at her house. Kind of took her mind off things for a while—the way her days drifted into a pattern of predictable monotony.

But Jessica had a feeling today would be different. When she approached the river, she knew she was right.

What was going on? Why all the screaming? She made her way toward the angry crowd gathered on the cobblestone street along the waterfront and outside the gable-roofed Wayward Inn. Some of the men raised their fists and shouted obscenities. Women clustered in small groups and gazed at something further up. Jessica strained to find out what the commotion was about, pushing her way past the crowd. Tinker, a tall, muscular former slave, now working as a hired man for Skipp Forester, wrestled with Skipp for a tattered Union flag hoisted on a six-foot wooden pole. A white man pushed a colored man holding a canvas sign that proclaimed in crude, printed letters "We Wants To Fight The Rebels." Five other Negroes, two of them women, their backs against the front of the hotel, shouted back at the crowd pressing around them.

Skipp glared at Tinker and grabbed his arm. "This ain't no war for niggers," Skipp bellowed. "You ain't got no right to parade 'round like this."

Tinker pulled away from Skipp's grasp and clutched the flagpole close to his bare, bronzed chest. "Beggin' your pardon, suh. I got every right. I be free man, and this here be my war, too."

"Don't argue with 'im!" a white man shouted from the throng. "Send 'im back to Virginia. They'll take care of 'im there. Put 'im on a plantation plowin' fields." Cheers arose from some of the whites.

Someone handed Skipp a horsewhip, and he grabbed it. "You don't work for me no more," he sneered. "Now git, or I'll put some stripes on your back."

Jessica forced her way past the swarm of people. She reached Skipp just as he was about to bring the whip back. "What are you doing?" Jessica screamed, grabbing his arm. "Let Tinker be."

Skipp dropped the whip in astonishment. "Jessica! I got some personal business here with my worker. It don't concern ya."

She noticed gratitude in Tinker's large brown eyes and glared back at Skipp. "What did he do that deserves a whipping?" Jessica demanded, releasing her grip on Skipp's arm.

"This here's a recruitin' station," Skipp explained, pointing at the inn, "and niggers aren't allowed to enlist for the Yankee cause."

"Why not?" she asked, aware of the growl in her voice. "They live in this country, too."

"Ain't their concern," a man from the crowd cried out. "Their kind can't be trusted," another echoed.

"Y'hear that?" Skipp said, grinning like he'd won an argument. "All Tinker's doin' here is causin' trouble. We got plenty of white boys who wanna sign up for service. Don't need no niggers to do our duty for us."

Jessica returned a fierce look back at him. "You need every able body you can get these days. I'd enlist myself right now if they'd let me."

Skipp laughed. "You? Heck, a college lady like you wouldn't know which way to point a gun, let alone how to load it."

"That so? C'mon, Tinker, let's get out of here."

"Whatever ya say, Miz Jessica," Tinker said, shrugging his massive shoulders. He handed the flag to another colored man and followed her past the crowd already beginning to disperse.

As they walked, Tinker dug his hands into the deep pockets of his dirty overalls. He pulled out his harmonica and started playing "Dixie."

Jessica shook her head in disbelief. "You ought not to be playing that rebel song in Yankee country. Could land you in a heap of trouble."

"I knows some Yankee songs, too," he said, looking away from her as if feeling embarrassed even talking to a young white woman. "I gonna go back home'n play some more."

"Where's home, Tinker?"

"I don' have a real home. I stay in a shed behind the Phillips house on Mississippi Street. People live there say it fine with them."

Tinker must be referring, Jessica thought, to that wooden shed behind the house where Aunt Penelope lived before she moved to Toledo. Jessica stopped and turned to face him. "If you want to fight for the North, Tinker, you ought to. It's your right and your duty."

Tinker nodded. "I hope yah don' mind, Miz Jessica, but I gots to ask yah a question."

"What is it?"

"Well, that talk yah had about fightin' in the war? I mean, would yah do it if yah could?"

"Sure. Why?"

"Well," he said, slowing his pace as he followed a stone path leading to a main road, "I heard that yah was 'fraid to shoot Sam Toby when he was up to no good. Izzat true?"

"It's true," Jessica said, forcing the words out. Matt Lightfoot must have told Tinker about that, she thought. Matt and Tinker were still good friends, despite the fact that Lightfoot had purchased Tinker at a slave auction five years ago. Since slavery was no longer allowed in Kansas, Matt helped Tinker get a job.

Tinker became a blacksmith's assistant for Skipp, even though the former slave had learned to read and wanted a job where he could teach other Negroes to read.

"Now that I think of it," Jessica added, "Skipp is dead wrong about Negroes not being allowed to enlist."

"Why's that, Miz Jessica?"

"I read about it in the papers. Congress gave Lincoln the right to employ former slaves in the service of the Union army. Not to fight, but for doing other chores."

"But I *wants* to fight." The muscles in his jaw stiffened as he clenched his teeth. "I *must* fight!"

"Why?"

"Cause it be the only way to free mah family in Virginia. They's still slaves'n always will be 'less we win this here war." He turned to face her, his deep brown eyes probing hers. "An'if I may ask, Miz Jessica, why d'you wanna fight the rebels?"

The sight of a burning farmhouse flashed in her mind. "I've got my reasons," she said.

"Kin I say somethin,' Miz Jessica?" Tinker asked, his head bowed a bit as he shuffled down the main dirt road with her.

"Sure, what?"

"You don't put on airs like some folk do. I shore appreciate that."

Jessica smiled, moving closer to him. But Tinker stepped away, keeping a distance of several feet from her. Probably self-conscious about being seen walking too close to a white woman, Jessica thought.

A horse approached from behind and stopped. "Jessica!" a man called out.

Jessica almost didn't recognize the gray-haired Yankee cavalryman, sword in hand, shouting at her. It was Uncle George, but his beard had grown longer, his skin more leathery, and his dark blue eyes had lost their sparkle and vitality.

"Is that colored man botherin' you?" he asked, waving his sword in Tinker's direction.

"Of course not," Jessica said, anger rising in her throat at the very implication. "Only thing bothering me was not hearing from you."

"Been busy. Are you going back to your house?"

"No, I'd rather walk further with Tinker here," she said, turning toward the direction of the freed slave. Gone! She looked about and saw him running away. "Tinker!" she shouted. "Come back. It's all right."

"Never mind him."

"Going back to Ohio for good?" Jessica asked.

"No, I'm returnin' to Kentucky tomorrow. Joinin' up with Colonel William Reid's group, the 121st Ohio Volunteers. Looks like trouble is brewin' there."

"What kind of trouble?"

"I'll tell you about it later." He grabbed a leather pouch and handed it to her. "This here has some of the things your Uncle Adam left for you."

She took the pouch, undid the strap, and found three embossed leather cases. One contained a daguerreotype of her Ma and Pa, another of Adam and his daughter Claire, and third, a daguerreotype of Nellie. She felt like crying when she saw their images again, especially Claire's. *I killed that little girl!* No, she wouldn't think about that. The pain was more than she could bear.

Jessica put the three leather cases back in the pouch and hastily dabbed her eyes with her kerchief.

George cleared his throat. "He wanted you and your folks to have these if something happened to him in the war." He scowled as he waved a finger in her direction. "You'll see in that there pouch some legal papers. It has the documents that go with his house in Lawrence, which you rightly now own. But it's got some other papers that say you and your mom would inherit the majority interest in the Silas Drug Company upon his death. If I'm not mistaken, since you're the sole survivor now, it's all yours. But maybe you oughta check that out with a lawyer."

"What!" Jessica was flabbergasted. Her uncle's drug company? She didn't know the first thing about running a business. Wasn't that why Uncle Adam wanted to send her to college and have her work with him after graduation?

"You could sell your stock in Silas Drug," Uncle George suggested, "and you'd have a nice comfortable life."

"I don't want a comfortable life. I want to do something and be somebody."

"Well, you just think about it." His frown suddenly changed to a slight grin, as if he had just heard a joke. "Jessica, you won't believe this, but I spotted a lady soldier in our unit."

"What!"

He laughed. "That's right, a lady soldier. She was all dressed up like a man—pants, shirt, boots, the whole thing. All set to fight, she was. Wanted to kill some rebels. Got found out by a doctor when she became ill."

Jessica shook her head at the thought of a woman posing as a man. How strange!

"Oh," George said, twirling his long gray beard with his finger, "I also wanted to tell you about your friend, the one you used to call 'Apple Mary' when you were little."

"Mary Delaney?" Jessica wondered what had happened to her. Not a word from her since her last letter to Jessica about her leaving for Kentucky. Urgent business, Mary had said. Told Jessica she'd write later about it, but no other letter had come.

"Mary told me after the funeral," George said, "that she wanted to do more than just sit around at home while all this fighting was going on. Well, it seems she decided to go to Lexington."

"Lexington? Whatever on earth for?"

"She wants to learn about helping with the wounded. There's a hospital in Lexington that's willing to train her. Wants to be a nurse, but I think military regulations don't allow ladies to be nurses. Anyway, she can still help out. Like maybe she can get provisions for the male nurses, help cool down a fever, talk to the sick, that sort of thing. I've gotta admire that woman, though. Takes a lot of courage."

Jessica felt her face flush and bit her lip so hard it bled. She dabbed her mouth with her handkerchief during the uncomfortable silence.

"Take me with you to Kentucky," Jessica said.

"Why in tarnation do you want to go there?"

"I got no business being here by myself. Besides, maybe I could be of help to Reverend Lightfoot somehow."

His face soured. "Matt doesn't need any help. He can manage fine by himself."

"Well, maybe I can do something for the wounded."

He shook his head. "I don't want you there, Jessica. Too dangerous."

Jessica's muscles tightened. "Surely, there must be something a poor, helpless, defenseless lady like me can do for the Yankee cause."

Uncle George smiled briefly, tugged at his beard, and glanced about. "Look, you've got a business you can sell and take it easy."

"I don't want to take it easy. I want to do things, important things for the Yankee cause."

"Jessica, there are lots of things you can do here at home. You can write letters, raise money for the war effort, or get some food to send to the soldiers."

"Think little ol' me can do all of that? Sounds mighty important."

"Look, I know it's not to your liking, Jessica. But goin' down there is foolish for a woman."

"Mary did."

"And she's a fool for doin' it."

"You just told me she was courageous."

His face turned sour. "No sense even talkin' to you. Your Pa always said you were stiff-necked. You're just like Penelope, actin' more like a man than a lady."

Jessica turned to walk away, but Uncle George called out to her. "Wait, Jessica. I know things have been difficult with you bein' all alone now'n all. I promise I'll write and let you know how Mary's doin', if I see her."

"I'd appreciate that."

George Radford's eyes drooped, and the muscles in his face relaxed. "Pray for me, Jessica, will you?"

"I will," she said. She hadn't prayed since Ma, Pa, and Nellie disappeared from the face of the earth.

Besides, she didn't have time for prayers. Right now, she had to see if she had a right to Uncle Adam's drug company. And if she did, maybe she could help the Yankee cause by getting the medical supplies they needed. Even, perhaps, bringing these supplies over to the battlefield herself. It'd be an un-womanly thing to do. Aunt Penelope would be so proud of her.

Chapter 4

Late August
Lexington, Kentucky

As Mary Delaney laughed, the curls of her autumn-red hair stroked her round, petite face. "That's the honest truth," she said to her male patient, all bound with bandages. "Those grasshoppers just plumb bounced all over the place. Poor Miz Wilcott jumped in the river, thinking she was being attacked by bees."

"I ain't never been to Kansas," the man said, raising his head up on the pillow of the hospital bed. "Are the folks there still fightin' the Missouri farmers who want slaves?"

"That's what the papers say." Mary kept her smile up, but her sapphire eyes turned serious. "Kansas may be a free state but there's still a lot of bad blood being shed over this slavery thing."

The man fixed his gaze on her eyes, as if searching for some glimmer of truth in them. "Is it true what I hear about Richmond, Kentucky, fallin' to the rebels?"

"I'm afraid it is. Fact is, I'm not sure Lexington's all that secure now." She saw the worry lines on the man's brow and quickly added with a forced laugh. "But don't worry about that none. If the rebels take over this hospital, I aim to give them a piece of my mind."

After checking on the other patients, Mary went downstairs to pour herself a cup of tea. She still hadn't opened her letter from Jessica since she got it this morning. Now that things had quieted down for a spell, she carefully opened the sealed envelope. It had been a while since she had heard from her friend....

Lawrence, Kansas
August 14, 1862

Dear Mary,

> *This will be a short letter because I have more to do than I care to think about. I inherited Uncle*

Adam's business in Cincinnati, whereupon I has-
tened to that town to attend a board of directors
meeting. The men there thought I was a brainless
fool. They tried to convince me to retire all my stock
and leave the company. They said this business was a
man's domain and a lady such as me would not
know how to run it.

I informed them that it did not matter to me
since I would be disbanding them and appointing a
new board. Not only that, but I hired Penelope Phil-
lips to manage the affairs of Silas Drug while I am
gone. I cannot tell you how shocked they were by my
action. Hopefully, I will be able to return later to Cin-
cinnati to take a direct hand in the firm. My initial
plans are to go to Kentucky soon after I return from
the nation's capitol.

Surprised? Yes, I hope I will be able to see you
again when I personally bring needed medical sup-
plies to the battle lines. However, first things first. I
must hasten to take a train to Washington and meet
with the chief of the Army's Medical Department. I
hope to obtain a contract for the sale of medicines
and medical supplies and reap a tidy profit on the
transaction. However, my main interest is to help the
Union cause.

I hope to see you again. I sometimes dream about
the times you were Apple Mary and I was holding the
ladder for you as you picked them off the tree at our
farm. I'll keep myself posted on your whereabouts
through Uncle George. He thinks highly of you. I only
wish he felt the same way about me.

Your friend,

Jessica

"Mary," a husky voice called behind her, "I got some urgent news. Can I see you downstairs?"

The captain held his black felt Hardee hat in his hands and bowed slightly to Mary when she saw him. "It is quite important, ma'am."

Mary swallowed hard. She had heard rumors about a rebel invasion of the city. She hoped this wasn't the news she'd been dreading.

The captain gestured toward a wooden bench outside and waited until she was seated. "It isn't lookin' good," he said. "Major General Nelson was unable to stop the rebels from headin' north to Lexington. Looks like Smith's troops will be here in a day or two."

Mary placed her hand to her mouth and gave a muffled cry. She had toiled at this hospital since July and had made many friends in town. She couldn't imagine this town surrendering to the rebels.

"Our regiment is leaving later this afternoon," he continued. "We have orders to destroy our storehouses and ammunition depot. My orders include abandoning this hospital." As if reading her mind, he added: "We'll try to get the wounded to another military hospital."

"Then I should go with them. The nurses need me."

"Indeed they do. That's why I'm sticking my neck out and askin' if you'd join our regiment in our march south. Union commanders don't look kindly on women workin' in the battlefield. But, Miss Delaney, you've done a commendable job, the way you helped the nurses in the unit."

"Thank you," Mary said, "but I don't do this for praise. I just want to help give our men some hope."

Mid-September, 1862
Topeka, Kansas

Otto Heller looked down on Clover Street, from the window of his third floor office at Heller Publishing Company. All sorts of people rushed by, in horse-drawn carriages or walking, in a hurry, always in a hurry. In a way, the rapid growth of Topeka reminded him of what he had heard about Frankfurt, Germany. Having immigrated to America in 1820 when he was a year old, he only knew about Frankfurt from what his father Helmut had told him.

Otto glanced at a now-tattered book on his desk, atop financial statements, sales plans, and proposed book cover jackets. This book of poetry was the only tangible memory of his father that he had left. Helmet impressed upon him a philosophy which Frankfurt's famous resident, Johann von Goethe, had about life. "Goethe felt we should never be boastful," Helmut told Otto, handing him this book of poetry. "There's a poem in here where he wrote about that. Hope you will read it whenever you feel you're more important than any other human being."

Helmut was right. It was easy to get caught up in one's own self-importance and forget the things that really mattered. Since joining the Underground Railroad, Otto had taken several trips through Missouri, en route to stocking bookstores, and risked his life bringing escaped slaves to Kansas. No one at his firm knew about it, and people would probably think he had taken leave of his senses if they ever found out.

People like Henry Thoreau were also correct, he thought, as he examined a copy of Thoreau's *Collected Papers*, which Heller Publishing had just reprinted with that title. Otto was particularly touched by Thoreau's lecture on civil disobedience. Thoreau, he recalled, raised the question as to whether, when unjust laws exist, one should be content to obey them. As far as Otto was concerned, the answer would always be an emphatic "no."

His swivel chair squeaked as he brought himself closer to his desk. "Well," he murmured, "back to business."

He no sooner started reading his latest financial statement than there was a knock on his door. Evelyn, his receptionist, with an embarrassed look on her face, opened the door part way. "Sorry, Mr. Heller, but there's a man here who insists on seeing you. I told him you were busy, but—"

Otto looked up, his eyes narrowing. He hoped it wasn't a pushy salesman. Evelyn had explicit instructions not to allow salesmen into his office. "I'm very busy. Who is it?"

A medium-built Negro male pushed the door wide open. He wore a checkered shirt and denims that were tucked into his boots. His narrow eyes darted away from Otto's. "Begging your pardon, Mr. Heller," he said, looking down at the carpeted floor, "but I need to see you."

Evelyn, the lines in her face echoing her exasperation, started to apologize. "I ordered him to leave, but—"

"Never mind, Evelyn," Otto said, focusing on the man, who had taken a couple of steps toward his desk. "I'll see what he wants. Close the door, will you?"

"But—" Evelyn said, looking at the Negro, then at Otto.

"Don't worry. Just close the door."

After his receptionist left, Otto leaned forward in his desk and gestured to the man. "Have a seat, Mr.—?"

"Fowler, Jim Fowler."

"I somehow know you," Otto said. "Your face and name are familiar."

"You should know me," Fowler said. "Six years ago you delivered to me and my wife Teresa, a young boy, an escaped slave, for possible adoption. You said you had been callin' him Lazarus 'cause when you found him, you thought maybe he was dead."

Otto grinned in recognition. "Of course! How's Lazarus coming along? He'd be what right now—about fifteen?"

"He'll be sixteen in January. But he lied about his age and joined up with Yankees. Got a letter from him. Told me things were just fine in Kentucky. He wishes they'd let him use a gun. But he thinks playin' a drum is fine, too. It may help the Yankees fight better."

"Took a lot of courage for him to enlist."

Fowler smiled. "You gave him a good example about courage. After all, you helped him escape, even though you were breaking the law."

Otto felt his face flush from embarrassment. He placed his hand on a copy of Thoreau's *Collected Papers*. "This man confirms what I've already felt—that one needs to break the law if the law itself is unjust." He handed the copy to Fowler. "Here, why don't you take this volume, with my compliments? It makes for good reading."

"Thank you, Mr. Heller."

Otto noticed the way the Negro shifted his weight from one foot to the other as he held the book with both hands. "Jim, you appear to be a bit nervous. Is there anything you need?"

"Yes, there is. Teresa and I just moved to Topeka in hope of finding work. We've been blessed with a baby, but things are difficult lately."

"How can I help?"

"Can you find me a job? You know, of course, that I can read and write well. Perhaps there is a job you can offer me. Anything. It doesn't matter."

Otto folded his hands and leaned back in his chair. Things were tight right now. He had all the employees he needed. Well, he was putting out a new magazine, and the typesetter he had was already working two shifts. He'd be taking a chance with Fowler, who had no experience in typesetting. He hoped Fowler was a quick learner.

Otto promised he'd do what he could and that he'd get back to him in a day or two. After Fowler left, he thought about Lazarus, how ill the boy looked when he had found him...how one slave woman, unrelated to the boy, tried to revive the child....

The woman had opened her dress and offered Lazarus her full breast. The boy's eyes were half open when she directed her nipple to his lips. Soon he was sucking eagerly. "It be milk for mah own child," she said, her eyes swollen with tears, "but mah child gone now, done get killed by a rattler, so you drink from me."

Otto tried to get back to reading his financial statement but couldn't. Instead, he opened up the tattered book on his desk, and read Goethe's lines again....

> "Once too, a child, not knowing where to turn,
> I raised bewildered eyes up to the sun,
> as if above there were an ear to hear my complaint,
> a heart like mine to take pity on the oppressed."

In six weeks he'd be making another trip—the last one, he had promised Helga. Since he needed to get to Wichita to open up a branch office, this would be his one opportunity. He'd take a much longer path to Wichita—by way of western Missouri—in hope of finding escaped slaves to take back with him to an underground contact in Fort Scott. Otto assured Helga everything would be fine and not to worry. But Otto couldn't shake off his own fears of being captured.

The next day
Dry Ridge, Kentucky

Six soldiers from a Kentucky infantry accompanied two supply wagons as they made their way south toward McCook's troops. One wagon carried Parrott shells and solid shot cannon projectiles while the other brought critical medical supplies. Two artillerymen drove the mules pulling the ammunition. Behind them was the medical supply wagon driven by John Howell and Jessica Radford.

Jessica mopped her brow with her handkerchief, thankful that the sun was falling into the parched farmland in the west. Soon they'd have to camp for the night.

John accepted the canteen Jessica offered him and took a swallow. He handed it back to her. "Who's managing the company while you're gone?"

"My aunt, Penelope Phillips. I think she's doing a better job of running things than I could. Of course, I don't think she gets along too well with the board members."

"Because she's a woman?"

"Not only is she a woman, she's half colored at that. Her slave mother was killed soon after she gave birth." She pursed her lips and turned to him. "I sometimes wonder if Nellie's mother is still alive."

"Who's Nellie?" John asked.

Jessica tightened her grip on the reins. "Never mind. I didn't mean to mention her name."

They rode on for a while in awkward silence. John cocked his head as he smiled. "I still can't believe you wanted to do this."

"You mean drive this wagon? Second nature to me. I used to drive a hay wagon on my Pa's farm."

"But this is no hay wagon," he said, "and this is no drive on a farm. There're scavengers and renegades out here who'd blow our heads off in the name of the rebel cause. Dangerous business, especially for a lady.

58

Jessica turned to him and smiled. John Howell looked more like a rugged frontiersman than an ordinary hospital steward. His unshaven face revealed a prominent nose, while his deep-set blue eyes, arched by his long, thin eyebrows, showed intelligence and deep thought.

"It's a good thing," Jessica said, "that I own this wagon and these supplies. Otherwise, they wouldn't have let me make the trip."

"You told me you drove a hard bargain back there in Cincinnati."

"Yes, but I wish I didn't have to. Sometimes I wished I'd been born a man. People wouldn't be fussing so much about my doing things I'm doing."

"Like fixing that broken axle yesterday?"

"Nothing to it. It was just a crack. Easy to patch."

John laughed. "You're not like any other woman I know, that's for sure."

"I'll consider that a compliment, Mr. Howell." She noticed that they were approaching a thick stand of cedars on the right side of the road. "I'm going to stop right here," she said, bringing the horses to a halt.

"Whatever for?"

She handed him the reins. "I have my reasons."

He shouted to the artillerymen ahead to halt while he reined the mules to a stop. "Mind if I inquire as to why you want to stop, Miss Radford?"

"I drank a canteen of water four hours ago, and you're asking me why I want to stop?"

"Well, this is an odd place, Miss Radford, in the middle of nowhere."

"Doesn't matter," she said, getting off the wagon. "I'll be back." She walked briskly toward the grove of trees. As she squatted discreetly behind a bush, she could see him in the distance, sitting on the wagon platform with his Springfield rifle glued to his hands. When she returned minutes later, he was still surveying the landscape as if expecting an attack at any moment.

"You oughta not go anywhere alone without protection," he said when he saw her approaching. "Dangerous around here. That's why we've got soldiers going with us."

"Well," she said, laughing as she climbed back on the platform, "there are times when a woman needs to be alone." She dug her hand in her dress pocket and pulled out her Colt revolver. "Besides, I've got this to keep me company, Mr. Howell."

He glanced at it and signaled to the artillerymen up ahead to resume. "Nice piece," he said scratching his angular chin. "Y'know how to use that, Miss Radford?"

"Fired it only once, by accident. Only thing I ever used much was my Pa's shotgun on the farm when he showed me how to shoot deer."

"A shotgun's a lot different than a pistol. I oughta show you how to use that thing."

At twilight, when the supply train stopped for the night, Howell insisted on giving Jessica shooting lessons. He held her Colt .31 in his right hand while supporting it with his left. "You have to use two hands," he said. "You need to keep it steady because the recoil could be powerful." He took aim at the top of a picket fence. "Like this," he said, exploding a round, drilling a hole into the fence. He handed her the revolver. "Now you try it, Miss Howell."

Her hand shook as she took the gun from him. Only once had she ever fired Sam Toby's gun, but here she was, about to make a fool of herself. "Maybe I should do this in the morning," she said.

"Nonsense, Miss, Howell. It's still light enough. C'mon, raise it up now with both hands and aim."

She did as he suggested, but her hand wavered. *I didn't mean to shoot you, Claire.*

She lowered her arms and felt her face burn with humiliation. "I'm sorry, Mr. Howell. I just don't feel like doing this right now."

A week later
Memphis, Tennessee

Before the slave auction began, Sam Toby scanned the news from the *Memphis Dixie Bulletin*, looking for any news about his brother Roger and the Twenty-Third Tennessee Infantry Regiment. Finding none, he thumbed past stories about

60

various rebel victories and noticed a piece about a Negro regiment being formed in Kansas. Somethin' about a Yankee abolitionist who was opposing the Secretary of War by organizing a Negro regiment in Kansas. Well, wasn't that somethin'? Puttin' the colored in the military to fight against the South.

What's this? An article about some slaves escapin' from New Madrid? Let's see. Yeah, slave owners puttin' up a nice reward for their return. He'd have to get back to catchin' more slaves. Still good money in that. Too bad the Underground Railroad was stealin'em and movin'em up North.

Once he got some good money for Nellie, he'd go back to roundin' up some more. He watched as wagonloads of slaves stopped near the platform where the auction would be held. He felt bad about having to sell Nellie, but he knew he could get a good price for her, and he really needed the money. He was pressed to pay his huge gambling debt, and this curvy sixteen-year-old slave girl was the only asset he had.

He wished he had money like the plantation owners and planters had. He'd have a lot of slaves, some for fixin' things, some for cookin' 'n cleanin', and some for lovin'. It'd be like money in the bank, too, 'cause he could sell 'em anytime.

The baldheaded auctioneer stood on the platform, his thumbs under his suspenders, calling for everyone's attention. "Serious bidders," he shouted, "are allowed to walk by each nigger on this stage and ask questions and inspect their bodies. But only serious bidders, please, 'cause we have a business to run here, not a show."

Down the long line of unchained slaves standing on the ground, to the left of the stage, Sam looked around for Nellie. One of the slaves he recognized was Phoebe, the rebellious woman who liked to sing hymns. Probably her owner couldn't take her stubbornness anymore, Sam figured, and was selling her.

Next to Phoebe was a slave girl whose head was turned away from the crowd. Sam kept his eyes focused on her. Could it be? Yeah, it was her, all right. She turned and seemed to look directly at him, not smiling, not frowning, just staring at him with a blank look. White men on horseback, holding long whips in their hands, trotted back and forth in front of the slaves, but Nellie kept her gaze steady on him.

Sam was glad he hadn't whipped her, although he had been tempted. Whip marks might bring down the bidding price 'cause it meant she'd be trouble for the new owner. He watched as the bidding started, with some bidders getting on stage to ply the slaves with questions, like "Do you take orders good? Kin you keep quiet when you work? Ever try runnin' away from your mastah?" Some of the bidders squeezed the backs and buttocks of the slaves, looking for signs of welts or sores. One burly, shirtless white man in a straw hat demanded that a slave boy, who looked not more than eight years old, pull his trousers down so he could inspect his genitals. The boy obeyed, while a slave woman standing nearby wrung her hands and shrieked, "That's mah son. If y'buy him, buy me too. Please, mastah! Buy me too!" The man bought only the boy, and the woman, having fainted, was dragged off the platform by two white men.

Sam noticed Phoebe bending down and whisperin' something to Nellie, who simply nodded. This made him uncomfortable as he remembered how the gunboat mate was suspicious of Phoebe. *Could be she's singin' some sort of message. I hear that these Negroes will do that.*

Suddenly, Phoebe ran to one of the guards standing at the end of the stage, grabbed the man's arm, the arm holding a long whip, and started to sing:

Slavery chain done broke at last
Gonna praise God till I die.

The guard struggled with the woman. A commotion rang out from the crowd. A horseman charged down toward the platform shouting obscenities. The guard pushed Phoebe away and aimed his carbine at her. A white man stood nearby, probably the master who was selling her, and screamed at the guard not to shoot. The guard paid no attention and blasted away at Phoebe. One shot. She staggered and dropped to her knees. Another shot brought her down. Two bullets, like thunder, slammed into her, both in the chest. In the confusion that followed, the other slaves started to scatter, but two more horsemen galloped by, shooting their rifles in the air.

Two men on horseback rounded up the slaves. Two others mopped up the blood on the platform and carried out Phoebe's body. The auctioneer, his face ashen, raised his hands in the air and called for silence. "This auction will continue soon as we do another slave count. Too bad we lost one slave, but we will not tolerate dissention. No sir!"

Sam didn't have to wait for the recount of the slaves. Nellie was nowhere in sight. Gone. He tried to get the auctioneer's attention, but people in the crowd told him to be quiet. They wanted to hear the results of the recount. Finally he heard what he knew would be the case.

"We have a missin' slave girl," the guard who had killed Phoebe announced. "But don't worry none. We're gonna get the dogs after her. We'll bring that nigger back. Let's go on with the sale."

Sam left immediately. He knew better than those slave sniffin' dogs where Nellie might have went. He'd find her and teach her a lesson she'd never forget.

Early October
Eighth Kansas Volunteer Infantry
A Union camp southeast of Louisville, Kentucky

When Lieutenant Matt Lightfoot approached the Negro workers' tent, one of the men jumped up at attention. Lightfoot returned the man's salute, glad the man knew how to follow military procedure.

"Private, is Tinker in?" Lightfoot asked.

"He out there by the trees, suh," the Negro said, pointing toward the grove of trees nearby. "Want me t'get 'im for yuh, lieutenant?"

"Never mind. I'll go there."

Matt Lightfoot hesitated to disturb Tinker, who stood, playing "John Brown's Body" on his harmonica. Lightfoot had second thoughts about having persuaded Tinker to join the infantry as a general maintenance worker. He hated to see Tinker unhappy. Tinker wanted to fight for the Union. But Negroes—whether slave or free—were excluded from carrying and firing weapons while serving in the military.

"Sorry to disturb you," Lightfoot said, "but I missed you at the services I held yesterday for our company. I was hoping you'd join us in song."

When Tinker turned around, Lightfoot saw tears in the man's eyes. "Is everything all right, Tinker?"

"Yes Mastah, I mean lieutenant," smiling with embarrassment as he slipped his harmonica in his pocket. "I'm sorry, but I keep forgettin'."

Lightfoot couldn't blame him. Tinker had been his slave for four years before he gave him his freedom.

"I was just standin' here, ponderin' things," Tinker said, turning back to look at the line of chestnut and evergreen trees fronting him like a battle line. "I was thinkin' how nice it was for you to teach me readin' even though most mastahs didn't allow it for their slaves. I was thinkin' 'bout that because I jest saw something one of the white soldiers had. He let me read it for mahself. It was 'bout Lincoln. He gonna issue some kind of proclamation next year to free all of the slaves."

Matt Lightfoot put his hand on Tinker's muscular shoulder. "You've already been a free man for more than a year now I guess."

Tinker turned his large sad eyes at his former master. "I know and I 'preciate that, suh. But if Nellie lived, she'd be free for sure."

"You miss reading stories to that child, don't you?"

"I do. She like the 'Song of Hiawatha.'" He closed his eyes tight and paused. "'Love the sunshine of the meadow, love the shadow of the forest, love the wind among the branches.' Then there was something 'bout the rushing of great rivers."

"Excellent," Lightfoot said, grabbing his hand and shaking it. "Maybe with a little more work, I can make an English teacher out of you."

Tinker grinned from ear to ear. "I don' think so."

"I bet you miss not seeing Jessica around, don't you?"

Tinker grew serious. "I do. I pine for Miz Jessica 'cause she a good woman. But I hear she leave Kansas. Do yah know where she go?"

"Last I heard, she was pickin' up a load of medical supplies in Cincinnati and headed over into Kentucky."

Tinker's eyes sparkled. "That mean I might get a chance to see Miz Jessica again?"

"Don't know."

Matt Lightfoot wished he did know. He missed her more than Tinker did.

One week later

Lazarus didn't feel much like talkin' to the men in the neighboring tents. Not that he had anything against white folk. He just felt like spendin' his free time tryin' to read what he could of a book Teresa had mailed him: *Collected Papers*, a collection of lectures by some man named Henry Thoreau. It was difficult, though. The sentences were long and he couldn't make out all the words. Maybe he'd go back to another book he had taken along with him—*Uncle Tom's Cabin*. Teresa had read part of this book to him and had underlined words she felt important. It didn't matter that he couldn't read all the words, she'd say; just read the words you do know.

"Think carefully about what these words mean," she'd add. "People use words when they make laws. People use words when they wage war. And people use words when they settle their differences."

Lazarus closed his eyes as he lay on his bedroll in the tent. He moved his tongue over his lips, first the upper one, then the lower. He was hungry again. There never was enough food here, and the food they had was tasteless.

Mr. Fowler, he thought, didn't think words were as impor-tant as action. "Lazarus," he'd say, "words alone didn't build this country. It was action. Pioneers ventured into the wilder-ness to homestead and build a new life. It was men who had the courage to go against the British and resist them with their own lives."

Mr. Fowler say one thing'n do another, Lazarus thought. Why don' Mr. Fowler allow him to join up with the Yankees? "Not right," Lazarus murmured. "Not right 'cause he knows I got to do somethin'."

He heard the spirited playing of a harmonica outside his tent and got up. Sounded like "The Battle Hymn of the Republic."

Opening the flap of his tent, he spotted a tall, muscular Negro man, his boot on a tree stump, playing away on his harmonica.

Lazarus stood facing him, his boot pounding out the beat as the man played. Soon Lazarus found himself whistling along for accompaniment.

The man stopped playing and grinned at the boy. "Yah likes it, son?" the man asked.

"Sure do. You play good."

"I thanks yuh, young fella," the man said. He extended his hand. "How d'ya do? I don't believe we met before."

"My name's Lazarus. What's yours?"

"Yuh kin jest call me Tinker, son. My mastah gave me that name long ago, but I still likes it."

"You a slave?"

"No suh, No slaves in the Union army, son. No slaves here at all."

Early morning
Loosahatchie River
18 miles northeast of Memphis, Tennessee

Hiding in the tall grass on some farmer's land, Nellie had eaten the last of the carrots she had pulled out of the ground yesterday and rested against the trunk of a tall loblolly pine. Yesterday there were fish in the river, and she tried catching them with her bare hands. Henry Radford used to catch 'em in a net, and she wished she had one. Eating nothing but raw potatoes, carrots, and beans that grew in the fields, she missed the occasional fish or meat Sam would drop in her dish.

Yesterday she finally stopped calling for Sissy. Maybe Sissy thought she was dead, too. Just like Jessica probably thought she was. Maybe being dead wasn't so bad. After all, there really was a heaven. Sissy told her that once and said not to worry. It was a better place than over here.

"I been lucky," she murmured. "They ain't gonna get me. I'm gonna run and run and run till something happens. I be free. I not a slave. I used to have papers that say I be free."

"Jest run'n run, girl," Phoebe had tol' her. "Make them legs of yours go fast like a deer in the woods."

When Nellie heard the gunshots behind her, she sprinted from the slave auction. She prayed that Phoebe wouldn't be killed, but in her heart she knew when she heard the gunshots that the woman was murdered. Phoebe died so she might live. Jest like what the preacher-man Lightfoot said 'bout Jesus, "He died so that we might live."

"Well," Nellie murmured, "this here girl ain't gonna die. Jest to show 'em, I'm gonna make sure I ain't gonna die. Even if I feel like goin' to heaven, I ain't gonna give 'em the satisfaction."

A strong arm grabbed her from behind. She screamed, swinging her hands to shake off her captor. "Lemme go!" she yelled.

"Hey, that anyway to talk to yah friend?" the man growled. "I jest wanna have some fun with yah."

Nellie turned around. Her heart pounded like a cannon.

Sam Toby, sneering, pointed his gun at her.

She knew she wouldn't escape this time.

Chapter 5

That evening
Two miles north of Springfield, Kentucky

Small campfires pierced the dark horizon when Jessica returned to the tent she shared with Mary. Sentries on duty marched along the small hills on either side of the camp. An owl hooted. Jessica wondered why she felt both embarrassed and elated. Why should she be embarrassed, she wondered? Surely, no one had seen her in the wooded area, alone with John Howell minutes earlier….

Jessica had pressed her back against a large cedar as he glided his hand across her small bosom. "I shouldn't let you do this," she said, her lips inches from his. "I've read stories about men who try to seduce ladies to lose their virtue."

"And what happens to the ladies in these stories?" he asked with a teasing smile on his lips.

"Well, they eventually fall in love—I mean—oh, I don't know what I mean."

His lips inched closer. "You know what, Miss Radford?"

"No," she said, not backing away.

"When it comes to love, you need to read less and experience more."

Before she could respond, he pressed his lips against hers. She closed her eyes, conscious of the way her heart was fluttering, aware of his tender fingers pressed against her breast. His breathing became heavy. "I want you," he said, his hand unbuttoning the front of her dress.

Grateful at hearing a voice calling out to someone at the camp, Jessica gently pushed him away. "I'm not ready for that experience, John."

"I think you are," he said, running his hand over her long sleeve. "And I think you're worth waiting for."

After she buttoned her dress, she walked back alone and felt like whistling. Life took on a new meaning when someone cared about you. And John cared about her—even if he only wanted to have his way with her. She wished she had more time to think things through. What did she know about him? Not much. In fact, he had told her he was going to be gone the next few days, but refused to tell her why. What was he hiding?

The moon silhouetted an outline of trees on a steep hill in the distance. The sound of crickets added to the loneliness of the night. The few soldiers who were awake were sitting quietly by their fires, speaking only in whispers when they talked. A sentry guarding one part of the compound looked closely at Jessica before letting her pass through. Jessica, barefoot, felt the day's heat trapped on the ground while mosquitoes bit her mercilessly. She raised the hem of her simple black dress to avoid getting snagged by the underbrush.

Uncle George had expressed his displeasure at Jessica's teaming up with some hospital steward to bring medical supplies in from the Silas Drug Company in Cincinnati. He wrote to tell her she was a stiff-necked, stubborn fool. He said she was just like Penelope in many ways. Once she had set her mind to do something, her ears were closed.

Still, in that same letter, he had grudgingly told her the company and unit where Mary was working as a nurse. Perhaps just to irritate Jessica, he concluded his letter by saying, "Mary's doing a wonderful job. When this thing is over, I hope the War Department gives her a commendation of some sort."

Well, no matter, Jessica thought. Her Uncle George would always be the exact opposite of her Uncle Adam. According to Uncle George, women were weaker beings, mentally and physically. Too bad Uncle Adam had died. He would have been so proud, the way she bargained with the Yankee military in selling them the medicines they needed. And he would have been proud, too, that while she was here helping out, Penelope was in Cincinnati running the company.

Jessica poked her head into the tent. Mary was just putting away her knitting. "Any luck?" Mary asked.

"No. I checked with the sergeant on duty. Not only are we not rationing water, we're plumb out of it."

"I've been doing a rain dance for Jesus," Mary laughed, "but maybe I'm not doing it right."

Jessica began undressing. "You remind me of that cheerful, optimistic little girl named Apple Mary. Do you really believe that Jesus is going to get us through this?"

"I most assuredly do. Don't you?"

"No." Where was Jesus, Jessica thought, when those vermin murdered Ma, Pa, and Nellie? "Look, Mary, I do believe there's a time for praying and there's a time for action. Now's the time for action. We better get some drinking water tomorrow, or we're going to be dead mighty soon."

"Any word from our leaders as to what they plan to do about this?"

"No," she said, laying her dress on a couple of boxes, "as far as I know, we're gonna have to spend time first looking for water before we can engage the rebels."

Jessica plunked her aching body on a wooden folding chair and sighed. "I passed by a soldier this morning lying by the side of the road. Thought maybe he was just resting but when I lifted his head, it was all sunburned. I mean he was as red as blood. Mouth was all cracked and parched. Nothing anybody could do for him; he was already gone."

Mary picked up her knitting. "What medicines did you bring with you?"

"I gave my list to John Howell, and he's going to give it to the company quartermaster. A range of items, such as magnesia, cotton oil, and soap. But I also brought in a large supply of bandages, iodine, powder of opium, spirit of ether, and morphine."

"Good. We've been low on those things."

Jessica got up and undid her petticoat. "I've heard of the good you're doing here, Mary. My uncle tells me you once helped a surgeon take out a musket ball from a man's stomach. I don't think I could do that. I'm not cut out for nursing. I'm probably more prone to do some fightin'."

Mary's eyes widened as she stopped knitting. "Fighting? Fighting is for men, not for women."

"I don't see why. It doesn't take any special talent to load a musket and fire."

"Jessica Radford! I am surprised at you. Would you actually fire a weapon at someone?"

70

"Maybe," Jessica said dryly. "My Ma was always against guns. Pa was different. Figured if a person rightly deserved it, he should be killed. Told us it said so in the Bible when they used to stone sinners. Could be I take after him."

After hanging her petticoat next to her dress, Jessica decided to catch her friend's attention. Wearing men's trousers, Jessica stood in front of her, smiling.

"What in tarnation!" Mary exclaimed, first frowning, then bursting into laughter. "So you've taken to wearing women's and men's clothes—all at the same time?"

"It's too bad I have to hide this under my dress. Someday, I suspect, it will be fashionable for women to wear men's trousers."

"That will never happen," Mary said. "Besides, I enjoy wearing dresses. Makes me feel like an attractive woman."

Jessica put her hands on her hips. "I'd feel like an attractive woman even if I were stark naked."

Mary giggled. "And you'd *look* like an attractive woman if you were stark naked."

Jessica smiled, ran a comb through her hair, then turned back to Mary. "My uncle tells me that Reverend Lightfoot is here. Have you seen him?"

Mary looked up at her. Her shadowed cheeks showed lines of strain on her face. "I've seen him. He asked about you last time we talked. He wondered how you were."

"Did you happen to tell him about my new role as a medical purveyor?"

"I did, and he admires you for it. Says it is a courageous thing you're doing."

Jessica blushed. "Really? He said that?"

"Are you two romantically—?"

"No, of course not! I have problems with Matthew, such as the fact he used to own slaves. And he always seems to be preaching religion to me when we meet."

"Did you tell him about John Howell?" Mary teased.

"Nothing to tell. Mr. Howell and I only spent a couple of weeks together traveling." But, Jessica thought, it was that last day before arriving here that lingered in her mind....

"Let's sleep under the wagon tonight," Howell had suggested after they ate by campfire.

"That wouldn't be proper," Jessica replied.

"I didn't think that 'being proper' was part of your vocabulary, Miss Radford."

She noticed that look of longing in his eyes. "Call me Jessica."

Later that evening, they slept under the wagon. She thought of encouraging him to do more than simply touch her in the right places, but she didn't. Her parent's values about "saving" herself for marriage kicked in at the wrong time, so they ended up talking before drifting off to sleep.

John was right. She needed to experience more and read less. It'd be especially true in order to one day become a successful writer. There were things about John she liked—his self-assuredness, his gentleness, and his intelligence. Maybe she wasn't in love with him, but she could imagine it, imagine someday feeling his warmth and experiencing those forbidden pleasures. It was both frightening and wonderful.

"You're hiding something from me, Jessica," Mary said. "I can tell by the way your eyes get glassy like that. When we were little, you never kept secrets from me."

"Mr. Howell is nice. That's all I'm saying about him."

"So you're not going to tell Matthew about him since there's nothing to tell."

"That's right," Jessica said, feeling her body tingle, imagining what it'd be like to make love to John. "And if I did, Reverend Lightfoot would likely be jealous. But it'd serve him right."

Jessica extinguished her lamp and slipped her tired body under the blanket.

"So maybe," Mary said, after a long silence, "you don't want to see Matthew anymore?"

"Like I say, I don't know how I feel about him. Especially since he enlisted. He told me in one of his letters that he's not only wanting to preach but that he intends to fight as well." Jessica bent forward and slid her fingers under the blanket, rubbing her legs, wincing at the cuts, bruises, insect bites on her bare skin.

"The way I look at it," Mary said, "ministering to Yankee soldiers is like fighting for the Lord."

"Y'know what the trouble with you is, Mary?"

"What?"

"You're always trying to make a bad thing sound like a good thing."

The three Union officers sat around a roaring campfire. General William Terrill, a tall and stern-faced 28-year-old, laughed when General James Jackson kidded him about his youth. "You're goin' into your first battle as a young general," Jackson said, running his fingers over the wide brim of his slouch hat. "Think you can handle it?"

"With all due respect," Terrill said, casting a respectful glance at Jackson as well as Colonel George Webster, "I've been in the army long before this war started. The Union is glad to have me on their side."

"I know," Webster added. "with you being a Virginian, you could have easily been a rebel."

Jackson pressed his back against the tree. "I wouldn't have been surprised if you had joined the other side."

Terrill's eyes widened. "I beg your pardon?"

"What I mean," Jackson said, "is your brother James is fightin' for the Confederates. How did that happen?"

Terrill's face fell a little. "It's a long story. Fact is, my father disowned me for sidin' with the Yankees."

A silence fell among them as the timber in the fire continued to snap and pop. "Water's gonna be a problem," Webster said. "The creeks we saw back there are dryin' up."

"Hope there's some in Doctor's Fork," Terrill said.

Jackson shook his canteen and a little water sloshed inside. "Rebels will be lookin' for water in the same places we are. Could get ugly tomorrow."

More silence. A long silence.

"Do you think," Terrill finally asked, "that one of us will be wounded, maybe even killed, when this battle is over?"

"It could happen," Jackson said. "but we should be more concerned with the lives of our men."

Webster rubbed his knuckles together and took a quick look at Terrill. "I like to play the odds. We've got more than twenty thousand men out there in the field. It's pretty unlikely you, me, or Webster would get killed in battle."

"I wish I could agree with you," Jackson said.

"Why is that?"

"I have a horrible feeling about tomorrow. A very horrible feeling."

Jessica woke up with a start. She must have slept through reveille. Mary was gone, probably attending a morning meeting with the medical staff. Jessica hurried to get dressed. Grateful for the horse Howell managed to procure for her yesterday, she untied it, looking about in vain for John. She rode out toward a group of men standing at attention as the chief surgeon addressed them. The sun had just inched up from the farmland in the east. Jessica saw Mary standing by herself at the end of the group.

Jessica dismounted and approached her friend. "Morning, Mary."

"Looks like we got here before the sun did."

"Have you seen Mr. Howell?"

Mary shook her head. "He's nowhere around. Didn't you tell me he was going to be gone for a few days?"

"Yeah, I did. But I thought I'd at least get a chance to say goodbye."

Mary returned a knowing smile but said nothing.

"Well," Jessica said, mounting her horse, "I best check with Sergeant Walker about medical supplies. Maybe he can tell me where John is headed."

"I doubt he'll have time to talk with you. I hear we're moving to Perryville soon."

"I'll be ready for it." Jessica said, riding off. About a half mile down she saw Major Radford seated on his horse, standing atop a small hill. Her uncle looked grand in his uniform, as if he were born to wear it, when he led men through the meadows and farmland to victory. His blue frock coat was wonderfully adorned with yellow trim, while his sleeves were embroidered with a looped braid that ran almost the entire length of the coat. His black boots and saber's scabbard gleamed in the sun, and Jessica thought he looked more like a general than a major.

Major Radford trotted his horse behind a line of field commanders inspecting the troops. The Yankee soldiers, arranged in blocks, some twenty men wide and fifty deep, stood at attention, their carbines on their shoulders and cartridge boxes and pistols in their belts. Behind them was the artillery brigade, where several 12-pound Napoleon cannons would each be pulled by a six-horse team. Five young men with snare drums marched at the edge of the field, playing a monotonous rat-a-tat-rat-a-tat while the commanders trotted their horses through the wide spaces separating the clusters of Yankee soldiers.

"I thought I'd find you here on the hill, away from all of this," a man's voice said behind her.

She turned to see a man of medium stature, friendly eyes, black hair cropping his high forehead....a man she knew would eventually find her.

"Why, Reverend Lightfoot," Jessica greeted with a smile, "aren't you supposed to be with Colonel Wessells's regiment?"

"I've been temporarily reassigned here, Miss Radford. After dismounting, he tied his reins around the trunk of an apple tree and approached her, grasping his rifle with one hand. "I'd like to think that it was 'cause the colonel felt these troops needed some spiritual enlightenment. Or maybe it was cause he wanted me singin' a few patriotic songs with this unit."

"Or maybe my uncle agreed to help you find me."

Lightfoot grinned. "He did. He told me your brigade was on its way to Perryville. I thought maybe I'd rejoin Webster's unit once we got there. Been writin' any stories?"

"No time. Someday I aim to get serious about it. I'd like to write like Emerson or Hawthorne."

"And you will," Lightfoot said, smiling. "Tell you one thing, Miss Radford, you're real good with words."

Jessica paused. "What are you holding there?"

Lightfoot followed her gaze to the carbine he held in his right hand. "Oh this? This here is a Sharps breechloading carbine the colonel gave me. Thought it'd be easier for me to use than one of them old-fashioned muskets."

Her mouth soured. "It'll make killin' much more efficient, I suppose."

"Shucks, Miss Radford. I don't condone—"

"That's quite all right," she said, folding her hands in front of her. "I'm glad you were able to find me. Like I say, I haven't been writing much. Course, in this war, there isn't much of anything good to say. Not much to sing about either, is there?"

"Slaves sang about hope in Jesus all the time."

Jessica glowered at him. "I wouldn't rightly know that, seeing as how I never owned any slaves."

Matt rubbed his hand over his chin. "Well, I best be goin'."

"I reckon so."

He turned, walked to his horse, and stopped. "Jessica," he said, looking at her with sad eyes.

"What?"

"Never mind." He got on his horse and rode away.

Early afternoon
A field northwest of Perryville, Kentucky

Jessica and Mary stood atop a grassy mound, safely back behind the soldiers. Jessica, looking through field glasses, observed General Terrill's Union Brigade forming a line against the Confederates who were crossing the tree-lined Chaplin River. One rebel brigade was in the lead, marching steadily through the open field while the Union's artillery battery positioned its cannons to confront them. The sun, peering through the clouds, cast an eerie white circle on the Union line. It was as if God were favoring the Yankees right now, Jessica thought.

"Don't you just wish," Mary said with a lilt to her voice, "that someone could just jump in the middle of all that and say 'come on men, let's put those guns down and talk'?"

"It would never happen. The rebels are too fond of killing. My pa used to say it's in their blood."

"With that attitude," Mary said, "you ought to be down there yourself, blasting away at the enemy."

"Sometimes I doubt I'm doing enough for the Union cause."

"There are times I wonder the same thing," Mary said. "I'm supposed to help nurses fix up the wounded so they can get shot at again. So what's the point of this war anyway?"

"Don't really know. Some say it's to protect state's rights. Others say it's to abolish slavery."

"So we're going to do that by killing everybody?"

Apparently so, Jessica thought, as she watched the armies jockeying for position. Yankee soldiers found whatever protection they could, behind trees, near bushes, behind fences, a chicken shed, or rock piles.

"It sure is awful quiet out there," Mary said as she turned her attention back to the battle lines being drawn below. "Maybe the battle's been called off, and we can all go back home now."

"I don't think this is anything to joke about."

"If I don't joke about it, I'll go crazy."

Jessica just nodded.

Commanders barked orders while their subordinates obeyed them. To Jessica, it resembled a chess game on a massive scale, with each side trying to outguess the other. The Union guns, together with batteries all along the Union line, opened fire. A series of explosions broke the awkward silence of the valley.

Mary looked again through her field glasses. "Alas, it's happened! God save our Union!"

After the first round of volleys from the cannons, scores of rebel soldiers fell to the ground, many screaming in agony. Rifle shots, like short claps of thunder, erupted all along the riverbank. Shots were returned, and white puffs of smoke blew across the trees. Lieutenant Colonel John Martin, further down the field, gave his horse a swift kick and galloped away, shouting orders.

The two women raced toward a small grove of trees. There, they found Timberlake and Johnson, two assistant surgeons with whom Mary worked. "We better find the others and get ready for the wounded," Mary shouted to them.

Timberlake kicked his boot into the dust. Johnson took a long drink from a canteen. "I never operated on anybody before," he said. His hand shook, sloshing water out of the canteen.

"Jessica and I could sure use some of that water," Mary said. "My mouth feels like a desert."

77

"Sure," Timberlake agreed. "I got an extra canteen of water for you ladies." He went to his horse to get the canteen and handed it to Jessica.

"How did you manage to get any water?" Jessica asked, taking a swallow before giving the container to Mary.

"Dead rebel," Johnson said, matter-of-factly. "If we find 'nough of them murderin' rats, we'd have 'nough for our horses."

Jessica could hear Pa saying, the night he was killed, *"It's about time they learn how to deal with murderin' rats."* As far as she was concerned, there was only one murdering rat—Sam Toby. He had to be out there somewhere.

Two hours later
Starkweather's Hill, near Perryville, Kentucky

Lazarus stumbled, but picked himself up again, beating his drum as best he could. The Yankees in front regrouped to five or six ranks deep. Retreat, advance. Retreat, advance. The explosions all about him rattled every nerve in his body. Blazing lights of reddish-golden flame, burning trees, grapeshot hissing like angry snakes. Further ahead, bugles pealed, officers shouted orders to advance or hold position, men staggered, cursed, and crashed through the thickets. A deadly scream pierced the sky, then another, sometimes several at the same time.

Lazarus slowly moved on, as if in a horrible dream. Ahead of him were uneven rows of Union skirmishers shooting, loading, here and there screaming as they fell backwards into merciful grass coffins. A corps commander, his eyes ablaze with fury, screamed orders as he followed his charging lines. Cannon fire erupted from rebel and Union sides alike, filling the afternoon sky with smoke, hiding the sun. Lazarus was sure he'd soon lose all his hearing from the constant booms of exploding shells.

The color bearer took a musket shot in the throat, and turned around, his eyes wide with horror, before he dropped to the ground. A Negro man, whom Lazarus did not immediately recognize, grabbed the tattered Union flag and raised it high. "Let's fight to the finish!" he yelled.

He turned around, his eyes meeting Lazarus's. "C'mon, son, beat that drum hard!"

"Tinker?" Lazarus said, stumbling just as a bullet whizzed past his ear. He picked himself up and flung himself at Tinker's legs, bringing him down. "Are you crazy?" Lazarus pinned him to the ground with his knee. "Yuh wanna get killed? Yah got orders to stay back away from the front lines."

"This here is my war'n yer war," Tinker said, gasping for breath, his eyes dancing wildly. "We needs to free our niggers."

"Look aroun' yah, Tinker. Men gettin' killed left'n right. Can't free the niggers if you git killed. Need to live so's we kin fight mo' battles."

"Maybe yer right." Tinker raised himself up to a crouching position. He turned to Lazarus and, raising the flagstaff, he punched it into the soil. "But I don't wants ta leave this here flag layin' on the ground. Now, let's git." With that, he ran, hunched over, down the end of a field of barley and toward an apple orchard.

Lazarus tossed the drum to one side and scurried after Tinker. His boot caught on something, and he fell headlong next to a dead Union lieutenant. He looked up for Tinker and found him stopping to grab the flag of the First Tennessee that lay on the ground. Tinker stood up, hoisting the flag high and hollering, "They's on the run! They's on the run!" A soldier in gray had come up from behind a boulder. Lazarus thought quickly. The dead lieutenant had a Starr Army revolver in his belt. On impulse, Lazarus pulled it out, his hand shaking. Mr. Fowler had once scolded him for taking his gun and killing a raccoon with it....

That's a living creature you just shot. With a pull of your finger, Lazarus, you denied it the right to live.

But *he* ain't got no right, Lazarus thought. He fired off a shot, the recoil jerking back his arm. The man in gray turned toward Lazarus, gun in hand, then plummeted to the ground.

Tinker whipped around, looked at the rebel who had just been killed and, mouth open in astonishment, gazed at Lazarus. "Where did you learn ta shoot like that, son?" he asked.

"I jest pretended he was a racoon, that's all."

"I don't get it."

"Never mind," Lazarus said.

Tinker removed his cap and scratched his head in amazement. "You done saved my life, y'know that?"

"I know," Lazarus said, embarrassed. Killin' rebels wasn't so bad after all.

Jest think of them as vermin.

Chapter 6

Union General Alexander McCook paced the kitchen of the two-story house and cussed in disbelief. "I have never seen such obstinate fighting before," he told his aide. "Seems like the more we tear them apart with our guns, and the more we cut them down with our swords, the more they fight."

"When will Buell send in reserves?"

"Frankly, I hope he knows by now that we've got a major battle going on." He pressed a crude map against the tabletop and moved his finger on it. "You say Cleburne's already crossed Doctor's Creek?"

"Yes sir."

"Hope our artillery holds against Cleburne on those slopes. Good position for us. But I'm worried about Lytle's men on Mackville Road. They're taking quite a beating from the rebels. C'mon, let's see if Gilbert's coming with reinforcements. We've gotta stop Cleburne."

McCook stormed out the door, with his aide following behind. The valley was filled with smoke. Cannons from both sides of the fray were booming. The yells and musketry of the men running across the open field echoed across the valleys and against the ridges. Bodies lay strewn about the farmland like misshapen dolls.

McCook took in the view with his field glasses. "This is what hell must be like," he said.

Lieutenant Matt Lightfoot shouted to the others in the brigade to hold their position. A captain grabbed his arm. "Can't do that. Best to fall back and regroup."

Matt Lightfoot retreated with the others toward lower ground but wished he could have stayed with the wounded and prayed. But there was no way to do that and still stay alive. Bodies had been dropping all around him this afternoon. One man had received a bullet in his eye and cascaded to the ground, blood oozing out of his eye socket. Another man had been blown apart by cannon fire, his detached arm sailing through the air. Lightfoot had seen enough. He prayed to God to have mercy and bring all of this to a peaceful end.

A bullet whizzed by, knocking off his cap, and Lightfoot instinctively landed with a thump on the dusty ground. His carbine, having flown past him, lay in a row of beans, some ten feet away.

He crawled on his stomach toward his carbine. When he got near enough to grab it, a heavy boot stomped on it. Lightfoot looked up. Grey uniform. Young man. High cheekbones. Long black hair. Prominent nose. Possible Cherokee features.

The man in gray lowered his rifle and took aim. Instinctively, Lightfoot raised a hand for mercy. "*Tsa-la-gi-yi?*" He guessed and hoped that the rebel understood Cherokee.

The rebel opened his eyes wide in surprise.

Lightfoot repeated his question. "*Tsa-la-gi-yi?*"

The rebel nodded, raising his gun. "*Ashehi.*" He was indeed Cherokee.

Lightfoot raised both hands, begging for peace. "*Nivwa dohi yadiv.*"

The rebel grinned, lowered the gun, and aimed it at Matt Lightfoot.

Instant thoughts of death blared through Matt's mind. Death. Blackness. Eternity. Heaven? Hell?

A tremor shook his body, waiting for the bullet. But the rebel turned the gun away from him, pulled the trigger, and shot into the ground. He laughed and took off running.

"*Nivwa dohi yadiv!*" he shouted back, repeating Matt's word of peace. "*Nivwa dohi yadiv!*"

Matt shivered from jarred nerves reverberating throughout his body. Death. He had always preached about facing death without fear because of the promise of an eternal reward. Yet he had not faced it bravely himself.

Sam Toby noticed two Confederate soldiers enter the tavern. One grabbed a chair at a table across the room and laughed at some remark the other had made about the ineptitude of the Yankee's General McClellan. He glanced briefly at Sam, and returned his attention to the other soldier.

Sam leaned forward at his table to get his brother's attention. "Roger, all I hear 'bout these days is what an idiot the Yankees have as a general. I'm tired of hearin' 'bout how Jeb Stuart rode 'round the Federals and got McClellan to retreat. All anyone talks 'bout these days is our Confederate commanders. I'm gettin' mighty tired of all this here damn war talk, and I don't even give a mule's rear end 'bout this stupid war."

The two soldiers seated at the other table looked in Sam's direction, but he cast them an angry stare in return.

Lieutenant Roger Toby, looked as if he had just been insulted. "Listen," he said, his eyes narrowing, "I don't care if yaw *are* my twin brother, this war's not stupid. Men are dyin' out there in the battlefields 'cause they want to be free from power-mad Federals. Lincoln and his bunch just want us Southerners to be his servants. Don't yaw ever call this war stupid!"

Sam felt his muscles tense, annoyed that his brother was always so uppity, just 'cause after grade school Roger went on to high school while Sam barely finished the sixth grade. Sam figured that's probably where Roger got those stupid ideas about slavery. He had lived with their wealthy, abolitionist-minded aunt in the next county the whole time he went to a private school there. After Roger joined the Twenty-third Tennessee Regiment soon after the war broke out, he was promoted to lieutenant and now was even more uppity than before. Well, Sam thought, he wouldn't stand for that.

"I guess I'm an expert on knowin' 'bout what's stupid," Sam answered, glaring at his brother. "After all, yer term of military service is over, and now you're free to go back to yer bank job. But you're thinkin' about reenlistin'. If that ain't stupid, I don't know what is."

83

"This war's important, Sam. More important than runnin' the bank here."

"Yah think I'm a fool 'cause I'm jest a bounty huntah." He bunched his fist like a mallet. He never could stand his brother. When his brother returned home to Tennessee years ago, Sam headed for Missouri just to get away from him. But Sam failed at all the jobs he tried—telegraph office clerk, mule driver, and horse trainer.

Roger glared back at him. "Sara asked me once why yaw hate slaves so much. I told her it was because some slave on Pa's tobacco plantation stole your horse'n money'n then run away."

"Yah tol' yer wife right. That's why I hates them niggers."

"Sam, slaves are just like yaw and me."

"No they ain't," Sam barked. "They's dirty, no brains, nothing. Hey, why yah on this talk 'bout slaves? I 'member yah used to like one in particular."

Sam knew why his twin brother suddenly seemed embarrassed. Roger wanted to forget about the time when, newly married to Sara, he made love to Nasha, an attractive, bosomy eighteen-year-old slave at Pa's plantation. Sam came into the barn and caught him in the act....

"Havin' fun, Roger?" Sam had asked, while Nasha, her wide eyes reflecting her terror, grabbed a blanket to cover herself. Sam, his hands on his hips, burst out laughing. "Roger, you've always tol' me how good you felt 'bout slaves. Didn't know this was what yah meant by that."

Sam laughed again, while his brother pleaded with him not to say anything to Sara about this. Sam swore he wouldn't.

"Can we talk about something else?" Roger asked, "like maybe the war? Yaw oughta be interested in it, Sam. I hear rumors that Nathan Forrest is plannin' to move into western Tennessee sometime this year and wipe out Grant's railroad supply line. That'd be something, wouldn't it?"

Sam grinned back at him with disinterest. "Yah for makin' war'n I'm for makin' money. I think I have the better deal."

"I don't think so." Roger studied him for a moment. "Sam yaw oughta get your own place someday. But yaw never stay in one place for long, do yaw?"

Sam turned serious. "Fact is, I gotta move on, get more slaves. But I got a problem, Roger, and I need yah to help me with this one."

"What?"

"Like I says, I gotta be free to go back to bounty huntin'. Good money in that. But right now I'm tied down with a slave girl I own. She done run away, but I found her and brought her back."

"Why do yaw need a slave girl anyway?"

Sam just grinned.

"You mean yaw and her—?"

"Sure, Roger, why not? Yah did with Nasha, didn't you?"

"That was different."

Sam laughed. "No, it ain't. Problem is yah think yah better'n me'n yer not. We come from the same mold."

Roger bit his lip, as if repressing an urge to argue with him. "Who is this slave girl of yours? Where is she?"

"Her name's Nellie. A real prize she is, if yah know what I mean," he said with a wink. "She's kinda strange, though, like sometimes I'll see her kneelin' with her hands t'gether like she's prayin' or something. She acts like a child sometimes."

"So why are yaw tellin' me all this?"

"I wants to sell her to yah. I'll make a deal. Seven hundred dollars and she's yours."

Roger's mouth dropped open. "What! Yaw can't be serious."

"Six hundred then. I know yah got plenty of money'n can afford her."

"Where is she?"

Sam stood up. "C'mon, I'll show yah." He paid for the beers and headed over to the boarding house nearby. Roger followed him up the stairs and waited for Sam to unlock the door.

"She's in this bedroom," Sam said, moving to a door which led from the kitchen. He unlocked the door and ushered Roger in. There, lying on the bed, was a Negro girl in a white chemise, her eyes closed, her legs brought up in a fetal position.

"She's a-sleepin' right now," Sam whispered. "Listen, she's worth the money, Roger. She'd be more fun than Nasha."

Roger traded stares with him. "What'll happen if I don't buy her?"

"If I can't get a buyer, I'll jest get rid of her."

"Yaw mean—"

Sam nodded. "Sure. No one would cry over a dead nigger."

Roger dug his hands in his pockets, looked at Nellie, then at Sam. "Let's get outta here'n let her sleep."

Roger returned to the kitchen and waited while Sam locked the bedroom door. "Well, Roger, whad'ya think? She worth it?"

"I dunno. I can't be unfaithful to Sara."

"Yah were before. Why is it any different now?"

"Yaw don't understand. I'm a changed man."

"Forget it then. I jest thought you'd be interested in her."

Roger's hand shook as he wiped his brow with a handkerchief. "But I *am* interested," he said, his voice quivering.

"Then you'll buy her?"

He glanced at the bedroom door. "Yeah," he said, wooden and distant. "Just have the signed papers ready for me tonight."

Nellie had given up hope of ever seeing Sissy again, but she came as a flash of light that melted into the form of a young Negro girl in a flowing white gown. Sissy's hair was as black as hers, her copper skin soft and smooth, her auburn eyes flooded with gentleness.

"You are safe now," Sissy said. Her voice was tender and caring. "No need to be afraid."

"Jessica done say you not real. You not help me when I cry for you."

Sissy smiled. "Evil men do bad things. But you are safe now."

"I don't believe you," Nellie said. "Why do you lie?"

Sissy vanished immediately and didn't return when Nellie called for her. But Nellie sensed the presence of a white light

86

burning through her eyelids. Startled, she opened them to find herself lying in a strange bed, sunlight warming her face. She looked around, confused by being in a room she had never seen. It was much larger than the one where Sam had kept her confined. Dark blue curtains framed the large window and next to her bed was a small table with a glass vase and daisies in it. On the powder-blue wall facing her hung two paintings, one of a winding river flanked by trees, a river that reminded her of the Missouri, where a man named Otto had discovered her. The other was a painting of a Negro kneeling on one leg and around him were some words. But what did it say? She pulled the covers from her. As she shuffled toward the wall, the wooden floor creaked beneath her feet.

She strained her neck looking up at the painting. "Am I not a man," she read aloud, "and a brother?" The painting looked like a slave beggin' to be free, she thought. What was this doin' here? Didn't Sam hate slaves?

Nothing was familiar here in this room. Where was she? Last thing she remembered was Sam Toby forcing her to take something he called "medicine" that made her sleepy. Sam then said something about takin' her to her new home, so this must be it. His new home.

She stumbled to the door, expecting to find it locked, but it wasn't. Had her mastah forgotten? Wasn't he 'fraid she gonna run away? Confused, she opened the door and entered what looked like a kitchen. In one corner of the room, between a fireplace and a window was a cupboard, its doors open, exposing plates and dishes. To her right was a wood-burning stove and in the center a fancy wooden table with four chairs.

She tiptoed to another door and opened it. Sure 'nough, there he be—Sam Toby snoring his fool head off in the bed. By now, she was used to Sam crawling in bed with her every morning, making her play with him and get him all excited. The first two times when she refused, he slapped her and beat her with his fist. Since then, she expected he'd demand this of her every morning, so she made it part of her routine.

Today would be no different, except that this morning she'd be crawling into *his* bed for a change. After closing the door, she took off her chemise and crawled under the covers.

She commenced to make love to him like Sam had told her to every morning.

Vacillating between sleep and reality he suddenly awoke with a start. "No, Nasha! Don't do that!"

Holding his face in her hands, Nellie asked, "Mastah Toby, who be Nasha?"

"Yaw don't understand," he said, pushing her away, "I'm not your master."

"Yeah, yuh are," she said, confused. Why was Sam playing this game with her? "Yuh tol' me I gotta do this every mornin' afore we eat."

The door flew open and a woman of medium stature and dressed in a petticoat entered. "Roger, I heard voices—" She stopped, frozen. Her gray eyes widened as she looked at her husband and then at Nellie. The woman's hand, still grasping the doorknob, trembled.

"Wait, Sara!" Roger cried, pulling himself up to a sitting position. "I was gonna tell yaw about her last night but yaw were asleep,"

But Sara left, slamming the door behind her.

Chapter 7

Late afternoon
Outskirts of Danville, Kentucky

The sun was about to be swallowed by a distant hill in the west when Jessica shoved open the door of the Presbyterian Church. While Sergeant Walker unloaded the rest of the medical supplies in the church foyer, Jessica stepped outside to get away from the screams of the wounded. She heard their cries for help, even with the large doors closed behind her. Dropping her tired body on a wooden step, she pressed her hands against her ears.

Even this church had to be part of the horror of war, Jessica thought. What Daniel Defoe once said was true— "Wherever God erects a house of prayer, the devil always builds a chapel there." This was a monument of hell, with men dying and with surgeons acting more like butchers in treating the wounded.

Jessica dabbed her wet eyes with her handkerchief. How could her friend Mary put up with nursing these men back there in Perryville? For the past hour or so, wounded Yankees from the battle ten miles away had been carted to this church, surgeons running about like lunatics trying to determine who needed to be treated first. Nurses deciding for the surgeons which ones were beyond hope and likely to die. She didn't want any part of this. Delivering medicine was one thing. Putting up with all this suffering was quite another. Not having eaten all day, she felt weak.

To help herself get rid of those negative thoughts, she tried to think about what she would be doing right now if she had returned to college. She recalled the four-story brick building she had seen on her way here. Caldwell Female Institute they called it. A school for women. Ma always wanted her to finish college. But now Ma was gone. Pa, too. No, Jessica had to think about what should have been. She should have been at school right now, learning things. Maybe learning about running a business or reading things written by scholars. She hadn't even opened a book since she left Cincinnati.

A shriek of agony from within the church. Jessica forced herself to ignore it.

She wondered how her friend Amelia Read and her husband Fred were doing in Lawrence. In none of her letters did Amelia ever talk about the loss of their infant. Instead, she always referred to her trust in God when things did not bode well. Yet Jessica was more interested in how she helped her husband Fred in his partnership with Lathrop Bullene when they ran the Bullene and Read Dry Goods store. Jessica always had the impression that Amelia was not at all like Penelope. Amelia loved the written and spoken word, but in an artistic, creative sense. While Amelia apparently had the ability to help Fred run a business, Jessica felt Amelia's real calling was elsewhere—perhaps as a teacher or as an actress in a play. In a way, Jessica felt Amelia was a reflection of herself—helping to run a business when what she really wanted to do was something else. In Jessica's case, it was writing stories, maybe one she'd write about a man like John Howell, where the heroine questioned whether she was simply infatuated with a particular man rather than in love with him.

She had grown fond of Mr. Howell these past two weeks. Not enough time to know him, but she knew enough to want his company. A handsome, virile, intelligent man, a man who had aroused something in her she didn't know she had–physical desire for him. Next time he had his hands on her, she might not resist giving herself to him. But where was he now? He had disappeared from the camp without saying goodbye. Well, he'd have some explaining to do when she saw him again.

Another scream from the wounded.

With a groan, she got up to see if Sergeant Walker had finished unloading. She opened the church door. A sea of noises surrounded her.... "More morphine.... Can't do it.... We're almost out.... Doctor, don't cut it off.... No, don't!... Don't do it!

Everything turning gray. Getting dark. Walls closing in. Walker's voice—"What's wrong, Jessica?"—was a distant echo. Footsteps rushing toward her. Falling. Falling.

That evening

The last place Mary wanted to be was here, with surgeons and nurses treating a growing number of casualties in a barn lit now by oil lamps. Night had fallen, but she could still hear intermittent gunshots echoing in the valley, even though she was two miles away from the battle. The white cotton fabric covering her dress was spattered with blood. The screams of the dying and wounded rang out from one end of the barn to the other. Twice she had to leave the barn to vomit—once when she saw how a shell had opened the intestines of a man, another time when a man shrieked in pain as they sawed off both of his arms.

She tried not to think about John Howell, who lost his leg to an exploding shell. Union soldiers had found him near Doctor's Creek, wounded as he tried to escape from Cleburne's rebels. General Sheridan paused briefly at the makeshift hospital and, after visiting the wounded, told her that Howell had helped the Union cause before. "Thanks in part to his information," the general said, "we were victorious at Mill Springs and Fort Henry. But it's tragic he didn't learn about Bragg's supply strategy for this campaign."

Mary couldn't believe it. Wasn't it more tragic that Mr. Howell had lost so much blood that he might die? But the general left before Mary could respond. What would she tell Jessica, who was assisting the quartermaster with supply deliveries? Mary pushed open the barn door to get away from all of this. Occasional spurts of grapeshot that echoed through an otherwise peaceful meadow still unnerved her, but not as much now as when the battle first started. Given enough time, she thought, one can get adjusted to practically anything. But she almost gagged when a light breeze carried along a pungent smell of gunpowder intermingled with sulfur. At dusk she had made out clouds of smoke and ant-like men scurrying about, engaged in battle. Now the black of evening would soon descend on the horror like a merciful curtain.

Just outside the barn, Mary found a man doubled over, sitting on a cracker barrel, weeping. She approached him, and hoped to console him as best she could. When he raised his head to look at her, she was stunned. It was Matt Lightfoot.

"My word, Matthew, what's wrong?"

Matt Lightfoot dried his eyes with his sleeve. Shaking his head, he looked down at his folded hands, his lips struggling for the words.

"Please, Matthew."

He got up and put his arms around her. "Ma'am, I shouldn't be here," he said, hugging her.

"Nonsense, Reverend Lightfoot. How can you say such a thing? It was indeed courageous of you to be on the battle-field today."

"No, it wasn't." He pointed to a carbine leaning against a cracker barrel. "See that there gun of mine? I never fired a shot with it. I pretended I did, but I never fired a shot. I couldn't see myself sending some soul to eternity."

She kissed him on the cheek. "I admire that in you, Matthew."

"No, nothing to admire," he said, pulling away from her. "I never did learn my lesson, Miss Delaney. After all these years..." His voice trailed away.

"Matt, I think you—"

"When I turned eight," he interrupted, "my father put me in charge of guiding a group of boys about my age toward sacred hunting grounds. But I ran away when I saw a snake. He was disappointed with me. Told me I shirked my responsibilities and let fear take over. Made me memorize a Cherokee saying: *Fear has its use, but cowardice has none.*" He looked up at her. "I'm a coward, Mary. That's all I am."

"That doesn't make you a coward, Matt."

"Yes it does Mary, it does. I've got a sacred duty to lead my men, to be an example for them. But all I've done today is watch men die."

Mid-morning, the next day

Private Trumbull and Corporal Newcomb had piled the twelfth dead Yankee on the pine platform of the wagon when Sergeant Steinberg told them it was all the mules would carry.

Trumbull took off his hat and wiped his brow with his dirty sleeve. He scanned the numerous bodies still littering the valley. "What are we to do with all them dead rebels, sergeant?"

"Let 'em rot there for all I care. It's more important we give our own men a decent burial."

Newcomb, with a bandaged right arm, winced as he scratched an ear. "Them folks need a decent burial, too. They's got families."

Sergeant Steinberg stomped over to Newcomb, going nose-to-nose with the corporal. "They're only worthless rebels. They disgraced the Union. They don't deserve no respect. You hear?"

Trumbull put his hat back on. "How many dead d'ya think we got, sergeant?"

"No tellin'," he answered, surveying the littered landscape. "Hundreds fer sure. Maybe thousands. Them rebels killed our commanders, damn pigs!"

"Which commanders?"

"Three that I know of. A colonel—Colonel Webster, and two generals. One was Jackson and the other a young feller that got promoted to general not long ago. A man who went by the name of Terrill, William Terrill. Promising commander they say. That's why I want them dead rebels to rot in hell."

Mid-morning
Two miles east of Perryville, Kentucky

"You had me worried yesterday, Miss Radford," Sergeant Walker said with one hand on her waist as she rode side-saddle with him. "You just plumb fainted right in the church foyer. Thought maybe you had come down with typhoid."

"I'm fine now. Nothing like a good night's rest."

Walker looked at her with wise eyes. "General Buell is gonna need more supplies soon."

"You told me about that yesterday. I telegraphed Penelope about it to start making arrangements."

"Good. But I don't see any need for you to go back to Perryville."

"I've got to see someone there."

"Your friend, Miss Delaney?"

"Yes." But she especially hoped to find John. He was all she could think about this morning.

"Received a message this morning," Walker said, with a happy lilt to his voice. "Hope it's true."

Jessica turned to see his slight grin. "Good news?"

"Excellent news. Bragg withdrew his armies from the field and is now headed back to Harrodsburg. Rumor has it that his troops are movin' south to Tennessee. If it's true, the Union would control all of Kentucky."

They rode on, Jessica thinking all the while what she would say if she saw John again. No, not *if* but *when*. And if he was still away, she'd wait for him to return. No sense returning to Cincinnati for medical supplies if she didn't first give him a chance to explain himself to her. To explain why he shut out one part of his life from her when he disappeared without a word. She'd forgive him, but only after she let him know how hurt she was. Then she'd go back with him to Cincinnati for more supplies. The quartermaster sergeant had already told her yesterday someone from Buell's staff would contact her as to where to drop off the next shipment. The sergeant said he would see if he could arrange it so Mr. Howell could meet her at her plant in Cincinnati. Then she and Mr. Howell would be returning to Louisville by riverboat rather than by a wagon to Perryville like they did the first time. Still, Jessica thought, they'd be together and she and John would—"

"Oh, no!" Walker exclaimed as they rode into the clearing. The farmland was strewn with bodies, many in gray. Yankees were picking up their own dead and piling them in carts. A choking stench of death hung in the air. Music, a chant of some sort, drifted off beyond a ridge. The morning wept with a sickly gray overcast.

"It's worse than I imagined," Walker said, slowing his horse.

The song grew louder as they approached the ridge. Two dogs ran down a cornfield, chasing each other, oblivious to the sadness gripping the rolling fields.

As he neared a gathering of mourners, Walker stopped his horse so Jessica could dismount. Reverend Lightfoot was leading a small group of soldiers in song:

The strife is o'er, the battle done,
the victory of life is won,
the song of triumph has begun.
Alleluia!

Seeing Jessica approach, Lightfoot stopped singing while the others continued.

"Miss Radford! It is so good to see you. I was quite worried about you."

"I'm only sad I wasn't here to help Mary. How is she?"

"Not doing very well. She may need a few days' rest. Quite a strain."

"Where can I find her?"

"I'll take you to her." He offered her his arm.

She shook her head. "I'll just follow you."

Lightfoot led her to a small tent and opened the flap. Jessica was stunned to see a woman with a ghastly pallor, shallow cheeks, her hair in disarray, lying on a cot.

Jessica rushed to her side. "Mary?"

Mary opened her eyes and offered a weak smile. "Hello, Jessica." She coughed. "I'm happy to see you."

"Are you—?" Jessica couldn't say it. "Dying" was such a horrible word.

"No. I spoke to a doctor here who told me I'm suffering from exhaustion. A little tea, crackers, and soup, and I should be as good as new."

"Had I known how severe this battle would be," Jessica said, "I wouldn't have left you."

"But you had a duty to deliver those medicines, and I had a duty to help the surgeons." She coughed and brought her right arm down to grab an envelope beside her. "John Howell asked me to give this to you. It's a letter he wrote. He had to dictate it to someone, since he couldn't write it himself." She handed Jessica the envelope.

Jessica's hand shook as she took it. "Where's John?"

Mary turned her head to one side.

"Where's John?" Jessica repeated. Her voice was shrill, anxiety pounding her veins.

95

Mary stared at her friend, then closed her eyes. "He died early this morning."

Jessica turned and left without saying goodbye, the heel of her boots stabbing the ground. She stopped long enough to read the few words John had dictated to Mary:

Dear Jessica,

> *It doesn't look like I will survive, so I must bid you farewell with this letter. It is good that you were not here to witness my agony, but I must tell you something that has been on my mind for quite a while. You know I do care for you deeply, but I am indeed grateful you had not succumbed to my base desires. I should have told you that I have a wife back in Ohio, and I—*

What! Jessica tore the letter into small pieces. Married? Why did he deceive her? Numb, she walked a considerable distance, oblivious to stares from some of the soldiers and medical people.

A crow sat on a tree limb not more than twenty yards away, cawing. Jessica took out her Colt revolver and held it just like John had told her to. Killing a living thing would be easy for her now. She pressed the trigger... once... twice. The crow dropped softly to its grassy grave.

Two days later
Stanford, Kentucky

Lieutenant Colonel Martin thumbed through some papers on his table as Tinker and Lazarus stood at attention. Tinker's knees shook while Abernathy took his time poring over his documents. Finally, the lieutenant colonel looked up at the two former slaves.

"This is a bit out of the ordinary," Martin said. "We normally don't like to transfer our men to other units unless there's a critical need."

96

"I understand, suh," Tinker said.

"But I also understand your need to fight and not just dig trenches, set up camp, and do chores."

"Yes suh. I wants to fight, suh. So does Lazarus here."

Lazarus's eyes lit up. "I do. I wanna fight them rebels, too."

"Why, you're just a boy," Martin said, eyeing him carefully. "I can't allow you to handle a weapon."

Lazarus looked like he was about to object when Tinker took over. "I understand, suh," Tinker said. "That's why Lazarus can be of help to us doin' other things."

"Hmmm." Martin rubbed his chin, looking at Lazarus, then at Tinker. "It says here both of you are from Kansas, so I guess it makes sense you should both want to join the First Kansas Colored. I've been told there are now some five hundred fugitive slaves in that unit. They're all ready to fight and die for their freedom. Of course, you're not a fugitive slave."

"But I still wants to fight, suh. I was a slave once'n I wants to help others be free, too"

Martin finally smiled. "I understand that, Tinker. And I admire you for that. The men in our unit say you know how to load and fire a musket. Is that right?"

"Yes, suh."

"The First Kansas Colored crossed the Missouri border last week, on their way to break up a gang of rebel bushwhackers."

Tinker frowned. "Beggin' yuh pardon, suh, but—"

"Bushwhackers," Martin explained, "are men who'd rob and kill innocent people just to get rid of us Yankees. They're a dangerous lot, and you and your friend here will be risking your lives."

A vein bulged in Lazarus's neck. "I don' care, suh. Mah life not worth nothing anyway if Tinker'n me don' get them rebels."

A hint of admiration shone in the lieutenant colonel's eyes. "I can transfer you both tomorrow to a Kentucky regiment headed that way."

Tinker felt like dancing about the room. "God bless you, suh."

Martin stood up, eyeing Lazarus carefully. "As I said, however, you won't go as a fighting man. You understand that, don't you, Lazarus?"

Lazarus nodded, his eyes betraying his disappointment.

Martin turned his focus to Tinker. "We need more men like you who want to save our Union. Good luck—to both of you!"

Vernon County, Missouri

Sam Toby congratulated himself as he cornered the young Negro hiding against the side of a brick building. Sam pointed his gun at him, and the tall slave screamed, holding his arms up high. "Don' shoot!" he begged, his large eyes pleading for mercy. "Don' shoot!"

"If it wasn't for the reward, I'd shoot yah all right. What's your name?"

"Salem. Mah name's Salem, suh."

"Salem, huh? Well, you're one of the two niggers that done run away from his master. I aim to take both of yuh in if I kin find the other one, too."

The slave dropped to his knees and cradled his head in his arms. "Please, suh, I don' wanna go back. My mastah will beat me. I beg you let me go."

"Get up on your feet," Sam snapped. "I don't like stinkin' beggars."

Salem took his time getting up, all six-foot-four of him. His muscles rippled under his sweat-soaked cotton shirt and his broad shoulders made Toby wonder how strong this man was. No wonder the master wanted to give two hundred dollars in reward money for him.

"So yah don't want to go back," Sam said, waving his gun at the slave. "Would yah be interested in making a deal with me?"

"Deal?" Salem asked, as if he had never heard of the word.

"If yah tell me what I want, I might let you go. How's that?"

Salem blinked in surprise. "Yeah, anything. But please let me go."

98

Sam whipped out the wanted poster from his pocket and held it in front of the slave. "I wanna get this other nigger. The one in this here picture. Tell me where I can find him'n I'll let yah go."

Salem shook his head. "Don' know."

"Then you're comin' with me. Put your hands behind your back."

Tears oozed from the man's eyes as he put his hands behind his back while Sam snapped on handcuffs. "I don' wanna go back to mah mastah. Please!"

"We had a deal," Sam said, "and yah didn't perform. Now go to that wagon up yonder. I'll be followin' right behind yah."

Salem took three steps and stopped. "I knows where he is, suh."

Sam smiled. "Yah do? Where?"

He bowed his head, ashamed to face his captor. "He mah brother. We done made a promise that we would meet where the Cypress River and Miami Creek join t'gether, up in Bates County."

That was probably about fifteen miles north of here, Sam figured. "Why in blazes do yah wanna go there?" Sam asked.

"We hear that there be a colored regiment from Kansas. They gonna be fightin' the rebels there. Figured maybe mah brother'n me kin join up with them and we both be free."

"Does he go by the name Ishmael, like it says on this here wanted poster?"

The slave nodded. "That be his name. He got it branded on his leg 'cause he done escape before."

"Yah been very helpful."

"Then you let me go?"

"We talk about it later. C'mon." Nothing to talk about, Sam thought. All I want to do is get yah turned in for the reward money.

Chapter 8

The first thing twenty-nine-year-old Penelope Phillips put on after her bath was her pearl necklace. The snowflake-white color of her pearls was a nice contrast to her skin tone, which was in-between olive and pale coffee. She was as proud of her long neck, upturned breasts, and petite frame as she was of her mulatto heritage. No way was she going to be ashamed of being half-colored. When people gawked at her, she stared back at them. She wished she could hold up a sign that said, "My colored momma became free the year I was born, so quit looking at me like that."

The only thing she regretted was not having known her mother, who had died a year after Canada outlawed slavery. But her father, a successful white Ontario businessman, instilled in her a belief she could be anything she desired, but she had to work within the system. "Try to get your way without men realizing they were giving in," he had said. "And if things get tough, get out and start over."

Too bad George Radford never realized what she really wanted when he had married her.

Well, she didn't need George anyway. She had a natural talent for business and, after her divorce, found she could get by on her own. Even as a child, she always got the better end of a trade. Today Jessica was going to make an announcement to the board of directors at Silas Drug. Penelope hoped that the news was going to be what she thought it'd be.

Through the boardroom window, Jessica watched the downpour slash in sheets against the brick buildings across the street. People scurried on the street below, caught in the sudden thunderstorm. Jessica reflected on how she and Mary had begged for rain to fall on the parched land near Perryville, how water was so scarce they could only find it in the canteens of dead soldiers. Now, when she no longer needed it, water poured from the heavens in buckets. She waited until Penelope Phillips and the other four board members were seated before she started. The four men sat together, while Penelope sat at the end of the table, facing Jessica. Jessica figured, smiling at her idea, that these men acted as if women had some kind of social disease. They probably thought it odd that two women would be business executives, rather than doing domestic chores and having babies.

"You already know," Jessica said when all eyes were on her, "about my desire to significantly contribute to a Union victory. While I still desire to make a worthy contribution to the cause, I don't see how my personal involvement in moving supplies to the battlefront will be meaningful."

She never thought she'd be saying this right now. She hated John Howell for deceiving her like that. Still, he didn't deserve death. Had he still been alive and had he not told her his secret, things would have been different. But it had all changed now. If she couldn't personally kill these Southern butchers for murderin' John, she wanted no part of the war.

Penelope raised her hand to speak. "Miss Radford, your personal involvement in bringing medical supplies to the front is, of course, unnecessary. As you know, we've set up a good distribution system with the Union Army, and—"

"Miss Phillips," Jessica said, interrupting her, "you are to be commended for helping Silas Drug run so efficiently during my absence in Kentucky. In fact, that is one of the matters I wanted to talk to all of you about." She paused, taking time to look at each face in the room. "I've decided to resign."

Heads turned. Looks of surprise from everyone except Penelope. Jessica had already confided in her about her decision while en route to the office.

"Because of that decision," Jessica continued, "I'm going to turn the reins over to Miss Phillips. I will be tendering my stock holdings in Silas Drug to her."

Heads swiveled toward Penelope, who continued smiling. A board member shook his head in apparent disbelief.

"Shouldn't you have discussed this with the rest of us before making your decision?"

"I don't see why. Miss Phillips is perfectly capable of running this business. You should consider yourselves fortunate to have her at the helm."

Penelope approached Jessica in her office after the meeting adjourned. "What will you do now, Jessica? Buy another business?"

"No. Now that I have some financial independence, I'd like to pursue a dream of mine."

"What's that?"

Diamond drops of rain splattered Jessica's office window. "I want to enroll in college. There are a lot of things I want to learn before I become a writer."

Penelope pressed her lips together and fingered the pearls of her necklace. "Someone once said that books are a wonderful font of knowledge, but all true learning comes from personal experience."

"Probably true, but I would like to learn about other aspects of life."

After Penelope left, lightning flashed through the deep purple sky. Jessica closed the drapes as she reflected on how things had changed this past year. There was no Ma or Pa or Nellie, no home to go to—and all because of that bastard, Sam Toby.

October 27
Butler, Missouri

It was late in the afternoon when Otto Heller and his assistant David Carter left Butler with a four-mule-team peddler's wagon filled with primers, popular books, ballads, and pamphlets. So far, their disguises as Confederate sympathizers had worked. They wore tattered grey trousers and had stuffed their pockets with Confederate bills. Otto had a rebel flag sewn on his broad-brimmed black hat, while David wore a dark grey forage cap.

"Remember," Otto had told his sales manager, "both of us are just a couple of Southerners peddling reading material." By adding a few pro-slavery books to his wagonload, Otto hoped to persuade suspicious folks that neither of them were abolitionists or jayhawkers. But once he and David got to

Wichita, Otto planned to burn the pro-slavery books and stock the shelves of his new bookstore with other materials.

"Haven't spotted any runaways so far," Carter said, taking the reins from Otto. "Maybe we should turn west and head back to Kansas."

"Maybe. But let's think about that tomorrow." Otto scratched his ear and laughed. "Still can't get over the fact you been in the underground all these years."

"And I can't believe you've been makin' these runs yourself all these years."

"Glad to have the company," Otto said.

"If that map you showed me's correct, we'll be crossing Miami Creek soon."

"Yes," Otto said, "and I think we ought to stop there and have a look around. Those two could be hiding there by the creek. I once found a little girl on the bank of the Missouri."

Nellie, he thought. Yah, that was her name. But was she dead? Jessica thought so. She insisted, in her last letter to him, that Nellie couldn't possibly still be alive. The girl had been kidnapped and never found.

The sun was rapidly descending behind a row of walnut trees in the west. The sky was pinkish blue. The air was still and unusually warm for late October.

"I was just thinking," Carter said.

"About what?"

Carter scratched his round chin. "About that 'wanted' poster we saw in Harrisonville. The owners must want their slaves pretty bad. Big reward money for the both of 'em. I suppose it's 'cause the two Negroes are able-bodied young men, good for heavy chores."

Otto nodded. "Interesting names—Salem and Ishmael."

"Do you suspect they've been caught by now?" Carter asked.

"I hope not."

In the twilight sky a coyote wailed. Carter glanced briefly at Otto. "I hear some bushwhackers here in Bates County killed a couple of farmers yesterday."

"That might be true." Otto sensed his own fears surfacing and shifted his attention to a book on Bible names he recently

103

helped edit. After a minute's reflection, he turned to Carter. "'God that hears' and 'perfect peace.'"

"What's that?"

"Those slaves' names. *Ishmael* means 'God that hears' and *Salem* means 'perfect peace.'" I rather partial to *Ishmael*. Reminds me of a character in a recent book I read. *Moby Dick*."

Carter grinned back at him. "You sure do a great deal of reading."

"A good publisher has to know what's being put out to the public."

"I agree." Carter scratched his chin again. "Y'know, we must be right by that creek by now. I think we oughta get out'n look around for those slaves."

Before Otto could answer, the distant sound of horsemen and bugling echoed through the valley. Carter reined the mules to a stop. "What's that?"

"I don't know," Otto said. "Let's get this wagon off the trail and see what that is." After hitching up the lead mules to an apple tree, Otto and David cautiously proceeded toward the sound they had heard. Otto took along his rifle, hoping he wouldn't have to use it. If those were enemy soldiers out there, he wouldn't have a chance, rifle or no rifle.

It was still light enough to see a brownish-green meadow beyond the trees—and tiny figures of men arranged in block patterns. Four men on horseback trotted about the field.

"Confederates?" Carter whispered, crouching behind a tree.

"Too far to tell. Look over to your left. See the creek?"

"Yeah, I see it. Maybe we ought to take a quick look there'n get out of here 'fore they spot us."

Hunched over and darting from tree to tree, they edged their way to the creek. The water made a gurgling sound as it rippled over the stones in its path. Trees that had fallen over the bank of the creek made it inviting to just sit by the water and daydream. If it were still daylight, Otto thought, he might be able to see fish swimming in that creek. It would be like that autumn morn years ago when he and Helga had celebrated their honeymoon in Tennessee. He caught a pike barehanded in the river.

From the corner of his eye, Otto thought he saw a movement in the bushes near the bank. He turned toward it. The bush moved again!

David drew his gun, but Otto silently motioned for him to put it back and rushed toward the bush. Immediately, a Negro man dressed only in faded and torn overalls stood up, raising his hands and shrieking: "Don' kill me, mistuh, don' kill me!"

"Well, I'll be," David said, running to Otto's side.

Otto whistled in amazement. "Sometimes you just get lucky," he said, to no one in particular.

The slave's almond-shaped eyes looked straight ahead, as if he were at attention. His square jaw was firm and determined. The bruises and cut marks on his hands told Otto this man was a fighter and a survivor.

"What's your name?" Otto asked.

"Ishmael. I go by the name of *Ishmael*."

Otto grinned as he thought of the Melville novel. "'Call me Ishmael.'"

Ishmael frowned as he looked back at Otto. "Why do I call you that?"

"Never mind." He noticed the slave still had his hands up. "Relax, Ishmael. You can put your hands down. My friend and I won't hurt you."

Ishmael put his hands down, but his eyes widened in disbelief. "You are. You rebels. You take me back to mah mastah. I no wanna go to mah mastah."

Otto turned to David. "It's these outfits. We certainly don't look like Yankees."

David gasped, looking behind Otto. "He's runnin' away. We gotta stop him!"

Ishmael darted toward the trees, but Otto quickly brought his rifle up to his shoulder and shot a hole in the tree trunk that Ishmael had grasped. Ishmael immediately dropped to the ground, and for a moment, Otto thought he had killed him. But Ishmael, looking like a mass of misery, pushed himself up with painful slowness, his legs trembling, eyes drooping, bruised arm gripping the tree trunk for support. "Kill me," he said. "I don' care no more. I ain't a-goin' back to mah mastah."

"We will not kill you," Otto said. "David and I, we're with the Underground Railroad. We intend to bring you and Salem back to Kansas."

Ishmael's eyes flickered with suspicion. "Salem? That be mah brother."

"According to the wanted poster, both you and your brother escaped from the same master. You must know where your brother is."

Ishmael shook his head. "Sure don't. We was s'posed to meet somewhere where the Cypress and Miami waters come t'gether. I was headin' that way when you come."

David shifted his gaze to Otto. "That'd be further south of here. We oughta go'n look for him."

"We will have to take Ishmael with us."

Once they came to the waiting mules, Otto got Ishmael to agree to hide in the false bottom of the merchant wagon. "I have room for you in this compartment," Otto said, after David lifted the three-by-five-foot plank floor. But you'll have to lie still in there, understand?"

Ishmael nodded. "I'm powerful hungry."

"I've got some dried beef and biscuits down in there."

"I thanks yah," Ishmael said, smiling before lowering himself into the hold.

"I will let you know when you can come out. Got that?"

"I thanks yah," Ishmael repeated.

Otto climbed off the wagon. "David, put that board back on and cover everything with books. I'm going to tend to the mules."

Ten minutes later, Otto and David were driving their wagon further south toward the Cypress River. A half moon hanging from the black sky helped guide them, but Otto sensed that David was just as nervous as he was. "I'd stop to camp for the night," Otto said, "if it weren't for Salem."

"I dunno," David replied. "I think we were just plumb lucky finding Ishmael. We're more likely to find a bag o'gold on this road than to spot another runaway late at night."

"You may be correct in that, but if we don't try we probably won't find him.

"Halt!" An angry, demanding shout. Silhouettes of men on horseback appeared out of the cornfield, from both sides of the road. Otto, his heart pounding like thunder, reined the mules to a standstill.

Three men approached the wagon. The moon's glow revealed their faces—all sinister, all looking as if they were thirsting for a fight. The lead man sported a mustache and wore a sailor's necktie. He appeared to be in his twenties; the others seemed older. A body draped across a handsome tan horse looked to be a slave.

"Where y'all headin'?" the lead man asked. He held two revolvers, one of them trained on Otto.

"Goin' on down to Joplin," Otto answered, trying to adopt a more casual and Southern manner of speaking. "Hopin' to sell some of these books down thar."

"What're your names?"

"I'm Jack Riverton," Otto said, glad that he had prepared himself for an alias. "And this here's my partner, Paul Dirks."

"Looks like you're rebel soldiers. What unit are y'with?"

"Unit?" David said. "Why, we're not—"

Otto elbowed him. He thought he had made it clear to David that he'd do all the talking if they were challenged. "Matter of fact," Otto said, "we signed up with the Missouri cavalry when the rebellion first started. But we didn't reenlist. We're just travelin' salesmen now."

There was a long pause and Otto worried that his answer didn't go over very well.

The young man with the mustache moved closer to Otto. "Do yah know who I am?" he barked.

"No, suh," Otto said, trying to sound calm. "Should I?"

The man laughed and the others followed suit. "You can't be serious, Mr. Riverton. Everybody in these parts knows me by now. Name's Captain Quantrill, William Clarke Quantrill to be exact. These two fellows are my lieutenants, George Todd and William Gregg."

"We aim to make some mighty good money catchin' slaves," Todd said, pointing to the body on a tan horse. "In fact, we just paid seventy dollars to a slave catcher who caught this one. We'll still make a nice profit when we deliver this nigger to the owner."

"The man didn't want to sell him to us at first," Gregg added, rubbing his rough face, "but I believe we convinced him to consider joinin' our team. Right now, he's out there lookin' for the other one that got away. There's darn good money in fetchin' slaves."

Todd got off his horse. "Sure hope you fellas aren't with the underground, cause if you are, we'll kill both of you right now."

"Look," Otto pleaded, "we're nothin' but book peddlers. We got nothin' to do with the underground."

"Get off that wagon," Gregg said, dismounting. "I want to see what you've got inside."

Quantrill whirled at Gregg. "Look," he snapped, "I give the orders around here. You got that?" Then he looked up at Otto and David. "He's right, though. Get out from there, Riverton," he said, looking at Otto. "You too, Dirks," he added, pointing to David. "We're gonna have a look around."

After climbing off the wagon platform, Otto and David traded glances. Otto hoped that Ishmael was smart enough not to make any noise while these bushwhackers rummaged through the stock. If not, he and David would have to make a run for it through the cornfield, but he doubted they would get very far.

Two men carried off stacks of books from the wagon and handed them to Quantrill, who dropped them to the ground.

"Careful with that," Otto said. "We've got to sell those things. Those books and periodicals can't be damaged."

"We're not gonna harm your precious books," Quantrill said. "If you ain't got any niggers in here, we'll send you on your way."

Todd directed the attention of Otto and David to the slave's body. "The slave catcher who caught this one for us tol' me the nigger's name is Salem. He had to get the nigger to drink a half bottle of his whiskey just to knock him out."

"I wish you'd believe me," Otto said. "We're not harborin' any slaves."

"Maybe," Gregg said, sneering, "and maybe not. I know all the tricks the Underground Railroad uses—puttin' up niggers in smokehouses or hidin' them under stacks of hay or diggin' tunnels for them to escape. Like Captain Quantrill here says, if you're with that group, you ain't got a chance with us. If he's here, we'll find him."

"Well, that's the last of the books," Todd said, digging through the wagon. "Ain't found nothin'."

"Maybe that's because you didn't look hard enough," Gregg said. "Mind if we take a look inside, Captain?"

"Go ahead," Quantrill said, taking out his gun to prevent any escape by Otto and David.

William Gregg jumped up and looked around the wagon. He walked back and forth across the length and width of the empty wagon. He stopped at the center of the floor. "Hear that?" he asked. "Sounds hollow to me. Something here under the floor."

David turned ashen. Otto tried to figure the best way of escape. Gregg, inside the wagon, had a gun in his hand. So did Quantrill. No way of getting away from here alive.

"Lookee here," Gregg said, raising the false bottom of the wagon. "I was right."

Otto closed his eyes. *Goodbye, Helga. And Emma and Mitzi—take care of your mother. I love you.*

Two days later, early morning
Island Mound, Bates County, Missouri

"We can't always be t'gether, son," Tinker said. "Lieutenant Gardner ordered me. Gotta go with him and some o' the others to rally the skirmishers. Yah understand?"

Lazarus dropped his eyes in defeat. "I understand. But I don' like it."

"Tell yah what," Tinker said, digging in his knapsack. "I read some more of that book yah done lend me." He handed Lazarus a copy of Thoreau's *Collected Papers*. "I made lots of notes about things I think he was sayin'. Listen, yah gots to read what I think he say 'bout John Brown." He paused for a moment. "I even knew a lady," he added, "who met him when he be still alive."

Lazarus didn't appear to be impressed as he took the book from him. "Thank you, but I wish I could go with you. Hate what I'm doin' here."

Tinker couldn't blame him. Lazarus had spent his day doing manual labor—digging trenches, foraging for food, and dismantling the tents—while other Negro soldiers in the First Kansas

Colored Regiment engaged the enemy with random skirmishes. Latest word was that Captain Armstrong had driven the enemy some four miles from camp. These slaves showed they could fight, and Tinker knew Lazarus was aching to be part of it all.

"I'm comin' back to camp," Tinker said, adjusting the rifle on his shoulder. "I promise."

Tinker wished he could have done something for his friend. After all, Lazarus did save his life, and he owed him for that. But rules was rules and Tinker had no say about them. He hurried to join the lieutenant and some twenty other skirmishers. As far as he knew, they'd be heading south of the mound where they were encamped, searching for the enemy.

After what seemed like hours of brisk walking, his legs hurt so much he thought he'd drop. He was thankful Lieutenant Joseph Gardner ordered the men to rest when they got to the top of a small hill.

Tinker sat on the grass and Gardner dropped down next to him. "We've got to retake our picket ground," the lieutenant said. "Can't let Cockrell and his bandits keep it."

Tinker studied him for a moment. Joseph Gardner was a white man in his forties. Full beard. Long nose. Intense eyes that pierced your very soul. All Tinker knew about him was his abolitionist leanings.

"May I say something, suh?" Tinker asked, hoping he wasn't being too forward with an officer.

"Certainly. What is it?"

"This here war's 'bout slavery, don' you think?"

"It truly is. That's why I'm even fighting here. The way I figure it, I could've been a dead man anyway, seeing as how pro-slavers were after me. Why, three years ago, they posted a $500 reward for my capture, dead or alive."

"What fer?"

"Because I once helped an abolitionist named John Doy escape from a St. Joseph jail." He grinned, but there was a deep sadness in his eyes. "It didn't help much when I tried later to get another man named John Brown out of a Harper's Ferry jail." He paused and rose to his feet. "We best get moving. It'll be dark soon."

The lieutenant joined two other officers and trotted down the hill, with the Yankee skirmishers. The others, mostly Negroes, followed. "Spread out," one of the officers shouted as the skirmishers entered a forest thick with cedars, pines, spruce, and maple trees. "Keep your wits about you," Lieutenant Gardner ordered. "If you see something moving toward you that doesn't look like a Yankee, shoot."

Tinker, hunched over, looked through the sky-blue spaces between the trees, searching for any sign of the enemy. The tall grass grabbed at his ankles, but he pushed on, aware of the other colored troopers, their faces as solid as stone, also pressing forward. A flock of sparrows flew past him, and Tinker raised his rifle, stopping himself just in time from pulling the trigger. A light breeze rustled the leaves. Tinker kept on. Legs tired. Breathing hard. Forcing himself. Must go on. He worked himself into a rhythm. Slave they be. Set them free. Slave they be. Set them free.

Tinker stopped. There it was again…A movement, to his left, behind a tree. He dropped in the tall grass and slithered toward a fallen log. Just ten yards ahead was a man sitting on the ground, leaning against a tree. A horse neighed. Tinker again examined the spaces between the trees and saw a saddled gray mount further back.

Tinker drew his gun as he approached the man, who apparently was either asleep or drunk. The man's black hair resembled a nest that encircled his large head. His skin was leathery, his eyes were closed, his gun tucked in his belt. By his side was a broad-brimmed gray hat.

Tinker pointed his gun at the man's head. "On yer feet, mistah!"

"What the—!" The man's dark eyes flashed back at him. He reached for the gun in his belt.

"Yer a dead man," Tinker shouted, "if yah go fer that dere gun."

"Whatever you say," the man responded, both hands pressed against the ground. "But I don't think you're gonna pull that trigger. You're a coward. All men of your kind are cowards."

"What's yer name, mistuh?" Tinker asked, both hands on his gun.

Mr. Saul Tobin to you, nigger."

Tinker flinched. Name sounded familiar, like that feller Miz Jessica said killed her folks. He wanted to pull the trigger right there, but couldn't. "Get up'n turn around. Where're Colonel Cockrell's men?"

Saul Tobin got up, laughing. "Colonel Cockrell? How would I know 'bout him? I'm one o' them independent bushwhacker types. More interested in huntin' slaves than fightin' white folk."

Tinker couldn't stomach him anymore. "Hands up! Turn around!"

"Whatever you say." He turned around and put his hands up, pressing them against the tree. "Is your master lookin' for you, boy?"

"I don' have a mastah. I be free."

A crashing sound. Tinker turned away at the sudden sound of volleys. Musketry echoed through the woods. The men under Lieutenant Gardner's command must have met the rebels. He was about to turn to face his prisoner when he felt two strong arms crushing him. He grunted and rolled to the ground, pushing Saul Tobin's gun away from his face. Saul tried to grab his neck. Tinker reared back, punching him in the eye. Saul strengthened his grip on his gun, and Tinker used all his force to push the barrel away from him. Saul swore, spitting on him, but Tinker bent his hand back.

Tinker's finger slipped onto the trigger. He felt his wrist weakening. More effort. He would need every ounce of energy to—.

The gun went off, the sound ringing in Tinker's ears. Saul Tobin's face changed into a mask of disbelief. Blood oozed out of the right side of his chest. Shaken, Tinker got up and kicked Saul's gun away. Saul tried to pick himself up with one hand, the one not covered with blood. "Don't leave me like this," Saul cried. "Please, I don't wanna die! Don't leave me."

At first, Tinker walked, then ran. He didn't want to think about the man back there. He didn't want to hear his cries for help. He'd sooner save the devil himself than that hateful creature.

But the man's groans still echoed in Tinker's mind. "Please, have mercy!"

112

No, Tinker told himself. No mercy. Have to hurry. Must get back. Slave they be. Set them free. Slave they be. Set them free.

Chapter 9

Two days later
Fort Scott, Kansas

Senator James H. Lane removed his cap, placed it on his desk as if it were a table centerpiece, and leaned back in his chair. He had the demeanor of a college professor. He looked up at the opposite wall as if he were contemplating a significant thought. An apologetic smile crossed his face as he turned to Otto Heller and David Carter, who sat facing him. "I'm terribly sorry for the inconvenience we've caused you," he said, "but since you were dressed like rebels, my officers naturally assumed you were the enemy."

"I'm glad we cleared that up," Otto said.

Lane smiled. "I find it remarkable you were able to hide that slave in the hold of your wagon. What's even more remarkable is that you didn't get caught."

"We came mighty close though," David said. "When I put Ishmael down in there, I decided at the last minute to cover him up with a load of our dirty laundry and trash. I told him I hoped he wouldn't get ill from the stench. I can't explain it, but I had a strong feeling we were going to be searched, and I didn't want anything to go wrong."

"I wish you would have told me," Otto added. "I nearly died when that bushwhacker lifted that platform in our wagon. When he saw the heap of dirty laundry and garbage in that hold, he didn't want to bother going through it to look for a slave."

Senator Lane laughed. "Ah, the mysterious powers of the sense of smell."

"How long must Ishmael be detained before he can leave, Senator?" David asked.

Lane pulled out his pocket watch and looked at it. "Oh, I'd estimate another two hours. After he has a bath, they'll feed him, and one of our doctors will check him over. You say you're delivering him to a Fort Scott family?"

"Yes," Otto said. "After that, we set up our books and other merchandise in Wichita, and then it's back home to Topeka."

"I guess you can say I'm the recruiting officer for the Kansas regiments here," Lane said, "and I'd be mighty pleased if Ishmael would consider joining us."

"You'll have to ask him that yourself, sir," Otto said.

"I will. I've heard some very flattering reports about the First Kansas Colored. Those slaves can fight."

One week later
Chattanooga, Tennessee

Sara Toby insisted on going alone to the Woman's Auxiliary at their church. "There's no sense in you going with me, Roger," she said as she put on her coat. "You might as well stay home with Nellie."

"Yaw want me to take care of Nellie?"

"Yes, of course." Sara studied him for a moment as if reading his mind. "I trust you, Roger." She turned to leave but stopped. "Oh, there are clean towels in the closet. Put one in Nellie's room so she'll have it when she's done with her bath."

"I still say it's too bad Nellie can't go with yaw," Roger said. "That girl never gets to leave the house."

"How can she, Roger?" Sara asked. "People would ask questions, and we'd have to say she's our new slave. But she's not our slave. She's no one's slave. She's a child of God."

Sara gave Roger a quick kiss and left for the carriage, where the driver was already waiting for her. What an understanding wife he had, Roger thought. When she caught him in bed with Nellie last week, she was furious. But she had accepted his explanation about Nellie mistaking him for his twin brother Sam.

"None of this would have happened, however," Sara mentioned, "if you would have told me you intended to buy Nellie to save her from Sam. You should have said something to me."

Sara was right about that, he thought. But what haunted him now was how Sara had said "I trust you." He thought he read something else in her sad eyes. Had Sam told her about Nasha?

He picked up a clean towel from the closet and took it to Nellie's room, intending to toss it on her bed. When he approached her room, he heard her voice filtering through the space of her partially-opened bedroom door. Who was in the room with her? He peeked through the opening to see her standing, with her back toward him. She was naked except for a silver chain around her neck. It was probably the beautiful chain Sara had bought Nellie so the girl could wear her medallion—the same medallion Nellie carried in her pocket when he bought her from Sam.

She remained standing at the foot of her bed with outstretched arms, apparently looking at the wall while talking....

"Yes, Sissy," she said, "I am happy."

She nodded. "Yes," she said again. She put her arms to her side, but remained standing, seemingly oblivious to Roger's presence behind her.

Nellie was having another conversation with her invisible angel, Roger thought. This young lady should not be having invisible playmates, but Sara convinced him to let her be. Maybe it was Nellie's way of contending with the horrors of slavery.

Roger put those thoughts away as he stared at her soft skin. He admired its subtle freshness, her nice legs, her supple waist, her graceful back, her smooth, plump buttocks. Droplets of water graced her body like morning dew on the petals of a rose. As he continued to stare at her, the distant memory of a female slave crept back into his consciousness....

"I love yaw," he had told Nasha as they lay together in the barn. "I want yaw always."

"You nice man," she replied, holding his bare shoulders, bringing him closer to her.

Roger loved the way her warmth hugged him. "I wish yaw didn't have to go back to my pa's farm."

"Have to," she said, her smile disappearing. "He my mastah."

After a few moments of forbidden pleasure, he looked deep into her eyes. Eyes that said she could never love him. She was property. Someone else's property.

"Do yah love Sara?" she asked.

"What?"

"Do yah love her?"

Roger looked away. Sara. Why did Nasha have to ask about Sara? Guilt rushed through his veins like ice water.

Seeing Nellie like this—naked, attractive, and vulnerable—his guilt returned like an explosion. Sara's words, spoken again today, taunted him. "I trust you," she had said. A simple sentence, rich with meaning. Roger took one more look at Nellie. Naked or not, she was, as Sara had put it, "a child of God."

Roger placed the towel on the floor near the door opening and tiptoed away from the room. A half-hour later, he was in the kitchen, looking at pictures through a Wheatstone stereoscopic viewer. He had purchased this intriguing product earlier this month. By inserting duplicate daguerreotypes into this device, he could look into the viewer and see three-dimensional objects. Pictures of people, buildings, and animals seemed almost lifelike.

Nellie entered the room, wearing the red dress and the white bonnet Sara bought her two days ago. "Do yuh like it?" she asked, smiling while she moved about the room like a peacock.

"Very much."

She stopped dancing about the room. "Sorry my door not closed when yuh come. Yuh was standin' dere long time 'fore you left."

Roger swallowed hard. "How did yaw know? Your back was turned the whole time."

"Sissy tol' me. She say yuh weak but yuh still a good man."

"Your angel probably knows me better than I do."

Nellie cocked her head as if she didn't understand. She pointed to the Wheatstone device. "What is that? What are yuh doin' with it?"

"I'll tell yaw. Come over here and look in this viewer. Tell me what yaw see."

She peered into the viewer at two pictures of a waterfall. "Oh," she said, dragging out the sound. "Oh," she repeated and turned to him. "How come I kin see things behind the water and behind the trees?"

117

"That's what's called 'depth.' It makes things look real." He removed the two daguerreotypes and inserted two more. This was his favorite. Two paired daguerreotypes of dead Yankees on the Antietam battlefield. A marvelous victory for the Confederates. He wished he could have been there.

"Nellie, this device fools yaw into thinkin' yer seein' things in three dimensions. Take a look at another picture. I'll show yaw what I mean."

He touched the nape of her neck as she again peered through the viewer. This time there were no "Oh's" coming from her lips.

"Y'see," he said, "yer left eye is lookin' at a picture from one direction while yer right eye is lookin' at the picture from another direction."

"Yuh mean different ways of lookin' at the same thing?"

"Yeah, sort of like that."

She continued looking through the viewer a long time before raising her head. Her face had lost its smile, her lips now had the sourness of vinegar. "Like this picture? Like it says to me about dead daddies? Chillun with no daddies?"

Early November
Columbia, Missouri

The college president's room was simply furnished, except for the fireplace mantel. On it loomed a porcelain statue of an angel. Jessica had heard that Joseph Rogers was a devout Christian, rising every day at four in the morning to study the Bible. She hoped he wouldn't expect the same from her.

Two things were certain, Jessica thought, he was both frugal and handsome. He wore his tattered suit well, and his mustache was meticulously clipped so as to converge with his neatly-trimmed short beard. His eyes sparkled with intelligence as he pointed to a framed daguerreotype on his wall. "This was our class of 1857," he said, standing in front of his large chipped desk. "About one hundred fifty students. Our enrollment has shrunk due to this ongoing War of Rebellion. It appears that if you enroll, there will be only fifty-seven ladies attending Christian College."

"I'm amazed that you've managed to keep this college open," Jessica said, walking over to the window, "despite the conflict."

Rogers adjusted a sleeve of his frayed coat. "We're going through a financial crisis. Many of our faculty are not even sure they'll be paid because of the low enrollment."

Jessica didn't see a soul outside—neither walking down the shady walk nor seated on the outdoor benches. The girls who went here full-time, Jessica imagined, were probably well shielded from the horrors of the war around them. Their entire world likely consisted of nothing but books, lectures, meetings, research, and study. Hundreds of miles away, some soldier was probably stabbing another with his bayonet or sword, or a man's body was being shattered by the explosion of musketry. Peace? Here was peace—but in a vacuum.

"You won't see students loitering outdoors," Rogers said, joining her at the window. "Security is a vital concern here. We take every precaution and allow students to be off-campus only for Sunday services." He looked at her for a moment. "I hope none of this alarms you."

"I'm not afraid," she said, returning his gaze. "Coming from Bleeding Kansas, I've already been in this war long before Fort Sumter."

He moved away from the window. "Miss Radford, I see from the letter you wrote that you attended one year at a small private college in St. Louis. What were your aspirations at the time?"

"To help my uncle run his business."

He put his finger to his chin. "And is that what you want to do now?"

Jessica thought about that for a moment. When Uncle Adam's business dropped in her lap, she had a chance to shape and build it. The business never interested her. The people did. Her hunger to create stories about people still lingered.

"I want to be a writer," she said. "Maybe a college education would help me learn more about the important things in life."

Joseph Rogers, pacing the room, stopped and looked at her, a faint smile crossing his thin lips. "That's an admirable goal. There aren't many successful female writers these days."

"I aim to change that."

The smile on his face widened. "Miss Radford, you are of course a Christian, are you not?"

Matt Lightfoot had once asked her that same question. She had been baptized, and she had read excerpts from the Bible and missed very few Sunday services. But when her parents were slaughtered, she had parted ways with God.

"Yes," Jessica answered. "Why? Is it a prerequisite?"

"Not really, but Christian worship is strongly encouraged. You'll find that the women here gather for chapel every morning and also attend a Bible lecture in the evening. Would that pose a problem?"

"Not at all." *I'll just pretend that I'm devout.*

Toledo, Ohio

He disliked having to return to his elegant but empty Italianate house with its low-pitched roof and elaborately carved windows and surrounds. On military leave, George Radford knew he'd have to put it up for sale. He doubted there'd be any buyers. This war had cost more than lives; it cost people jobs and money.

Everything here was just the way it was when he left it to join the Ohio Volunteers. The parlor, with its patterned sofa, the two chairs that Penelope bought at an auction....

Penelope. He wished he could stop thinking about her and the divorce. In retrospect, maybe it was more his fault than hers. He hadn't loved her when he proposed, but he loved her charm and beauty. She was also willing to please him in bed. But Lawrence, Kansas, was her town, not his. He missed his boyhood town of Toledo, and many of his friends were still there.

On condition they keep their house in Lawrence, Penelope finally agreed to move to Toledo. "I'll always want to think about coming back someday," she had told him. "You've got your friends in Toledo, but my heart will always be in Lawrence."

George realized his mistake soon after visiting familiar faces in his Ohio hometown. If they didn't say it in words, they said it in their actions. Why did he marry a mulatto woman? Was he out of his mind? Didn't he realize how many attractive *white* ladies were available? And would he have dark-skinned children with Penelope?

Then there was her wanting to buy a small business with money from her inheritance after her parents died. "Are you insane, woman?" he had said. "Women don't run enterprises. Men do." After several explosive arguments, she backed down and never broached the subject again.

He wandered into the kitchen. The wood-burning stove. The oak cabinetry containing imported china. The large wooden table that sat eight, although the Radfords rarely had company.

Then here was the bedroom, with its heavy blue curtains, Oriental rug, the large poster bed, thick mattress. On that bed were memories of how he resisted making love to her when she was most likely to ovulate. "No children," he shouted, drowning out her cries for affection. "I can't risk bringing any colored children into the world."

Further down the hall was a spare room Penelope used as her study. Frilly lace curtains over the window. A bookcase once filled with books on science and technology and business, all books Penelope devoured. A roll-top desk, stacks of papers, several pens, a wicker lamp. "My business office," Penelope called it. George hated her business office. Women were not supposed to be smarter than men, but Penelope was, especially when it came to business matters. She knew it. He knew it—and he despised her for it.

Here, too, was where he had asked her for a divorce, telling her he had no use for a stubborn, independent woman. She was gracious about it. Let him keep this house but insisted on retaining the house in Lawrence. Didn't demand any money from him. She simply disappeared from his life. No letters, no visits.

He lowered himself on the chair of her "business office." Had he made a mistake? Should he have remained married to her? Why should he have cared what other people thought of their marriage?

Maybe he *had* made a mistake. What use did he have for this empty house? The war ruined everything. Other men had lovers to come home to. He hadn't even lain with a woman since his divorce.

Through her office window he looked up at the tall elm in his yard. Branchless. Alone. Cold.

Bowling Green, Kentucky

General William Rosecrans, accompanied by seven officers, rode in the middle of the open field. The captains in each company called for the troops to stand at attention and present a military salute. Rosecrans paced his stallion past the long columns of men, tipping his hat occasionally to signify he appreciated being their new chief commanding officer.

Matt Lightfoot was glad General Buell would no longer be in charge. From reports he had heard about Buell's incompetence at Perryville and about Rosecrans' recent victory in Corinth, he felt confident the men were in good hands. Maybe Rosecrans and his Army of the Cumberland would help bring a quick end to this bloody conflict. Matt hoped so. He had been counting the days when his term of service would expire next August. But it was only because of Mary Delaney's ability to face this senseless carnage that he continued on.

After his regiment camped in Smith's Grove, Matt took a doctor's advice and had a warm bath at the army hospital. Finding it didn't help much to relieve the pain in his back and legs, he put on a robe and went to a vacant room to lie down.

He congratulated himself on his good fortune at not getting caught at attempted desertion the previous night. His commanding officer knew nothing about Matt's flight from the campsite, his tripping and rolling down a hill like a rock...and his painful retreat to camp. Maybe, Matt thought, it was God's will that he remain in the military, but he couldn't understand why. What words of comfort could he provide those men who sought him out, terrified at the prospect of being killed? Matt had felt the same terror the day that Cherokee rebel was about to shoot him.

A knock on the door. Matt ignored it. Another knock. Probably another soldier seeking him out, wanting his comfort. He thought of rising and getting dressed, versus lying here, free from pain as long as he remained still. "Come back later," Matt moaned.

"Would you rather I come by later?" a soft voice answered. It was Mary!

Matt turned his head to one side. "I didn't know it was you, ma'am. Please come on in."

"Hello, Matthew."

He felt her weight when she sat on the cot, and he relished the gentle touch of her hand on his back.

"I heard about your pain from one of the men ," she said, "so I brought some mineral spirits. Would you mind if I massaged you?"

"Not at all, ma'am."

"Then let me first take this off," she said, as she pulled off his robe and covered him with a sheet.

Matt felt awkward. "But I—"

"It's totally proper. After all, I'm a nurse's assistant."

Matt couldn't argue with that logic. He felt the rush of cool air on his backside as she removed his robe. Humming, she got up from the cot, and a minute later he felt her body ease back to the cot, closer to him this time as he could feel her dress fabric tease his bare skin. The mineral spirits soothed him as she, still humming, caressed him up and down his spine.

"How did you hurt yourself, Matthew?"

"Well, Miss Delaney—" he started, but stopped. He didn't want to lie, so he'd tell her a half-truth. "I fell yesterday. Rather clumsy of me, tripping over a rock like I did. I must have hurt myself, the way I fell."

"I'm sorry to hear that. Where exactly is the pain?"

"My lower back and legs, ma'am."

"Just relax, Matthew. I'll help you feel much better." She ran her fingers down his lower back, her hands having the grace and the softness of velvet. As she continued massaging him, he imagined himself in heaven. Her gentle hands were now stroking his buttocks and upper legs. Soon he was aroused, finding himself wanting her, but wondering whether

123

he should tell her to stop. After all, he was a minister, and he didn't want to sin. Besides, he still had feelings for Jessica, didn't he—even though she had been seeing John Howell? But Mary was so kind and comforting. How could he tell her to stop something so wonderful?

"You sure have a nice touch, Miss Delaney."

"Why, I appreciate that, Matthew. I'm delighted I'm able to help you feel better." She went back to humming again.

Groaning with pleasure at her touch, he wondered for a moment what it'd be like making love to such a gentle woman. "Pardon me for saying this, but you sure are pretty, Miss Delaney."

"Nonsense. Not as pretty as Jessica."

"Shucks, ma'am, I'm talkin' about being pretty on the inside."

"Such foolishness. Now get some clothes on," she said, her dress rustling as she moved past him. "I've got other rounds to make."

"You might be right about one thing, Miss Delaney."

"What's that?"

"I'm quite fond of you."

"I could tell," she laughed, tossing a towel at him.

The sudden blast of a bugle and a drum roll got Matt's attention. General Rosecrans sat on a white horse addressing his troops with a megaphone. "Men," he said, "I applaud your heroism and your devotion to the Union cause. Our recent victory in Corinth is a precursor of future victories for the Union."

Several men in each regiment shouted their "Hurrahs" and clapped. Rosecrans waited for the noise to abate before speaking again through the megaphone. "The President has promoted me to Major General and has given me command of the Fourteenth Corps of the Union Army. Those men who know me will realize I will pursue this War of Rebellion to its bitter end. As you all know, General Bragg and his band of bloodthirsty Confederates have been driven from Kentucky. Now I intend to drive him out of Tennessee and out of this entire land if God be willing."

More clapping and hurrahs from the soldiers. Rosecrans gave an attendant his megaphone and raised his saber into the air. More shouts from the immense throng of soldiers surrounding him and his staff.

Matt didn't join the others in their enthusiasm. His mother would have told him it was wrong for him to be here. The spilling of all this blood served no useful purpose. Dying this way was not noble. God didn't create us so we'd be butchered on a battlefield.

But he was, after all, a military man. And he had taken an oath of loyalty, hadn't he? How could even he have thought of desertion earlier? No, his Cherokee father had drilled him on the importance of obedience to your superiors. And obey he would from now on.

He'd just have to quiet that nagging, still voice within.

Chapter 10

A week later
Topeka, Kansas

After exchanging pleasantries with Mr. Heller's assistant at the Heller Publishing Company, Penelope Phillips looked in the mirror to ascertain that her hair was not mussed up. She smiled at the way her black hair swept across her forehead, making a statement against the contemporary fashion of parting one's hair down the center. Her darker skin most likely didn't appeal to others, but as far as she was concerned, she was as attractive as any other thirty-year-old. Maybe more so. In fact, she was proud of her skin. Why should she cover her arms with those ridiculous long sleeves? And what was wrong with wearing a dress that was just a few inches above the ankle? If people thought that made her look like a trollop, then so be it.

"Mr. Heller will see you now," the assistant said, looking up at her with disapproval.

Penelope grabbed the box she had on the chair next to her and strode into his office with it. Otto stood in front of his desk, ready to greet her.

"I appreciate your making the long trip from Cincinnati, Miss Phillips," he said, bowing as he kissed the back of her extended hand.

"I had other business here anyway, Mr. Heller. I'm meeting with some officers in Topeka about supplies for bandages. And I'm also here to visit some friends of mine in Lawrence—including my niece, Jessica Radford."

Otto's eyes took on a glint of recognition. "Oh? She's your niece? How has Miss Radford been? I haven't seen her in quite a spell."

"Fine. As I mentioned in my letter, she sold me her stock in Silas Drug and returned to Lawrence. I know she plans on going to college. Smart lady."

"I know. You two are so alike, you could have been sisters," Otto said, grinning. He took the box she that she had

126

been holding and placed it on his desk. Gripping the back of a chair, he offered her a seat. "I understand your niece recommended my establishment to you. I appreciate the referral." He went to a seat behind his desk. "We run a fine enterprise, but I'm sure there are equally qualified publishers in Cincinnati."

"True," she said, gazing briefly at the nature painting on his wall, "but I'm particular whom I hire. I love dealing with someone I can trust, and I highly value Miss Radford's high opinion of you and your enterprise."

"I'm indeed flattered, Miss Phillips." He placed his hand on the box on his desk. "I assume your visit has to do with the brochures and announcements you'd like for us to print."

"It does. While Silas Drug has been quite successful in selling its products to the military, I need to think about the future. After the war's over, I'll need to focus on sales to the civilian population. But it requires I plan ahead." She got up and opened the box, revealing a wire basket containing bottles of liquids and powders. "What this is," Penelope explained, "is an example of home remedy medicines people can own. Should they be in need of a tincture of iodine for a cut, or medicine to soothe an upset stomach, or something to help relieve congestion, they'd find it all here, in one convenient basket. What I need to do, Mr. Heller, is find the best way to communicate this to the civilian population."

"Through paid public announcements, I assume?"

"Yes, in newspapers and handouts in public establishments. I've even considered the possibility of printing such announcements on large boards and somehow affixing them to public coaches." She lifted a large envelope from the box. "In fact, I've drawn up several alternative approaches to getting my message out. Not only that," she said, dropping a stack of printed papers on his desk, "I've highlighted my targeted sales areas, listed the newspapers serving those areas, and indicated the costs for a half-page display announcement. It's all there."

Otto shook his head as he shuffled through the pages. After a while, he put the papers down and placed his hand to his chin, grinning.

"Well?" Penelope asked, wondering if his smile was mocking her.

"Jessica told me you had a mind for business. I can see that myself. You are amazing."

Penelope relaxed. She could probably trust this man with handling her account.

The next day
Lawrence, Kansas

Jessica dipped her pen in the inkwell and wrote another line:

> *The Yankee lieutenant stood at attention*
> *while the colonel's daughter faced him at reveille.*
> *"This is the man I was telling you about, father,"*
> *she said. "Please send him to my tent."*

Jessica laughed and scratched the last line. No, she wouldn't have him sent to her tent. It was too contrived. Jessica wished she could write stories that flowed better, stories such as those written by the Brontë sisters. Emily Brontë would probably set a much better scene, and Charlotte Brontë would likely have her heroine meet her man in a more believable fashion.

There was a rap at the door and Jessica went to answer it. Penelope, dressed stylishly in a light blue bonnet, dark blue cape, and black dress smiled back at her. "Hello, Jessica."

"Penelope! Come on in."

After taking Penelope's things, Jessica brought her into the kitchen. "Have you had your visit with Mr. Heller?" Jessica asked, ushering her to a chair by the table.

"I did. The man is a delight to talk with. He's the only man I've ever met who didn't raise his eyebrow at the idea of a woman running a business."

"Yes, he is rather remarkable. I just finished making tea. Would you care for some?"

"That'd be fine, but I can't stay long. I'm curious to see what you might have done to Adam Silas's house."

Jessica brought in a tea tray and set it on the table. "I didn't make many changes. Added another bookcase in the dining room and an ottoman in the parlor. Changed the drapes. New rug. But other than that, it's the same as my uncle kept it."

"I noticed the daguerreotype of Claire in the hall. That must have been taken the year she died."

Jessica was about to pour the tea into Penelope's cup when she spilled some of it on the table. "Oh, I'm sorry, Aunt Penelope. How clumsy of me. Did I get any of it on you?"

"No, I'm fine. Claire was such a sweet child. She was only four or five when I watched her. Made her laugh a lot with the games I made up especially for her. I still can't believe she was murdered. You know, I hope someday they find that horrible person who shot her."

"Maybe they never will." Jessica set the teapot back on the tray and hoped her friend wouldn't notice yet another spill, this time on the floor. "By the way, how are things at Silas Drug?"

"I wish I could say things were fine, but they're not. My all-male board of directors wants me out of the company. They didn't say so, of course, but I could read the telltale signs. They've been rejecting all my proposals, including the last one I made concerning home remedy medicines. Actually, that's what I went to see Mr. Heller about. I intend to run an intensive campaign with that product."

Jessica flicked a strand of hair from her eyes. "I'm confused. How could you run that campaign if the board rejected your proposal?"

"I outflanked them," she said with a playful wink. "I asked my chief accountant to hide $2,900 in fictitious expenses so I could put that money where it's needed—in this project."

"Isn't that illegal?"

"Technically, I guess. But it's for the good of the firm. After I get this product launched and it becomes a success, the funds will be restored in the company anyway. And if the project fails, I'll just sell all my assets and replace the $2,900. I can't lose."

"I don't know. That'd make me a bit nervous."

"I'm a risk-taker, Jessica. That's why I love running a business. Only thing I'd love better is living a lot closer to you. You're the only one I know who really understands me."

"Maybe that's because we're too much alike."

Mid-November
Vernon County, Missouri

Tinker still missed the shed he called "home" on Mississippi Street. At least there he was alone with his thoughts. Here at the camp it was hard to get away, so he felt lucky he had found some privacy where he could write his letter to Jessica. He wished he could get someone to help him write this. But how could he let another soldier in on his shame? That man—his name sound like the one that killed Miz Jessica's folks—make him angry. I don' want to listen to his cries for help. Will the Good Lawd punish me?....

> *Dear Miz Jessica,*
>
> *I be happy where I be. We got another Negro in our camp. His name be Ismela or Ishmael, or somethin like that—I have trouble with names. He be a slave, but a nice man find him and bring him to Kansas. Now he join First Kansas Colored and he and me become good friends. I teach him cards and he teach me dice. He learn game lookin at how his master play it. But he free now and he be happy.*
>
> *Miz Jessica, I feel bad. I shoot rebel and not save him from dying. He call me names so I leave him in woods. He cry for help, but I don' come back. I forget his name, but it sound like that man that kill yer momma and daddy. He a mean man, but I mean, too, and not come back when he call me. Don' know now if he alive or dead. When I shoot from faraway, I don' feel bad. But when I shoot so close I kin see his face, I feel bad.*

He read his letter again one more time, checked Miz Jessica's address in Lawrence, and ran to drop it in the sack before the mail was picked up. He had second thoughts about

130

the letter when he returned to his tent. Maybe Miz Jessica would think it strange he worry 'bout the life of another rebel. But when the man beg for help and you don' help him, it seem wrong.

He took a deep breath as he stood outside his tent. Look at that mornin' sky. Clear. Birds singin'. Life goin' on like nothing happened. A time for fishin', lyin' down on the bank, pole hangin' low over the water, sun sparklin' the surface.Damn war!

November 26
Columbia, Missouri

Dear Mr. Heller,

I apologize for not writing you sooner, but I thought I should advise you as to where I am currently residing. Since the new semester at Christian Female College begins next January, I won't be able to enroll until then. However, I have taken residence here in Columbia and am auditing several classes to get some idea of what the teachers and the courses are like. The students complain about all the writing they must do for English composition, but I think it is marvelous, particularly since the teacher expects you to write on a wide variety of topics. I also like their history class but am not too keen on classical geometry.

I have not been to Lawrence for a while, and I am certain I must have a mountain of mail waiting for me there. Fortunately, I am relying on a good neighbor to check on my house there while I am away. Hope all is well with you. Let me know if my aunt took my advice about using your firm for her printing needs.

I hope you and Helga have a wonderful Christmas.

Best regards,

Jessica Radford

December 12
Topeka, Kansas

Dear Miss Radford,

I am fortunate to have received your new address in time as I have some dire news to relate to you. Helga has taken seriously ill. She is growing considerably weaker each day with fever and nausea. The doctor believes she has contracted typhoid and does not hold out much hope for her recovery.

My dear, sweet Helga! If she dies, I don't know how I will continue to exist. She has been everything to me. I spend every moment I can telling her how much I love her.

I must ask you for a favor, Miss Radford. If it would be possible, would you assist me with the children? Perhaps you may remember I have two daughters—Emma, who will be six by the end of December, and Mitzi, who turned eight three days ago. If you cannot make it, I will try to contact someone else, but at this moment, I do not know who.

Please pray for Helga. I hope the doctor's diagnosis is in error and that she will recover soon.

Sincerely,

Otto Heller

December 17
Nashville, Tennessee

Stepping over railroad tracks, trotting past a saddle shop and dry goods store, walking down a row of red brick houses, Tinker managed to keep Lazarus within sight. Tinker knew

Lazarus would be upset if he knew he was following him this afternoon. But Tinker felt he had an obligation to protect the boy who had once saved his life. When Lazarus told him about having to do his captain a favor by purchasing a razor strap and lathering soap at the edge of town, Tinker was suspicious. Why was Lazarus so eager to go? It was after Tinker pestered him for an answer that Lazarus admitted he wanted to visit a known bawdy house in town.

"Don' do this," Tinker had said, grabbing Lazarus's sleeve. "These folks be Southerners. They hate us colored, 'specially Yankee colored."

Lazarus forced his friend's hand away. "It be safe. Yankees patrol the streets here. Don't worry 'bout me none."

Before Tinker could object again, Lazarus took off running. "I be back by dark," he shouted.

After receiving permission from the captain to follow Lazarus for his own protection, Tinker lumbered after him, almost losing sight of Lazarus after crossing a wooden bridge. Some boys, Tinker thought, got stupid when they became men. Lazarus not thinkin' right. Too much danger in these here parts. Bad 'nough, when a boy has ta risk it fightin' rebels. Why risk it lookin' for a hussy?

Lazarus had second thoughts about visiting a prostitute after he took off. Sure, the Union occupied the city, well patrolled by Yankees. Maybe he should feel safe, taking advantage of his excused absence by going through town, looking for Lillian Porter's house, the one with the white slats and green gables. But maybe Tinker was right about this. Here he was, Lazarus thought, a young Negro drummer boy, resented by white Southerners who still lived here. Would they try to kill him, despite his military uniform?

All he had in his knapsack was a blanket, a book Tinker had returned to him—Thoreau's *Collected Papers*, and a knife. The knife really wouldn't do him much good for protection, he thought. It was a shame the regiment thought he was too young to be trusted with a revolver. He might need it here.

Tinker warned him this was foolish'n dangerous. Maybe, Lazarus thought, he should just buy those items for his captain

133

and return to camp. But if he didn't get to the bawdy house, he'd always wonder what he missed.

The smell of smoked ham wafted through the open door of a restaurant. Moving his tongue over his lips, Lazarus wished he was back with the Fowlers' havin' supper. He was gettin' mighty tired of dry vegetables, dried beef, and stale biscuits.

Somewhere in the distance, a church bell tolled four past noon. Two small children, playing in front of their house, gaped at Lazarus, and one of them pointed at him. He smiled back, but a lady scolded them. "Now you know better than to pay attention to niggers."

Lazarus shook his head. When would people treat him like a human being? That's why he needed to fight this damn war...to set the *minds* of people free'n not just the slaves.

He turned the corner and saw the house, just as one of the white soldiers in his company had described it, a two-story frame house, with white curtains and green steps that led to the main door. He stopped when he got to the front of the Porter house, debating whether he wanted to go in or not. Just then, two white Union privates exited the front door, laughing. Words like "that tall one was gorgeous" or "that other one's a freak," or "next time I'll take the blonde" spilled from their lips as they passed by Lazarus without giving him a moment's notice.

Lazarus decided since he had come this far, he ought to go in. No tellin' what would happen in this here war. What if he done got killed'n never know what it be like to make love to a woman? He swallowed hard and stepped inside.

He entered a large room, his boots thumping embarrassingly against the worn wooden slats of the floor. Along the right side of the saloon were a bar with four stools, a number of bottles of liquor, a large mirror—and a man with shaggy white hair and an unkempt mustache glaring back at him. To his left stood four white ladies—one with an ugly scar across her cheek—all four in colorful cotton dresses. The ladies stared at him. Lazarus felt like dropping into a ditch.

"Hey, boy," the man said, "you're too blasted young to be wantin' a drink."

Lazarus bristled at the remark. "I'm not here for a drink."

The man grinned and leaned on the bar. "Then you're wantin' to have a lady, are you?"

Lazarus nodded, feeling as if his mouth were glued shut. He should have never come.

"Well, we don't want your kind here, know what I mean?"

Lazarus felt almost relieved. He'd just thank the man, slither out of here, and head back to camp. But a woman's voice called out just then. "Just a minute, Emmett!" She wasn't one of these four ladies Lazarus had already seen, but another woman, maybe in her fifties, wearing a nice satin and lace gown. Her styled red hair had a silver headpiece, and she wore white teardrop earrings.

"My name's Lillian Porter," she said, unsmiling and businesslike. "I run this place. Do y'all have money? Not that worthless Confederate paper but Yankee money?"

"I has got five dollars, ma'am," Lazarus said. Maybe it wouldn't be enough and he could go.

She smiled, but just a little. "That'd be fine. Come with me." She sauntered to the other side of the room where the four white women stood, their eyes on him. "This young man is looking for a lady today. Which one of y'all will give him a good time for five dollars?"

Three of the ladies shook their heads and walked off. The lady with light brown hair parted in the middle and a scar on her cheek remained. Her hands were folded in front of her. "My name's Rose," she said, staring at the floor, "but some folks call me Miss Scarface."

In addition to her distracting scar, Rose had a round face, protruding nose, thin lips, and small neck. She was unattractive, but Lazarus figured she was, after all, a woman and he needed the experience. "I'll go with her," he told Lillian Porter.

The man with the shaggy white hair shouted back: "No niggers here, Lil!"

"Quiet, Emmett," Lillian shouted back. "Money is money. I'm running this place, not you." She turned to Lazarus. "Never mind my husband. He don't understand business."

Out of the corner of his eye, Lazarus saw Emmett take a long swallow from a whiskey bottle.

"Follow me," Rose said. Her red dress rustled as she hurried up the steps and moved down the hall. "I hope you won't regret it. Most men don't want me." She led him to a six-by-eleven-foot room, with just enough space for a cot, a chair, and wardrobe. "We can have some privacy here."

She stood for a moment with her hands on her hips. "Well?"

"Well, what, ma'am?"

She held out her hand. "I don't do this for free, y'know."

"I'm sorry, ma'am. Of cuss, you want my money." Lazarus, dropped his knapsack on the bed, and pulled out a book as he searched for his cash.

"Oh, you're one of them slaves who can read?" Rose said, picking up the book with one hand while holding out the other for her fee.

"I can read a little," Lazarus said, handing her his five dollars. "My friend Tinker wrote me notes to help me understand it better. He stuck 'em inside the pages."

"Maybe after we're done," she said, dropping his book on the cot, "you can read some for me."

"I'd like that, ma'am."

She dropped on a chair and stuffed the roll of bills into her shoe. "You been a Yankee soldier for long?"

"No, not long, ma'am."

She got up and untied the ribbon in her hair. "They don't let colored fight for the South, y'know." She turned and struggled with the hooks on the back of her dress. "Can you help me, please?" she asked.

"Yes, ma'am." After Lazarus undid her hooks, she slipped out of her dress, but he sat on the cot, facing a small curtained window. No sense embarrassing this lady by watching her undress, he thought. He peered outside but there wasn't much to see. Rocky soil, a few houses further away, a road that meandered to a creek.

The rush of footsteps up the stairs. A sudden pounding on the door. "Hey, boy!" Emmett's voice boomed. "I want yah outa here right now. I don't want no niggers in this place."

Lazarus felt his gooseflesh crawl. He ought to leave. No sense in—

"Leave him be!" Lillian's voice screamed. "He paid his money. Leave him alone."

Lazarus half turned toward the door and caught a glimpse of Rose in her petticoat. "Maybe I oughta—"

"Forget him," Rose said. "He's just a drunken old fool. Let's just you and me have some fun."

Lazarus returned his gaze to the window. Maybe Rose was right. It appeared the man didn't run the bawdy house; Lillian did. Lazarus figured he should just forget about it for now. He'd be safe.

Clothes rustled behind him. A hanger made a wooden sound. More rustling of clothes. Was it proper for him to turn around yet? His adoptive parents taught him to treat all women with respect, so he felt strange being in the same room where a lady was undressing. Perhaps he shouldn't be here. Besides, five dollars was more than a half-month's pay. How could he spend it for something this foolish?

The bed creaked. "What's your name, Yankee?"

He continued staring out the window. "Lazarus."

"Like after the man they say Jesus raised from the dead?"

"Yeah, something like that."

A momentary silence passed between them. Lazarus waited for his cue. Was it proper to gaze at her if she was still undressing? Better to wait.

"Well, Lazarus, are you gonna view the merchandise or not?"

He turned to look. She had a wonderful body. Her skin was as smooth as ivory as she sat facing him on the bed, her back against a wall, her feet pressing the mattress, her hands on her knees. A gentle fragrance of cherry blossoms wafted through the air.

She grinned as he looked at her. "Are you embarrassed, Lazarus?"

He nodded. Maybe he could tell her he made a mistake and leave. He didn't even care about the money.

She rose from the bed and threw her hands up in exasperation. "C'mon," she said, her face drawn and tired, "let's get this over with. Take off all your things. I haven't got all day."

"Yes, ma'am," he said, getting up to remove his clothes. Wanting to act proper in front of this nice white lady, he avoided looking at her as he put his clothes away. With each layer of clothing he discarded, he still didn't feel anything but cool air tingling his skin. Maybe they could just talk. But about what? The war? Her miserable life? His frustrations?

"This your first time?" she asked, stroking his neck.

"Yes, ma'am." How did she know?

She moved to the edge of the bed and sighed. "There's always a first time for everything." Her eyes focused on him with an intensity that made him uneasy. "How old are you, Lazarus?"

He didn't care to lie anymore. "Fifteen."

"Fifteen? That's about the age I was when I lost my virginity. C'mon, sit next to me and relax," she said, patting the mattress.

He lowered himself next to her, feeling her soft thigh pressing against his. "Why did the other ladies walk away from me, ma'am?"

"Don't you know?"

"Because I'm colored?"

"Of course, honey. They probably figure you got some kind of disease or you're a runaway slave or something. They only like to fool around with white men."

Lazarus's blood boiled. When will people stop treatin' him different?

"Know why I didn't walk away?" she asked, drawing her face close to his.

He wondered about that himself. "Why?"

Just then, Emmett's voice roared through the closed door. "Listen woman, no nigger Yankees here. Understand?" It sounded as if he were shouting at his wife.

Lazarus felt his pulse thumping inside his arms. Gots to leave. White man angry.

"Get outa here!" Lillian screamed. Then footsteps banging down the steps. An object hitting a downstairs wall.

"I'll be back, woman!" Emmett shouted just before the outside door slammed like a thunderbolt.

Lazarus's heart raced. He looked at Rose. She don' look scared. Maybe it'll be fine.

Rose, with a smile that seemed forced, ran her fingers over his body. "Good. He's gone. That Emmett's a little crazy at times."

Lazarus took a deep breath. It be quiet now. "Ma'am, you were sayin' about why you didn't walk away—"

"Because I know what it's like when people hate you," Rose said. "People call me Miss Scarface because that's the first thing they notice about me."

Lazarus looked away for a moment. He didn't want her to think he was staring at her. He knew what it was like for people to judge you by your skin.

"But," she continued, "I'm still a human being, and I have feelings. It's too bad people find me disgusting because they don't like my face."

Lazarus put his arm around her waist. "*I* don't find yah disgustin', ma'am."

"Thank you for sayin' that. Means a lot to me. Sometimes I think for a lady like me to look like I do is probably worse than being colored."

Lazarus was about to disagree with her when she asked him to lie on his back. "I think you're ready, Lazarus." She knelt over him, cupping her breasts with her hands. "These are swollen with milk and they're tender. So before we start foolin' around, I want you to promise to be gentle."

The slave woman he had seen six years ago flashed into his mind.

"I don' want yah to die, child," she had said, opening the top of her dress.

No, Lazarus thought, I now fifteen, I be a man now. Need to make love to woman. I be a man.

"It be milk for mah own child, but mah child gone now, so you drink from me."

Lazarus's mind darted from thought to thought. Did he want to *make* love to a woman? Or did he *want* the love of a woman?

He wanted the love, he reckoned, like the love he got six years ago. If he could only relive that moment in the barn with that woman—a complete stranger, escaping from her master.

"I loves you and wants you to live. Drink, lil' boy. I gives you love'n food."

Lazarus closed his eyes, trying to recapture that memory. Forget bein' a man fer now. Be a boy again. Remember how sick you was? She gave you life. All comin' back now. The hunger. The cold. Her smile. Her breast. Her words. The warmth of her milk on his lips.

Lazarus looked at Rose. "Ma'am, would it be proper for me to—?"

She frowned. "To what?" A smile formed on her face, and she shook her head in disbelief. "Well, I'll be! Is that what you want?"

He nodded, embarrassed. This was a stupid request. He shouldn't have made it. After all, he wasn't a little baby, and women only nursed babies, didn't they?

"Well," she said, the look of surprise still in her eyes, "I guess there's no harm in it, even though it is a little peculiar."

"I understand, ma'am. Sorry I asked."

"Wait. You'd be doin' me a favor—but promise me you'll be gentle."

"I promise, ma'am."

Rose patted his head as he drew in the warm, white fluid. It was like being nine years old again. In a cold barn, hungry, and the slave woman offering him her breast so he could survive. Her words came back....

"Your momma done get taken back. I wish I could be your momma, honey child."

Rose pressed him closer to her. "You're too young to be shootin' with the men, aren't you, Lazarus?"

He looked up at her. "I just play the drums, ma'am. But I really wants to fight. If I'm gonna die, I'd like to do it fightin' rather than drummin'."

"Truth be told, honey, I'm a Yankee at heart," she whispered. "I don't want slaves, cause I'm one myself, in a way. But you're lucky, Lazarus."

He looked up at her. "What yah mean by that?"

"Lazarus, you already got some of the Yankees fightin' for your freedom. I ain't got nobody fightin' for mine."

Unexpected, heavy footsteps, like bricks, hit the stairs. A gunshot. Another explosion, with a bullet whistling through the locked door. "I'm comin' in, nigger!" Emmett's voice boomed. The door weakened from the pounding.

Lazarus pulled away from Rose, his heart thumping so loud it was like cannon fire in his ears. Rose screamed, falling over backwards, as the lock to the door gave way.

Lazarus's blood turned into ice. This not the way he wanted to die.

Crouched behind a huge sycamore in the yard of the two-story Victorian where he saw Lazarus enter, Tinker gasped when he heard the gunshots. He got up and looked up at the second story window, where he thought he had heard the noise. "Oh Lawd, no!" he shouted.

Without hesitation, he ran to the front door, pushing it open, brushing past a man with white hair and a wild look in his eyes, his face drenched in perspiration. The man had a carbine in his hands and cursed at Tinker before fleeing out the door. Four women stood at the bottom of the stairs, their faces lined with shock and worry. One of the ladies, a red-head dressed in a fine satin and lace gown, was hysterical, flailing her arms, screaming: "Emmett! You murderer!"

One of the women pointed at the stairs, and Tinker raced up the steps toward a room where the door had been sheared off its hinges. Lazarus lay on the floor, naked, a gunshot wound to his lower abdomen, his head held by a naked lady with large breasts who kept saying "Honey, don't die, don't die."

"Oh, Lawd!" Tinker exclaimed, his face awash in tears as he dropped to the floor by Lazarus.

"It happened so fast," the woman said, choking. She stood up and grabbed a sheet from the bed to wrap herself with. "He killed this dear boy for no reason, 'cept he was colored."

Tinker lifted Lazarus's head and cradled it in his hands. "This not the way you wanted to die, son. This not the way."

"He was just a boy," she moaned, the sheet slipping from her trembling hand as she touched her breast. "A boy wanting his momma."

Tinker's hand moved toward Lazarus's bleeding abdomen. "You save my life, son, and I still owe you." He examined his own bloodied hand and stared hard at the woman. "This boy died fighting a renegade rebel," Tinker said. "Y'hear me?"

The woman, clutching the sheet tightly, looked down at Lazarus. "I'll do whatever he wants."

"He want to be buried fightin' fer the Union. That what he want. That what he get."

Christmas Eve
Topeka, Kansas

Otto's eyes were filled with pain. "I wish she could have at least seen one more Christmas."

Jessica put her arm around him as they stood by Helga's black casket at the funeral home. Emma Heller, who would turn six next week, sat in a chair, pressing her fingers together and murmuring. Her eight-year-old sister Mitzi looked up at Jessica with tearful eyes. Jessica wished she could give her an answer as to why God had to take her mama away.

"Otto," Jessica said, her voice choked, "I know how hard it is when you love someone."

His face wrinkled in agony. "I'm not sure I can go on without her, Miss Radford."

She looked into Otto's grey, tired eyes. "I will always be here for you, Mr. Heller. If there's anything at all I can do for you—"

"You've done a lot for me already, Jessica." He took out his handkerchief and dried his eyes. "Nice of you to help out last week with the children. I really appreciate that."

"But perhaps I could do more. I'll stay as long as you need my help."

"I would greatly appreciate that. I realize you are still in mourning over the loss of your parents, and I am just a bother."

"No, you are not a bother," Jessica said, trying to sound as if she truly meant it. She thought about the dress she had on—the same black mourning dress and veil Mary had given her. This was the dress Jessica had worn at her parent's funeral. She hated it.

She put her hands together and paced the floor. She was glad she had stayed at his home last week. All Otto did was sit by the window and stare out, apparently not concerned about his children. She made the meals, helped the girls get dressed, and took them to school. What would he have done had she not arrived when she did?

She returned to face him. "My greatest pain, Mr. Heller, is not knowing whether Nellie is dead or alive. That remains an immense burden for me. I think of Nellie every day."

He looked at her with questioning eyes.

"Nellie," Jessica repeated. "That little Negro child you rescued five years ago—in fact, five years from this day."

A hint of recognition swept over his face. "Oh, yes. I had asked you about her in one of my letters. You told me you believed that she was—she was—"

"Killed? Yes, Mr. Heller, she was. I'm sure of it. The man who kidnapped her is evil, and murder would not be a problem for him."

Same day
Nashville, Tennessee

Tinker took scant notice of Ishmael, who was shivering and shifting his weight from one boot to the other while the wind gusted across the cemetery. The headstone was simple, Tinker thought, maybe too simple—Lazarus, 1847-1862, Army of the Cumberland.

Ishmael, still stomping his boots as he stood at the gravesite, placed his large hand on Tinker's shoulder. "Did yuh see him get shot, Tinker?"

"Yeah. Like I tol' the captain. Lazarus done shot back at the rebel before he died." Tinker bit his lip and looked about him at the barren fields, the noonday sun sneaking up from above a thick cloud, and the Union camp in the distance. Death was sure cold and empty, like this here wind sweepin' across the land. "Yeah," Tinker said, digging his hands into his pockets. "He was a brave b-b-" He paused to correct himself. "He was a brave man."

Evening of the same day
Chattanooga, Tennessee

Nellie awoke after a short sleep. A bright light lit the room like a thousand candles. Soon, a form began to take shape.

The familiar form of a young girl wearing a white satin gown appeared. Her hair had the color of coal and the texture of pure silk. Her dark copper skin was radiant and soft. She seemed to be about ten years old and her eyes sparkled with warmth.

"I wish you a joyous Christmas," Sissy said, appearing at the foot of Nellie's bed. "I'm happy you're in a good home."

"I am, too," Nellie said, "but I miss Jessica."

"Jessica is going through a lot of pain right now," Sissy said, her voice the softness of a feather. "She's sad because a friend of hers has lost his wife."

Nellie lowered her sad eyes. "When can I see her again?"

"I wish I had an answer for you," Sissy said, looking up—not at the ceiling but beyond it, as if she were looking at heaven itself, "but I don't. It's not for me to say. A lot depends on the free will of other people. Understand?"

"You mean we make our own mistakes?"

"Exactly. Humans will make mistakes, but God always tries to make something good come out of it anyway. Sometimes He directs His angels to help do that."

"You tol' me once that you was an angel. But how come you ain't got no wings or one o'them halos?"

Sissy smiled. "Angels don't have to have wings, and they don't have to wear halos. They just have to be good servants of God."

"You is an angel with dark skin, like me. Are you a Negro?"

Sissy smiled, her face growing more radiant as she did so. "Yes, my skin is dark. But angels come in all different shades. All colors are precious to God. You are as precious to Him as the Indian, the white man, the Chinese."

Nellie turned to stare at a painting on her wall, a painting of a slave beggin' to be free. The words on the painting asked, "Am I Not a Man and a Brother?" That man slave could have been her father. He was probably as good a man as any of them there white folks. So, she thought, ain't that slave both a man and a brother?

"The answer is 'yes,'" Sissy said, reading her thoughts. "No one should be a slave to anyone. God does not consider us slaves for Him. Why should we have slaves for ourselves?"

Nellie fingered the silver chain around her neck. "I always happy when you come, Sissy."

"That's a nice medallion, Nellie. I think you should give it to Roger Toby as your Christmas present."

"This?" she asked, holding it up toward the angel. "This mean a lot to me, Sissy."

"But since it means so much to you, giving it to him will mean so much more to God. And it will have a special meaning to Roger."

"I'll give it to him for Christmas."

"Good, Nellie. And ask him to wear it every day to remind himself how dear you are in God's sight, and he should never ever think of hurting you."

"I will, Sissy. I hope you never leave me."

"I'll always be here for you."

The clock outside Nellie's room chimed twelve times.

All at once, glorious music vibrated through the house. Sweet violins, proclaiming trumpets, soothing clarinets…all sorts of instruments teaming their voices in praise of the Glorious Birth. Nellie was flooded with music. The walls were alive with it.

Sissy lifted her arms toward heaven and sang "It Came Upon the Midnight Clear," and although Nellie had heard this music before, she had never heard these words to that song:

"Yet with the woes of sin and strife,
the world has suffered long;
Beneath the heav'nly hymn have rolled
two thousand years of wrong;
And warring humankind hears not
the tidings which they bring;
O hush the noise and cease your strife
and hear the angels sing."

Sissy sang the last two stanzas again and again, each time fainter than before:

"O hush the noise and cease your strife and hear the angels sing."…

"O hush the noise and cease your strife
and hear the angels sing."

145

Then she waved goodbye with her small arms, smiling at Nellie. "Have a joyful Christmas," she whispered as she floated toward the window, evaporating into a pinpoint of light

"Don't go!" Nellie cried, jumping off her bed and racing to her window. "Come back, Sissy!" She yanked the curtains back, hoping to find her angel friend outside. But all she saw were large snowflakes, drifting in the night air like white crystals hanging in space, not wanting to meet the white blanket below.

It snowed like this five years ago, Nellie remembered. She nearly froze on the banks of the great Missouri. Her mother had been taken by the white slavers. But that nice man came, just as Sissy had promised he would, and brought her to the Radfords. It was the best Christmas present she ever had...

...to finally know what it was like to be free.

1863

"...Death holds all parts together."
--Walt Whitman, *Leaves of Grass*

Chapter 11

Early January, 1863
Stones River, Tennessee

Matt had just finished hanging his wash on the line when he noticed Mary nearby. Her hands were folded in front of her and her lips betrayed a teasing smile. "Well," she said, "if I knew you were that handy with household chores, I would have hired you as my man-servant."

"Shucks, I'm not that handy, really," Matt said, making a foolish attempt at a laugh. He forced his hands into his pockets, hoping she wouldn't notice how they were shaking. In his mind, he could still hear the guns, canisters, and cannons—even though Bragg's Army of Tennessee had already retreated away from Stones River and toward Shelbyville and Tullahoma. Yesterday was the first day the fighting had ceased, but all day he had been helping bury bodies of the dead.

"What do I have to do to get you to relax?" she asked, walking toward him. "The fighting's over, Matt."

"For now," he said. "For now, it's over. How many more blasted dead do I have to pray over and bury before it really *is* over? I can't sleep at night thinkin' about men I once talked to, men with big dreams whose hopes are now gone forever."

Mary's face lost its smile. "You don't have to tell me about that. I know all about tragedy. I've seen a surgeon warm his hands over an open gash in a man's stomach. And two days ago, a soldier killed himself once he realized his manhood was forever destroyed by canister shot. We should at least be thankful for this lull in the fighting. Maybe both sides will come to their senses."

Matt put his arms around her. "I'm sorry, Mary. I'm a bit out of sorts because of Tinker. Tried to console him over the loss of his friend. He can't get over the fact the boy's dead."

She pulled away. "You mean Lazarus?"

"The same. Murdered by a man in a Nashville bordello, although Tinker told his captain a different story."

"Oh my," Mary said, putting her hand to her face.

149

"Found out about it yesterday from a woman named Lillian."

"Lillian?"

"Owner of the bordello Lazarus visited. She's settled outside this camp with a trumpet named Rose, the lady who saw Lazarus get murdered. Tinker found Rose crying over the boy's body. Since Rose wanted to follow Tinker back to camp, Lillian decided to accompany her, and the two of them have been following our soldiers ever since we left Nashville."

Mary's eyes narrowed with suspicion. "Why would the owner of a bordello talk to you?"

Matt sensed his face burn with embarrassment. "Because I'm a minister and Tinker's friend. She feels rotten about this whole thing since Emmett, her husband, was the one who did it. Wanted me to tell her if God would forgive her for not turning him in."

"What did you tell her?"

"Told her to read Psalm 86. 'The Lord is good and forgiving and abounding in kindness to all who call upon Him.' That didn't seem to make an impression on her, so I told her if she didn't turn Emmett in, the man might murder someone else."

"What did she say to that?"

"Said he'll be murdering more men anyway because he joined a rebel unit in Tennessee." He turned away from Mary and stared out into the open field. He had wrestled with this question before. Lillian, he thought, only served to illuminate it for him.

"What's wrong?" Mary asked.

"I guess I don't know the difference between what Emmett did to Lazarus compared to what Emmett will do to some stranger out there on the battlefield. Does the Fifth Commandment distinguish between these two situations?"

The next day
Topeka, Kansas

Otto Heller's kitchen was warmed by a large wood stove. In it, maple tree limbs crackled with the noise of hungry flames. Jessica looked about the kitchen before taking the kettle off the stove. She found this room comfortable, despite the dampness and the pungent odor of burning wood. It reminded her of a January evening in Waverly, Missouri when she, at five years old, took her baths in the kitchen.....

"If yuh wash her any more," Pa had said as Ma scrubbed Jessica in the metal basin, "all her skin will come off and she'll have none left."

"I wouldn't have to do this, "Ma replied, "if you would've kept an eye on her. What was she doing in the muddy chicken coop by herself anyway?"

"I dunno. That girl's got a mind of her own, I reckon. She don't listen to nobody."

Jessica tied on an apron after Emma and Mitzi climbed into the tub of water. "Now you girls will have to get nice and clean for me," Jessica said, pouring in another kettle of water, "so you'll look pretty when your father comes home."

Emma Heller grinned as she sat in the tub with Mitzi. "Are you going be here forever, Miss Radford?"

"I don't think so," Jessica said, handing a bar of soap to Mitzi. That was a good question though, Jessica admitted. It had been two weeks since Helga's death, and Otto was still dependent on Jessica to help out with the children and take care of meals. When Otto came home tonight, she'd have to tell him about her need to return to Columbia, Missouri, to start classes.

"But I'm not even sure I want to go," Jessica mumbled as she poured water over Emma's flaxen hair.

"What did you say?" Emma squeaked, her eyes closed while water drenched over her face.

"Nothing." Jessica realized she might decide *not* to go. Could she really focus on her studies while there was the unfinished business of avenging the murder of her family and finding Nellie's body? The Yankees had to win this war. They just had to. How else would all slaves be set free?

Things might have been different, she thought, if only John Howell had lived. She would have still been there with the Yankees, doin' her part deliverin' supplies just so she could be with him. But now she was here, away from battle, not doin' anything to help the Union. She felt only shame when she remembered what she had told Skipp when he abused Tinker for wanting to fight. "You need every able body you can get these days," she had told him. "I'd enlist myself right now if they'd let me."

But the only way she'd want to help the Union was by fighting the rebels herself. Being a nurse or even driving a medical supply wagon wouldn't satisfy her.Nor would making cloth for uniforms nor sewing flags nor rolling bandages. No— it had to be shooting back at the enemy. She wanted to personally cause those rebels to fall. Too bad those fools in Washington thought all women were such helpless creatures that they couldn't be good soldiers.

Jessica helped the girls get dressed and hurried to make supper. Otto, she thought, will need to hire a maid servant to do these chores for him. Whether or not she returned to Columbia for college, she couldn't keep doing this. Tonight she'd tell him.

The clock in the dining room chimed seven times. What was keeping Otto, she wondered? Supper was ready, the children were at the table, and he still wasn't home. "We'll just have to eat without your daddy," she told the girls as she served up the ham and potatoes on their plates.

Mitzi's face was unsmiling as she looked at her food. "Did God really say it was time for mommy to go to heaven, like Daddy says?"

"I suppose He did." But Jessica didn't believe it herself. How could the Lord allow this misery? What good was spending all that time going to church and worshipping Him when good people like her parents were murdered? If there was a God, why did that monster Sam Toby continue to live while her parents were now in their graves?

By the time the clock chimed nine, Jessica had put away the dishes and prepared the girls for bed. This was the first time since the funeral that Otto had failed to return home on time. Perhaps he had an emergency at his publishing house. Maybe a last-minute deadline change. Perhaps a problem with a press. But none of that would have kept him away so long.

"Where's Daddy?" Emma asked before Jessica extinguished the lamp by the girl's bed.

"I don't know, Emma. He might be working late."

"I wish he could tuck me in."

"I know, sweetheart. Good night." She blew out the candle and tiptoed down the stairs to Otto's study. She found a book on his desk and sat down to read, hoping she'd forget worrying about him. It was Walt Whitman's *Leaves of Grass,* and there were two slips of paper sticking out from the pages of the book. Out of curiosity, she opened the book at the page where the first slip was inserted and read:

> *I am the hounded slave ...I wince at the bite of the dogs,*
> *Hell and despair are upon me ... crack and again*
> *crack the marksmen,*
> *I clutch the rails of the fence...*
> *My gore drips, thinned with the ooze of my skin,*
> *I fall on the weeds and stones,*
> *The riders spur their unwilling horses and haul close,*
> *They taunt my dizzy ears...*
> *they beat me violently over the head with their whip-stocks.*

In the margin, along the vertical side of the book were names, apparently penned by Otto:

Cicely, Moses, Ruby, Lewis, Mattie, Dicer, Johnnie, Willis, Lazarus, Torch, Devin, Kitty, Hilda, Anna, Milo, Zeke, Daisy, Nellie, Libby, Bruno, Chester, Elvira, Hetty, Patches, Bobolink, Annie, Abel, Poona, Adam, Taffy, Ishmael.

Jessica's eyes widened in shock. She counted the names. Thirty-one. Maybe these were thirty-one slaves Otto helped escape as a conductor for the Underground Railroad. Lazarus was named here. So was Nellie. Otto never talked about the slaves he helped set free, but here was a written record. Perhaps he would be upset if he knew she had seen this.

There was another notation in the margin. What was this? *Hebrews 13, 2-3.* Did that have something to do with all those slaves he helped free? Well, maybe she'd look up that scripture later.

She was about to close the book when she decided to see what page that second slip of paper led to. She found it easily. The words in the passage were underlined:

> *"Great is Life, real and mystical, wherever and whoever;*
> *Great is Death—sure as life holds all parts together,*
> *Death holds all parts together.*
> *Has Life much purport?—Ah, Death has the great-*
> *est purport."*

The familiar Whitman passage came back to her...she had mentioned it to Mary months ago, on the day of Ma and Pa's funeral. She had forgotten about it since then, but now that she read it again, she wished she understood it.

A sudden rap at the door. Jessica's heart thumped. Otto! She flew to the door, almost overturning a lamp.

Otto Heller, head bent low, feet dragging, was supported by two men, one white, one colored. A third stranger was there as well, a young white soldier smartly dressed in an officer's uniform. "Ma'am," he said, tipping his forage cap, "I'm Lieutenant James Pond and a friend of Mr. Heller. I witnessed the attack. Fortunately, these two men were kind enough to come to my aid and bring him here."

"What happened?" Jessica asked, her voice rising as she made way for them to get through the doorway.

The other white man looked up at Jessica with a gray face, his brown eyes tired, bloodshot. "I heard gunfire. The lieutenant here chased the attackers, but by the time we got there, they were gone. By the way, my name's Carter, David Carter." He grunted as he helped the Negro carry Otto to the bedroom. "This other man here is Jim Fowler. We both work for Mr. Heller."

While the two men placed Otto on the bed, the lieutenant shifted his attention to Jessica. "Happened kind of sudden, ma'am. I spotted my friend Otto from across the road and was about to call out to him, but then some ruffians grabbed him and hauled him to the ground. By the time I got there, they had given him quite a pounding."

154

"We were at the livery stable when we heard the noise," Fowler said, getting a pillow for Otto's head. "The lieutenant was shooting at them as they ran off."

"Lucky the lieutenant got to Mr. Heller when he did," Carter added.

Jessica gave a muffled cry at the sight of his bloodied face and ran to the kitchen for a towel. She returned and mopped up the blood from his nose and cheeks. One of his eyes was badly swollen.

"Did you see who did it?" she asked.

"I've seen one of them before," Lieutenant Pond said. "I can't place that face with a name, but I recognize him."

"I suspect," Fowler said, "the beating had something to do with him meeting Jim Lane."

Otto groaned as he shifted his weight on the bed. He opened his eyes halfway. "Where am I?"

"You're at home," Jessica said. "Maybe I should call the doctor."

"No," Otto protested with another low groan. "I'll be fine. Just need to rest a little." He put his head to one side as if he intended to sleep.

Jessica got up from the bed and looked at Fowler. "You were saying something about Mr. Heller meeting someone named Lane?"

"Yes, ma'am," Fowler said. "Senator James Lane. He used to be part-owner of the *Kansas Crusader of Freedom*, but recently he contacted Mr. Heller about publishing some abolitionist pamphlets. I guess they're all part of his efforts to get rid of bushwhackers crossing into Kansas."

"I suspect these were proslavery thugs who did this to Mr. Heller," Carter added.

Jessica offered them a drink before they left, but they refused. "I've got to get home to my wife," Fowler said. "This war's already taken a toll on my family now that Lazarus is gone."

"Gone?" Jessica asked.

"Killed."

Jessica held her breath for a tense moment. "Lazarus? Tinker's friend?"

"Yeah," Fowler said, looking away, "my boy died fighting. I'm proud of him."

"But," Jessica said, "Mr. Heller never mentioned a word to me about Lazarus dying."

After the three of them departed, Jessica went to the outhouse in the back yard. When she returned, she overheard two of the men talking on the front porch....

"Yeah," Carter said, "Otto knows a lot of things he never talks about."

"I thought he had given up slave catchin' after Helga died," Fowler said.

"He wanted to. But he had to rescue Salem. After all, that slave was Ishmael's brother. Family's important to Otto. Real important."

"I know," Fowler said, sounding as if he were choking on his tears. "That's how he felt about me and my wife adopting Lazarus. He told me he was giving us the son we had always wanted."

"Well, you can be proud of one thing, Jim."

"What's that?"

"Your son wanted to fight to free the slaves—and he didn't mind dying if he had to."

The next day
Cincinnati, Ohio

"At best," Benjamin Robles told Penelope, "you've been guilty of malfeasance of office and misappropriation of funds. At worst, you've been guilty of embezzlement."

Penelope Phillips gave a passing glance at the legal volumes in his office before turning toward the window. It was a man's world out there, she thought, among all those multistoried brick buildings. Business was exclusively man's domain even if a lady was more capable of running it. Well, it certainly reflected the philosophy of the board of directors at Silas Drug.

"As I mentioned," Penelope said, "all I did was direct our chief accountant to alter our financial statement so stockholders wouldn't question it."

"You're referring to that $2,900 investment into your home remedy medicine project?"

"Of course. I knew the board wouldn't approve it. But after they saw the results of our market entry, they'd consider it a blessing. I did it for the good of the company, not for my own personal gain. The firm will be the ultimate benefactor, not me."

The attorney got up from his chair and paced the room. He stopped in front of her, his eyes dark with resolve. "Now see here, Miss Phillips. You're fortunate that the board hasn't yet notified the authorities about your crime. If I were you, I would take them up on their offer."

"I wouldn't call it an offer. I'd call it extortion."

"Call it what you like, but it's a sure way to escape prosecution."

Penelope glared back at him. "So you agree with them? You agree I should resign my position with Silas Drug?"

"As well as liquidate your share holdings and return the $2,900 you've embezzled."

She folded her hands in defiance. "And for that, they're willing to correct their books and forget the whole thing. Is that your understanding?"

"It's preferable to going to jail, in my opinion, Miss Phillips."

"In a way, I feel I'm already in jail."

"How's that, Miss Phillips?"

"My ability to run a business being questioned because I'm a lady. I'd call that being in jail."

January 10
Westport, Missouri

Sam Toby, with a massive crop of brown hair hugging his large face, took another swallow of beer in the almost empty tavern. A brown-and-black dog, wagging its tail, nudged its way between Sam and Larkin Skaggs. Skaggs, a middle-aged man, bald in the center with an outcropping of scraggly hair at the ends, put his newspaper down. "Tell that mutt to get out of here. He just wants some of your crackers."

"If that's what he wants, Larkin," Sam said, flashing an angry glance, "then that's what he gets." He grabbed a couple of crackers from the dish and fed them to the dog. "Poor guy probably's hungry."

"Is that like the mutt yah tol' me yah once had?"

"Yeah, sort of," Sam said, petting the dog. "Except mine was what they call a terrier. He had these pointy black ears that would go up sometimes when I called him. I'd say 'Hey, Animal.' That was his name, Animal. I'd say Hey, Animal, 'n his ears would go up'n he'd bark at me. Funny dog." He leaned back in his chair. "Anyway, Animal died on me last year. Got poisoned. Sure do miss'im."

Sam tossed the dog a few more crackers and turned his attention to Skaggs. "Anything important in that damned abolitionist paper you been readin'?"

"Yup," Skaggs said, opening the *Kansas Weekly Tribune* to the third page. "Look at this here picture. Is that the same feller who's been stealin' slaves'n bringin' 'em over to Kansas?"

"Damn right that's him," he said, looking at a picture of Otto Heller standing next to two little girls.

Larkin took a swallow of beer. "Don't know too much 'bout him. But he's the one who's been talkin' to that Lane feller. Thought maybe we'd beat'im up bad'n teach'im a lesson. It's that Lane fella I wanted to get, though. Would've shut him up fer good."

Sam's dark eyes, arched by his bushy eyebrows, studied his comrade and the muscles in his jaw twitched. "Yah know as well as me, we couldn't have done that. He had four soldiers with'im, two on each side. If that damned Yankee lieutenant in his fancy uniform wouldn't have come when he did, we could've put a few bullet holes into Mr. Heller."

Sam pushed himself up from his chair, wincing in pain and cursing. "Damn chest still hurts. That damn Heller hit me hard. If I ever see'im again, I'll blow his brains out."

"What do you think Quantrill is gonna want tah do next, Sam?"

Sam Toby stroked the coarse hair on his face. "Now how could I know that? I just joined his men last month. Besides, I hear he only tells his lieutenants what he's thinkin' about. But I suspect that we'd be doin' Quantrill and his lieutenants a real service in gettin' this other feller, this here slave stealer, Otto Heller."

"Can't do that now," Larkin Skaggs said. "Todd ordered us back to Bates county."

"Yeah," Sam growled, "but we'll be back in Topeka again." He grabbed the newspaper and ripped out Otto's picture. "Says here that those girls are his two chillun. Nice thing to know."

The next day
Cincinnati, Ohio

While waiting for her train at the station, Penelope laughed to herself about her performance yesterday in front of the board. She showed up in a spectacular white lawn eyelet dress with a high neck and full pleated skirt. With her hair swept up, and her thin waist elegantly corseted, she strutted back and forth across the room. "Gentlemen," she had said, "how have you really perceived me since I took over this enterprise—as a business leader or as an attractive woman?" She stopped, grabbed a vacant chair, and hoisted her leg on it. With a quick movement of her hand, she raised her hemline several inches above the ankle. The men gasped, jumping up from their chairs in protest. "Oh, I guess," she added, feigning surprise, "this is how you really see me—an object of desire. Well, perhaps I should have you all arrested for leering at me."

After a shouting match where the men objected to her outlandish behavior and she, in turn, cited their underhanded tactics, she told them she'd agree to their demands. "But I want you to know," she said, after signing all the necessary papers, "that you have to live with your consciences. What you're all guilty of is extortion and blackmail—and I hope your business rots!" With that remark, she left the room and slammed the door behind her.

It was over, Penelope thought. She'd be going back home to Lawrence, Kansas, to reconsider her future. Maybe once she removed herself from the business jungle, she'd be able to think rationally. First, however, she'd stop in Topeka and visit with Mr. Heller at his office. Last she heard was that Jessica was caring for Mr. Heller's children at the Heller residence, wherever that was.

Penelope wished she had known earlier about Helga's death. She would have gone to the funeral. Still, she'd find out where Jessica was staying and pay her a visit. It would be good to see her again. Maybe they could start another business together.

January 14
Brentwood, Tennessee

The cabin Lillian and Rose had rented lay just outside the Union compound, across a ravine, and Tinker found it easily. A humorous hand-drawn sign outside said "Closed for Horizontal Refreshments," but he realized that only pertained to customers.

Rose was wearing a red cotton dress with white ruffles when he arrived. Her face powder lessened the intensity of the scar across her cheek. Her eyes were cold, angry. "We're closed, sir. Didn't you see the sign?"

"I did, but I be here on other business."

Sudden recognition swept over her embarrassed face. "Tinker!" She looked beyond his shoulder, as if seeing if there was anyone else with him. "Lillian's not here, so maybe you can come in."

Tinker didn't know what she meant by that. Did Lillian not want him here? Maybe it didn't matter. Rose let him in, didn't she? Besides, he wasn't planning on staying long.

Facing him as he entered was a small parlor containing two purple cushioned chairs, a small varnished table and a cabinet containing glassware. Along one corner of the room was a wooden bookcase, and along the other, a stone fireplace. Above the fireplace was a large framed daguerreotype of President Lincoln, which Tinker thought odd with these women being Southerners. Maybe they were trying to make a favorable impression for their customers.

"We need to be quiet," Rose said. "Jay's asleep."

"Jay?"

"My two-year-old son. Now that I'm on the road, I take him with me."

160

"But—" Tinker didn't understand why she would raise a boy under these awful conditions.

Rose put a warning finger to her mouth. "Shhh. Just follow me," she said, her voluminous skirts and crinolines rustling as she walked toward the bedroom.

Tinker followed her into a room containing a four-poster bed with a thick white comforter and two pillows, a plain wooden chair, a small dresser on which stood a white ceramic vase. There was also a closet, the door to which was open, revealing dresses and women's undergarments.

"This is my bedroom," she said, as Tinker examined the freshly-painted walls. He wished he lived in a room like this. The only "house" he knew—the shed behind the Mississippi Street residence in Lawrence—was smaller than this room.

"I thought the war'd be over by now," she said.

Tinker studied a painting of a bowl of fruit on the wall. "Me too."

"I wonder about the Union, sometimes."

"How's that?" Tinker asked, still surveying the room.

"Well, the Union lost to the rebels down south in Galveston. Looks like they're losing more and more battles these days."

Tinker turned around, about to tell her he hoped to change all that, when he was taken aback. She was now dressed only in her undergarments.

"Hold on," Tinker snapped. "I'm not here for that."

She looked both surprised and disappointed. "Then what *are* you here for?"

"I'm here 'bout Lazarus. He had a book with him when he saw you the day he got himself killed. I forgot all 'bout it at the time, but I'm here to get it back. Yah got it?"

Her eyes betrayed her guilt. "Yes. I kept it because it's the only thing I have left to remind me of him. I'd like to keep it."

"I needs it back, Rose. I wants to return it to the Fowlers—those nice folks who adopted him. They need somethin' to remember him by too."

"I suppose you're right." She opened the bedroom door. "Follow me."

She led him back to the parlor and picked up a volume from a small bookcase in the corner of the room. "This must

161

be what you're referring to," she said, handing him a copy of Thoreau's *Collected Papers*. The cover was spattered with dried blood.

"I apologize for its poor condition.," she said, bringing her chair closer to him. "My hand was soaked in blood when I picked it up that day, that awful day!" She dabbed her eye with a handkerchief.

"I don't care none 'bout that," Tinker said, running his thumb through the pages. "My notes are still here. Wonder if Lazarus ever read them?"

"Don't know if he did or not. I read a few things from the book. I even made some notes of my own in the back."

Tinker turned to the inside cover of the book. There were several sentences he guessed were written by Rose's hand. "I likes this one," he said. "'Time is but the stream I go a-fishin' in.' Makes me think about the day all of this is over. When we gots no more war and we gots no more slaves, I can be free to do what I wants to do."

"And what is that, Tinker? What do you want to do?"

Through the parlor window, Tinker watched a small cloud in the blue sky. It reminded him of a boat on the sea, a boat heading for the mainland. "Some day, I wants to marry a nice woman, have chillum, and own a piece of land. I wants to see what I can do with my own life with no one gettin' in my way. I wants to see—"

A child's wail reverberating through the walls interrupted him.

"Oh my stars!" Rose exclaimed. "Jay's awake. I must attend to him." Taking quick steps, she hurried out of the room.

Tinker got up and cradled the book in his arm. Rose returned, holding the hand of a mulatto child. "This is Jay," she said. "He just learned to talk but only knows a few words." Rose ran her fingers through the boy's disheveled blond hair. "Jay, this gentleman's name is Tinker."

Jay stared wide-eyed at him for a moment. "You a slave?"

"No," Rose laughed. "He's not a slave." She glanced at Tinker. "Sorry, but you resemble his father a little."

"He be a slave?"

"He *was* a slave."

Tinker rubbed his chin. "You mean he be free now?"

Rose turned her attention to Jay. "Tell Tinker how old you'll be next year."

The boy grinned and showed him three fingers.

"Where's his father now?" Tinker asked, miffed that Rose had ignored his question.

Rose looked at a clock on the wall, and avoided Tinker's gaze as she returned her attention to Jay. "I think this boy's hungry," she said, removing a shoulder strap from her chemise before easing herself into a chair. She offered her breast to the boy, who cradled it with both hands as he sat in her lap.

Tinker started for the door. "I best be goin', ma'am."

She gently stroked Jay's head. "Maybe you're right. Lillian will be coming soon."

"Yah keep sayin' that. Does Lillian mind mah comin' here?"

Rose just gazed at him with a blank expression. It wasn't until he reached the front door and turned for one last look that he saw an incredible sadness washing over her face. "I'm glad," she said as she continued nursing Jay, "I could give Lazarus something special."

"What's that, ma'am?"

"Same thing I've always given Jay—a momma's love."

Evening, two days later
Chattanooga, Tennessee

The crash of thunder woke Roger Toby from a deep sleep. He turned to find Sara rolled over to one side, fast asleep. Layers of rain slashed the window, and Roger decided to get up and see if the windows upstairs were closed. Roger stopped down the hall when he saw a yellow radiance illuminating the staircase landing. Could he have forgotten to extinguish the lamp upstairs?

When he got to the top of the stairs, he saw the glow of candlelight coming from Nellie's room. The door was partly open, so he tiptoed in without knocking. Nellie was sitting on the side of her bed, staring out the window, occasional flashes of white from the lightning brightening the sky. Each clap of thunder sounded like the lash of a whip and Nellie trembled.

"Nellie," Roger whispered, "are yaw all right?"

"Don't like thunder, Mr. Toby."

He sat down next to her. "Nothing to be scared of, child. Yaw safe here."

She looked at him with puppy eyes. "I know. Sissy tol' me."

"Sissy tells yaw a lot of things, doesn't she?"

Nellie nodded. "Like she tol' me to give yuh my medal for Christmas."

Roger fingered the coin-shaped bronze medallion hanging from his neck. "I like it, especially since your name's inscribed on the back of it. I wear it all the time."

Nellie returned to staring out the window. "I safe but I still scared. Hate thunder. When I was little, mah mastah punish me and mah momma real bad. He chain us in with the pigs outside to punish mah momma'n it rain'n thunder like this all night. I scared then. Real scared."

Roger saw a book lying on her table. "Maybe I can read yaw something. Would yaw like that?"

Her face lightened as she handed him the book. "Tinker used to read this to me."

Roger examined the cover. "Hmmm. *The Song of Hiawatha?*"

"Yeah. I like that."

"Where do yaw want me to start?"

"The part about making peace. That's Sissy's favorite."

Roger thumbed through the pages, thinking maybe he'd just read anything from it. He was tired and wanted to get back to sleep. But she stopped him. "Right there," she said, "where the corner of the page is bent."

Roger focused his eyes on that section of the poem and began reading:

I have given yaw lands to hunt in—

Nellie giggled. "You read funny. When Sara reads it, she says 'you,' not 'yaw,' and she reads it real slow-like."

Roger shrugged. "Well then, let's see if I read it better than Sara." He started over, reading slowly, pausing after each sentence, and allowing the meaning of the words to sink in:

I have given you lands to hunt in.
I have given you streams to fish in,

I have given you bear and bison,
I have given you roe and reindeer,
I have given you brant and beaver,
Filled the marshes full of wild-fowl,
Filled the rivers full of fishes.
Why then are you not contented? Why then
will you hunt each other?
I am weary of your quarrels, Weary of your
wars and bloodshed,
Weary of your prayers for vengeance, Of
your wranglings and dissensions;
All your strength is in your union, All your
danger is in discord.
Therefore, be at peace henceforward....

Roger stopped reading when he noticed Nellie was sound asleep. He returned the book to the table and blew out the candle.

As he left the room, he noticed it had stopped thundering.

Chapter 12

January 17
Lawrence, Kansas

After picking up her mail from the post office, Jessica arrived at her Indiana Street home. It wasn't as large as the Griswold home down on the corner of the street, but it was a welcome sight—a white Victorian structure with an enclosed patio. A giant oak, with its leafless tentacles, dominated her fenced front yard. She wished it were summer so she could again see her lawn populated with buttonbush. This would ordinarily be a peaceful place, Jessica thought. But with the war going badly for the Yankees and Kansas being threatened by invasions from Missouri to the east and from Indian Territory to the south, she felt anything but peaceful. It was unfortunate that Mary was still helping out with nursing and Matt was still fighting somewhere in Tennessee. Had she not gone to Topeka last month to help pull Otto through his loss, she'd probably have been in college right now, forgetting all about the war. But it was too late for that now. She had already written to Joseph Rogers concerning her intention not to enroll this year. Maybe when the war was over she'd go back.

Emma and Mitzi were reluctant to return with her to Lawrence, not wanting to leave their daddy, but Otto explained to them it was the best thing and said he'd only be away for a while. But to Jessica he elucidated his plans for finding a new, more secure home for them near Topeka—one that would give them more protection from intruders. Then he'd return for the children.

Jessica questioned the wisdom of that decision. For one thing, he was exposing himself to danger every day he stayed there at his home. For another, she didn't feel comfortable with the idea of temporarily caring for his children in Lawrence. True, with the threat the border ruffians had made on his life, his daughters wouldn't be safe in Topeka. But would they be any safer here in Lawrence, with the constant threat of an invasion from pro-slavery marauders?

Well, Jessica was at least happy to be home once again. Maybe she could visit with her good friend. Last she heard from Amelia Read was that her husband had dissolved his partnership with Mr. Bullene and was buying another store.

Jessica was glad to be back in Lawrence. It was a small town of about 2,500 people, but it had a strong sense of community. People felt free to express their beliefs and help each other out. Like back in 1858 when Pa learned a Federal marshal might be paying him a visit because someone claimed he was hiding a slave. Under cover of darkness, Pa had taken Nellie to his friend Benjamin Johnson, who hid Nellie in the cellar of the Johnson House Hotel until the danger subsided.

Jessica placed the small bundle of letters on the kitchen table before showing the children a guest room where they'd be sleeping. She realized there would still be a considerable amount of work needed to be done in order to get this house ready. She hadn't been here since she left a month ago to visit Otto, and the place was dusty and had a damp odor of neglect.

She stopped in the parlor to check herself in the mirror. With the money she made from Silas Drug, she could now afford the best. She had ordered this one from New York—a black silk dress, with undersleeves and collar of black crepe. She didn't much care for the sheer, black lace collar and wished it were white instead. At least she no longer wore that hideous black veil. In time, she'd buy colorful earrings and dare anyone to look askance at her. Certainly she missed her parents, but to be chained to black mourning clothes for a year was like a prison sentence.

Returning to the kitchen, she sorted through her mail, mostly requests for donations to the war effort or paid announcements of store openings. But she noticed a letter from Tinker by the way he addressed her as Miz Jesika Radford. As she opened it, she saw it had several postmarks on it. It must have had difficulty getting to the right address. She would have to write Tinker back and apologize for being so late in responding. She was about to read it when she heard a knock on the door. Stuffing the letter in her dress pocket, she went to answer the door.

"Surprised to see me, Jessica?" Penelope beamed.

167

"Indeed I am! What are you doing here?" Jessica found herself envying her aunt's dark blue cotton dress and light blue feathered bonnet. Only four more months, Jessica thought, before she could toss her black clothes out for good.

"Can't a lady pay her dear niece a visit?"

"Of course, but I mean, you came all the way from Cincinnati. And how did you ever know I was here?"

"Remember writing to me about Helga's death? You told me you were staying with Mr. Heller after the funeral to take care of matters. I wanted to meet you, but since I didn't know where you were, I paid a visit to Mr. Heller. He told me you had just left for your home in Lawrence with his two daughters."

"As a governess for his children," Jessica interjected.

"Yes. He also told me about the awful beating he had taken. Makes me think we're living in a barbaric society these days."

"Indeed we are. Please come in. You'll have to tell me all about how things are progressing at Silas Drug."

Penelope spent the next thirty minutes on the settee discussing how she was forced to resign her post at Silas Drug and sell her stock to avoid prosecution.

Jessica put her hand to her cheek. "My word! Will you be all right? What will you do now?"

"Don't fret about it. I'll find another business. Maybe something here in town."

"Do you intend to live at your old place?"

Penelope nodded, taking another sip of tea. "Yes. Looks like we'll be neighbors." She glanced about the parlor, taking everything in. "I see you've made a few changes here, but it still looks very much as it did back seven years ago when I used to watch Claire. In fact, I sat in the same rocker where you're sitting. I really miss that child, don't you?"

Jessica's stomach turned sour. *Sam Toby killed her, not me.* "Would you care for more tea, Penelope?"

"No thank you. How are the children taking to their new environment?"

"Why don't you ask them yourself? Mitzi! Emma! Come here. I'd like you to meet someone."

The two girls entered the parlor, with shy grins on their faces. Penelope welcomed Emma on her lap and stroked Mitzi's long brown hair as the eight-year-old showed her a pencil drawing she had made. "Oh, what's this?" Penelope asked the child.

Jessica spoke up for the little girl. "That's probably the sketch she made. She worked on it when we took the stage-coach here. She didn't want to let me see it until it was fin-ished. It's supposed to be her image of Lawrence, Kansas."

"Then I don't understand this, Emma," Penelope said, frowning at the drawing. "What is all of this?"

"These are the houses on fire," Mitzi said, tracing it with her finger. "They're burning because some bad men came into town with torches."

Penelope shook her head. "Where do these children get such horrible ideas?"

"Shows what she thinks of this war," Jessica said. "Mitzi must have gotten the idea from some pictures she saw in the *Kansas Weekly Tribune* last month. Some farmhouses near the Missouri border were set ablaze by bushwhackers."

Penelope sipped her tea during the unpleasant silence that followed. After she placed her teacup on the table, she lifted Emma from her lap. "Well, I should be going," she said. She bent down and gave each of the girls a hug. "These children are adorable, aren't they? George and I could have had children, except he was afraid of—" She pursed her lips and betrayed a slight sadness in her hazel eyes. "Your uncle was always concerned our children might turn out to be colored."

Jessica walked her to the door, wondering what kind of mother Penelope would have been, given her penchant for business. Maybe a good one. She seemed to like children. "Penelope, what's Uncle George doing these days? Haven't heard from him in a while."

"He wrote to me when I was in Cincinnatti, saying he hoped to get a furlough someday to see me. I never wrote back to him."

Otto was glad to learn that his friend Lieutenant James Pond was still at Fort Leavenworth for training exercises. He hastened to see Pond and thank him for his help. With Senator Lane's influence, Otto experienced few obstacles in securing clearance from an aide to Colonel Barstow, the 3rd Wisconsin Cavalry commander,

As soon as Otto entered the small unadorned room, James Pond bounded from his chair with both a handshake and a smile. "Mr. Heller, I was concerned about you. How have you been? Have a seat."

Otto eased himself into a chair. "I'm fine. Nothing broken. Lot of bad bruises, however. It hurts when I move around."

Pond stroked his finger across his chin like a violin bow. "It's been a few years since you left Wisconsin, hasn't it?"

Otto collected his thoughts and arranged the pictures of his friendship with James Pond's father in his mind. "Yes—ten years ago, I believe. Miss those days I had with Willard. Of course, I've always considered you a friend, too, even though you were a boy then."

The lieutenant nodded. "I guess I thought of you more like an uncle then. You've helped me get interested in reading. I appreciated that."

"And I appreciated getting your letters after I moved to Kansas. Looks like you've been living a full life—typesetting, editing, prospecting, and a dab here and there in politics." He put a finger to his lips as he gazed at his young friend in uniform. "As I recall, you even told me you joined John Brown in his fight against slavery. Lucky thing you parted company before he got captured at Harper's Ferry."

"See? That's the kind of influence my father and you had on me," he said, taking off his forage cap and stroking his full head of hair with his fingers. "I guess when it comes to freeing slaves, I'll do anything. But you and my father deserve a lot of credit. He used to say the two of you made a good team in the Underground Railroad. He wasn't too happy when you left Wisconsin to get married."

"I've been out of touch with Willard. How's he been?"

"Fine." His face got serious as he played with the rim of his hat that he held in his hands. "Otto, did you get a good look at the men who beat you?"

"The only one I remember was the one I punched in the stomach. Looked familiar, but I don't know why."

"Well," the lieutenant said, leaning forward, "I got a real good look at one of them, maybe the same one you hit. I couldn't remember where I saw him at first. But it came to me as I was riding back with Carter and Fowler that night. I saw his name on some wanted posters last year when I was in Kansas. Name's Sam Toby."

"Sam Toby?" Otto's mind spun. The wanted poster—yes, he remembered seeing it. Otto riveted his attention on the lieutenant. "What do you know about this man—Sam Toby?"

The lieutenant gave that some thought. "Well, one of our scouts said a man fitting Toby's description was seen riding with Quantrill through Westport. Might not necessarily mean he's officially joined those border ruffians."

"What else?" Otto asked, the muscles in his hands tensing.

"This man Toby's apparently killed innocent civilians. His most recent murder was that of a couple in Lawrence last June. I believe their names were Henry and Rachel Radford."

"What!" He was stunned. All Jessica had ever told him was that three of the four men who had murdered her parents were caught and executed. This must have been the fourth man—still on the loose.

"Are you feeling all right, Otto?"

"I'm fine." Otto stared blankly back at the lieutenant. What would he tell Jessica? Or should he tell her, knowing she might put herself in danger if she tried to seek him out?

A week later
Murfreesboro, Tennessee

Mary nudged her horse toward the small ridge on the outskirts of the camp, where she thought she had heard the commotion. Sure enough, when she made it to the top, she saw two men exchanging blows. A man with broad shoulders and muscular arms landed a punch at Matt Lightfoot, sending him to the hard, pebble-strewn ground. "You don't belong in

171

this army," the man bellowed, taunting Matt to get up on his feet.

"Men!" Mary shouted, dismounting. "You're to fight the enemy, not each other."

The man bowed politely toward her and stroked his beard, a menacing smile still on his thick lips. "With all due respect, ma'am, this man's a traitor. He desrves to be horsewhipped."

Matt pushed himself up off the ground and brushed himself off. "Mary, I'm sorry you had to see this."

The man took a step toward him, raising his fist. "I oughta teach you a lesson. You Cherokees are all alike. You're all brothers, fighting against us."

"Please!" Mary pleaded. "What's this all about?"

The man walked toward his horse, cursing. "I don't care to hear his explanation. They're all savages."

Matt waited until the man rode away. "This isn't the first time I got this kind of hatred from our own men, Mary."

Mary furrowed her eyebrows. "What happened?"

"Well, this morning the captured rebels were lined up for roll call. Must have been a couple of hundred of 'em at least. Anyway, as I was passing by on my way to breakfast, I heard one of the prisoners shout '*Ama, oginali, aquaduli ama!*' I recognized this as the Cherokee tongue. The man was asking me for water. So I came over to him and asked '*Hitsalagis?*', which meant 'Are you Cherokee?' and he nodded that he was. So I asked an officer nearby if the prisoner could have some water. Well, the officer gave me this ugly stare, as if to say 'This is none of my business,' but he gave the man a cup of water. The prisoner thanked me, and I wished him well and went on my way."

Mary smiled. "That was nice of you."

"I thought so, too, but another lieutenant followed me out here and cursed me for fraternizing with a prisoner—an Indian at that. When I informed him I was part Indian myself, he lost control of himself and started punching. He said that Cherokees like myself were traitors, that the South was getting a lot of help from that tribe in fighting against us. That was about the time you came by."

Mary closed her eyes and felt the afternoon sun go deep inside her. It was bad enough, she realized, that men killed each other with bullets and cannon fire. They also had to kill each other with unkind words. "Mr. Lightfoot, I once read an article where the writer questioned white man's superiority to the Indians. He said that before white man discovered this land, the Indians were still running it, there was no debt, no jails, men were free to hunt and fish all day and women did all the work. Then along came the white man thinking he could improve the system."

Matt laughed. "Have you ever thought of acting in a comedy play?"

"That might be my next career."

Matt gazed in the direction of a natural arch formed by an even row of pine trees. "Miss Delaney, there's a small cave under a hill down there. I go there sometimes when I want to be alone. Would you care to join me?"

"Certainly."

They mounted their horses and rode past the trees, veered to the right between a V-shaped limestone rock formation, and stopped at the mouth of a cave surrounded by tall grass. "I came across this place purely by accident one day when it was raining," Matt said, tying up his horse. "Found it was a good spot for me when I wanted to get away from the dice, poker games, swearing, and drinking and just be alone."

He grabbed a horse blanket and laid it on the stones at the mouth of the cave. "It might not be the most comfortable place to be, Miss Delaney, but it sure is pretty here."

"I hope you don't have any perverse designs on this lady," Mary teased as she sat next to him.

"The only design I have on you is to tell you you're very pretty."

"Not as pretty as Jessica."

"Prettier." He placed his hand on hers. "In fact, I'd like to get to know you better, Miss Delaney."

"I'd like to get to know you better, too," she said without hesitation, much to her surpise. She felt a twinge of guilt, realizing he perhaps still cared for Jessica. "Matt, you've never told me anything about why you became a minister. Didn't you say that when you were a little boy you lived on a reservation with your Cherokee father and white mother?"

He picked up a stone with his free hand and moved it around with his fingers as if he were contemplating an important sculpture. "Miss Delaney, about twenty-five years ago my family was forced to leave our home. We lived in Tennessee then, but we had to head out for Indian Territory south of Kansas. Many people in the Cherokee Nation died along the way. All sorts of disasters—starvation, cholera, smallpox…My mother called our trip the 'trail of tears.'"

"How old were you at the time?"

"Only eight, but I remember it well." He put his arm around her thin waist. "Some of us refused government food because we didn't want the soldiers to think we accepted this cruelty. And some of the food they gave was foreign to us, like wheat flour, which we didn't know how to use."

Mary leaned her head on his shoulder. She could almost feel his inner rage over the memory.

"I saw a young mother," he said, his voice getting sour, "carry her dead child all day long, looking for the right place to bury it. And near the end of our long journey my father—" He paused long enough to clear his throat. "—my father was beaten, robbed, and murdered by white men who hated our kind." He turned to Mary, rage building on his face. "I was so angry, Miss Delaney, I was so angry I wanted to kill every white man I saw."

Mary watched a sparrow fly toward a nest on a low branch of an elm. Family was important even with birds, she thought. "Matt, what was your father like?"

"A good man but a stubborn one. He favored the old Indian manners and had no sympathy for slaves. But he was a wise man. He taught me how to respect animals, how to forage for food, how to listen to nature to tell when the weather would change. 'Matthew,' he'd say, 'learn from your elders. They have already made their mistakes. You need not repeat them.' When he died, he left a big hole in my life."

"So how did you ever become a minister after such an experience?"

His furrowed frown began to evaporate. "I owe that to my mother. She became a Christian after he died and taught me

174

the importance of forgiveness. It's because of her that I entered the seminary, intent on spreading hope to people in despair." He shook his head and smiled. "Of course, the way I've been behaving in this war, you'd think I've given up all hope myself."

"It's been hard on me too, Matt. I've had times when I just wanted to get on my horse and ride as far away from this war as I could."

"Why didn't you?"

"Because in the eyes of some of the wounded, I was their only hope."

"You're my hope, too," he said, his lips dangerously close to hers.

"We'll always be good friends, Matt."

"I'm not talking about just being friends," he said, placing his hand on her knee. "I need you, Mary."

She felt the warmth of his hand even through her layers of clothing. An uninvited thought flickered in her mind—what would it be like to make love to him? What would his manhood feel like inside? Would he be gentle and caring as he gave himself to her? Embarrassed at even entertaining such a notion, she pulled away from him. "I've got to be going, Matt," she said, getting up. "I still have wounded and sick soldiers to tend to."

Late January
Topeka, Kansas

Penelope surveyed the bar, crowded with military men, as she sat at the table across from Otto. She returned the few surprised stares she received from them with challenging stares of her own. She wasn't sure if they didn't like the fact she was a woman or a mulato, but what difference should it make to them? If they didn't like it, they should go to another bar.

"Look, you don't need to apologize," she told Mr. Heller. "I'm the one who left you stuck with a project I couldn't fulfill. At least my check should compensate you for your out-of-pocket costs in preparing those brochures for me."

Otto took another sip of burgundy and returned the wine glass to the table, his fingertip running across the rim as he studied her. "I thank you for that, Miss Phillips. I'm only sorry you had to leave your firm. What will you be doing now?"

"I'm considering a business opportunity in Lawrence."

Otto Heller's eyes were gray and tired. "I'd sell you my own printing business, but several of my associates already expressed an interest in forming a partnership and taking it over."

"What!" Penelope exclaimed, her voice rising. "Why this sudden change? Why would you want to sell your business? It's your life."

Otto shook his head. "Not any more it isn't." He leaned over the table, whispering: "As I was leaving the office two nights ago, someone took a shot a me."

"Oh, no!"

He sat back in his chair and dismissed her concern with a wave of his hand. "I'm all right. Whoever did it was evidently a poor shot. But I can't take another chance. Now that Helga's gone, I worry a lot about the children." His melancholy eyes searched the bar and then he looked down at his empty wine glass. "I'm leaning toward not searching for a home here in Topeka like I told Jessica I would. Of course, that would mean moving to another town and getting a new occupation."

Penelope captured a thought floating in her mind. She stared at Otto, studying him, his sunken eyes, his prematurely graying hair, and his soft, kind face. "As it turns out," she said, "I'm thinking of opening up a store in Lawrence. Remember that home remedy medicine kit I was going to test when I was with Silas Drug? I still think it's a good idea, and I have other ideas the public would appreciate. For one thing, I could develop attractively prepackaged medicines that people could buy right off the shelf. Maybe I'd get into other merchandise as well."

Otto raised a questioning eyebrow. "That's fine, Ms. Phillips. But what has that to do with me?"

"I could use a partner in my enterprise, especially one who is more adept at business finance than I am. Someone like yourself, Mr. Heller."

Otto shook his head, grinning. "But I don't know much about running a general merchandise store. Besides, it would probably make more sense for you to team up with Jessica. Don't you think? She's already had that exposure."

"Except she's really not interested in running a store, or any business for that matter. She made that clear to me a few days ago when I discussed the idea with her. She intends to be a writer. But she's also concerned about the battles the Union has been losing, and she'd like to fight in this war." Penelope laughed. "Knowing Jessica, she'll probably figure a way to do that, too."

Otto appeared to be mulling Penelope's proposal in his mind. "I don't know, Miss Phillips. It would mean enrolling the children in a new school in Lawrence."

"Next week is registration. It could be done."

Otto scratched the back of his neck. "Yes, I suppose if it were possible for me to work during those hours that Mitzi and Emma would be in school—" He took out his pocket watch. "Listen, it's getting late and I've got to take care of a few things." He rose and went around the table to hold the chair for Penelope.

"Thank you," she said, getting up. "So will you consider it?"

"Indeed I will. I'll give it some serious thought."

Two days later
Murfreesboro, Tennessee

"Don' pay no attention to them," Tinker told Ishmael after the others laughed at him for trying to take the pot with only two pairs. "Cards is hard tah learn. Three of a kind beat two pair, but I know is hard for you tah learn. But you'll catch on."

"I don' like cards anyways," Ishmael said, glaring at the men seated on the ground. "I wants to fight but we jest sittin' around here." He got up and made his way toward the tent, and Tinker followed him. One man was playing *Battle Hymn of the Republic* on his harmonica, and Tinker wished he could join him. But it was more important that he help Ishmael quit feeling bad about himself. Ishmael hadn't made any friends here, and Tinker never asked him about his momma or poppa. Maybe now was the time.

"You got any family, Ishmael?"

Ishamael stopped and turned to face Tinker with large, brown, questioning eyes. "Well, I see my brudder Salem last year 'fore the slavers took him. I don' know 'bout my momma or pappa. Never seen them. But I used to have a sister."

"A sister?"

"Yeah. But then she, then she—" Ishmael's face wrinkled as if he were about to cry. "Her mastah kill her six years ago when she say no 'bout doin' something bad. She pray and sing fer her Jesus to save her. But He don' save her." A tear rolled down his cheek, and he appeared embarrassed as he looked away. "Mastah want her to do a bad thing with me, but she say no. Then he make me look when he kill her. She cry and bleed all over before she die."

Tinker felt a chill run through his own body. No wonder Ishmael complained of nightmares. "What did he want yah to do, Ishmael, that was so bad?"

His face was awash with tears. "I can't say. Very bad. Very bad." He wiped his tears with his sleeve, looking around perhaps to see if anyone saw him crying. "Why do the Lawd want us to be slaves?"

Tinker placed his hand on Ishmael's large shoulder. "Someday we be free. I'm sure that's what the Lawd wants. To be free someday."

But we should be free now, not someday, Tinker thought. The President give slaves the Emmancipation Proclamation. Matt say it only freed slaves in the South. He say there be 'bout a million slaves in Union that still not be free. But Matt think it be a good thing 'cause now Negroes can fight fer the Union like real soldiers. Maybe now there be more colored fightin' for freedom.

Ishmael turned toward his tent, but Tinker stopped him with a friendly grab of his arm. "Yah tol' me today wuz yer birthday. Right?"

"That be right."

"Then maybe yah ought to celebrate it," Tinker said. "Yah gotta forget about all this."

178

"I am.I gots five dollars. Gonna go see that lady yah tol'
me 'bout."

"Rose?"

"Yeah. I be 'fraid she maybe won't want to see me."

Tinker grinned. "Don' worry none. Tell her yah my friend.
She be nice to yah."

Ishmael stuck his hands deep in his pocket to keep them
from shaking when a white lady in a red dress and a scarred
face opened the door to the cabin. He guessed it might be
Rose from the way Tinker had described her to him. "Hello,"
she said, irritation arising deep from her throat. "What do *you*
want?"

"I be a friend of Tinker's," Ishmael explained. "My name
be Ishmael. Are you Rose?"

"Yeah, either Rose or Miss Scarface, but I'm busy right
now."

Ishmael flashed the money before her face. "I pay, Miz
Rose. I gots five dollars."

"You do?" Rose looked out the door. "Anybody with you?"

"No. No one with me."

"Come on in then, but be quick about it." She trotted
through the parlor, giving Ishmael a hand signal to follow her.
"Maybe we can make this fast," she whispered once she got to
her bedroom. Let's see that money again."

Ishmael showed her the money. She grabbed it and put it
into her dress pocket. "C'mon, take your things off and let's
get it over with."

"Rose!" A female voice shouted. "You got a nigger in
there?"

Ishmael's heart pounded in his throat. Rose had panic
written over her face. "I've got to lock this, and we need to be
quiet," she whispered, moving toward the door. "Lillian don't
want no niggers here. Says it's bad for business 'cause the
white soldiers don't come here when they find out."

Lillian pushed open the door before Rose had a chance to
lock it. "Rose!" she screamed, flicking a strand of her red hair
away from her face. "I told you after you done your business
with Lazarus, no more niggers. You didn't listen, and you let
Tinker come here anyway."

"But he only came to take a book belonging to Lazarus. That's all he come for."

"Then what's this here nigger doin' in your room? Is he coming here to pick up a book, too?"

"I'm sorry, Lillian," Rose said, breaking into sobs. "I could really use the money."

Lillian glared at Ishmael. "We don't want your kind here." She then turned her hostility toward Rose. "Where's his money, woman?"

Rose dug in her pocket and handed her the five dollars. Lillian forced the money into Ishmael's shaky hand. "Here, take this and get out!"

"Yes, Miz Lillian," he said, pushing his way past her.

"Why did you come here anyway, you filthy nigger?" Lillian demanded. "Get outa here."

He stopped long enough to stare at her as he glowed with rage. He would have choked her with his bare hands if it weren't for the sound of a little boy crying somewhere in the cabin.

"You deaf or something?" Lillian said. "I told you to get outa here! We don't want your kind."

Nuff o' this damn war, he thought. No different than bein' a slave, even if I be a Yankee soldier. "I only come 'cause it be mah birthday, Miz Lillian," he said, his chest heaving. "Prob'ly mah last birthday."

By three that afternoon, Rose sat alongside Jay on a grassy knoll overlooking the Union camp. The boy waved a stick in each hand and laughed as a drumbeat sounded in the distance. He struck the ground with the sticks and looked back at his mother for approval.

"You might be a drummer boy just like Lazarus," she told him.

Jay smiled. "Laza—? Lazarus?"

Rose nodded. "That's right. That was his name. A Negro man, just like—" Rose stopped short of saying "just like your father." Jay's father, Shanty, was a young man of seventeen. Unlike Lazarus, Shanty was never free. Rose, entrusted by her stepfather to feed and clothe the slaves he owned to work his plantation, spent private time teaching them to read. But she

180

never expected to fall in love with Shanty. For weeks, they'd meet at the tall black oak near the riverbank and make love under the stars. After Rose told him she was pregnant with his child, they talked foolishly about escaping together to the North. But that all changed one day. A gun blast from her angry stepfather put Shanty into an early grave.

The sound of musket fire shattered Rose's thoughts. Soldiers at the camp had just fired their muskets into the air as part of their daily drill.

"Guns," the boy said, pointing at the soldiers far away.

"That's one word I don't want you to learn, Jay. I hate that word."

The night sky was specked with stars as Lillian left for the outhouse some fifty yards away from the cabin. An unexpected sound. She stopped. Was that the rapid crunch of dry leaves behind her? Could it be an animal of some sort? She turned to look and thought she saw a shadow passing through the branches. Her heart humming with fright, she hastened her steps but felt the shock of two strong hands grabbing her shoulders, pushing her down to the grass.

Before she could shout for help, she felt a gag being tied tightly around her mouth. As she lay on her stomach, she wailed through the gag, kicking her feet, feeling the pressure of the man's knee on her buttocks. The man grunted as he jerked her hands together behind her back and tied them.

Lillian felt her dress being pulled. The sound of fabric ripping. Was he using a knife to slash away her clothes? What did this monster want? Money? She'd give him all she had. If only he'd let her talk. She tried to roll to one side, but the pressure of his body on hers prevented it. More ripping, tearing. An enormous pain seared through her body. She screamed through the gag, feeling her own hot breath through the cloth. Help me, please, she mentally pleaded. Won't anyone help me?

After he was through with her, she lay crying in agony, her whole being convulsing, throbbing, shivering. Finally, she was able to roll over on her back.

It was then that her attacker stuffed money inside her gag before running away.

181

Chapter 13

Early February
Southwestern Cass County

"Listen," Sam Toby said as he slapped the old rancher cowering in the tool shed, "these here leg irons are cut. Don't tell me you ain't got no slave here."

"Jest shoot 'em," Larkin Skaggs said, belching as he took another swallow from his whiskey bottle. "He ain't worth talkin' to."

"Please don't," the old man said, holding his knees as he sat on the dirt floor, pressing his back against the wooden side of the shed. "There're no slaves here. I don't know how those leg irons got here."

A large gray-haired dog stuck its nose in the tool shed and barked.

"Is that yers?" Toby asked.

"Yeah, name's Killer."

"C'mon here, Killer," Toby said, "I won't hurt yah."

The dog took cautious steps toward Toby and sniffed his hand when Toby held it out to him. "Yer a big dog," he said, "but you ain't no killer, are yah?" He petted Killer, and the dog responded by moving its tail.

"I had one like that," Toby said. "I like dogs. They always respect yah. Never give yah trouble like people do."

"Will you let me go?" the man asked, a look of fright pulsated from his eyes.

"No, I can't let you go. Not unless yer gonna be honest with me."

A commotion, a shrieking woman and a boy's demanding shouts, interrupted him. The dog barked.

"Send Killer home," Toby ordered.

"Killer," the old man said, "git now. Go on, git out!"

The dog barked once and left. A boy about sixteen wearing a butternut shirt and jeans forced an elderly lady in a plain black cotton dress into the entryway of the tool shed. "This here lady," the boy said, "doesn't want to give me her jewelry. Stubborn ol' cuss she is."

"Jest rip it from her, Jesse," Skaggs told the young Jesse James. "Takes a man, not a boy, to know how to do things right. No wonder Quantrill's not sure 'bout takin' you in yet."

"Is that right?" Jesse snarled.

"Yeah, that's right. Better take some lessons from yer brother Frank. Least he's a man."

"Now hold on a minute," Toby said, stepping in between them. He raised the woman's sleeve from her wrist, revealing a silver bracelet. Her hand shook when he tried relieving her of her diamond ring. "Tell yah what, woman—if yah give me the bracelet, the ring, and yer earrings, I'll let yer husband go free."

Skaggs began to protest but Toby shut him up and stared at the frail woman. "Well," Toby said, "what'll it be?"

"All right," she said, her face softening into painful sadness, "you can have these. But I was only wearing them for our wedding anniversary. We came back from a party, and—"

"Shut up, lady, "I don't care 'bout that," Toby answered. "Jest let me have the rest of it'n he goes free."

Her eyes hollow with grief, the woman removed her golden earrings, silver bracelet, and diamond ring, and gave them all to him.

"Have her empty out her pockets," Jesse James suggested.

"Good idea," Toby said. "When yah rob someone, make sure yah get everything."

She pulled out of her pocket a handkerchief and a rosary, one with large red beads and a silver cross. "That's all I got. Wait! Not that rosary. I got it in France. Blessed by the Lady herself, at Lourdes. That's where Bernadette saw the Lady five years ago. Please don't!"

"I dunno what yer talkin' about, woman. What lady?" She started to explain, but he told her to shut up. He held the earrings and ring in one hand while he stuffed his pocket with the rosary and bracelet. "If yah can afford tah go tah France, yah have lots of money'n won't miss any of these things." He felt the weight of the earrings, convincing himself they were gold, and squinted at the large sparkling diamond. "I bet we get five hundred for all o'these," he laughed.

"That's quite a catch," James said, drooling.

Sam Toby turned toward Skaggs and James and signaled them to leave. "Let's go fellas. We got what we came fer."

The woman, James, and Toby took several steps toward the house, but Skaggs remained behind in the tool shed. "I wanna talk to the ol' man some more," Skaggs said, taking another swallow of whiskey.

As the woman paused at the door to her house, her palm on her forehead, Jesse James mounted his horse. "What does he want to talk to that old man about?" James asked, staring back at the tool shed.

"Don't know," Toby said, stooping as Killer ran toward him barking. "He sometimes gets crazy when he drinks." Toby smiled at the dog. "And yah isn't no killer, yah mutt. Yah just bark a lot."

As he waited for Skaggs to return, Sam heard gunshots—two of them. The dog yipped at the sound and ran, barking, toward the tool shed.

Sam was sure Skaggs had just killed the old man. Good shootin,' Skaggs, Sam thought. The man was probably a Union sympathizer anyway.

Early the next morning
Eight miles southeast of Nashville, Tennessee

Hunched over with his Sharps carbine at the ready, Ishmael made his way toward a two-story white frame house where he had first heard the commotion. It sounded like two men arguing. He told himself this was none of his business, but spurred by curiosity, his legs moved on toward the building. Perhaps the people inside were Southerners who'd take him in as a slave. He'd take his chances on running away again once he recovered his strength.

Ishmael, yah talk like a fool. Yah don' come all this way, fightin' for freedom only to lose it again.

But what could he do? Where would he go? Back to camp, to face charges of desertion—and worse, rape?

As he drew within a few feet of an open window, he heard a man ranting, "Admit it! You took the money, didn't you?"

184

"No, I didn't, mastah."

"Liar!"

Ishmael raised himself up to the window ledge. The burly white man drew back his arm and struck the young slave with his fist. The Negro struggled to pick himself up from the floor. The other man cussed and went for his pistol lying on the kitchen table.

Ishmael brought the barrel of his weapon to the ledge, grateful it was already loaded. The eyes of the young slave, wide with shock, were glued on Ishmael's carbine.

The white man cocked his revolver as he aimed it at the slave. "I don't need no liars workin' for me."

Ishmael squeezed the trigger, and the explosion rang in his ears. The white man fell to the floor, blood growing a rapid circle on his white shirt. The slave got up, gaping first at his dead master and then out the window at Ishmael. "We all dead men," the slave shouted. "Run for your life!"

Ishmael dashed toward the front door. The slave, perhaps about Lazarus's age, almost ran into Ishmael as he exited. "My mastah's brother comin' down from upstairs," the slave said, a wild and frightened look in his eyes. "He gonna kill us both now."

Ishmael didn't bother to turn around as he and the slave ran for the tall grass. He dropped prone on the ground as a bullet whizzed past him. The slave, lying next to him, was breathing heavy. His forehead was drenched in sweat.

"Yah got a name?" Ishmael asked.

"Simon."

"Trees up ahead, Simon. Can yah get there?"

"Hope so."

Simon ran with him toward a forest of pine trees. Adding to the shouts and sporadic gunfire behind them was the faint sound of the hooves of a horse. From the corner of his eye, Ishmael could make out Simon hunched over, bounding for the trees. "Almost there," Ishmael cried out. "Little ways to go."

Ishmael ran without stopping until he made it deep within the forest. He reloaded his gun and turned around to look for Simon. He had assumed the slave was nearby, and was surprised after several minutes of searching, Simon was nowhere about.

Just as Ishmael was about to call out for him, he heard the young slave's cry for help. Ishmael ran to the edge of the forest. There, he met his worst fear. The young slave was frantically waving his arms in the air. A white-haired man on horseback and wearing a black chesterfield, blue jeans, and dark boots held a shotgun at Simon.

Ishmael crouched and aimed for the man's chest.

"I didn' kill yah brother," Simon growled. "How come yah can't believe me?"

"Cause all you niggers lie," the man shouted back. He took aim with his shotgun.

"No!" Ishmael cried out.

The man jerked his horse around to face Ishmael and fired off a shell at the instant that Ishmael squeezed the trigger. The man fell off his horse, shrieking in anguish.

Ishmael grabbed his left shoulder, searing with pain. Simon's mouth dropped open and he took a step toward Ishmael.

"Run, Simon," Ishmael shouted. "Head for Nashville. The Yankee's will take care of yah there."

Simon turned around, standing for a moment as if trying to decide whether to stay or run.

Then he ran.

Early February
Lawrence, Kansas

Although the morning sun beamed its radiance through her bedroom window, Jessica didn't feel quite like getting up. She felt lost these past couple of weeks, as her only "job" now would be to do what she thought she always wanted to do—to write her novel.

But she missed the children; they were back with their father. Gone were the happy screams of Emma and Mitzi. No longer were they insisting she read them a story after breakfast. There were no more strolls with them to see small farms along Henry Street and observe a cow or two grazing. She missed those leisurely walks with them toward Massachusetts and Berkeley, where they could watch the cavalry recruits practice their drills. It was on one of those days that Emma had asked her a painful question.

"Miss Radford, why aren't you a soldier?"

"Because," Jessica had answered, "the army doesn't think women make good soldiers."

"Why?"

"I don't know, Emma."

Jessica knew she'd make a great soldier. She was no longer afraid of using her Colt revolver. For the past few days, she had ridden to the woods and practiced her shooting. She also picked up a book discussing military strategy used by Americans in the Indian wars. Well, if the Yankees didn't want her only because she was a woman, it was their loss.

After donning her petticoat and hoop skirt, she searched through her closet and picked out a black silk dress she had bought from a New York clothier. She had only worn it once since coming to Lawrence as there was a torn sleeve, but she finally got around to mending it yesterday.

She struggled with the buttons as she thought about Mr. Heller's decision to rent the second floor of Penelope's house on Mississippi Street. It was foolish for Otto to succumb to the threats of those border ruffians and sell his business in Topeka. However, she had to admit Mr. Heller was rightly concerned about the health and safety of his two little girls—although she questioned whether Lawrence had all the proper security provisions necessary. The town offered little protection against intruders. Mayor Collamore made matters worse by not allowing citizens to carry firearms but requiring them to be stored at the armory. While a tiny military garrison had been placed across the river, it would be of little use if Lawrence were attacked. Lawrence was indeed vulnerable, Jessica thought, but what town *was* truly safe during this war?

Jessica's skirts swished as she went to the kitchen to brew coffee. Penelope's decision to sign a one-year lease for the store from Mr. Sutliff was perilous, Jessica thought, but Penelope was convinced "New Necessities" would be a successful retail operation. And Mr. Heller's arrangement to be a minor partner with Penelope's operation made sense. As Jessica understood it, New Necessities would eventually offer items to the general public not readily found in other store outlets—

such as medical kits, pewter vaginal douches, scented antiseptic lotions, and juices prepackaged in small bottles. In addition to helping Penelope wait on customers, Mr. Heller would keep books, pay bills, make purchases, and review written contacts. This would give Penelope the freedom to excel in the areas where she was best—finding the right products to sell and selling them.

Jessica relaxed at the table with her cup of coffee. She hoped that the understanding Penelope and Mr. Heller had regarding the children would work. After school hours, Mr. Heller would pick up his daughters and take them home. If Penelope had to work into the evening, he would also prepare them supper and put them to bed. So far, this arrangement seemed to be working, but Jessica insisted that if a problem ever arose, she would be available to help out.

By nine o'clock, Jessica transferred herself to her writing desk and reviewed what she had written the day before:

> *Lucy didn't care what Paul thought of her, she was going to go behind enemy lines and see for herself. But how would she do this? She couldn't very well crawl on her belly in her dress. And stowing a gun in her pocket would present a problem should she suddenly be attacked. No, it'd be better if she dressed like a man. But if she did so and was caught, she'd no longer have the protective status of being a lady.*
>
> *Lucy decided to throw caution to the winds. She'd do it for the good of her country.*

Jessica recalled stopping at this point yesterday because she wasn't sure this was realistic. Would Lucy really be able to get away with this charade? Wouldn't it be obvious to anyone in the way she talked and behaved that she was a woman? Hmmmm. She remembered Uncle George telling her once about a woman who had dressed as a male soldier. Jessica should have asked him how long this woman served in the military before her identity was found out.

She reached into her pocket to pull out a handkerchief and discovered a letter there. A letter from Tinker. What was this doing here? The curtain of her mind slowly opened. This was the dress she had worn when she had picked up her mail upon her arrival in Lawrence that day. She must have put this letter from Tinker into her dress pocket, intending to read it later.

She pulled the letter from the open envelope. Tinker's words struck her like a thunderbolt:

He call me names and I left him in woods. He cry for help, but I don' come back. I forget his name, but it sound like that man that kill yer momma and daddy. He a mean man, but I mean too and not come back when he call me. Don' know now if he alive or dead.

Jessica gasped... *that man that kill yer momma and daddy...* Sam Toby! Could Tinker have actually confronted Toby as he fought the rebels back in November? She searched for all the information she had accumulated on Sam Toby. Within minutes, she found it. One of the items was a letter from the sheriff expressing his apologies for not being able to locate him after an extensive search following the capture of three of the men who had murdered her family. She also came across a newspaper clipping showing some of Quantrill's men, including one who resembled Toby, although it didn't give a name. The third item in the folder was a copy of a "Wanted" poster of Sam.

There'd be no hope of finding a soulless hog like Sam in this big country, but if the rebels allowed him to fight on their side, they were just as guilty as he. The blood of her murdered parents were on their hands because they tolerated such senseless slaughter. Why, there were even stories in the newspaper about Confederate renegades like Bill Anderson and William Quantrill who took pleasure in killing innocent civilians. Fact was, she thought, the rebels were all butchers. Besides, she always believed that slaves should be free—why *shouldn't* she fight for what she believed in?

Why couldn't she be in the ranks of other soldiers killing the enemy? But how could she, as a woman, be allowed to do that? She wouldn't. Yet, George Radford once told her about a woman who fought as a man for the Yankees....

"That's right, a lady solider," George had said. "She was all dressed up like a man—pants, shirt, boots, the whole thing. All set to fight, she was. Wanted to kill some rebels."

Hmmm. How would she go about doing this? How and where would she enlist? Would she be able to get away with it—and what would be the consequences if she got caught? Yet, the possibility intrigued her.

Later that afternoon, Jessica drove her carriage to school and picked up the children. She was glad Otto had told her yesterday he and Penelope would be going to Lecompton on business today. Jessica welcomed the diversion, hoping it'd ease her torment over Tinker's revelation.

"Why are we stopping here, Miss Radford?" Mitzi asked as Jessica reined her horse to a stop on Massachusetts near Berkeley Street. Seven men with the Second Colored Regiment were on the grounds doing exercises before Reverend Snyder, the lieutenant in charge of the regiment. Snyder stood stiffly in front of his men but tipped his cap when he noticed her.

"I just want to watch for a minute, children." She couldn't help but think of Matt Lightfoot as she watched Snyder go through his routines with the men. What was Matt doing now, without her? She missed him and wondered if it was because John Howell was now gone. Maybe there was more. Maybe she never gave herself a chance to know Matt. She could wait until he returned to Lawrence next August, but if she could somehow enlist in his unit....

"What would you say if I became a soldier?" Jessica asked Mitzi.

Mitzi put her hand on her mouth as if she were stifling a laugh. Emma grinned. "That's silly," Emma said. "You'd look funny in a dress and carrying a musket."

Indeed she would, Jessica thought as she envisioned herself charging the enemy while raising her petticoat to avoid tripping on a rock. Maybe if she ran down the battlefield dressed only in her chemise, she'd shock the enemy into submission without firing a shot. She ought to suggest that to Mary next time she wrote. Her friend always enjoyed a good laugh.

A half hour later, Jessica followed the girls up the steps of Penelope's house on Mississippi Street, which she was now sharing with Mr. Heller. It was a two-story Colonial with Doric columns, double entry door, and a fenced-in white porch. Mr. Heller occupied the upper floor and Penelope the lower, but both had the same floor plan. While Penelope's home was extensively furnished, Mr. Heller's was simply adorned. In his parlor he had only two chairs, and in his dining room, a simple wooden table and three chairs. In his small kitchen he used tin plates rather than porcelain china for dishes, while his study consisted of only a desk, chair, oil lamp, and two walnut bookcases.

Jessica shook her head when she entered his study. It was littered with papers. This was one fault Mr. Heller had—lack of organization. After checking on the children in the parlor, Jessica went to his study to clean it up. Then she'd straighten up the other rooms as well before starting supper. Mr. Heller would be home in a couple of hours and if she worked swiftly, she'd have time to relax with a book prior to his arrival.

She hadn't intended to read that letter on his desk, but her eyes caught a name written on it as she was about to place the letter on a pile of other papers. It was a letter to Mr. Heller from Lieutenant James Pond....

Dear Mr. Heller,

You had asked me to find out anything further about Sam Toby, the man who attacked you in Topeka. While I told you when we last met that Toby was seen by our scout riding with the Quantrill gang, I still do not have any intelligence on the movements of that murderous villain. He may be with the Quantrill gang or he may have joined a regular Confederate unit. I lack sufficient information to be able to tell you with certainty which course of action he had taken. As you know, he is wanted for murdering the Radfords near Lawrence. It will be difficult to capture him, especially if he is now deep in enemy territory. I wish I could be of more assistance to you in this regard....

Jessica stopped reading and slammed the letter on the desk. So, Mr. Heller had learned from Lieutenant Pond that Sam Toby had murdered her parents. Why, then, did Mr. Heller keep it a secret from her? Why did he not tell her that he had confronted Toby that evening? Was he so insensitive he didn't think it mattered for her to know this?

Jessica was quiet during supper and answered Mr. Heller's questions briefly.

Emma was quick to pick up on Jessica's emotional turmoil. "What's wrong, Miss Radford?" she asked. "Are you angry? Did I do something wrong?"

"No, Emma," Jessica answered, with a reassuring pat on the child's shoulder, "you didn't do anything wrong. I'm just tired, that's all."

Otto frowned as he patted his chin with a napkin. "I know I've put you under a bit of a strain, Miss Radford. Perhaps you'll want to retire early tonight."

"I don't understand you, Mr. Heller," Jessica said, rising from her chair. "I don't understand you at all." She raced out of the dining room, fuming.

She was about to leave the house when Otto came up behind her. "Please, Miss Radford! What's wrong?"

"Why didn't you tell me Sam Toby was the one who attacked you? You knew that he killed my parents, yet you said nothing to me about it. What other secrets have you been keeping?"

Otto drew back, appearing defeated. He raised his hand to touch hers, but she backed away. "I'm very sorry, Miss Radford. I only withheld that information from you because I didn't want to upset you."

"Didn't want to upset me?" she mocked. "What do you think you're doing now?"

"I keep a lot of things buried in me, Jessica. That's just the way I am."

"Now it's your chance to tell me *everything*. Where do you think Sam is hiding?"

His eyes drifted past her face, pondering the question. "I wish I knew. Obviously, since you've read my letter, you know Toby was last seen with Quantrill's men. But for all we know, he might have also joined a Confederate regiment somewhere.

Impossible to say." He searched her face as he gently touched her shoulders. "Believe me, Miss Radford, I want him caught as much as you do."

Unsmiling, Jessica looked directly in his eyes. "I've made a serious decision, Mr. Heller. My friend Mary Delaney is with the Eighth Kansas Volunteer Infantry in Tennessee. I want to be there with her—but as a private."

Otto released her shoulders and took a step back. "What!"

"You heard me correctly. I can fight as well as any man. When I was younger, I tamed a wild horse, built a barn, skinned a deer, cut down trees, and drove a plow down the field. I've even been practicing shooting at targets with my Colt. Darn good at it, too." Resentment was building in her voice. "You know, Mr. Heller, I've probably done more things by the time I was nineteen than most men."

Otto cracked a smile. "I actually admire you for that, Miss Radford. I've always believed in equality. That goes for men and women as well as colored and white folk."

She stepped closer to him. "I know that about you, Mr. Heller. You've done some mighty good things about freeing slaves that I never hear you brag about."

Otto's eyes widened in surprise. "You know about that?"

Jessica nodded. "You've exposed yourself to great danger in doing so."

"I don't know if I can continue doing that, now that I'm Emma and Mitzi's only living parent. I can't afford to put myself in harm's way any longer."

"But I can, Mr. Heller. I can't see myself writing stories while the Union is struggling for its very survival. I've learned even Walt Whitman expressed a desire to serve the Union as a male nurse."

"I see your point," Otto said, scratching his chin. "But I think what you want to do is risky, extremely dangerous, deceitful, and very unbecoming a lady of your station."

Jessica was about to object when Otto, widening his grin, stopped her with his stern finger pointed toward her face. "But, as I said," he continued, "I believe in complete freedom not only between coloreds and whites but between men and women. If you want to dress up as a man—" He paused. "By the way, have you chosen a name for your new role?"

193

"Actually, I've given it a lot of thought. I need to use a name I could easily remember. So I think I will name myself Walter Brontë, since my favorite writers are the Brontë sisters and Walt Whitman."

Otto tilted his head thoughtfully. "Walter Brontë. I like it. Good, then if you want to dress up as a man, I'll ask my good friend, Senator Lane, for a huge favor. 'Senator,' I'll tell him, 'I know a gentleman named Walter Brontë who sorely wants to enlist as a private specifically with the Eighth Volunteer Infantry. Can you open the right doors for him? He can handle a Colt and follow orders better than anyone I know.'"

"Thank you, Mr. Heller," Jessica said, kissing him on the cheek.

"Just don't get yourself killed," he said. "You'll need to finish that novel of yours when you return."

Chapter 14

Mid-February
Murfreesboro, Tennessee

Ever since Ishmael had disappeared from camp, Matt Lightfoot was certain he'd never be found. Thousands of men had deserted Yankee camps and were never found, so Matt thought Ishmael would be counted among that number. But just two days ago, as he washed his face in the creek, Matt heard someone call out to him from behind the bushes....

"Reverend," the raspy voice said, "I needs to see you."

"Ishmael?"

The tall Negro emerged from hiding, his blue trousers muddied, the lapel on his dark frock coat torn. A bloodied cloth was wrapped around his left arm. His right hand trembled as he held a Sharps carbine and leaned against a tupelo tree. "I done wrong," he said, his face frozen with fright. "I run away, but I come back. Maybe you help me?"

Matt pulled a gun from his holster. "First drop that weapon. Then we talk."

Ishmael let go of his weapon and staggered toward him, falling once and slowly picking himself up again.

"What happened to your arm, Ishmael?"

"Someone shoot me. Maybe a surgeon could fix it for me." He held Matt's arm. "You hafta help me. I don' wanna be in this army anymore."

"I'll get you medical attention, Ishmael. But I'll have to turn you in." He looked away from Ishmael's tear-filled eyes. "You're guilty of desertion and need to pay for your crime."

Ishmael dropped to his knees and looked up at Matt. "Please, Reverend, I beg you—please help me get my arm fixed up'n let me escape. You mah only friend."

Matt recalled his own attempted desertion one night...how he ran from the campsite, tripped over a rock, tumbled down a hill, and retreated back to camp. He understood Ishmael's desire to escape.

He studied Ishmael's soulful, pleading eyes, but his father's sharp command on the importance of obedience echoed in his mind. "I can't do that, Ishmael."

"Let me go then. I needs my freedom."

"Sorry," Matt said, training his pistol on Ishmael. He ignored the small, still voice taunting him about what Jesus had said about the unforgiving servant…"I cancelled your entire debt when you pleaded with me." But this was different, Matt argued with himself. He had a sworn duty to bring Ishmael back to camp on charges of desertion. Military justice required it.

Two days later

At least Miss Delaney would eventually realize he had done the right thing, Matt thought as he hurried to the tent where Ishmael was being held prisoner. When he turned Ishmael in for desertion, he had no idea Ishmael was also guilty of raping a prostitute. Mary had upbraided Matt for not looking the other way when it came to Ishmael's only apparent crime of desertion. "Must you always follow regulatons to the strict letter of the law?" she demanded of Matt. "Couldn't you have looked the other way for your friend?" But once she learned that Ishmael had confessed to the horrific crime of rape, she begged the military court to waive capital punishment and instead consider incarceration because of Ishmael's cruel treatment as a former slave. The court turned down her impassioned plea.

If only Ishmael had met with him before going on this rampage, Matt thought, perhaps he could have talked Ishmael out of his anger. But that was the past. Today would be Ishmael's last day on earth. Matt entered the large tent and took scant notice of an armed guard nearby. Ishmael, with bowed head and bound in chains, squatted on the ground. His heavily bandaged left arm hung limply by his side. He looked up, his face expressionless as Matt dropped on the ground across from him.

"How's your arm, Ishmael?"

"Surgeon took out the bullet. Arm be infected. But that don' matter none now."

"I'm sorry it turned out this way, Ishmael."

"Mah fault," Ishmael said, glancing away from him as if embarrassed by his presence.

"Did you have a good meal?"

"It look good, suh. But I can't eat nothing much 'fore I die."

"Ishmael, why did you rape Lillian Porter?"

"I dunno. I done bad. I know that. But what she say make me feel bad. I came to this infantry 'cause I thought I be free. But I not free. Never free with white folk. I still a slave."

The early morning sun beamed a narrow stream of light through the tent opening and warmed Matt's cheek. Ishmael, he thought, would never see another sunrise. "Tinker's been taking it hard," Matt said. "Blames himself. Says he never should've encouraged you to see that harlot."

Ishmael glanced at Matt briefly before he bowed his head again. "It not be his fault. And I sorry now I did what I did. I so sorry."

"God forgives all sin, even yours, Ishmael."

"I knows that. I sorry to God, too." He covered his head in his hands.

Matt looked about the tent, at the small writing table, Ishmael's cot, and at the officer who sat on a cracker barrel near the tent entrance. "Ishmael," Matt said, "you told me once that you had a sister, but your master killed her because she didn't want to do something bad. What was that all about?"

Ishmael's dark eyes were like solid marble beads, lifeless, empty. "Mah sister be only ten years old. But he want to watch me do with her the same thing I did to Miss Porter."

An icy stream of disbelief surged through Matt's veins. Rape? Her master wanted to watch Ishmael rape his sister?

Matt forced himself to change the subject. "You said you had a brother, didn't you? Wasn't his name Salem?"

Ishmael nodded. "Yeah, that be his name. He back with our mastah now."

"No, he's not," Matt said. "He got rescued by someone from the Underground Railroad. He heard about you being in the infantry and decided to enlist." Matt took a deep breath, knowing what he'd say next was difficult. "I don't know how to tell you this, Ishmael—" He stopped and inhaled deeply. "Salem will be coming here next week."

Ishmael broke down in tears. "I don' want him to know the bad thing I done."

"I'll come up with something to tell him. I'll ask my commanding officer not to reveal anything about this to Salem."

"I shore 'preciate that, Reverend. I want yuh tah give him mah rifle." He pointed toward the corner of the tent. "It be there with mah other things."

"I'll be sure Salem gets it."

The guard stood up from his cracker barrel. "Your time with the prisoner is over, lieutenant. I must escort him to the gallows."

"Give me one more minute, please," Matt said. "Ishmael, you've been forgiven by Jesus, and when you die, you'll be in heaven."

Ishmael looked away. "I don' know 'bout that, Reverend. I bad man."

"Trust in Him. I've been prayin' for you."

"I thanks yuh fer that." Ishmael pursed his lips, his eyes focusing on Matt for a moment. "Reverend?"

"What?"

"Pray for Simon that he be free."

"Who's Simon?"

"A slave I know. He be a young man. Lot to live for."

"You never told anyone about who shot you and why. Care to tell me now?"

"It don' matter none, Reverend."

A quiet moment followed. Matt was conscious of his own breathing and the song of a meadowlark filtering through the tent.

"Ishmael, what was your little sister's name?"

"Her name be Sissy."

Matt placed a reassuring hand on Ishmael's shoulder. "I'll pray for Sissy, too."

"Don't have to pray fer her none, Reverend."

"Why's that?"

"She already be in heaven."

Before leaving the tent, Matt picked up Ishmael's cartridge box and rifle. It was a carbine with the word FREDUM carved deeply into the wooden stock. Too bad, he thought, that Ishmael never got a chance to use it to help free slaves.

Early March
Chattanooga, Tennessee

Every seat in the small theater was taken. Roger Toby estimated there were perhaps sixty people attending the minstrel show. As he sat through the performance, he took ocassional glances at Captain Robert Patterson, seated next to him. Patterson appeared to be enjoying the performance, laughing with the crowd as Zip Coon, a free Negro attempted to put on airs...or, as Jim Crow, carelessly tossed the peaches he himself picked into another slave's bag.

The entire performance disgusted Roger, particularly the closing scene. Here, Cookie, a Negro girl probably about Nellie's age attempted to "buy" Lester, a middle-aged white farmer so she could marry him.

"Can't afford me," Lester announced. "Besides, I should be buyin' *you* instead."

"I kin afford yuh more'n yuh kin afford me," Cookie declared, pulling out a bunch of bills from her dirty canvas bag and tossing them on the stage. "I'll tell yuh what, Lester, I'll give yuh fifty cents fer every time yuh'n me fool around. And I'll give yuh another ten dollars fer every child yuh give me." So if yuh give me eight children, I'll give yuh—" She thought for a moment with a stupid look on her face. "—I'll give yuh eighty dollars and fifty cents."

Lester dropped to his knees on the stage, running his hands through the money. "But these are all Yankee dollars and I ain't no Yankee."

"And I ain't no colored," Cookie said, wiping the black greasepaint from her face.

"But I need a slave," Lester replied, looking terribly sad. "I really need a slave."

"Well," she said, putting a finger to her cheek, "if yuh marry me, yuh got one."

The audience cheered and clapped, but Roger kept his hands to his side. How, he wondered, could they exhibit such a cavalier attitude toward slavery? It reminded him how his brother Sam considered Nellie as property, whom he could dispose of at the point of a gun if he cared to.

When the performance was over, Roger met Captain Patterson at the exit. "My first minstrel show," Roger said. "And probably my last."

"Well, Roger," Patterson said, "not all folks enjoy the same thing. It's a shame you don't, but listen, since I'm staying at the boarding house next door, why don't we chat a bit? I mean, it's not every day I get a chance to talk with an old friend who wants to reenlist in the Army of Tennessee."

Roger agreed and followed Patterson up three flights of stairs to his friend's living quarters. Patterson opened two windows in his parlor and a breeze from the street below ballooned the lace curtains. A captain's hat sat on a straw arm-chair in the corner. A copy of *The Daily Chattanooga Rebel* on the dining table headlined Lincoln's signing of the Conscription Act.

"Can you imagine that, Roger?" Patterson said, pointing to the paper. "Those Yankees must be getting desperate for manpower since they are forcing men to enlist. Maybe the Confederates are doing too good a job killing off their soldiers." He sat down at the table and offered Roger to join him.

"I guess it's a war fought by poor men," Roger answered, taking a seat across from him. "Apparently, one can be exempted from military service if he pays a $300 fee or else sends a slave in his place."

Peterson scanned the paper and shook his head disapprovingly. "Well, Roger, I don't rightly care what the Federals do. But I'm concerned about the way our side is running this war. I see in the paper a lot of opinions being expressed about General Bragg's ability to lead the Army of Tennessee. Some think he spends more time arguing with his generals than planning strategy. One thing's for sure, it was a mistake for him to blame his retreat from Kentucky on Hardee and Polk."

"Don't know anything about that. What I do know is I'm pleased by your recent promotion to captain." He extended his hand to Patterson. "Congratulations."

Patterson shook his hand, but his face remained serious. "Thank you, Roger. Not sure if I deserved it all that much.

They needed someone to replace James Sinclair. You know, of course, he was killed in the Stones River campaign near Murfreesboro, do you not?"

"I read about it. Tragic. He was a good man, and I was glad to have served under him."

"I feel the same way. His shoes will be mighty tough to fill. He was a brave man...and a good leader." He leaned forward on the table. "Just between you and me, we shouldn't have lost Nashville to Rosecrans and we should have won in the Murfreesboro conflict. Bragg could have sent more of Breckinridge's divisions across Stones River. And it cost us dearly in Confederate lives just to push the Yankees back over the rock bank across McFadden's Ford. This Stones River conflict was a disaster. I just hope Bragg won't repeat his mistakes. Better yet, I hope Davis has the foresight to find a suitable replacement."

Roger laughed lightly to break the tension. "I'm quite impressed with the abilities yaw offer to the cause. Too bad they didn't promote yaw to general when they had the chance."

Patterson's face broke into a slight grin. "I'm not so sure that would have been the right course of action, Roger. But I'm glad you decided to reenlist with the Twenty-Third Tennessee Infantry Regiment. It's good to have you back. How did your wife take the news?"

"Not very well," Roger said, reflecting that Sara was so angry she refused to talk to him for two days afterwards. "But she believes as strongly as I do that the South needs to break its ties from the Union. We need our independence from Federal tyranny."

Patterson returned a thoughtful stare. "We're also fighting for our freedom of choice—to not let government interfere with our freedom to own slaves. Isn't that right?"

Roger debated how to answer his friend. Which was more important, he thought, one's freedom to own slaves or a Negro's freedom to live with dignity? "Captain, I don't believe we have to be in like mind as to *why* we're fighting for Davis and the Confederate States. I only think it matters we help achieve ultimate victory."

The recruiting sergeant took a cursory glance at Jessica after scanning an official-looking letter before him. "So, Walter Brontë," he said to her with telltale annoyance in his voice, "I see you're getting special attention from Colonel Martin himself." He again studied the letter. "Seems he wants you to be processed into the Eighth Kansas as a result of a recommendation for active duty from Senator Lane." He widened the smirk on his face as he looked up at her. "So what makes you so special, Mr. Brontë?"

Jessica tried not to show annoyance in her voice, which she lowered to sound as masculine as possible. "Well, sir, I'm not special. But I have a friend in the Eighth Kansas whom I wanted to be with."

"A friend? What's his name?"

"It's a lady, sergeant. A lady who goes by the name Mary Delaney. She's an assistant nurse with the Eighth."

"Oh," he said with a playful wink, "a close companion of yours?"

Jessica let the remark pass, her eyes glazed over, waiting for him to stop taunting her. He went through a few more questions with her, confirming Walter Brontë's name, age, place of birth, indication of any handicaps, whether he could read or write, and what his occupation was as a civilian. For this last question, Jessica had to think quickly. "A writer," she answered, remembering to keep her voice low and masculine.

"Well, you won't have much time to write on the battlefield, Mr. Brontë." He had her sign the enlistment form. Jessica stopped herself just in time, almost poised to sign her real name. Instead, she took her time to pen her new name. It would take some getting used to.

"After you are sworn in, you'll be Private Brontë with the Army of the Cumberland," he said, handing her a card. "Now take this to the supply depot for all your gear."

The supply depot was actually a warehouse of military goods, and through an open door, Jessica could see endless rows of military material. Dressed in trousers, shirt, and boots, she stood in line with several other men. Now that she wore men's clothes, she felt good since it reminded her of how she used to dress on Pa's farm when she'd help work the field. The only thing she'd miss was her long hair, now cropped short to resemble a man's cut.

She followed a line of men down a row of tables, where she collected an infantryman's overcoat, neck stock, forage cap, kerchief, knapsack, uniform trousers, wide belt, sack coat, shirt, brogans, stockings, tin canteen, and blanket. As soon as she received her last piece of equipment, she was ushered to a room, ordered to stand in line with the other men, place her equipment at her feet, and raise her hand for the oath of service. After being sworn in by an elderly adjutant, she and the others were told they'd be leaving for Lexington, Kentucky, in the morning.

"Oh, Private Brontë," the adjutant called out to her as she was about to leave for the barracks, "I need to see you."

Jessica swallowed hard. Had her identity somehow been found out? "Yes?"

"You and one other man are the only ones bound for the Eighth Kansas. So you'll need a special ticket to take a train to Bowling Green upon your arrival in Lexington." He searched the pocket of his coat and handed her an envelope. "It's in here. Don't forget reveille is at 5 o'clock tomorrow. Good luck, private."

"Thank you," Jessica said, breathing easier. She still couldn't believe she had made it this far. Thank God, she thought, that her voice and her movements didn't give her away. Her bunk was at the end of a long row of cots. Carrying her equipment, she walked passed the men, avoiding eye contact, wondering if there would be any other hurdles she'd have to overcome before she finally set foot in Tennessee. There were.

She asked one of the men where the outhouse was, and he directed her to the latrine at the other end of the barracks. Jessica hurried in that direction, pushed through the door, ready to shield her eyes if necessary. Thankfully, there was no one else inside. Yes, privacy or the lack thereof, she thought, would definitely be a problem in an all-male infantry. facing an all-male infantry.

Since Penelope was tied up with business, Otto left the children in the care of Thomas and Mary Guest on Mississippi Street before leaving for the *Kansas Weekly Tribune*. He was looking forward to paying his old friend, John Speer, a visit. He hoped John could steer him in the right direction. Those recent threats from proslavery advocates against David Carter of Heller Publishing worried him. Until now, Heller Publishing had always kept a low profile, but ever since he had published those abolitionist pamphlets for Senator Lane, Otto felt he had enraged the ruffians from Missouri.

The *Kansas Weekly Tribune* was on Massachusetts Street between the Simpson Bank and Brechtelbrauer's Saloon and across the street from the Eldridge House. Otto remembered when Speer first started the paper as the *Kansas Pioneer*, later changing it to the *Kansas Tribune*, and earlier this year, to the *Kansas Weekly Tribune*. But Speer's spirited free-state, abolitionist's voice never changed in all that time. It just got more strident.

No sooner had Otto entered the foyer than a neatly dressed gray-haired gentleman greeted him. The man's face broke into a friendly smile. "How are you, Otto?" John Speer held Heller's arm as he shook his hand. "What has it been eight, nine years?"

"It'll be nine years this coming October," Otto answered.

"C'mon in to my office," Speer said with a friendly lift to his voice. "I'm glad you decided to put down roots in Lawrence. You never gave me any particulars in your letter why you sold your business in Topeka. Problems?"

"That's what I wanted to talk to you about," Heller said when he entered Speer's modest but well-organized office with neatly piled stacks of newspapers and correspondence on a long table against the wall.

John Speer sat on the edge of his desk rather than take his chair behind it. That was one thing Otto liked about Speer—he put on no pretenses and wanted his friends to feel instantly comfortable. "Two of my sons," Speer said, "John, Jr., and Robert, are going to make great printers someday. I keep an eye on John, of course, since he works for me, but I hear nothing but good things about Robert's job as a printer at *The Republican*. William, my third son, is different, however. I think all he wants to do after he finishes school is travel. I keep telling Will there's no future in that."

"How's your wife Elizabeth?"

"Oh, she's just fine. And my daughter Eva's doing fine, too. You know, I think Eva is still proud of the fact she was the first girl born here in Lawrence."

"Well, then," Otto said, chuckling, "we ought to erect a statue here in her honor."

John laughed and offered him a cigar, which Otto refused. John lit one for himself. "Otto, it's been a long time since you helped me get *The Kansas Pioneer* off the ground. He took a slow, relaxed puff of his cigar. "From your letters, it looks like you've moved to Kansas, got yourself married, and now have two daughters. By the way, how are things going with you and Helga?"

Otto's face fell. "I apologize for not writing to you these past several months, John. I didn't tell you Helga passed away last December."

"Oh, I'm sorry to hear that. I know Helga wanted you to quit the Underground Railroad. You told me she was always worried about you."

"Well, after rescuing a slave named Salem, I quit being a conductor. I worry too much about my two children."

"Just curious—have you followed up on any of the slaves you've rescued?"

"A few of them. "Two of them—Ishmael and Lazarus—are dead. Possibly a third is also dead—a girl named Nellie. Another one I intend to follow up on is Hetty. Matter of fact, after I leave here, I'm riding to Olathe to see how she's doing."

John Speer, his face turning serious, paced the room. "Otto, you alluded earlier to problems you had back in Topeka. What is that all about?"

Otto told him how bushwhackers had apparently learned of his abolitionist activities. He mentioned the beating he had taken from the ruffians, subsequent threats to his life, and how he decided to sell his business and move to Lawrence for the sake of his children. "I find it quite interesting that the new owners of

Heller Publishing," Otto continued, "are being similarly threatened. I think it all stems from those abolitionist pamphlets we printed three months ago for Senator Lane. I'm no longer with Heller Publishing, but I feel a responsibility for the safety of the people running it."

"Hmmm." John glanced at Otto, and then looked away, putting a forefinger to his bearded chin. "I'm not sure how I can help you. The printing and publishing business is in a dire state of affairs right now with all the plundering and murdering going on. I'm quite a target myself, as you realize. People credit me for helping make Kansas a free state, and the things I've published haven't been very favorable for proslavery sympathizers."

Speer then asked Otto for specifics about the recent threats the new owners of Heller Publishing had received. After Otto filled him in on that, Speer promised he'd meet with him to discuss it further. "Maybe you'd like to join Elizabeth and me for dinner some time."

"That'd be fine. I'd like to bring someone with me as well. A lady by the name of Penelope Phillips."

"Oh?" His eyebrows lifted teasingly. "A lady friend of yours?"

"Just a business partner." Otto didn't feel like telling Speer he now thought of her more as a close personal friend.

Late afternoon, the same day
Olathe, Kansas

Hetty, a pretty nine-year-old Negro girl with short frizzy hair, giggled as she coaxed a chicken to move so she could retrieve an egg underneath. She stopped when she heard Abigail call out to her outside the chicken coop. "What is it, Miz Abbie?" Hetty asked.

Abigail stepped inside, her hands on her hips, curls of her blond hair caressing her forehead, and her blue eyes smiling along with her thin lips. "You have a visitor, Hetty. You can finish that up later."

"A visitor?" Hetty put her basket of eggs on the haystrewn floor. "Who?"

"You'll have to come and see for yourself." Abigail Martin, Hetty's thirty-year-old white caretaker, walked with the girl to the house. "It's someone you haven't seen since last year," Abigail said. "He came to pay us a visit."

"Oh, I know who it is!" Hetty ran ahead of Abigail when she saw him seated on a wooden bench. He waved at Hetty and the girl waved back.

"I just came from Lawrence to pay you a visit," Otto Heller said, picking up Hetty and placing her on his lap. "How's everything? Is Miss Abigail treating you fine?"

"Miz Abbie is fine," Hetty said, grinning. "She teach me numbers and history and composition and everything."

Abigail sat on the bench next to Otto. "She's doing well in school with other colored children. Of course, I also happen to be her teacher, so I make sure she learns." Abigail returned her attention to Otto. "My brother Chester and I can't thank you enough for what you did, Mr. Heller."

"Well, I really don't deserve—" he said, his voice trailing off. "By the way, how is Chester?"

"He's out somewhere in Tennessee fighting the rebels."

Hetty gave Otto a big squeeze. "Will you come live with me. Mr. Heller? I miss you."

"No, but tell you what—I'll come again for another visit just to see you." He tickled her neck until she giggled. "You know, Hetty, you remind me of another little slave girl I brought back six years ago. Her name's Nellie."

"Nellie? Will you bring her with you next time you come?" she asked sweetly.

"If I could, my child, I certainly would."

"Mr. Heller," Abigail said, all smiles as she shook her head, "If it weren't for you, this little girl would have surely been taken back to her master, and Chester would have been killed."

"Don't thank me. Thank the Lord I was fortunate to be in Olathe last September when it happened. Heard the shouting and gunshots from my room at the hotel. By the time I got to my horse, I saw the horsemen coming around the bend in the road."

"I remember. Chester was asleep in the other bedroom. If you hadn't come by when you did, they would have surely killed him for harboring a slave."

"I'm just glad I knew where to find you," Otto said.

"I was scared, Mr. Heller," Hetty said, looking into his eyes as she ran her thin arms around his neck. She remembered how Otto woke her up from a deep sleep and how he had lowered her and Chester into the deep well on the Martin farm. "You'll be fine, child," Otto had told her. "Just don't make any noise."

It seemed to last forever, Hetty recalled. It was dark in that well. Chester, holdin' her tight, whisperin' to keep quiet. Sound of horses. Men shoutin' at poor Miz Abbie. Demandin' to see a slave they was sure was here on the farm. But Miz Abbie she just plumb tol'em to leave as there were none here.

"Honestly," Abigail told Otto, "I didn't know if that Quantrill mob would catch you in the barn with all those clothes piled on you. I thought surely they'd tear the place apart and find you."

"The good Lord must have been looking out for me that day," Otto smiled. "Only one thing that worries me, though."

"What's that?"

"I don't think Quantrill and his murderers are through with us yet. Sure hope I'm wrong about that."

Chapter 15

Late March
Bowling Green, Kentucky

Jessica lay awake in her bunk, ready for the hated bugle call for reveille. She never realized how difficult training exercises could be. Every day seemed to offer the same routine. After reveille came roll call, inspection, drill, breakfast, march, drill, lunch, skirmish exercises, drill, weapons training, march, and supper. She could still hear her sergeant snapping at her: "Private, dress up that line!...Quick march, Brontë, faster!...Check the inside of that musket, Brontë, clean it!"..."Brontë! Answer when I call your name!" This last one was particularly humiliating when she allowed herself to forget she was now Walter Brontë. It first happened a week ago when she checked in at the Lexington station gate for her train to Bowling Green, Kentucky....

"Let me see your ticket, private," the stationmaster had said.

Jessica turned around to see whom he was addressing. "Sir," the stationmaster repeated his demand with some irritation in his voice, "your ticket please."

"Oh," Jessica said, realizing that she was the "private" and the "sir" he was addressing. She apologized and handed him the envelope. He scanned the ticket, stamped it, and informed her in a lackluster tone of voice that the train would arrive in about twenty minutes.

Jessica took her seat on a bench next to a Negro man about her age, square chin, long neck, his hands on his knees, and looking very stiff and uncomfortable in his regulation blue uniform. There was an intelligence in his eyes, and his skin lacked the roughness she had seen in Negro slaves. His nervousness, apparent from the way he twirled his forage cap in his hands, made Jessica think he was just like her—a new recruit who was a bit overwhelmed by all of this.

She couldn't resist asking him where he was headed.

"Murfreesboro," he answered, looking at her with eyes that displayed caution. "And you, sir?"

"Same place," Jessica replied, pressing her cap tightly against her skull when a breeze threatened to blow it off. "I understand that's where the Kansas Eighth went after leaving Nashville."

The man's eyes brightened. "The Kansas Eighth? That's my regiment too." He stuck out his hand. "My name's Devin, Private Devin Alcott."

Jessica shook his hand. "My name's Walter." Jessica paused, almost forgetting her new last name. "Brontë. Private Walter Brontë. But you can call me Walt." She noticed his nervousness had all but disappeared. "Devin, how did you happen to be assigned to the Kansas Eighth?"

"Truth is, I really wanted to join the 10th Kansas Volunteer Infantry, but they said slaves could only join a colored unit, so that's why I'm with the Eighth Kansas Infantry instead."

"But the Eighth is a pretty good unit, Devin. They've already seen action at Stones River and Perryville."

Devin made a slow nod, looking down at his feet. "That's nice to hear. Unfortunately, the military thinks that because I'm colored I must have been a slave. Actually, my mother and father live in the British colony of Québec. My mother used to teach music in London and my father had been a military attaché to King George IV. I know very little of that first-hand, you see. I was only five when we departed for Québec."

"If I may be so bold to ask, Devin, why are you here, fighting for the Union.?"

Devin rubbed his hands together as if warming them over a fire. "I met some slaves who had escaped across the St. Lawrence River. I couldn't believe the brutality they had suffered. I have seen hatred in Québec, where animosity exists between the French and English, but nothing like the cruelty slaves have suffered under their white masters. I resolved to do what I could to bring an end to it. I thought perhaps serving in the Union might be something I should do."

He scratched his chin, lost in thought. "You know, these slaves were as black as me, yet I've never known what it is to be treated like animals, as they were. When people look at me in America, it's as if they think I must have been a slave at one time or another."

Jessica shook her head. "It's a shame that we live in a society where people judge you by the color of your skin. I hope someday that will all change."

The reveille bugle call snapped her from her thoughts. She stretched and climbed out of her cot. At least today would be a bit different. The sergeant told them they'd be learning about the use of field artillery. He told them that they'd practice both loading and firing six-pounders. "You never know," he said, "when you might have to take over for a wounded artilleryman. So you might as well learn how to hit them rebels with rolling thunder," he shouted. "Show 'em no mercy. Wipe 'em from the face of the earth, men!"

The only men Jessica wanted to wipe from the face of the earth were Sam Toby and those marauders who had threatened to murder Mr. Heller. She had never killed a man before, but killing was something she had resigned herself to do. That's why she was here, she told herself.

Easter Sunday
Lawrence, Kansas

Penelope gave Otto's hand a gentle squeeze as she watched Emma and Mitzi join in the Easter egg hunt with the other children. She was glad Otto agreed to attend Mass at St. John the Evangelist with her today, even though he was a Lutheran. He seemed much more relaxed now that his friend John Speer was helping David Carter with Heller Publishing. By financing a move to a new printing plant in Ohio while dismantling the old one in Topeka, Speer helped ease the growing unrest over threats to the company by bushwhackers crossing from the Missouri border.

"It was nice of Father Favre Sebastian to do this," Otto said, amidst the shrieks of children running back and forth across the church lawn. "We need more of these diversions to get our minds off this war."

"I wonder how Jessica's making out as a man-soldier," Penelope said with a slight giggle. "I can imagine her having

211

to listen to men cussing and bragging at night. Of course, knowing how tough-skinned Jessica is, I think she can hold her own."

"I just hope she doesn't get herself killed in the process."

"I guess she's got the same kind of stubborn will you've got—bringing those slaves over here at the risk of getting killed. Helga must have been worried about you all the time."

Otto took a few steps away from the crowd, and Penelope followed him. "What's wrong, Mr. Heller?"

"Nothing's wrong," he said, stopping. He turned to face her, his hands in his pockets, his face looking a bit embarrassed. "I did have something I've wanted to discuss with you, but I just don't know how to bring myself to do it."

Penelope tried to make light of his sudden seriousness by giving him her biggest smile. "Well, can you tell me if it is something that will make me faint or cry or run out of here shrieking with laughter?"

"I don't know how you'll react to what I am about to ask you," he said, looking away. "Helga passed away almost four months ago. I still miss her terribly, so I hope this doesn't sound strange to you, but—"

"But what?" Penelope was worried. What could he possibly tell her that was so devastating?

"You and I work together well in business. We've also been able to work out an arrangement in taking care of my children, bringing them to school, picking them up, helping them with their lessons and all of that."

"Yes, and it has been working out well, as you say."

He placed his hands on her shoulders with a suddenness that alarmed her for a second. "Miss Phillips, I will always consider you a very good friend. My children do also. Mitzi appreciates the way you've been helping her out with her multiplication. And Emma really enjoys those long walks with you and Mitzi in the park. They talk about you all the time." He looked away for a moment and focused his eyes back on hers. "I know this is going to sound absurd, Miss Phillips, but Mitzi and Emma need a mother, and I wouldn't mind even raising them up as Catholics, but—"

Penelope put her hand to her mouth. "Oh my! Are you about to ask me to marry you?"

He dropped his hands, crestfallen. "I'm sorry, Miss Phillips. I knew it was a ridiculous idea. I shouldn't have brought it up."

"Shouldn't have brought it up? Why not? Of course, I'd marry you, Mr. Heller. You're the dearest, sweetest man I've ever met. I am indeed flattered that you've even thought about asking me."

Otto's confusion showed on his face. "But how could you marry me? I've told you that I'm still in love with Helga. I mean, I'm quite fond of you, Miss Phillips, very fond of you, in fact, but—"

"Fondness," Penelope interrupted, drawing nearer to him, "often turns into love." She lifted her head, and he touched her chin with his fingers.

"Oh, Penelope," he said, embracing her with a kiss. "Oh dear, sweet Penelope!"

Two days later
Murfreesboro, Tennessee

The only two people Jessica wanted to meet after her arrival this afternoon at the Eighth Kansas bivouac were Mary Delaney and Matt Lightfoot. While she was in training at Bowling Green, she had thought of ways she might reveal her new identity to both of them. She finally settled on simply meeting with each of them alone and telling them.

After learning where the field hospital and nurses were located at camp, she took the long hike across to the other side. She found Mary alone, sitting on a log, a quarter mile away from the hospital. Mary was engrossed in a book and apparently unaware of Jessica's presence nearby.

"Excuse me, ma'am," Jessica said, trying to sound as masculine as possible, "but could you please direct me to a lady named Mary Delaney?"

Mary squinted, shielding her eyes from the setting sun as she looked up at her. "Why, *I'm* Miss Delaney," she said. "What is it you want, private?"

"I'd like to go dancing with you," Jessica said, trying hard not to laugh. "Then later, we can walk out to the woods and spend the evening together—just you and me."

Mary stood up at once. "What! How dare you! Private, if you don't leave here at once, I'll report you to my commanding officer."

Jessica burst out laughing. "Mary, it's me! Jessica!"

Mary's face broke out into a puzzle. She looked hard and long, disbelieving. "Jessica? Can it possibly be? No. Jessica?"

"It's me. I'll tell you all about it, but let's you and I take that walk to the woods to avoid prying ears."

Later, Jessica explained her situation and told Mary she'd reveal her secret identity to Matt as well. "I wouldn't do that if I were you," Mary said, a worried frown creasing her forehead. "Matt may be a nice man, but he takes his military responsibilities quite seriously."

"How do you mean?"

"Matt revealed to his captain the identity of three men who had been tardy for roll call. He's also turned in two deserters since he's been here. One of them was his friend Ishmael."

"Oh my! What happened?"

Mary explained what happened to Ishmael. "I just don't feel confident about Matt not revealing your true identity. I think Matt is a wonderful man, but he's also quite loyal to the Eighth Kansas."

"How has Matt been otherwise? I haven't received any letters from him in a while. I wonder why?"

"Matt's fine," Mary answered, betraying a hint of guilt in her eyes. "I've gotten to know him a lot better these last couple of months."

A thought flickered in Jessica's mind that perhaps Mary had gotten to know Matt a little *too* well these past two months. Jessica dismissed it as absurd because Mary knew of Jessica's fondness for Matt—lukewarm though it might well have been.

But the possibility later bothered her.

The next day
Shelbyville, Tennessee

After Lieutenant Roger Toby checked the muster rolls of the Twenty-Third Tennessee Infantry Regiment, he reported to

214

the adjutant for Colonel Keeble. "The men are all present and accounted for," Toby told him, saluting.

"Thank you, lieutenant," the adjutant said, picking up a newspaper from his desk. He handed it to Roger. "Did you see this? Looks like the Confederate Navy stopped Admiral DuPont from takin' over Charleston Harbor. We not only sunk the Union's *Keokuk*, but we made DuPont retreat like a whipped dog."

"I wish I were with the naval forces right now, sir," Roger said. "At least they're seein' some action."

"Don't worry," the adjutant beamed. "I suspect when it gets warmer, we'll be on the march to Chattanooga."

"That's what Captain Patterson told me, sir."

Roger returned to his tent. This was the fifth day in a row the sky had been overcast. It was as if God refused to shed His light on this regiment and on this war. Someone outside his tent was playing "The Bonnie Blue Flag" on a banjo, while men sang the chorus:

Hurrah! Hurrah! For Southern Rights, Hurrah!
Hurrah for the Bonnie Blue Flag that bears a Single Star!

Roger knew that Southern fighting song well. An outdoor band in Sara's home town in South Carolina had played it almost two years ago. With Sara by his side as they sat on the grass, he watched the flag wave in the breeze—the bonnie blue flag, a blue flag with one star for South Carolina, a symbol of a growing cry for independence from the Union. The song brought back happier times that now were only painful memories. He wished they'd stop playing it.

Roger lit an oil lamp to kill the darkness in his tent. He dipped his pen into the inkwell and finished his letter to his wife....

> *...and so, my dear Sara, I hope you understand I felt it my duty to return to military service. I know it poses a hardship for you—particularly since you must also take care of Nellie. I worry about that young lady sometimes, the way she still talks to Sissy, her invisible angel. She needs to think like a woman*

215

and not as a child, and you need to encourage her to stop such foolish imagination. I suspect her loneliness created a space in her mind for Sissy, but I fear her delusions will only serve to hurt her as she becomes older. If my memory serves me, Sara, I believe Nellie has a birthday next month. I wish I could be there to help her celebrate it.

I will write to you often, and I have been cherishing every letter you have sent me. I hope this war will soon be resolved so the Confederacy can finally achieve its independence. It is only unfortunate that this must be done with the shedding of blood.

With all my love,

Roger

*   *   *   *   *   *   *   *   *

April 14
Chattanooga, Tennessee

My Dearest Roger,

It has indeed been difficult being here without you, but I realize how important it is for the South to win its independence. Nellie asks if you are still wearing her medallion she gave you for Christmas. She believes it will protect you from harm, and I didn't want to persuade her otherwise. I have been taking Nellie with me on trips to the market as well as to church. As you might expect, I was getting questions concerning Nellie, and people acted very surprised when I told them I did not consider Nellie as our slave but as our foster child. It was particularly disconcerting when our Baptist preacher, Reverend Thatcher, told me we had no business raising a young Negro lady as our own daughter. I told him I found it interesting that he owned two slaves whom he considered unfit to attend church services. Well, Roger, it appears that following that episode, I have

216

*been told to find another church. That is a good
idea, since I would like to find one where Jesus Himself was present.*

*There are growing shortages of cotton goods,
paper, ink, leather, glassware, dishes, and the like,
but I think we can make do without them. Two of
my dresses are wearing thin, and I will not be able
to replace them easily. But this is a small sacrifice
which I must face, given the tremendous sacrifice
shown by the fighting men, both North and South
alike, who have given their very lives on the battlefield. Oh, Roger, I am so fraught with worry, and I
pray every day for your safety—and Nellie does too,
in her own way.*

I love you always,

Sara

Mid-April
Franklin, Tennessee

All George Radford had heard about Lieutenant Colonel
Henry Banning was how well he had drilled and disciplined
the 125th Ohio. There were rumors that General Granger had
recommended Banning's transfer to the 121st Ohio. As he stood
at parade rest with the other men in his regiment, Radford
suspected this was the reason for the announcement to assemble, by company, in the open field this morning.

Banning congratulated the men of the 121st Ohio on its
splendid performance at Stones River. "You stopped the rebel
threat and succeeded in pushing Bragg deeper south."

The men cheered, but Banning cut them short. "I believe,"
he continued, "in discipline, in obeying orders to their fullest
extent, and in teamwork. These are the same principles that I
myself carried out as an Ohio lawyer. I further believe that
while we may have made errors in the past, errors of indeci-
sion and errors of poor execution, these will not be commit-
ted on my watch."

George guessed that the "errors" Banning referred to were
the inefficiencies of the 121st Ohio in the Perryville battle.

There was indeed lack of coordination, but how much of that could be attributed to General Buell himself?

Banning continued, "I want to thank General Granger for appointing me as your new commanding officer. I also want you all to know that we are gearing up to take Tennessee away from the rebels. And we will, so help me God!"

Cheers went up from the men. Major Radford joined in with them. He wondered, however, how much longer the 121st would be needed to protect the right flank of Rosecrans' army in Murfreesboro. If it would be a while before any new plans were put into action, perhaps he could get a short furlough so he could see his niece again. Whatever happened to her? The last time he had seen Jessica was last year, when she drove a team pulling her medical supply wagon to a Kentucky battlefield. He probably should have told her he admired her bravery, although he still thought she was foolish. She could have stayed back in Lawrence, out of harm's way. He wondered why his letters to her had come back to him. He had mailed one to her in care of Silas Drug in Cincinnati and another to her home in Lawrence, but each one came back marked "addressee unknown." It was as if his niece had disappeared.

During lunch, he thought about her again. The one other person who would know the whereabouts of Jessica was his ex-wife. He had learned that Penelope moved back to Lawrence after that article appeared in the *Kansas Weekly Tribune*—the one about her starting a new business. Yet Penelope never answered his last letter.

Well, if he got a furlough, he'd pay her a surprise visit—not only to find out about Jessica but to let Penelope know he still cared for her.

Late April
Murfreesboro, Tennessee

Jessica took Mary's advice and didn't reveal her identity to Matt. But she had found it awkward when he ran into her one morning at camp.

"Hello," he said, joining her for breakfast, "are you one of our new recruits?"

Jessica looked up from her fried eggs, biscuits and gravy, startled at seeing him so unexpectedly. "Yes," she said, trying to sound both masculine and nonchalant. "Brontë, Private Walter Brontë."

"Pleased to make your acquaintance. I'm Lieutenant Matthew Lightfoot." He paused, looking at her carefully as if he recognized her. "I'm also a reverend, so if you ever need anyone to talk to, I'm available."

"Thank you for letting me know, lieutenant."

He continued to stare at her. "I must apologize for not meeting you sooner, private, but this is a fairly sizeable company and I've been quite busy."

"No need to apologize, lieutenant," she said, giving him only a casual glance. "I really appreciate your taking the time to stop by."

He looked at her more intently. "Do I know you, Private Brontë? You somehow seem familiar to me."

"No," Jessica said, avoiding his gaze by focusing on her food. "We've never met."

That appeared to satisfy him as he turned his attention to the enormous clutter of tents spread out over the pasture. "I know the men are getting restless camped out here so long, but I'm certain we'll be movin' out soon."

"That is my understanding, Lieutenant Lightfoot."

"A key part of our success in this campaign will be getting intelligence on the enemy. It's a shame we lost Private Stuart last week."

Jessica looked up at him, frowning.

Matt returned an embarrassed smile. "Oh, I'm sorry, private. You probably were not aware of what occurred a couple of weeks earlier. Abernathy informed his staff that Private Stuart had been captured by the rebels near Shelbyville and shot as a spy."

"Oh no!" Jessica uttered instinctively, although she didn't know the man.

"Yes, but that is one of the dangers he knew he was getting into. Unfortunately, Lieutenant Colonel Abernathy needs an exceptionally qualified man to replace him. It won't be easy. Stuart was the best we had."

Jessica pictured in her mind a man spying on the Confederates and feeding information to Union leaders on his return.

It sounded indeed dangerous, but strangely thrilling as well. One could get killed by the enemy if caught, but one could also get killed on the battlefield just as well.

"How vital was he to Abernathy's plans, lieutenant?"

"Extremely. Ever since his promotion this year to lieutenant colonel, Abernathy's shown extreme caution. He wouldn't want to make a move without good intelligence on the enemy."

Jessica wished she could have met Private Stuart while he was alive. It would have been interesting to learn how he went about his duties.

Matt excused himself, thanking "Private Brontë" for the chat, and left for another part of the camp. If spies were all that important, Jessica thought, there ought to be more of them. Maybe that was the key to the Union ultimately winning this damn war—find out what the enemy was up to.

Early May
Lawrence, Kansas

Lawrence was a different town than when George Radford moved away from it seven years ago to take his wife with him to Toledo. There were many more shops now. As he rode his horse down Massachusetts Street, he was impressed with it all…St. Louis Clothing Store, Deners Ice Cream Parlor, Duncan & Allison Dry Goods, the *Kansas Weekly Tribune,* and the Eldridge House—which he remembered as the Free State Hotel before border ruffians decided to burn it down.

George Radford felt fortunate indeed that Banning had approved his ten-day furlough. The lieutenant colonel told him it would likely be a long time before he saw another furlough. Plans were underway to stop Nathan Forrest's relentless pursuit in reacquiring lost rebel territory. The Union drive to Chattanooga this summer would be perilous, and Banning would need every able-bodied man he had.

But for the time being, Radford could allow himself to forget about the war. After passing Pinckney Street, he spotted Penelope's storefront. Painted in bold red lettering was her sign: "New Necessities—for hard-to-find supplies." As he tied up his horse at the post, he rehearsed how he would tell

Penelope that he just happened to be in town on other business and thought he'd drop by.

The shelves inside were stocked with various kinds of merchandise—books, medical supplies, feminine products, lotions, fancy writing pens, Indian tapestry, paints, and knick-knacks. The items were grouped together on the shelves with prices prominently marked. Penelope, looking pretty in a black dress with a white collar and ruffled sleeves, stood behind a counter. She was talking to a woman in a colorful Indian clothing.

George couldn't believe it. What was an Indian woman doing in this store? Didn't Penelope have enough common sense to ask her to leave?

"Thalia," Penelope told her, "I can have those for you in about two weeks. But it may take longer, depending on the war situation. Supplies can be unpredictable."

"I understand," Thalia said. She thanked Penelope and left, avoiding George's stare as she passed by him.

Penelope was busy counting the money in her register. George waited until she was through. He approached the counter. "Hello, Penelope. It's good to see your business prosperin' like this."

Penelope's jaw dropped. "George! What are you doing here?"

He widened his grin. "I'm in town on other business, and I heard about your operation here. I was curious how it was workin' out."

"Well," Penelope said, stretching out her arms, "this is it, and it's working out fine."

George took a glance around. "I'm impressed. You certainly have a wide assortment of merchandise here. How about customers?"

"Got a lot of those too. Matter of fact, people are coming from all over to buy things here. Thalia, that woman who was just here, came across the river from the Delaware Reservation just to buy some special beads from me."

"You mean you actually encourage savages to enter your store?"

"Savages?" she said, her voice rising. "She's no more a savage than I am."

221

This was not a good start, George thought. He wanted to make a favorable impression on her, not rile her.

"I'm sorry," George said. "I assume, then, that business is good?"

"Very good, except my problem now is in getting certain supplies. Some things are getting more difficult to obtain, like certain fabrics. It's impossible now to get merino, for instance, and the price of cotton goods is climbing higher than a mountain."

"I can well imagine, with the way the war's goin' on," George said, letting his words drift off into an uncomfortable silence.

Penelope straightened a shelf behind the counter. "I suppose you're wondering how your niece is doing."

"I was in fact. How's she doing?"

Penelope went to another shelf. "Jessica's doing fine. A lot of folks, like her friend Amelia, have been inquiring about her as well. She turned around to face him. "Unfortunately, Jessica made me and Otto promise not to reveal where she is at right now."

"Otto? Who's Otto?"

"My fiancé."

"What!"

Penelope smiled as if she were enjoying this. "Otto Heller and I will be getting married soon."

George was stunned. He had not prepared himself for this.

"You can't," he said, his voice almost a whisper.

"Why not?"

"Because you and I belong together, that's why."

"I don't think it'd work out the second time around, George."

"How can you say that?"

"I can't change the color of my skin. Besides, if I invited a savage home for dinner, you wouldn't approve."

A week later
Lawrence, Kansas

"My husband Fred and I are very happy for you," Amelia Read said, as she straightened Penelope's wedding veil while

222

Penelope sat in front of her dresser mirror. "I'm pleased that you chose me to be your matron of honor. But it's really Jessica you should have chosen for your bridesmaid.

Penelope laughed as she stood up, looking as stately as a Rembrandt work of art—her light blue gown illuminated by the morning sun's rays streaming through the window. "Amelia, it'd be difficult having a man named "Walter Brontë" be my bridesmaid. Wouldn't it?"

Amelia brushed off some lint from Penelope's gown. "I still can't believe she wants to do that—dress and act like a man so she could fight in the war. She's got a lot more courage than I do—that's for sure!"

"We don't really know how courageous we can be until we're put in a position that requires it."

"Perhaps you're right." Amelia looked at her friend and nodded her approval. "Penelope, I still wish Jessica would be here for your wedding."

"I'll write her. By the way, you and Otto are the only ones who know about her little charade as Private Brontë. I didn't even tell her uncle."

"I feel honored. Don't worry, I can keep a secret. Have you decided where you will have the ceremony?"

"St. John's."

Amelia cocked her head at the answer. "The Catholic church? But I thought that because of your divorce you wouldn't be—"

"Mr. Heller has friends in high places," Penelope answered.

"How's that?" Amelia asked.

"While I went to a seamstress with the fabric I chose, he met with the bishop. Looks like I may not have a problem getting an annulment from my marriage to George."

"Mr. Heller's a good man."

"I know, Amelia. Meeting him was one of the nicest things that ever happened to me."

The sun, beginning to sink behind the hills, now drenched the pasture. Jessica took a deep breath, gathering in the scent of clover, glad summer was nearly here. Soon, the Army of the Cumberland would be on the move again. Calm such as this won't last, she thought. Soon they'd probably engage in some noisy, deadly battle somewhere. And there'd never be true peace until every single rebel was crushed. She was just one soldier doing her part in this war. But she had thought of a more thrilling way she could help ensure victory. The idea had gnawed at her for some time. Maybe she'd confide in Mary—after she was through with this chess game.

Jessica pressed her "Private Walt Brontë" forage cap tighter on her forehead, stalling for time as she looked at the chess piece Mary had moved minutes earlier.

"It's your move," Mary said, pointing to the chessboard between them. It was a faded board, one that Mary had brought along with her but rarely used.

"I know," Jessica said, about to move her rook before switching to her queen. "There you go, Mary. Checkmate."

"You're too good at this game," Mary said after looking over the board carefully. "Maybe you ought to go back to playing poker with the men."

"I played a game with Tinker the other day. He doesn't suspect a thing about me."

"Tinker? Hmmm," Mary said, putting the chess pieces and board in the box, "I haven't talked to him in quite a while. How's he been?"

"He's still feeling guilty over Ishmael's execution. Blames himself for fixing him up with a trollop. By the way, he heard that those two prostitutes, Rose and Lillian, have left our camp and are on their way to Shelbyville to meet up with the Army of Tennessee." Jessica laughed. "I guess prostitutes don't mind what side they join, as long as they get business."

"It's a good thing that trash is leaving." Mary rose up, holding the chess game while gathering her long, sweeping skirts about her. "I can't believe Lillian wanted to be forgiven after what she'd done to Ishmael."

Jessica got up as well. "What are you talking about?"

Mary related Matt's account of Lillian Porter meeting with him, asking if God would forgive her for not turning in her husband. "Matt later told me how Lillian refused entertaining former slaves because it was bad for business. Ishmael left her cabin and went to Tinker, sobbing like a child, telling him how she devastated him with her cruel mouth."

Jessica felt an instant hatred for Lillian Porter, although she had never met the lady. "I hope I never see her," Jessica said, fuming.

Mary stood as still as a headstone in a cemetery as she looked at the setting sun. "Well," she said, forcing a smile back at her friend, "how does it feel to be Private Brontë? You're getting into character so well, you'll have a difficult time being a lady again."

"You may be right. I think I've picked up some bad habits. I know more swear words now and have taken a liking to beer and whiskey."

"Jessica!"

"Shhh!" Jessica said, her finger over her lips. "You're the only one who knows who I am. Don't ruin it."

"Well, you shock me sometimes," Mary said, lowering her voice.

"I've got something else that will shock you. I've been giving a lot of thought to the noble way Private Stuart served our unit. I hear he had been spyin' for us for several months before he got caught. I'm thinking of asking Lieutenant Colonel Abernathy if I can take his place."

"What!"

"Shhh! Lower your voice."

"That is an idiotic idea."

"Look at it this way," Jessica said, "I know that being a spy is certainly dangerous. But it can't be any more perilous than running on a battlefield with nothing to stop a shell from killing me."

"I don't know," Mary answered, glancing at her friend. "What do you know about spyin' anyway?"

"I could learn. I've thought about this a lot, and I have an advantage other men don't have."

225

"*Other* men? You're beginning to sound as if you've become one yourself."

"Well, when you wear their pants, eat with them, talk with them, and sleep in the same tent with them every evening, you begin feeling you're one of them."

Mary shook her head in disbelief. "What advantage would you have as a spy?"

Jessica looked to one side and thought she saw a soldier standing by a tree, staring back at her. They were no longer truly alone. "Wearing a good disguise," Jessica whispered, "is crucial. So if I dress like a woman, I just might be able to get away with it."

Mary was about to reply, when Jessica interrupted her. "Shhhh. That man walking toward us—he's—yes, he's Matt. You haven't told him about me, have you?"

"Of course not." Mary stared at him as he approached. "Looks like he's upset about something."

"Hello, Mary," Matt said, tipping his cap at her. "Is this private bothering you?"

"Not at all. We're just having a conversation."

Matt's face was stern as he faced Jessica. He saluted her and she returned the salute. "Private Brontë, I don't know how you've gotten past the sentry, but you've gone beyond the camp perimeter. If you don't leave immediately, I'll have you arrested."

"Yes, sir," Jessica responded, wondering why Matt made a big deal out of her being a few yards outside of the campgrounds. Jessica turned on her heels and left, relieved that Matt didn't know who she was. Mary was right. Matt was too much of a military man to be trusted with such a secret.

Mid-May
Lawrence, Kansas

"You've been acting very suspiciously," Otto said when his new bride put a "Closed" sign outside the store and coaxed him to let the bookkeeping go until tomorrow. "I suspect this may have something to do with my birthday today."

"My lips are sealed," Penelope said with a noticeable twinkle in her eye.

"You win, boss," he said, closing his ledger. "I suppose you're not going to tell me where we're going."

"The Johnson House," she said.

"Are you sure folks at that hotel will let a peace-loving man like me inside?" Otto chuckled, knowing its reputation as the headquarters for the Jayhawkers.

"If not," Penelope laughed, "I'll provide them with a list of all the slaves you've freed. That'll impress them."

Otto walked hand-in-hand with Penelope toward the three-story Johnson House on Vermont Street. He admired her more than he could say. He'd always love Helga, of course, but there was something special about Penelope. She had this will to live life to its fullest, to squeeze out every drop of joy she could from it. And she wasn't willing to let anyone get in her way. That included her ex-husband George Radford, who sat in the last pew in church during their wedding. He acted very civil, yet reserved, after the wedding, shaking Penelope's hand briefly and then whispering something to Otto he'd never forget, "Don't make the same mistake I did, Mr. Heller. Accept her for who she is."

Otto wouldn't think of doing anything else, of course. Penelope had a mind of her own, yet she often asked him for advice. He didn't know if it was because she really wanted it or whether she just wanted him to feel important. It didn't matter. She seemed happy. Mitzi and Emma now had a mother. And he enjoyed being with her. The only thing he felt badly about was that he hadn't yet consummated their marriage. Penelope told him to relax, he'd get over it. But Otto was worried. She coaxed him, teased him, but he still couldn't perform for her in bed. He loved her in many ways, but when it came to physical love… well, maybe she was right… he needed more time. But he hoped that her patience wouldn't wear thin.

Penelope interrupted his thoughts by stopping at an empty lot on Vermont Street. "Every day I pass by this weed-infested lot," she said, "imagining what it will look like once we build our new home here."

Otto stared at the lot south of the Methodist church and across the street from the Johnson House. It was his wedding present to Penelope, but he wished he could have provided her the actual house to go on it as well. Yet the business was doing well, and he was sure that perhaps in a couple of years they could start the groundbreaking work for a two-story, stone-and-brick home with a porch, mansard-type roof, and dormers.

"I want to show you something," Penelope said, pointing to a patch of tall jimson weeds fronting a grassy mound of earth at one end of the large lot. "There's actually an abandoned cellar in here."

"I don't see it. Where is it?"

"Over there." Penelope directed his attention to a large flat piece of stone. "That stone guards the entrance to the abandoned cellar. I happened to come across it quite by accident last week. Plenty of room down inside. Looks like it could accommodate as many as two dozen people."

Otto laughed. "I'll keep that in mind if I ever want to host a party."

Benjamin Johnson, the proprietor of the hotel, greeted them at the entrance and directed them to a large room down the hall. As soon as they opened the door, several people shouted "Surprise" and "Happy Birthday, Otto!" Emma and Mitzi were at the front of the gathering, their hands up, begging to be picked up. Otto lifted his daughters up, one on each arm, and smiled at the sea of faces.

"Our house wouldn't accommodate all of them," Penelope explained, "so that's why I rented out the reception room of the Johnson House."

"Maybe we should buy a larger house," Otto quipped, lowering his daughters to the floor so he could take the glass of punch John Speer was handing him.

"Good to see you again," John said with a twinkle in his eye. "Never did believe that story you gave me about Penelope being just your business partner."

Otto smiled back. "Sometimes business partners become marriage partners."

"You know my wife Elizabeth, of course," John said, pointing to a lady in an attractive red cotton dress standing next to him. "My sons, however, couldn't be here today. All three are working today."

After wishing the Speers well, Otto allowed Penelope to guide him to a man examining the binding of a large volume on a bookshelf. "I even persuaded your favorite bookseller, Edward Fitch," she said, "to join us today."

Ed gave Otto a friendly pat on the arm. "I wish all my customers were like you, Mr. Heller. I'm willing to bet you bought every poetry book I have in stock."

Otto was about to make a comment when Penelope directed him to a serious-looking man with a thin, gray beard, standing alone, away from the crowd. "I'm not certain," Penelope said, "if you know Reverend Hugh Fisher."

"I don't believe we have met," Otto said, smiling.

"Maybe it's well that we haven't," the reverend said, shaking his hand. "You see, I've served as chaplain to Senator Lane's Jayhawkers, and I don't think the bushwhackers are terribly fond of me right now."

"You don't have to worry about that," Otto replied. "I know they're not terribly fond of me either."

"The problem is," Fisher quipped, "people like Quantrill and Anderson have a reputation for eliminating men they're not fond of."

Chapter 16

Early June
Murfreesboro, Tennessee

Jessica, as Walter Brontë, made her way toward the guards at the door of a house that served as Colonel Martin's head-quarters—telling herself she had to do this. She tried not to show her nervousness by looking straight in front of her. It was, in fact, Otto's recent letter that convinced her to proceed with her plan. His last few sentences were especially encouraging...

> *"You need to do the right thing, despite the obstacles that come your way. I still remember the words John Brown once spoke: 'So long as another human being is kept in bondage, we cannot allow ourselves to rest.'*
> *Godspeed, Walter Brontë. Penelope's prayers as well as mine are with you."*

After agreeing to serve as her sponsor, Mary spent time with her reviewing army manuals concerning fortifications and armaments. Then she submitted Private Walter Brontë's name to Martin's officers at the Eighth Kansas. "I hope my reputation here carries some weight," Mary remarked to Jessica. "The soldiers here honored me as their 'Daughter of the Regiment,' which means they hold me in high regard. Even Lieutenant Colonel Abernathy once paid me a personal compliment."

"Halt!" the sergeant of the guard shouted. The huge man stood in front of her, rifle in hand, and looked as if he ate nails for dinner.

"I have urgent business with Colonel Martin and his staff," Jessica said, returning a cold stare.

Another soldier ran over to the sergeant and whispered something in his ear. The sergeant nodded and grunted at Jessica that she could enter.

Lieutenant Matt Lightfoot stood in front of a table where Colonel James Martin and five other uniformed men were seated. Matt's face was surprisingly expressionless, and Jessica wondered whether he had forgotten by now about that trivial incident two weeks ago. Perhaps Mary had persuaded him that Private Brontë didn't realize he was outside the campground perimeter.

Although she had previously met Martin before he was promoted to full colonel, she didn't know four of the officers in the room. She appreciated Matt's introduction of the men seated at the table: Lieutenant Colonel Abernathy, Captain Laighton, Major Schneider, and Quartermaster Bancroft. She saluted them all and then took her assigned seat facing them.

They bombarded her with questions..."Why did you enlist?"..."What did you do before you entered the service?"..."Why did you choose this regiment?"..."What is the reason you want to be a Union spy?"..."Which weapons are you intimately familiar with?"... "What kind of mortar is used in trench warfare?"..."What do you think of the ideology of the Confederate States?"..."What is your opinion of Jefferson Davis...of General Lee?"

They were particularly interested in her answer to one question they had asked: what would she do if caught by the Confederates and tortured? Jessica carefully phrased her answer. "Nothing they could do to me," she said, "would force me to betray the Union. I have pledged my life for the Union when I took the sacred oath, and I am willing to die that the Union may be preserved."

Slight smiles crept over the faces of the officers after she said this. She felt a headache coming on, but fortunately, Colonel Martin spoke up, "If every one of our soldiers was this informed and this motivated and this loyal, we'd have the best damn regiment in the military. I think my colleagues will agree with me that you, Walter Brontë, are a credit to our regiment..."

Jessica thought she saw Matt cringe at this remark and forced herself to continue to look serious.

"...and as a result," the colonel concluded, "we will grant you an opportunity to embark on a secret and very dangerous mission to discover what you can about the Army of Tennessee."

Jessica then took a special oath given to espionage agents in the service of the army. Before she was officially dismissed, Abernathy told her she'd need to meet with his adjutant tomorrow. He would supply her with funds and be her main contact point for her mission.

"Thank you, sir," she said, saluting. She turned and left immediately. Matt Lightfoot was leaning against a stone column near the porch of the colonel's headquarters. "You know, private," he said just as she passed him, "I wish I could get over this feeling that I somehow know you."

Jessica stopped and turned. "Believe me, Lieutenant Lightfoot, you've never met Walter Brontë before."

"You realize, of course, that now you can indeed leave the camp perimeter to embark on your mission."

Jessica suppressed a laugh, not knowing whether she'd still sound masculine if she did. "Thank you for not bringing the matter up."

"It's Mary Delaney you need to thank."

"Oh?"

"Yes. She's persuaded me that you're the qualified man for this job."

"I'll thank her, lieutenant," she said, hurrying off before she'd burst out laughing. Most qualified *man* for this job? Maybe her fervent desire for equality with men had finally been fulfilled.

The next day

Devin Alcott closed his eyes as he fingered an imaginary piano, pretending to play *Ode To Joy*, which Beethoven had incorporated in his *Ninth Symphony*. The gurgling sound of water spilling over a tiny waterfall in the river was soothing. He felt as if he were no longer sitting on the bank of a river at a Union camp, but rather back in Québec, learning the piano from his talented mother. His father was too involved with the governmental affairs of the colony to bother with him, but Anna took on the role of teaching him classical music.

232

"There are many ironies in life," she'd tell him. "Take music, for instance. When Beethoven composed music to glorify the joy of being, he himself was utterly miserable." Devin never forgot her words. This war was an irony because Americans were slaughtering themselves in order to save their ideals. President Lincoln was an irony because his original priority was not to free the slaves but to save the Union at any cost— even if it meant *not* freeing the slaves. And for Devin himself, it was an irony that men assumed he was a slave because of the color of his skin. They didn't look beyond that to learn that he was probably smarter than most of the officers in this regiment.

Devin heard the rustle of leaves and stopped his imaginary fingering. He sensed there was someone standing behind him. He whirled around, relieved to see it was only Private Walt Brontë standing there, his hands on his hips, grinning.

"A little finger exercise there?" Brontë asked.

"I miss my piano. Haven't played it since I got here."

Brontë dropped down to sit next to him. "Well," Brontë asked, "have you considered playing for our drum and fife corps?"

"It's nowhere near the same kind of music that I enjoy playing."

"I know," Brontë said in a voice dripping with sincerity, "but our brigade dearly needs music to keep up the spirits of the men. I wish you had met Lazarus when he was alive. I hear he played the drum very well, even in the heat of battle."

"I might consider it."

"I'm glad you're in our brigade. You mentioned something last time about writing music. Is that something you'd want to do after you're mustered out of service?"

Devin nodded. "I'm not sure I can earn a living from it, but it sure gives me satisfaction."

"Well, you and I have something in common. You like to write music; I live to write stories."

"Hard to do when there's a war going on."

"I know." Private Brontë rubbed his chin, and Devin wondered why the man's face was always smooth. He must shave quite frequently. "Devin," Brontë added. "how's Tinker doing? I worry about him sometimes."

233

"Tinker? He used to keep to himself a lot. But I notice he's been doin' more things with Salem lately. Just yesterday he showed Salem how to hit a ball with a stick. Told him that was what the game rounders or baseball was all about." Devin laughed. "Only thing was, there were no balls available, so Tinker picked some apples off a tree and used those. Made quite a mess."

Private Brontë stood up and dusted off his pants. "I should probably say goodbye to Tinker," he said, his voice trailing off.

Devin stood up at once. "Goodbye? Where are you going?"

Brontë looked embarrassed and fidgeted with his hands. "Oh, did I say 'goodbye'? I meant 'hello.' With so many things going on with this war, I can't even talk straight sometimes."

Brontë walked away and Devin wondered about the mystery of this man who never talked much about himself.

Johnson County, Missouri

The sun had just come up over the high bluffs when Sam Toby left the tent carrying a pitcher of water, soap, towel, and a razor. Wearing only the trousers he had slept in, he wandered through the short grass to a mirror nailed to a tall walnut tree. As he shaved, he wondered how his brother Roger was doin' with Nellie. Did Roger make out with that slave bitch like Sam figured he would? Didn't matter. Roger always figured he was better'n him, but he wasn't. No sir. He, Sam Toby, almost looked like Roger, and if he put on that fancy gray uniform of his brother's he'd probably look exactly like him.

Problem was, Sam thought, Roger ain't got any common sense. What was the point of runnin' around an open field with a rifle in your hand, when you could do the same thing here when you were robbin' folk? With the stolen loot Quantrill divided up with all his men, Sam figured he was better off doin' this than catchin' slaves. Besides slave-catchin' was no good anymore. Too many niggers now were runnin' over to the Union armies to fight with them.

The faint sound of sobbing caught his attention. He wiped his face with the towel and listened. There it was again. Some fool lady cryin' her eyes out somewheres. Curious, he bounded down toward the stream. Sitting by the bank, her head in her hands, was Kate Clarke King, Quantrill's lady.

Sam stood behind her, his hands on his hips. She looked especially pretty to him this morning, but he figured maybe it was because he hadn't had a girl since he sold Nellie.

"Problem, Kate?"

Kate gasped as she rose up at once and spun around. She was wearing a tan dress and squeezing a wrinkled handkerchief. "Oh, it's you, Mr. Toby."

Sam came closer. "What happened? Why are yah cryin'?"

She pursed her lips and turned away. "We had an argument this morning."

"Wanna tell me 'bout it?"

Kate, fidgeting with her hands, gazed up at him for a moment. "Ever since we got married, Bill's been acting different."

"Married? Well, I'll be hog-tied. I didn' know that."

"Happened last week. He took me to a country preacher to make it official."

"I'm s'prised he didn' tell everyone."

"That's the way Bill is. Keeps a lot of things to himself."

"Yeah, he sure does."

Kate played with her sleeve. "I love William, or thought maybe I did. But sometimes he makes demands on me. Orders me around like I was his servant girl."

Sam moved closer and held her soft, round shoulders. "He don't deserve yah, Kate. I wish yah were my woman."

Kate searched his eyes, his lips dangerously close to hers. She gently pushed him away. "If he saw us like this together, Mr. Toby, he'd kill you. Lucky he got up early and left for town."

Sam laughed. "I know. I saw him leave. What's he gonna do in town?"

"Probably spend his money on some foolishness instead of on me."

"Well, if yah was *my* woman, I'd give yah anythin' yah would want."

She parted her lips into a slight smile. "Mighty kind of you to say that, Mr. Toby. You married?"

"Nope. But that don' mean I wouldn't like makin' a young lady like you happy."

She blushed. "I don't want to give you the wrong idea, Mr. Toby. I like Bill, but sometimes I—" She played with her sleeve again. "Sometimes I think I should've gone back to Blue Springs and finish my schoolin'."

Sam scratched his head. "How old might yah be, Kate?"

"Fifteen. My pa always thought a girl shouldn't get ready for marriage until she was at least seventeen."

"Well, yah look seventeen to me."

Kate's eyes turned serious. "I really wish things would work out with Bill and me. He don't care about some of the things I want. All he does now is complain as to how he can't keep track of his men anymore. I mean Todd, Pool, and Blunt and all the rest have their own followers. He feels he's losin' everyone's respect. All he talks about now is organizing a big raid somewhere—something that will get everyone's attention. I depend too much on Bill for everything. Maybe I ought to see other men once in a while."

Sam took her hand and held it loosely. "Well, yah can, y'know."

"What do you mean?"

"I tol' yah I wouldn't mind makin' a pretty young lady like yah happy." He kissed the back of her hand, and she instantly jerked it away.

"Mr. Toby!" she exclaimed, her face darkening. "I am not a lady of easy virtue. How dare you!"

"I thought maybe yah wanted to see other men," Sam said, walking away. "Guess yah don't."

"Mr. Toby!" she exclaimed in a more conciliatory tone.

Sam turned around. Kate seemed embarrassed as she moved a strand of hair from her forehead and took a step toward him. "I hope you won't think any less of me if I tell you I appreciate you taking an interest in me. I like that in a man."

"Thank yah, Kate. Damn, yah sure are pretty. Quantrill's lucky to have a young lady like yah."

"I enjoyed the pleasure of your company this morning, Mr. Toby."

Sam grinned. "Yeah, I'll be here whenever yah want me."

Two days later
Murfreesboro, Tennessee

Jessica checked herself in the mirror. She was pleased with this dress Adjutant James Love had obtained from an officer's wife yesterday. It was a grey cotton outfit with a brown collar, brown cuffs, and red buttons going down to the waist—and she loved it. This would be the first colorful dress she wore since her parents were murdered.

There was a rapid knock on her cabin door, and Jessica answered it.

Adjutant Love whistled his surprise when he saw her. "Private Brontë, if I didn't know any better, I'd swear you were the real thing."

Jessica removed her gray bonnet and shook her head playfully. "Well," she said, using her own feminine voice, "I'll take that as a compliment from such a fine gentleman."

Love laughed as he dropped into a chair. "That's good, private, real good. You've got that female voice just about right. Maybe you can add a Southern drawl to make yourself sound more like a Memphis lady lookin' for her cousin servin' with the Army of Tennessee in Shelbyville."

"Y'all mean lock this, honey child?" Jessica said, beaming.

"Excellent, but don't overdo it. Now remember, Brontë, your name is Vivian Andrews, and you're lookin' for your cousin, Clifton Whitehead, a Confederate soldier. They're not gonna find anyone by that name, so once you're there you can mingle with the ladies and try to learn what's goin' on. Find out where Hardee's and Polk's troops are, where they might be headed, how strong their cavalry is, what kind of munitions they've got—anything you can find." He looked her over carefully. "Brontë, do you have those papers I gave you yesterday, the ones that show your name as Vivian Andrews from Memphis—as well as a commendation from Davis himself for your generous donations to the war effort?"

"I got them. Also got those Confederate bills you handed me. The way inflation is climbing with rebel money, though, I

237

hope I'll still have enough by the end of next week to get food and shelter."

The adjutant folded his hands, frowning. "Frankly, I hope that's the only risk you're going to face. You can still back out of this, private. You know how high the stakes are."

"I do," Jessica said, feeling less confident now that she'd soon be traveling into enemy territory. I want to help the Union win the next campaign, and I'm well aware of the risks."

"Very good. We leave in a few minutes, so be ready." With that, he closed the door behind him.

Jessica exhaled deeply. She was grateful that she had been assigned to her own place at the far end of the camp. Espionage carried certain privileges. Obviously, it would have raised a lot of questions if Private Brontë were spotted disguised as Vivian while camped with the other men. Abernathy cleared another obstacle for her as well—what to do when Private Brontë didn't respond to reveille and roll call in the morning over the next several days. Her immediate superior was informed that Private Brontë was on special assignment.

The adjutant was outside, looking at his watch, when she exited her cabin. Not wanting to be pressured, she took her time fastening the strap to her saddlebag before mounting the animal. "Please hurry, private," the adjutant called, waving his arm to follow him, "I've got orders to escort you through our pickets immediately." Jessica took one more look at the campsite, etching the sight into her memory. "I'm coming, sir." She followed him, trotting past an artillery battery and behind a long stable of cavalry horses.

Both nervous and excited over the prospect of discovering what might lie ahead, she focused on the task ahead. She summoned Pa's voice. "Don't be afraid, child," he said, "because bein' afraid don't amount to nothn.' Better to try it'n not do good then to not try it at all." She was only seven, milking a cow for the first time.

Jessica and the officer made it to the outer rim of the camp, where a sentinel raised his rifle and ordered them to halt. "Easy, soldier," Adjutant Love said, "I'm escorting this lady through the lines." He handed the sentinel an envelope. "I've got orders from Colonel Martin himself."

After examining the document, the sentinel saluted and allowed them to pass. She followed the adjutant up to the top of a small ridge. The adjutant moved his horse next to hers and held out his hand. "Good luck, Private Brontë."

He left at once, the horse's hooves creating dust clouds in his trail toward camp, which now resembled tiny flecks of tents. She watched him until he was swallowed up by the encampment.

The last time she had felt this alone was when the sheriff told her that her parents' deaths were no accident. Bushwhackers had shot and killed her parents and set fire to the house. "I'm going to kill them myself," she vowed. "Every last one of them."

That memory she hoped to bury some day now infuriated her. Slavers like Sam Toby were butchers. If she couldn't kill Sam Toby personally, she'd at least see to it that the Union won this damn war. Danger or not, she'd do her part. She kicked her horse into a gallop. There was no turning back now. She'd use this time alone, on her way to Shelbyville, to rehearse her new identity—Vivian Andrews, a Memphis woman looking for her cousin. But what if they didn't believe her, what then?

From her map, it seemed to be only a thirty mile ride to Shelbyville. Jessica figured she'd get there before sundown. How would she get to know any of the ladies there? Would they ask her questions she couldn't answer?

Stop it, Jessica told herself. You'll do fine.

The sun was probably an hour away from setting by the time she reached Shelbyville, heavily fortified by rebel troops. Her heart skipped a beat when she saw two soldiers on horseback riding toward her. Confederates!

The man with a brown beard hugging his face spoke up first. "Halt! What business do you have here?"

"Easy, captain," said the other, a somewhat older and clean-shaven soldier. "Maybe the young lady is lost. Who are you, ma'am?"

"My name's Vivian Andrews. I'm just out to visit your encampment in search of my dear cousin, Clifton. Perhaps you know him? Clifton Whitehead?"

239

A wicked smile crossed the captain's face. "How do I know yer not a Yankee spy wearin' a lady's dress? I need to check yah out—check out everythin' about you."

"But sir—" the other man started.

"Lieutenant," the captain interrupted, winking back at him, "we got to be sure about this one. Maybe even make her take off that there dress of hers to be sure she's not a man."

"How dare you!" Jessica yelled, concealing her own nervousness, "I demand to know your name and rank. I'm the colonel's sister, sir, and he'll be mighty interested in knowing how you have just insulted me. Your name, captain!"

"Oh, ah, never mind," he stammered. "I—I didn't know the colonel even had a sister. My deepest apologies, ma'am. I beg you to allow me escort you to town."

Jessica's heart was still racing as the captain cleared her way past the other sentinels on duty. He seemed greatly relieved when she assured him she would not mention his indiscretion to the colonel. After parting company with her escort, she saw a young girl of about nine or so, talking to a soldier near the officers' bivouac. Next to him was a woman in a gray dress. All three of them stared at her as she dismounted and tied up her horse, but Jessica pretended to be oblivious to all this attention.

The soldier who had been talking to the young girl tipped his butternut-colored slouch hat when Jessica approached him. "Good evening,' ma'am," he said.

"Hello," Jessica answered, altering her voice to sound genteel, "mah name is Vivian Andrews, and I hope I'm not troublin' y'all."

"Not at all, ma'am," the officer said, smiling politely. "I'm Major Samuel Lancaster, and this here's my wife Edwina and my daughter Ellen. What can I do for you?"

"Can you assist me?" she asked in a gentle Southern accent. "I am searching for my cousin Clifton Whitehead. I do believe he's stationed here at Shelbyville, but I declare I had no idea this campsite was so large."

"Do you know what regiment Mr. Whitehead is with?" Major Lancaster asked.

"Oh heavens, no. Will that be a bother trying to locate him?"

"It will take some doing. I'm with the Fourth Tennessee Infantry myself. Actually, we consolidated with the 5th as a result of our losses at Murfreesboro. Both of our regiments are now reporting to Colonel Strahl."

"Do you have a place to stay?" Edwina asked.

Jessica looked down at the dirt road to emphasize the hopelessness of her problem. "Afraid not, Mrs. Lancaster."

"Well then, you can stay with us tonight. Does that suit you fine, Samuel?"

"It's all right with me," Major Lancaster answered.

"Ellen and I," Edwina continued, "will be departing for Dalton, Georgia, tomorrow. We're going to live with my mother there until we find a place of our own. Had a nice cottage in Nashville 'til those awful Yankees took over our quiet, peaceful existence. I hate them Northerners, don't you?"

"I surely do," Jessica said emphatically.

"Maybe Miss Andrews can sleep in Ellen's cot," Edwina said.

At that suggestion, Ellen made a disagreeable face.

"Oh, that won't be at all necessary," Jessica said with a grin directed at the little girl, "I much prefer sleeping on the floor anyway."

Ellen's eyes lit up in appreciation. "I'll let you sleep in my room," she said, smiling.

Later that evening she lay on the floor of a room lit only by a yellow moon peering through the window. She overheard the major in the next room tell his wife that reinforcements to Strahl's brigade would be arriving at the Shelbyville-Murfreesboro Pike in a couple of days. "We've got a strong cavalry protecting our right flank," he said, "but it looks like we're going keep our caissons in reserve near Fort Rains." He went on to describe his thoughts on how the Confederates might best hold off any attack of Tullahoma by the Yankees.

Jessica took a slip of paper from the inside of her shoe and made notes in the semidarkness. "What are you writing?" Ellen, in the cot above her, asked.

"Me?" Jessica thought quickly. "A poem. I'm writing a poem." Ellen's insatiable curiosity reminded her a little of Mitzi. Jessica missed them both—Mitzi and Emma, and she wondered for a moment how they liked their new stepmother.

Ellen continued to stare down at her from the edge of the cot. "Can I see it, Miss Andrews?" she whispered.

"Maybe later. Now hush and go back to sleep. I'm really tired after my long ride."

Jessica returned to her notes, wishing there was some way to come up with more specific information, but how could she do that? If she showed any interest in military matters, there'd be immediate suspicion as to who she really was. Best to keep her ears open and hope she overheard something important.

In the morning, Jessica was fed breakfast consisting of cornbread, jam, eggs, ham, and milk—thankful for the best meal she had in weeks. If officers' families ate this well, she wondered what the rest of the regiment had—pork rinds, dried apples, and stale bread? Major Lancaster excused himself from the table, telling Jessica he'd see what he could about learning where her cousin was. Jessica kept on eating after he left, but Edwina deluged her with questions. "Vivian, whereabouts in Memphis are you from? Do you have a family? What are you doing for the war effort?"

Jessica, as "Vivian Andrews," answered them as best she could, worried that Edwina might trip her up. "I'm still rather tired," Jessica said when Edwina asked her who were some of the women she knew who might also have been major contributors to the Confederate cause. "I'm afraid I didn't get much sleep last night."

"Indeed," Edwina answered, "Ellen told me you were busy writing a poem last evening. How nice that you're so creative! There's a desk and an oil lamp in the next room you could have used instead of writing in the dark."

"Thank you," Jessica said, "but it wasn't very important."

"I found one of your poems on the floor this morning," Ellen said, digging her hand in her dress pocket, "but I can't read it."

Jessica froze as she watched Ellen hand a slip of paper to her mother. "Can you read it for me, mother?" Ellen said.

"Ellen, don't bother your mother with such nonsense," Jessica said, reaching for the paper.

Too late. Edwina began reading it, frowning. Looking puzzled, she turned to Jessica. Ellen squeaked in anticipation

242

as she glanced over her mother's shoulder, perhaps believing Jessica had written a poem about her.

Jessica put one foot ahead of the other, ready to bolt for the door.

The same day
Chattanooga, Tennessee

Talk of an imminent invasion by Union troops was rampant, despite the heavy fortification of Confederate troops surrounding the town. People had stockpiled whatever products they could afford—particularly food—in the event Chattanooga's supply lines were cut off. Sara Toby knew better than that. Her husband was still stationed in Shelbyville, and from his last letter, she got the impression the Yankees were more likely to strike Shelbyville first. From what she understood, the Army of the Tennessee had some of the best fighting men in the South. Chattanooga would hold; she was sure of it. How dare these Tennesseans lose faith in their God and in their army by stockpiling!

After the Sunday service at her new Baptist church, Pastor Finley had asked Sara and Nellie to meet with him briefly in his office. Fearing another episode with a preacher who didn't like the idea of her bringing a Negro into his church, Sara prepared herself for the worst. "Now remember, Nellie," Sara told her, "I don't want you to be offended by any slave talk from the pastor. If he thinks you oughta be my slave instead of my daughter, that's his problem, not yours. And if he don't want you in his church, we'll find another."

Pastor Paul Finley, a man with a mound of well-combed hair on his head, welcomed Sara and Nellie into his small office. The bookcase to one side of the room contained some surprising texts: *Uncle Tom's Cabin*, *The Heroic Slave*, and *Our Nig, Sketches from the Life of a Free Black*. These were anti-slavery books! So were copies of *The Weekly Anglo-African* and *The Liberator* piled up in a corner of the bookcase.

"I like to get acquainted with new faces in my church," the pastor said, "so I thought we ought to have a friendly chat this morning."

243

"I understand, Reverend," Sara said. She was about to ask him about those provocative books and other publications in his office, when he turned his full attention to Nellie. "How do you like it here in Chattanooga, young lady?" he asked, grinning at her.

"I likes it fine," Nellie said, fidgeting with her fingers.

"I assume," Pastor Finley said, looking at Sara, "that she's a slave girl."

"Used to be one." Sara took a deep breath, not knowing what she might have to say next. "I consider her like one of my own family, not a slave."

"God bless you for that," he replied. "I've helped conduct four slaves into Kentucky myself, but I wish I could have done more."

Sara stared at him in disbelief. "You did what?"

Pastor Finley smiled. "Don't act so shocked. Not all Southerners believe in slavery. I see Jesus in every colored face."

Sara leaned back in her chair, surprised and relieved.

He glanced briefly at Nellie. "So tell me, Mrs. Toby, how's she doing?"

"Nellie's doing fine, except she talks about Sissy all the time now."

"Sissy?"

"Her invisible angel," Sara explained. "I tried to convince her she's getting too old for this sort of nonsense, but she won't listen to me."

Finley turned his attention to the girl. "Nellie, tell me about Sissy."

"Well," Nellie said, eyes downcast, "she my guardian angel. She once be a slave girl like me when she done get killed by her mastah."

Pastor Finley raised an eyebrow. "Why did her master kill her?"

"Because—." Nellie's eyes were filled with pain as she appeared to struggle for the right words. She fidgeted with her hands again.

Finley's eyes narrowed during the silence that followed. "Because why, Nellie?"

"Because he want her tah do something real bad with her brother Ishmael."

244

Chapter 17

Jessica still couldn't get over her good fortune as she helped Edwina and Ellen put their luggage in a wagon outside the cabin. That piece of paper, Jessica thought, must have slipped out of her shoe this morning as she was getting dressed. Good thing her handwriting was illegible and Edwina couldn't read it. "Next time don't write in the dark," Edwina had said good-naturedly, handing her back the note. "It's bad for your eyes." Fortunately, Jessica still recalled much of Major Lancaster's conversation last night, so she found some privacy and rewrote her information.

"I'm sorry our visit was so short, Miss Andrews," Edwina told her, "but since some of our soldiers are marching south, I thought it best for us to leave now. Ellen and I should be in Georgia by tomorrow."

The eight-year-old was all smiles as she looked up at Jessica. "I wish I could read some of your poems, Miss Andrews."

"My poems aren't all that good," Jessica replied. "Maybe you'll write your own someday."

After Edwina and Ellen departed, Major Lancaster stopped by. "Sorry, Miss Andrews," he said, "I won't have time to check the rosters of all our companies. However, we will be looking into the matter in a few days. If we can locate him, I'll be sure to notify you."

"I do appreciate your help in this matter, major."

"If you need any help with accommodations in the meantime—"

"Perhaps you know some ladies at this camp who would allow me to stay with them until I get word on the whereabouts of my cousin."

The major took off his cap and scratched his head. "That's a question you ought to have asked Edwina. Frankly, I don't know any other women here, except for—" He shook his head and laughed at his own thought. "No, of course you wouldn't want to be acquainted with them."

"Who?"

"A group of ladies who call themselves the Porterhouse Courtesans."

"The Porterhouse Courtesans?"

"A fancy name for some loose women based near this camp. It's being run by some lady named Lillian Porter. Don't know why we even allow them here. Some of the officers think they're good for the morale of the men, but as far as I'm concerned—"

"Lillian Porter?" Jessica interrupted. "Is that her name?"

"Yes. Why? Do you know her?"

"No, of course not." Why, she thought, did that name sound familiar?

The major's face betrayed surprise, perhaps at the very idea that a nice lady like Vivian Andrews would know that harlot.

Jessica decided to change the subject. "I was pleased to meet your wife and child. You have a wonderful family."

"Thank you, Miss Andrews. Excuse, me, but I must be on my way. I hope you will be able to locate your cousin."

After he left, Jessica recalled where she had heard that name. She remembered that Lillian Porter was the lady Mary had told her about—the woman who had devastated Ishmael with her verbal abuse. It certainly didn't give Ishmael the right to retaliate by raping her, but her gross insensitivity must have provoked him.

Jessica told herself to calm down, that she was on a mission for the Yankees, that her feelings toward this woman should not play a part. But she wondered if rebel officers who visited these trollops would likely reveal any sensitive military information in the heat of passion.

There was one sure way to find out, of course, but she couldn't see herself becoming one of these loose women. Well, the first thing she could do, she thought, would be to find the Porterhouse Courtesans and meet the ladies working there. If she at least pretended that she was interested in being a prostitute, maybe they'd be willing to tell her what sort of customers they accommodated. By the time she found the

246

Porterhouse Courtesans, Jessica was debating how she'd get such information without losing her virtue.

Lillian Porter, with her red hair rippling in the breeze, seemed happy to meet Jessica. "Oh, yes, Miss Andrews," she said in response to Jessica's question, "officers do visit us, but they're very selective of the women they choose. This might not pose a problem for you. With your looks, you'd have no problem snagging a generous officer."

"Thank you for the compliment," Jessica said, feeling her face warming with embarrassment. "May I talk with the other ladies in your—ah—establishment?"

"Certainly," Lillian said, walking with her toward a large two-story brick house she had rented. "Two of my ladies are presently engaged with gentlemen, but there are two others I can introduce you to now."

Lillian was right. There were only two ladies in the downstairs parlor when Jessica arrived. One of them was Danielle, a brunette who was slightly older than Jessica. The other was Rose, a lady with a disfigured face who, Jessica had learned earlier from her friend Mary, was the one who had witnessed Lazarus's murder.

"Have you ever done this kind of work before?" Danielle asked, as she stood by the window, dressed only in a red balmoral petticoat and white silk bodice.

Jessica hesitated for a second. "Oh, yes. Made good money doin' it in Memphis." Jessica wondered why she had just lied like that. She had no interest in being a prostitute, but still couldn't figure out any other way to get military secrets from those rebels who visited Lillian's bawdy house. "Do the officers," Jessica asked both of the prostitutes, "ever tell y'all things they're not supposed to—like their campaign strategy?"

"Yeah," Danielle answered, "sometimes they go on and on. They like to brag. A lieutenant once told me about a general's plans for an anticipated battle near Stones Creek. I wasn't interested, so I didn't pay any attention."

Rose groaned. "I never get any white officers. They don't like freaks like me."

"You're not a freak," Jessica said instinctively. "You ought not talk about yourself like that."

247

"I know I'm not pretty to look at," Rose said. "But Negro men like me. They don't call me 'Miss Scarface' like the white men do. They treat me like a real lady."

"Don't y'all go on talkin' about them Yankee darkies you slept with," Danielle snapped.

Rose, shooting an ugly glance at Danielle, rose from her chair. "Excuse me, but I think I hear my little boy cryin'," she fumed.

"Y'all have to excuse me too, Miss Andrews," Danielle said, looking at the clock against the wall. "I'm expecting another gentleman who wants to spend the entire evening with me."

"Certainly." Jessica headed for the door when Lillian burst in, all excited. "Delightful news, Miss Andrews. I hear Lieutenant Major Wilkins is comin' to visit in the next half hour." She opened a notebook and searched through it. "All of my ladies are busy with other customers, unfortunately."

"Maybe Rose isn't," Jessica suggested.

Lillian laughed. "Who? Miss Scarface? Are you kidding? We're talking about a lieutenant major here. He's over six feet tall and handsome as the devil. I'd have him myself except for the pain in my back and legs. Must be what happens when you get old."

Jessica put her hand on the door. "Well, it's getting late and I've got to be going."

"Going?" Lillian asked. "You're making a huge mistake in leaving right now, Miss Andrews. Lieutenant Major Wilkins will probably give you a generous tip. I think the only problem is he's got some twisted ideas about sex. Last time he wanted Danielle to blindfold him and ride him like a horse. He likes the unusual all right. Oh—and he talks a lot when a woman drives him wild. But you don't have to listen to him. Just make him happy. Don't pass up this great opportunity."

Lillian was right, Jessica thought. This would be a great opportunity for her—an opportunity to learn about Confederate plans for defending Shelbyville and Tullahoma.

"Well then, I'll see him," Jessica said, still hoping she'd somehow be able to get out of this uncomfortable obligation. Lillian thanked her, telling her she'd be going into town and wouldn't return until much later. After Lillian gave her detailed instructions on the kinds of services rendered for different levels of payment and showed her the upstairs room where she'd be entertaining Wilkins, she left, wishing Miss Andrews luck.

After Jessica headed upstairs to check on her assigned room, she heard Rose humming from another room. What was it, Jessica thought, that Tinker had once said about Rose? That Rose wanted the Yankees to win? If Rose was indeed a Union sympathizer, an alternative plan was possible. Jessica approached Rose's bedroom and knocked.

"Come in."

Rose sat nursing a curly-haired mulatto child about two years old. "This is my son Jay," she explained, "I usually feed him about this time in the afternoon."

Jessica felt like asking her who the father was and telling her the child didn't belong in this unhealthy environment. But this was none of her business. She was on an important mission and couldn't distract herself from it. But could Rose be trusted with an important secret Jessica would have to tell her? If not, Jessica knew her own life would be in terrible jeopardy.

After some polite conversation, Jessica came right to the point. "Rose," she said, speaking in a hushed voice, "I understand you're a Union sympathizer. I'm told you'd like nothing better than to see the South defeated!"

Rose turned ashen, her eyes as wide as poker chips. She dabbed her breast with a cloth, stood up, and placed her sleeping boy on a pile of blankets on the floor. "What are you saying, Miss Andrews? Are you accusing me of being a traitor? Who told you these lies?"

"Shhh. Hold your voice down," Jessica whispered. She went on to say she knew all about Lazarus's murder and Ishmael's rape of Lillian Porter. "Tinker told me you hate the Confederacy, especially with its leaning toward slavery."

"That's true." Rose pointed to the scar on her face. "I got this here from my stepfather. He caught me teachin' his slaves how to read and write. He was so angry, he came at me with a knife. Cut my face pretty bad before one of his friends stopped him. Well, I still don't believe in slaves, 'cause I feel like I'm one myself. Look at the way they treat me here—like trash."

"I see that. How would you like to get even?"

Rose's eyes showed a spark of interest. "Get even? What do you have in mind?"

Jessica spent the next ten minutes outlining her plan in anticipation of the lieutenant major's arrival at the Porterhouse Courtesans this evening.

The Confederate officer appeared at the house on time and Jessica greeted him in the parlor. After paying her, Lieutenant Major Wilkins grinned, stroking his mustache. "Did Miss Porter tell you, Miss Andrews, that I want something—well, something out of the ordinary?"

"Yes, and y'all will most certainly get the full treatment of mah special Southern hospitality," Jessica answered, putting on her best performance as a lady from the deep South.

After he entered her upstairs room, he wasted no time in getting undressed. "You're awful pretty, Miss Andrews. Where has Miss Porter been hidin' you all this time?"

"She likes to save her best women for her best customers," Jessica said as she unbuttoned her dress. "Like I say, handsome, I got something special in mind that I hope y'all like."

"What do you have in mind, my darling?"

"Well," Jessica said, hanging up her dress, "We're gonna play a prisoner-of-war game, with yer being a naughty Confederate officer who captures two Yankee women—who'll be me and a mystery lady. But I'm gonna hafta blindfold you first, darling."

"Who's the mystery lady going to be, Miss Andrews?" he asked, breathing heavier.

"Can't tell y'all, Lieutenant Major," Jessica laughed. "Otherwise, it wouldn't be a mystery now, would it?"

"No, but I don't want *you* to be a mystery too. I want to take a real good look at you."

"I most surely understand." Jessica removed her chemise, hoping the Army of the Cumberland appreciated her having to humiliate herself like this. "Now here's the game, Lieutenant Major. The mystery woman and me—yer two captured Yankees—are gonna turn the tables on yah. After y'all blindfolded and tied to the bed, I'm gonna ask some questions. Give me a truthful answer and me and mah mystery woman will do your bidding, if y'all know what I mean."

"I sure do know what you mean, Miss Andrews," he said, grinning.

After she blindfolded him, she directed him to lie on the bed. Rose quietly entered the room and helped Jessica tie his wrists to the headboard. After binding his legs, Jessica watched as Rose lay atop him, stroking his hair. "You're sure good lookin' for an officer," Rose said.

"Wish I could see you," he said, grinning with expectation.

"You can just imagine me," Rose answered, touching her scar. "Imagine me as the most beautiful lady in the world."

Wilkins laughed. "Are you and Miss Andrews *both* gonna fool around with me?"

"No," Rose said, cooing. "I'm doin' the foolin', she's doin' the askin', and you're doin' the talkin'."

"I'm not talkin' until Miss Andrews comes over here and gives me a kiss."

"Have it your way," Jessica said, feeling a bit nauseous at the very thought. Reminding herself she had to do this, she kissed the blindfolded lieutenant major as he pulled on his restraints, unable to hold her close to him. "The mystery lady and I just captured you, soldier, and now you're gonna have to answer our questions."

"Mighty glad to, if you give me what *I* want."

"Well first, y'all gotta answer our questions about yer military operations in Shelbyville and Tullahoma."

"What do yah want to know, sweet thing? Yah oblige me'n I'll oblige yah."

"I'm your mystery lady, and I'll be happy to oblige you," Rose said. After she let him have his way with her, she offered him a drink from a bottle of bourbon. During this "prisoner-of-war" game, Jessica asked him questions like where do you think the Yankees will strike first?…how will the Army of Tennessee protect its right and left flanks?…what kind of firepower did the Confederates have in terms of cannons and mortars?…what's their weakest position? Jessica silently signaled Rose to reward him with more of her charms each time Jessica felt his answer sounded truthful.

Wilkins appeared suspicious. "What are you two ladies," he asked, his voice slurring, "—Yankee spies?" Jessica backed off and repeated some raunchy joke she had heard from the Eighth Kansas.

The bourbon finally put him to sleep. Jessica, already clothed, helped Rose get dressed. "Congratulations, Rose" she told her, "you finally bagged a white officer."

But Rose's face was solemn as she took hold of Jessica's arm. "Listen—if you see Tinker again, tell him I think Lazarus was the nicest boy I ever did meet. Tell him that, won't you?"

"I will, Rose. I will."

Two days later
Murfreesboro, Tennessee

"Let me see if I understand this, Private Brontë," Colonel Martin said, after glancing at Captain Conover and Adjutant Love in the room, "you wrote here that the Confederates have established a fortified line along the Duck River, extending from Shelbyville to Wartrace."

"That's correct," Jessica said, pressing her hands together as she sat facing him, hating to be the center of attention.

Martin looked at a paper on his desk. "You wrote that the Confederate's right flank, consisting of infantry and artillery detachments, are guarding Hoover's Liberty. Let's see—and you also indicate that their largest troop strength appears to be in Shelbyville, followed by Tullahoma and Wartrace."

"Yes, sir. I've also gathered some insight on their weapon supplies."

"I'm not sure about that information, Private Brontë. Some of this artillery data seems to be inflated. I mean, it doesn't appear reasonable they would have on hand several boxes of spherical hand grenades and five dozen mortar shells. That'd be quite an accomplishment, even for us. Sounds like your source was a bit of a braggart. How did you come by this information anyway, Private Brontë?"

Jessica felt confident she had taken down everything Lieutenant Major Wilkins spouted in the heat of passion. While she discounted his obvious lies ("we Confederates outnumber the Yankees by five-to-one"), she was unable to distinguish between a lie and the truth for other matters.

"Let's just say," Jessica answered, "that I got a high-ranking officer rather drunk one evening."

"Well," Colonel Martin said, rising from his chair and saluting her, "you are to be congratulated, private. Good work!"

Later that day, Jessica found Private Devin Alcott outdoors, standing with his back turned toward her, playing "All Quiet Along the Potomac Tonight" on a saxhorn brass instrument. She remembered the words well—from a poem written by a woman named Ethyl Lynn Beers and entitled "The Picket Guard":

> "All quiet along the Potomac," they say,
> "Except now and then a stray picket is shot,
> as he walks on his beat to and fro,
> by a rifleman hid in the thicket.
> 'Tis nothing—a private or two now and then
> will not count in the news of the battle...."

Devin played the piece with such depth of emotion, Jessica felt like climbing to the top of a hill and shouting for people to return to their senses. This wasn't a war about generals or about strategy and battle maps and firepower. It was a war about slaves cryin' to be free and about common men dyin' to get them free.

When he finished playing, Jessica clapped. "You told me you played music," she said, "but I had no idea you were that good."

Devin turned around and smiled. "I took your advice, Walt, and I've joined the military band. I'm going to play this instrument before we do battle, but during the battle I'll resort to a trumpet since it's easier to carry on the field."

"A musical instrument is probably a lot more powerful in some ways than a rifle."

"That may be true." He sauntered toward her. "I haven't seen you for several days, Walter. Thought maybe you deserted us or something."

"If they didn't shoot deserters, I might have well done that. By the way, where's Tinker? Salem's been lookin' for him."

"Tinker? He's been keepin' to himself lately. All he wants to do is go back home."

253

Home? Jessica thought. Tinker had no home. Penelope told her in her latest letter that she had torn down that simple wooden shack behind her house to start a vegetable garden.

"The war's probably got him down," Jessica said, "like the rest of us."

After Jessica returned to her unit, she discovered mail addressed to "Private Brontë" from Penelope. Jessica tore open the envelope, eager for news from home:

Dear Walt:

> *I am indeed sick of these successive Confederate victories I keep reading about. There was that battle near Fredericksburg, another one at Brandy Station, and now, the latest one in Winchester, Virginia. The latter Union loss is especially painful because it now allows General Lee to march on north to Pennsylvania. The newspapers allege that General Hooker is placing the blame for that on his commander, General Halleck, so it will be interesting to see what develops. On the brighter side, I have been reading that West Virginia might soon be admitted to the Union, so perhaps when you receive this letter, this will already have occurred.*

> *Enough about the war, however. Otto and I have been quite busy with running the store as well as raising the two girls. Emma and Mitzi are already calling me "Mama," and I couldn't be more thrilled since I know they miss their real mother Helga, God rest her soul!*

> *I am upset that Mayor Collamore won't allow Lawrence citizens to bear arms for their own protection, contending that Lawrence has both a weapons armory and a recruit camp. I doubt these ancient weapons—even if we had ready access to them—as well as the presence of a few soldiers will help protect us. Sometimes I wonder if*

women would have more common sense when it comes to matters such as this.

Amelia wanted to let you know she prays for your safety every day. God bless you for what you are doing for the Union cause!

Respectfully,

Penelope Phillips Heller

That evening Jessica took a leisurely stroll around the perimeter of the camp, thinking about tomorrow, when they'd all be heading toward Shelbyville and Tullahoma. Rosecrans had apparently delayed moving his forces all these months because he wanted to prepare his men and not rush into battle without a concrete plan. The men had been getting restless, and she could feel their excitement when word went out they'd be heading south.

Colonel Martin thought well enough of "Private Brontë" to allow her to move ahead of the troops on scouting missions. After commending her for a good job of espionage, he told her he'd be pairing her up with an officer to search for enemy movements through the high hills and heavy timber growth. "This is as dangerous a mission as your last one," he had said, "and maybe even more so, because you won't have the advantage of disguise."

Jessica wondered who would be assigned with her for the mission, but she'd have to wait until the morning to find out. It didn't matter. She felt good about making a real contribution to the campaign. Whatever she discovered on her mission had to be helpful to the Army of the Cumberland.

As she approached the creek, she heard a man's voice and the sound of a woman giggling. The tall grass rustled softly in the evening breeze. The silhouette of a man, his arms resembling columns, bore down into the soil. Below him was the unmistakable body of a woman. Afraid of being seen, Jessica dropped prone to the ground.

"I need you," the man groaned. "It's been a long time for me."

"Matt," the woman said, "it's been an even longer time for me. I've never slept with a man before."

Jessica's heart raced. It was Matt Lightfoot, and that was Mary's voice! Jessica wanted to leap up, surprise them, and demand an explanation—but she had to remember she was Private Brontë.

"I've been thinking about you a lot," Matt said. "Thinking about what it'd be like for me to take you and—"

"Oh, Matt..." Mary sighed, "I want you too, but—"

"But what?"

"But what about Jessica? Do you still love her?"

Jessica closed her eyes. *Do you, Matt? Do you love me despite how I've ignored you these many months?*

"I thought I did, but I don't know where things are with her. She had, after all, favored Mr. Howell over me."

Jessica winced. *I'm so sorry, Matt. I've been such a damn fool. I don't think I've ever really been in love with Mr. Howell.*

"Mary," he continued, "I need to be one with you tonight."

"Oh, Matt!" Mary was breathing more heavily now.

"I promise to be gentle."

"I know you will, Matt."

"It will be a glorious feeling, Mary."

"Will it? I've been wondering what it'd be like to feel the power of a man's passion stirring inside of me."

Jessica had heard enough. She got up and sprinted back to camp, fighting the mist in her eyes and the angry pain in her heart. It was only three years ago that she had been introduced to Matt Lightfoot...

At her high school graduation picnic at South Park in Lawrence, Pa introduced her to a lanky, dark-haired man in a checkered shirt and dark trousers, wearing a straw hat at a jaunty, devil-may-care angle, and holding a long-stemmed pipe in his left hand. He looked odd, the way his harsh Indian features clashed with his friendly smile. "Jessica," Pa had said, "I'd like yuh to meet a friend of mine. Name's Matthew Lightfoot, or I should say Reverend Matthew Lightfoot."

"Miss Radford," Lightfoot said, reaching for her hand and kissing it, "it is indeed a pleasure."

"Matt's finished his seminary education," Pa interjected, "and he aims to become pastor of his own parish someday. Maybe settle down'n get married, right Matt?"

"Yes—when I meet the right lady, of course. Maybe I already have," Matt teased, grinning at Jessica, who knew her face had to be as red as a strawberry. "Your pa," he added, "tells me you like to write. That true?"

"I do, Reverend Lightfoot. I find life fascinating; I want to write about everything."

"Young lady," he said, "let your heart be your guide—not only in writing, but in life."

Jessica, sobbing quietly, stumbled over a rock in the darkness, as she ran toward a row of tents. Falling, falling, landing on the claylike surface of the ground. *Let your heart be your guide.* His haunting words stung her now, as did the small stones that scratched her face. It was only a physical thing with John Howell, she thought. She never obeyed her heart, never thought about giving her heart a chance with Matt. Now it was over. She picked herself up, not sure if she should hate herself more than she hated Matt at the moment, and limped to her tent.

Next day

After his company halted about ten miles south of camp, Salem sat on the ground, in the middle of some farmer's barley field. He examined the weapon in his hands. It was Ishmael's Sharps rifle with the word FREDUM carved into the wooden stock. Salem was proud of this gun, having been told his brother Ishmael had died bravely fighting off several rebels during a surprise ambush. Or was it during a formal battle? Tinker's version didn't match with Lieutenant Lightfoot's, but it didn't matter. Salem would carry on where his brother Ishmael left off.

Strange thing this mornin', he thought, when the lieutenant met Private Brontë. They was both goin' on ahead as advance scouts, but the private didn't wanna go with that lieutenant. The lieutenant got mad and ordered Brontë to go with him or face court-martial. Brontë went, but why did they hate each other? This whole war thing was strange. The enemy be out there, but sometimes the enemy be inside here.

It be a lot like what happening to Tinker now. He mad at everything—not just the enemy. He done tol' me he don' care no more if he die. Two of his friends—Ishmael and Lazarus—he say done get killed and for no reason. No reason, I say? How can that be when both men die with honor? He say "no," it not be an honor to die like they die, but he don' say what he mean. They both die fightin' for freedom. They both heroes, ain't they? But he say he don' want to talk 'bout it no more. I worry 'bout Tinker sometimes. He don' want to fight no more.

Same day, late afternoon
Shelbyville, Tennessee

As Lieutenant Roger Toby made his rounds, checking the sentries around the northern perimeter of the town, he had a vague feeling that General Bragg was wrong about this. Roger had heard rumors from some of the officers that Bragg rested his hopes in victory since he didn't think Rosecrans had much of a mounted infantry. There was also speculation of Lincoln's growing impatience with Rosecrans, who had spent the first six months of the year virtually immobile, camped around Murfreesboro. Would it result in the same problem Lincoln had with McClellan's earlier reluctance to attack? Roger wasn't too sure about that. After all, this gave Rosecrans extra time to strengthen his forces and make repairs to damaged bridges and railroad tracks—as well as perhaps, making Bragg uncertain whether he should detach many of his troops to help break the siege of Vicksburg.

Rosecrans didn't have much of a cavalry—that was the gossip the officers spread around, but Roger didn't believe it. One soldier who had spied on the Union had told Captain Robert Patterson that the Federal's Colonel Wilder had organized a mounted infantry brigade he called the "Lightning Brigade." Fast horses, determined fighters, and a new Spencer seven-shot repeating rifle—capable of shooting off seven cartridges in 15 seconds. No, the Union was not sitting around using old-fashioned weapons and strategies. This would be a tough battle.

Roger also didn't agree with some of the other officers that the main Union attack would happen here at Shelbyville. That idea didn't make sense to him when he looked at a map, seeing that the main Union plum would eventually have to be Chattanooga. Not that Chattanooga itself was all that important, but it was, after all, the intersection of several major railroads serving the South. That being the case, Roger could only suspect that Tullahoma would be the place for the next main attack—almost a straight shot southeast from there to South Pittsburg and over the main road leading to Chattanooga. As far as he could tell, Shelbyville bore no strategic value to the Yankees.

When he thought of Chattanooga, he couldn't help but think of Sara. It made him nervous to think of the possibility that the Yankees might eventually capture it. What would happen to Sara if she had to move? They had a house in Chattanooga. Would she just have to abandon it and flee with Nellie further south to Georgia? Roger relaxed when he realized that the sheer terrain surrounding the town, let alone the strong protection given by Confederate troops, made it unlikely that the Yankees would be able to penetrate that far.

But still, there was that possibility—and it refused to stop nagging him.

Same day
Bedford County, Tennessee

Jessica, as Private Brontë, refused to walk any further up the steep hill and dropped down to rest. Matt called out to her that a clearing was just over the ridge and that they ought to camp there for the night.

"Give me a moment," Jessica shouted. "My legs are giving out on me."

Matt, panting, returned from his higher position up the slope. "We'll rest a bit, but it's not much further."

"Sorry I gave you a difficult time of it this morning," Jessica said, checking her cartridge box to see how many shells she had. She had fired off a few shots earlier at a moving object, only

259

to find to her embarrassment that she had killed a deer instead of a rebel.

Matt shrugged his shoulders. "I chalked that up to the stress of the war." He dropped himself on the ground next to her. He scratched his beard as he surveyed the landscape. "Private, I meant to congratulate you on the fine job you did spyin'. Abernathy told me you won't reveal how you got that lieutenant major to talk so much."

"Got him drunk is what I did," Jessica said, trying to sound casual about it.

Matt shook his head in disbelief. "I don't know. It's hard to imagine an officer talkin' to a stranger like that. So you're not gonna reveal your secret, are you?"

"We all have secrets, lieutenant. You never told me about your secrets when it comes to the ladies. Are you seeing anyone special?"

Matt didn't say anything for a moment, and his eyes became glassy. "I am. And she's very special." He turned in Jessica's direction. "Private, have you ever—" He paused, his eyes appearing to be focused on some remote, distant point, "—have you ever respected a lady so much you refused to take advantage of her—I mean, even though you knew she'd give herself to you?"

Jessica's heart felt like a pebble skipping over water. *He didn't make love to Mary last night?*

"No, lieutenant, I've never had that experience," Jessica said, finding it difficult to get the words out, let alone trying to sound masculine at the same time.

"The lady I'm seein' is a virgin," Matt said, his voice cracking. "She told me she had always dreamt she wouldn't pleasure a man until she became his bride." He looked away. "I know I sound like a damn fool, but I didn't want to be the man who destroyed her dream."

"Do you love her?" Jessica asked, struggling to maintain her male voice.

"No, but I'm fond of her. She has a delightful sense of humor and is very caring, but—"

"But what?"

"But there's only one lady I thought I loved, but she's disappeared from my life."

260

At that moment it was difficult for Jessica to continue pretending to be Private Brontë. It took all her strength to resist kissing him and telling him that she never disappeared from his life.

Chapter 18

The rain started in the morning as a mist. However, in the afternoon it transformed into a sudden downpour over the large gap between two huge hills. Thunder clapped through the heavens. A cannon ball from a Federal battery whistled through the smoky air. A captain shouted to continue plowing through a web of tall trees.

Shells lobbed here and there as Tinker slopped ankle-deep in mud. When the men got to a grassy clearing, some slid face-down on the field, only to pick themselves up and wipe the mud from their eyes with their sleeves and continue on, like crazed animals.

Tinker wished Lieutenant Lightfoot were here by his side. He'd ask the lieutenant one question: *what was the point of this here damn march?* The army had 'nuff of a hard time gettin' the artillery through the gap'n the men were tired. Ten miles in this rain be like twenty miles in the sun.

The lieutenant, Tinker thought, be goin' back home in August. But he, Tinker, be here in this here unit 'til the end of the year. By then he be out. Well, he ain't gonna wait that long. First chance he got, he'd leave. Let 'em shoot him as a deserter, he don' care no more. And maybe the lieutenant don' care no more neither. Reverend Matt Lightfoot no longer "reverend." He done become a soldier-boy, follow the colonel like a sniffin' dog, not bendin' any rules, but goin' only by the book.

At least, Tinker, thought, if Mary be around, he could talk to her. But she'n the medical folk be following the troops a few miles behind. And Miz Jessica, the only other one he trust, she be gone. Oh yeah, there be Brontë. He fine, but I don' know him that good. They promote him to corporal yesterday but he not say much. Corporal Brontë keep to himself a lot.

Now he up in front of this here line, with the white scouts, not here with the black fighters, skin-black and clothes-black.

The captain ordered the men to spread out as there were sharpshooters hiding in the cedars. Tinker moved way toward the left side of the line, dropping to his stomach when he saw the glint of a rifle pointing in his direction from the side of a tree. The enemy shot once, twice, and a sergeant riding near Tinker fell off his horse, a look of disbelief shadowing his face. As he dropped into the muddy ground, his chestnut horse neighed, prancing away from the action, into the fringe of the woods.

Tinker saw the man by that cedar aiming his rifle at him, and he instinctively cut him down with a bullet. One less rebel killin' people today, Tinker thought, feeling more relieved than proud at the moment. He looked to one side, then the other. On his left was the sergeant's horse, equipped with saddle and saddlebag. To Tinker's right there was a wide empty space, the men having moved westward, perhaps obeying an officer's command that he himself didn't hear. The rain had eased up. Tinker felt if he were to make a move, it should be now.

He didn't give it any further thought as he took the next step. It was as if he were seeing someone else run toward the riderless horse, mount it, and reverse his direction, away from the battle—all in one easy motion. Three or four miles later, he saw Mary Delaney staring at him, her face in shock, as he rode by. "Tinker!" she screamed, "you're headed the wrong way!"

But he ignored her. Better she don' know he leavin' for good now.

The next day
Eight miles north of Shelbyville

Roger Toby had never seen such chaos before in the Confederate lines. A Yankee battery fired continuously at them, a major's horse reared as a bullet whizzed by his ear, and a lieutenant chased after a group of retreating soldiers, barking at them to return and hold the line. Another lieutenant shouted at Roger that George Thomas—that obstinate Yankee general who refused to be intimidated by superior rebel forces—had captured Hoover's Gap. If that's true, Roger thought, Bragg would probably retreat to Tullahoma. With skirmishers rumored to be advancing from both sides, Roger didn't have time to respond to the lieutenant.

Captain Patterson pointed to a ravine, just past a bank of cedars. Breaking through the noise of pounding hooves, gunfire, and yells from some of the men, he ordered his soldiers to follow him. "Take cover!" Patterson shouted as the enemy approached.

Nine or ten Yankee horsemen moved swiftly toward them, guns blazing in rapid-fire succession. Repeating rifles, Roger thought. This must be part of that Yankee "Lightning Brigade" he had heard about.

Patterson rose up from behind a tree. "Fire!" he yelled, waving his arm when the horsemen came within fifty yards of the staggered Confederate line. Patterson caught the first three bullets, one in his face and two in the chest. He didn't even have time to scream as the impact flung him backwards onto the wet ground.

Roger had turned his attention away for only a second or two when a bullet grazed his thigh and another struck his leg. The combined pain was severe, but he forced himself to crouch on his good leg as he yelled for his men to retreat. The horsemen had already passed them but were turning around, stopping, probably pausing long enough to reload. "Charge!" a man at the head of the brigade shouted.

Roger tried to trudge after his retreating men, but the pain was too intense, and he dropped to the ground. He heard the hooves of the Federal horses rushing toward him, and he made a feeble attempt to reach for his pistol and take at least one Yankee with him. Not able to get his gun, he closed his eyes and waited for a fatal bullet as the brigade rode past him—but the end never came.

The smell of gunpowder, hovering in the air like a shroud, assaulted his nostrils. He snaked his way along the ground toward the tree where Patterson lay in his own blood. The dead man's eyes were ghostly white, rolled back in their sockets, his lips frozen in the shape of a wreath, as if he had been cut down in the middle of his scream. This was the shell of the man—his once animated, lively friend—a man he had met again in Chattanooga, attending a ministrel show with him. He remembered how he told Patterson of his decision to reenlist. This was the same man who had plans for great things beyond the war. Now he was just a corpse.

Roger lifted himself up enough to cradle Patterson in his arms. "I hate this damn war," Roger said, feeling his heart burst."I don't give a damn who wins anymore!"

The afternoon light dimmed, dropping like a heavy curtain on the meadow. White clouds of death still hung in the air, but now they competed with ominous thunderclouds that had formed. After a heavy gust of wind, the sky opened and rain fell in torrents. In an attempt to cover his head as he sprawled on the wet ground, Roger opened his jacket. He felt something metallic pressing his chest. It was Nellie's heavy bronze medallion hanging from a chain on his neck. A lot of good that did him now. The war had left him; the men were gone, except for the dead ones.

He wrapped his wet fingers over the medal, remembering how he promised Nellie he'd wear it every day. It was just last Christmas that Nellie had given it to him...

"Sissy wants you to have this," Nellie had said, handing him her medallion and chain. "She say if you pray, God will hear you."

"How come yaw the only one who sees Sissy?" Roger asked.

"I ask her 'bout that once. She say it because she used to be a slave girl too, like me. She know how hard it was for me. She want to be special for me."

"Why does Sissy want me to have this medallion?"

"To remind you of her. She tol' me she once had one like this too."

Roger looked at Sara, who sent him a silent signal not to tell Nellie what he really thought about her silly invisible angel. "It's wonderful of yaw to give me this present," Roger said to Nellie, trying his best to appear grateful.

"I wish yaw did exist, Sissy," he murmured, rain washing over his face as he recalled the quotation from the Psalms on the medallion. "I could sure use an angel right now. I can't die like this, alone. Please help me."

He drifted off to sleep, despite the sharp pain in his thigh and leg. Drifting, drifting. *Something, somebody stirring up ahead. A figure? A soldier?* "Who's there?" he asked weakly, before blacking out.

She felt it had to be her lack of sleep and the whiskey a private shared with her that made her delusional. Jessica, now masquerading as Corporal Walt Brontë because of her promotion, saw things and felt things that weren't there. At breakfast this morning, while it was still dark out, she sensed the presence of Lazarus standing next to her, his face solemn, his hands ready to play his drum. Then later, as she marched with the others through the woods, she saw a man hanging from a tree. As she came closer, she recognized the executed man as Ishmael. She gasped, pointed him out to a nearby soldier, who looked in the same direction. But there was no man, no Ishmael. Only the tree. "Are you all right, Walt?" the soldier had asked.

And now, as she joined a wave of hollering Union soldiers chasing after the rebels in retreat, she thought she saw a large flock of small white birds flying overhead. It made her laugh to think maybe these were doves symbolizing peace and an end to this endless war.

Behind her a military band for the Army of the Cumberland played "Battle Cry of Freedom," and Jessica recalled how she and some of the men sang the chorus back in Murfreesboro:

> *The Union forever! Hurrah, boys, hurrah!*
> *Down with the traitors, up with the stars;*
> *While we rally round the flag, boys, rally once again,*
> *Shouting the battle cry of freedom!*

Private Devin Alcott had to be back there bugling with them, she thought. She could pick out his instrument from the rest of the band. He showed an unmistakeable artistry in the way he blew his trumpet.

But there certainly was no artistry to this war, she thought, dropping to the ground when a bullet whistled past her head. This was government-sanctified butchery, but necessary to root out devils like Sam Toby and his ilk from the world. She picked herself up and pressed on with the others.

An artillery company stopped on the left flank, loaded its heavy guns, and fired. Grapeshot peppered the sky as a light rain began to fall. Once or twice, the rebels took a stand, only to be broken up again with a volley from the Federal line.

To her right, a portion of Colonel Wilder's brigade charged on horseback down the line while some of the foot soldiers waved them on with their hats. If she had thought of it, she would have insisted on drilling for the cavalry. There was nothing like flying through the air on a steed with a weapon in your hand. Battle cry of freedom. That's what it was all about, she thought. Freedom was a right, not a gift. And anytime she caught herself thinking about not shooting at the enemy she thought of that. Killing was really a good thing if it freed mankind.

It began to rain.

"Spread out!" a major on horseback ordered when some twenty rebel deserters were spotted coming toward the Federal line. In the distance, Jessica saw the "Lightning Brigade" charge through a small cluster of rebels, firing in rapid succession. Several of the enemy fell, but only one Union horseman took a bullet. Some of the rebels ran in her direction, and Jessica dropped to the wet grass, rifle at the ready. She missed with her first shot and cussed as she reloaded. The figure she had shot at fled into the dense brush, and she chased after it, determined to get that rebel coward.

She rushed toward the brush, expecting to see him crouching with fear. Not there. She spun around with her rifle and thought she saw a figure dash down a small hill. "Hey, you milksop," she yelled after it, "come out here and fight like a man."

The figure disappeared behind a hedge, and Jessica ran after it. She leaped toward the hedge, ready to pull the trigger. Instead of a man, however, she found a young Negro girl— maybe 9 or 10 years old—in a bloody, ragged dress, crouching in fear. "He done shoot me!" she shrieked when she saw Jessica. "Now I gonna die!"

"What in tarnation! What are you doing here, child? How did you get here?"

She fell to the ground. "My mastah," she groaned as she lay on her back, "he done shot me 'cause I not do what he want."

Jessica noticed a growing red spot on the child's dress. It appeared the girl had been shot in the chest.

Oh, dear Claire! I've killed you!

No, Jessica reminded herself. That happened long ago, and this certainly wasn't Claire.

"Heavens!" Jessica exclaimed, dropping to her knees in front of the Negro girl. "Your master shot you? Why?"

Her eyes drooped. "He want me to do something bad with my brother."

Jessica didn't even want to know what "bad" thing the girl was talking about. "The bastard! I'll kill him. I swear I'll kill him."

"No," the girl replied, her voice weakening, "killin' only begets more killin'."

"We'll talk about that later, child. Right now, I've got to get you to a doctor." She took off her kerchief from around her neck and covered the child's face to protect it from the rain. This, Jessica thought, didn't make any sense. How could this little girl have run at all with such a wound to the chest? And what was she doing here—near a battlefield—anyway? Where was her cruel master?

Jessica lifted up the little girl, who seemed as light as a bag of feathers.

"Thank you, ma'am," the girl said, her sweet voice filtering through the kerchief on her face. "God loves yuh fer your kindness tah me."

A chill ran through her body just then. God loves her? What sort of thing is that for a dying girl to tell her? This child ought to worry about getting better. "I don't want you to die, little one." Surely, she thought, there had to be other Yankees back there who could help take this slave girl to a surgeon.

"Too late," the girl said, weakly. "I be all right. I go to a good place."

268

It had to be fever, Jessica thought. This child must have a fever the way she's talking nonsense. *What* good place? No such thing around here. Nothing but killing, nothing but anger, nothing but hate.

Jessica looked about her. Where was her regiment? As she recalled, there was a line of trees to her left and a high bluff to her right when she took off after the rebel. Yes, she thought, there it was. But where were the Yankees? It was pouring hard now, and the rain would make it even more difficult to find someone to help her, but she had to try. This girl needed a doctor. Jessica scurried to a spreading elm that offered some protection from the rain. She removed the kerchief and looked down at the child's face, but the girl's eyes were now shut, a peaceful smile on her lips.

"No!" Jessica shouted, shaking the girl's limp body. "Don't die on me." She exploded in grief and dropped to her knees, not caring that she was kneeling in mud. God, she thought, I can't take this anymore. *Why did You bring me here only to watch another child die?*

The rain had slowed to drizzle, but thunder rolled through the sky. Thunder, she thought, or maybe a drum roll for this poor girl's death. Jessica got up and struggled with her knapsack to remove a blanket. "Foolish child!" she muttered. "What were you doing here anyway? " As she turned to put her blanket over the girl's dead body, Jessica gasped. The girl was gone!

Jessica realized she must have been hallucinating again. Never again, she told herself, would she take whiskey after going three days without sleep. She'd have to hurry now to find her regiment or else they'll think she deserted them. The rain continued to drizzle as she trudged on in the direction where the troops were probably headed. She couldn't believe how vivid her imagination was. Yet, that child must have been a delusion. How light she was when Jessica lifted her up. That's it, Jessica told herself. No more whiskey, no more sleepless nights.

She heard the faint rumble of thunder in the distance. Black clouds, like angry fists, lined the western sky. Out of the corner of her eye, she noticed a man lying against a cedar a few yards away. His jacket was off, his head slumped over,

269

blood splotches on his gray lieutenant's uniform. Jessica would have gone by, thankful to see another dead rebel, but it was his face that stopped her. She took a good look at him. His face was large and rough, his bushy eyebrows forming a distinctive arch over his closed eyes. His large nose and coarse brown hair completed the picture of a man she had sworn she'd kill—Sam Toby!

She didn't want to bother reloading her rifle, so she tossed it off to one side. She grabbed her Colt .31 revolver. About to shoot him with it, she saw him stir. His eyes opened slowly, focusing on her, his lips parting in surprise. "What the—" he exclaimed. A moment of silence passed between them. "Are yaw gonna finish me off, Yankee?" he asked, his voice faltering as he raised his hands. "Or do yaw want to do the right thing and take me prisoner?"

"No, Mr. Toby, I'm gonna finish you off all right," Jessica said, coming closer, her gun aimed at his head," but, I'd like to see you suffer first."

The man frowned. "Mr. Toby? How did yaw know my name?"

A streak of lightning flashed through the darkening sky. The rain had stopped, as if listening for further instruction from the heavens. Another bolt of lightning illuminated the meadow for a brief moment.

"I never forget a face," Jessica said. "And I never forget a name. On your feet, mister!"

The rebel struggled to get up, using the trunk of the tree for support. "It's hard for me to stand. I got shot in a couple of places. Bleedin' a lot."

"How do you want to die, Sam? Should I hang you, shoot you, or set you on fire—or all three?"

"Sam?" The man furrowed his brow. "My name's not Sam. It's Roger. Roger Toby."

Jessica flinched. "You're not Sam Toby? You're a damned liar!"

"I'm not lyin.' I have identification here to prove it." He reached for his knapsack on the ground, but Jessica ordered him not to make a move.

"I'll get it," she said, stooping to grab his rucksack. She ransacked through the contents—a book, writing paper, a pen, letters, a Confederate buckle, some rope, a small knife, some Southern banknotes, and what looked like an official paper of some sort. She removed the paper and stood up.

He took a step forward and fell, groaning in pain.

"Hold it! One more move, Sam, and you're dead. I'd love to shoot you with this—your own gun."

"Don't know what yaw is talkin' about," he gasped, picking himself up. "Yaw got the wrong man."

"You don't give up with your lying, do you?" she said, tossing his rucksack to the ground. She took a quick look at the certificate. It claimed his name was Roger Toby, a Second Lieutenant with the Twenty-Third Tennessee Regiment. Could have been forged.

"You're a damn liar," she said. He *had* to be Sam Toby, she thought. She'd never forget that horrible face. But could she possibly be wrong? This man looked like Sam but didn't sound like him. Seemed more refined. Maybe she ought to— just a minute—what was that silver chain around his neck? "Hey, Toby or whoever you are," she said, her voice dripping with sarcasm, "what kind of jewelry are you rebels wearing these days?"

"Oh this?" he said, bending his head. "It's a religious medal. It's supposed to bring me luck, but it hasn't worked for me so far."

A thought raced through her mind. A religious medal? No, it couldn't be the same one, could it? "Turn around," she ordered, "and wrap your hands around that tree. I want to see what you're wearing."

He did as he was told, and Jessica unhooked the chain from the back of his neck. It was a large, round bronze object in the shape of a coin. She brought it up close to read the inscription. She struggled in the dimming light, but she made out the words: "For He has given His angels charge concerning thee, to keep thee in all thy ways." No, Jessica thought, was this the same one? Could it be? She flipped it around. The back side of it had—Oh Lord!—the back side of the medal had an all too familiar inscription—Nellie Radford!

"You pig!" she screamed. She ordered him to face her, but he crumpled to the ground as he did so.

"Get up, you bastard!"

271

"I can't," he groaned. "Just finish me off."

"What did you do to her, Sam?" she shrieked, not worried anymore about not sounding like Corporal Brontë. "Did you rape her before killing her? Are you happy you sent my parents to their graves?"

His eyes widened as he looked up at her. "What're yaw talkin' about? Who are yaw? Yaw voice sounds just like a lady's."

"That's because years ago I was the girl you almost raped." She'd never forget that day...

"Let's see what yah look like, Jessica. Take them clothes off."

She had begged him to stop, threatened him, but he just laughed at her.

"You'll do what, little girl? What will yah do to me?"

Jessica shook off the distant memory. "You asked me once what I'll do to you. I'll tell you what I'm gonna do to you." She stooped to pick up a knife and rope from among his belongings, still training her pistol at him. "I'm gonna tie you up, and then I'm gonna slice you like cheese, one piece at a time. You're gonna suffer before you die, you swine!"

The man was now sprawled on the ground, his leg and thigh soaked with blood. "Woman, yaw insane," he groaned.

He didn't resist as she tied his hands and feet. But he moaned the whole while, complaining about his pain.

A streak of lightning cut the sky into fragments. Jessica thought how this war gave people like this pig Sam Toby an excuse for killing people *off* the battlefield. She'd see to it that Sam never harmed another human being again. She'd send him straight to hell, just like she swore she'd do. "I'm gonna do this for Ma and Pa," she grumbled, tightening her grip on the knife, "and also for what you did to sweet, innocent Nellie."

A bright light burst like cannon fire before her, turning everything into a brilliant white. Jessica ducked for cover. An explosive sound of thunder quickly followed. So this is what it was like to be struck by lightning, she thought.

Just then she heard a voice. A sweet, childlike voice.

"That man did nothing bad to Nellie," the voice said. "Leave him be."

Jessica, shaken, grabbed her gun and picked herself off the ground. "What? Who's there?"

The figure of a little slave girl appeared before her—the same girl who had died in her arms. But this time, she wore a clean white gown—a dry gown—dry—despite the continuous rainfall! The girl's voice sparkled. Jessica's gooseflesh spread up her spine and she fell to the ground, stunned. She looked up, her heart pounding. What was happening?

"Don't be afraid," the girl said. "I want to thank you for your kindness. You stopped to show you cared. Now pass on your love to him."

"Go away, girl!" Jessica snapped, waving her Colt .31 at the wounded man. "I've got to do this." But she couldn't stop her arms and legs from shaking as she pulled the trigger. The gun failed to fire.

"No, don't do it, Jessica!" the girl ordered.

Jessica froze at the sight of the glowing image of the little girl. "What's going on here? How did you know my name?"

"That man you want to kill is Roger, Sam Toby's brother. He saved Nellie from harm. You ought to thank him for that."

"Who are you? What are you? Why are you here?"

The little girl stretched out her arms as her image began to fade. "Always keep this in mind: love is stronger than fear. Remember, love is stronger than fear."

"Who are you?" Jessica screamed. "Answer me!"

The girl smiled before she disappeared. "My name's Sissy."

Everything turned black just then, as if the entire earth had darkened. A sound. A clap of thunder. A touch. A breeze caressing her cheek, but no rain. Jessica opened her eyes. Twilight. A man lay on the ground groaning, his hands and feet tied, his pants leg red, soaked with blood.

"Please, God, forgive me,!" Jessica said, dropping her gun. She ran over to him and cut the rope from his wrists and legs. "What have I done, Roger? I'm so sorry!" Hoping she wasn't too late, she removed her muddy shirt and undershirt, ripping the latter into ribbons because it was cleaner. Using the knife nearby, she cut off his pants leg and tied his wounds as best she could to stop the bleeding.

Roger's eyes were closed, his head slumped to one side, and for a moment, Jessica thought he might be dead. She listened for a heartbeat. There was one, although it was faint. She'd have to get him to a surgeon, she thought. But how? Even if she did find one, they'd likely send him to a prison camp after he got well. From what she had read about prison camps, they were atrocious places. Roger deserved better. She had to think quickly.

A cool breeze gave her small boyish breasts goosebumps, and it was only then she realized she was naked from the waist up. What a sight she must be, she thought, laughing to herself. Here she was, a lady dressed in men's trousers and wearing no top for modesty. Well, at least she still had a blanket to cover herself with. She took a good look at Roger, who remained unconscious. The man had about the same build as she. Maybe, just maybe… Yes, she'd do it. She'd dress him up as a Yankee, toss his Confederate clothes away, and drag him to a main road.

"Sissy," she said aloud, pulling her blanket close to herself, "if you really want me to save him, you better help me find a field hospital for this brave soldier. I can't do this alone."

Chapter 19

June 28
Shelbyville, Tennessee

Jessica wore the same dress Adjutant Love had given her when she went on her spying mission weeks earlier. But today she was Jessica Radford once again. Corporal Brontë had disappeared—forever. This morning she'd be officially drummed out of the service, but she didn't mind. She was only thankful that yesterday morning the Yankees had discovered her, wrapped modestly in a blanket, near the main road. Complying with her request, they took her to Mary Delaney at the field hospital. There, she was able to tell Mary privately what she had done and convince her to agree with Jessica's story—that the wounded corporal they found was a Yankee and a friend of Mary's. As far as how Jessica had lost her military uniform, her explanation was that some rebels discovered she was a lady and that they had stripped off her clothing, intending to rape her, but she escaped.

While her immediate superior believed her, Lieutenant Colonel Abernathy reprimanded her yesterday for deceiving the army by pretending to be a man. "Do you realize," he asked sternly, "you've not only put yourself in harm's way, but you've jeopardized the safety of the other men in your regiment? You could have been captured by the enemy, and they could have blackmailed us for your safe return." Jessica felt like telling Abernathy that she also contributed to the success of the campaign, but decided against it. Better to just let matters lie.

As ordered, Jessica appeared in Abernathy's cabin following breakfast. She didn't want to hear any more lectures from the lieutenant colonel but was surprised when Abernathy warmly greeted her in a room he used as an office. "Now that we're alone," Abernathy said, grinning, "I just wanted to tell you I admire your heroism. There are few women who would have had the courage you did in risking your life for the sake of the Union."

"I don't understand," Jessica said, sitting across from his desk, "just yesterday you—"

"Yesterday some of my officers were present, and I couldn't tell you how I really felt. I didn't want to give the impression that I encourage this sort of charade. But I just wanted to personally congratulate you on your service to our cause."

"I am honored."

"I have another matter to discuss with you. About this wounded corporal you discovered the other day—"

Jessica fidgeted with her hands in her lap.

"You told me," he continued, "the man's name was Roger Toby and a friend of Miss Delaney's. But Miss Delaney herself doesn't know what regiment he's with. We couldn't ask him ourselves since he was not fully conscious." Abernathy scratched his chin. "But I found something quite curious."

"What is that, sir?" She held her hands together to keep them from shaking.

"When Corporal Toby awoke earlier this morning, he told the nurse he didn't want to be sent to a prison camp. Now why would he say such a foolish thing as that?"

"No idea, sir. Perhaps he is suffering from a fever."

He reflected for a moment. "This man also claims a lady had threatened to kill him. Was that you, Miss Radford?"

"How could that be me? Why would I want to kill a fellow soldier?"

"Yes, of course." He looked at her as if he wasn't fully convinced. Then he rose up from his chair and saluted her, much to her surprise. "This is for Corporal Brontë," he said. "I'm sure going to miss him around here."

"I will too, sir."

Jessica saw Matt Lightfoot outside the door when she left the lieutenant colonel. He lowered his eyes as she approached, looking hurt and angry, as if someone had betrayed his confidence. "I can't believe you tricked me like that," he said.

"I apparently fooled a lot of people," Jessica said, trying to sound casual.

"It was grossly unfair of you," he said, his face turning a shade red, "to encourage me to go on talking like I did about

Miss Delaney in your presence, making me believe you were a man named Walter Brontë."

"I'm sorry. I wanted to reveal my identity to you, Matt, but I was afraid you'd turn me in. I was on a mission that I didn't want to be stopped from fulfilling."

He jammed his hands into his pockets and looked out at the open field. "Have you accomplished your mission, Miss Radford?" he asked, his voice sounding cold and distant.

"I was on a mission of revenge," she said, reflecting on that fateful day over a year ago...the day she touched her Pa's casket and vowed that she'd get Toby for this if it was the last thing she'd ever do.

"Did you succeed?"

"No," she said. She bit her lower lip in reflection. "Thank God, I didn't succeed." She thought about the letters she took from Roger Toby's haversack. There really was a Negro girl named Nellie living with Roger and his wife Sara in Chattanooga.

"Jessica," Matt said, shifting to a friendlier tone, "I'm sorry about the way things turned out. Maybe when I see you in Lawrence next month, you and I could—" He clenched his jaw, looking as if he were struggling with what to say.

"I don't know, Matt. The war's changed me a lot. And it's changed you, too. Things may never be the same again."

July 8
Hickman, Kentucky

Tinker, dressed in stolen civilian clothes, assumed he was a free man when he made it to Kentucky. After all, Matt Lightfoot had told him about Lincoln's Emancipation Proclamation. So he was surprised when two men grabbed him after he left a general store in Hickman. "Where're your free papers, nigger?" the younger of the two asked. "Yeah," the older man said, "prove you're not a slave."

"Papers? I don' need no papers, suh. I free man from Kansas."

"Kansas?" the older man snarled. "Then what are you doin' here? Lost or something?"

277

Tinker had to think fast. He couldn't tell them he was a Yankee deserter. "Visitin' some friends, that's all."

"I don't believe you," the younger man said, grabbing his arms and forcing them behind. "Put those cuffs on him, Luke."

The older man named Luke took out a pair of handcuffs while Tinker struggled to get free. "Yah can't do this to me!" Tinker screamed. "I be free long time now."

"Think we can make it in time for the auction in Union City today?" Luke asked, clasping the cuffs on Tinker.

"If we hurry. This one's gonna fetch us some good money. He's strong, he is."

Just then, a neatly-dressed gentleman in a black derby called out to them: "Men, why are you badgering my slave? Leave him be!"

"Is this here nigger yours?" the younger man asked.

"You better damn well believe he's mine," the gentleman said, looking righteously indignant as he stared at him. "Take those cuffs off him now, or I'll have you arrested for stealing my property!"

Luke apologized as he released Tinker to the stranger's custody. The man turned to Tinker, wagging his finger at him. "I told you once before, Ezra, you don't go off wandering by yourself. See all the trouble you cause me?"

Tinker was thoroughly confused, but he didn't object when the man took his hand and escorted him to a rooming house at the end of the block. "Suh," Tinker said, when they entered the building, "my name's not—"

"Quiet," the man interrupted. "We'll talk in my room up-stairs."

Once they were alone, the man explained that he was with the Underground Railroad. "Kentucky's in a good position to bring slaves over," he said. "Y'see, we're the only state sur-rounded on three sides by rivers. So we do this all the time. Where are you headed, son?"

"Kansas, suh. Lawrence, Kansas."

The man took off his derby and scratched his head. "Kan-sas, huh? I've got a connection in Missouri, so I'll see what I can do."

"Beggin' your pardon, mistah, but ain't it true that Lincoln's 'mancipation Proclamation made the slaves free?"

"Wish it did. But the Emancipation only freed slaves from states that seceded from the Union. Since Kentucky never seceded, its slaves aren't free. Understand?"

Tinker shook his head. "No, suh. That make no sense to me, suh. No sense at all!"

Late July
Lawrence, Kansas

Father Favre Sebastian circled the date on his calendar: Thursday, August 20. He was glad Bishop Miege would be able to make it here a few days prior to the Confirmation scheduled for August 23rd. St. John the Evangelist was a rather young parish, but one going through a lot of trials because of the war and the constant harassment of Lawrence by border ruffians. There was strife even among some of his own parishioners on the slavery issue, although not as much as other Kansas towns experienced. Towns like Topeka and Lawrence tended to be far more supportive of the abolishment of slavery than others.

Father Sebastian reflected on the crucifix on the wall of his austere office. People came up to him all the time, confessing their sins of hate and despair. He couldn't understand hatred, but he could understand despair. This war was tearing families apart. Fathers and sons alike were going off to fight, some as far away as Virginia to preserve the Union, and in the process, abolish slavery. But at what price? According to one account, the recent battle at Gettysburg was the bloodiest so far. Altogether, some 50,000 men gave their lives in this single battle. Father Sebastian had been upset when one parishioner rejoiced that this was a "glorious Union victory." In his homily last Sunday, the priest countered by telling his parishioners that God had to be heartbroken over the loss of so many lives. As far as he was concerned, he could not celebrate this victory, knowing there were countless wives who now had no husbands, sisters who had no brothers, and children who had no fathers…the only ones left were the friendless, the orphans, the widows.

Father Sebastian knelt before the crucifix and wept.

"I swear you like the lumber business a lot more than groceries," Henry Grovenor remarked to his brother Gurdon as he checked off the shelf items at Grovenor Groceries. "A fellow can come up to you, tell you what kind of porch he's buildin' and you can describe for him right off what kind of wood to use and how to build it."

Gurdon laughed as he packed groceries into a wooden box. "Comes from learnin' how to build things when I farmed in Connecticut, Henry. I don't have to tell you times were tough back then. You either learned how to do it yourself or you didn't get it done at all."

Henry surveyed the stacks of lumber, sorted by gauge, as well as a few simple tools behind pickle barrels and bags of flour. "That's true, but we're gonna have to decide at some point what business we're in. I think if we could focus on the grocery end of things we'd be a lot more successful. Look what happened when Peter Ridenour joined up with Harlow Baker. The Ridenour & Baker operation is doin' quite well these days. I hear Harlow's even gettin' a loan to expand their grocery business."

Gurdon smiled. "I've got to give that man a lot of credit. Maybe when I get to be that successful, I'm just gonna hang it up. I'll just move back east and spend most of my time fishin'." He turned his attention to a customer who had walked in moments earlier. "Good morning, Will."

Fifteen-year-old William Speer waved his hand. "Morning. What's this I hear about spending your time fishing?"

"You a fisherman, Will?" Gurdon asked. "I hear there are some good-sized bass running down the Kaw this time o' year."

"Yeah, I guess so. My father's takin' me and Guy Smith, one of my friends fishin' at the end of August.

"Guy Smith—the German shoemaker's son?"

William nodded. "He doesn't have many friends."

"Well, I'm glad you're his friend," Henry said. "By the way, when you see your father today, tell him I didn't get last week's copy of the *Tribune*. Maybe he can save me that issue. I would like to see it."

"I'll ask him." He eyed a container of oatmeal cookies on the shelf near the register.

"They're freshly-made," Gurdon said. "Want some?"

Will shook his head. "I just have enough money for bread, sausages, and cider for lunch. My brother and his friend David are makin' me come here because they don't have time. Big deadline comin' up for *The Republican* and they've got to help with the printing."

"Think your brother Robert will someday be a great printer like your father?"

Will shrugged with disinterest. He handed Gurdon his written instructions on what to order for lunch.

Gurdon put the note down on the counter and opened up the cookie container. He placed several cookies in a sack and handed it to the boy. "Here, Will, my treat. By the way, where are you goin' campin'?"

"We're headin' up to St. Joseph on the 22nd of August. Father says it's beautiful there around that time of the year."

Jessica told Elizabeth Fisher she'd be happy to watch her three older boys while Elizabeth and her husband Hugh participated in a wedding ceremony in Leavenworth. "I'd leave you with my five-month son, too," Elizabeth said, "but I need to feed him, so we're taking him with us."

"Who's getting married?" Jessica asked.

"An officer with the Fifth Kansas Volunteer Cavalry. Reverend Fisher will be officiating at the ceremony." She looked back at the waiting carriage, her forehead deeply furrowed and her lips taut. "It always makes me nervous these days when we go anywhere."

"Don't worry about the children, Mrs. Fisher," Jessica said, hoping her own smile would relax the minister's wife. "I'll take very good care of them while you're away."

"I know you will. It's not that. I'm worried about Hugh. Just last week he received another anonymous letter informing him he's a dead man. Could be a bushwhacker. I know those ruffians hate him for his proslavery activities, but Hugh's also not well-liked by a lot of people, including some of his fellow clergymen. Why, one of them even accused my husband of mishandling church funds."

281

"That's absurd," Jessica said, gazing at a large flower bed in South Park, not far from the Fisher home. "I happen to know Reverend Lightfoot has always held him in high regard."

Unfortunately, Jessica thought, she no longer held Matt in high regard. She reflected on his obsession for following military orders to the letter.

"Well, I'd better be going," Elizabeth Fisher said. "Are you sure you'll be all right with the children?"

"I'll be fine. You just have a good time and don't worry about them."

After watching Elizabeth depart with her husband, Jessica took the three boys with her to South Park to play catch. Twelve-year-old John "Willie" Fisher tossed a ball up in the air and caught it with one hand. "Do you know how to play rounders?" he asked.

"No," Jessica answered. She remembered hearing about the game of rounders or baseball for the first time when Devin Alcott had mentioned it to her: *"...there were no balls available, so Tinker picked some apples off a tree and used those."* The thought made her want to cry. Things had changed so much since then. Tinker was now a wanted man, a deserter, and he insisted on hiding during the day in the rear of Penelope's store on Massachusetts Street.

"I would sure like to learn," Jessica added. "What about you two? Do you know how to play the game?"

Ten-year-old Charlie Fisher glanced at his eight-year-old brother Joey. "I'm pretty good at pitching, but Joey throws the ball like a girl."

The remark made Joey angry enough to push Charlie with both hands. "I don't throw like a girl!"

"You do"..."I do not"..."You do"..."I do not." The argument soon escalated to shoving, but Jessica quickly restored peace between them. "What if I told you," she said, "that sometimes a girl's as good as a boy in doing things, maybe even better?"

All three boys laughed at that comment. "Well," Jessica added, "do you think a lady might make as good a soldier as a man?"

"No!" they all shouted at once. "Women would be too scared to fight," John added.

Jessica had expected that response from them. Women weren't allowed to vote, let alone fight. Penelope told her that would change some day. Jessica hoped she was right.

Two days later

Otto was considering purchasing a settee at a furniture store on Massachusetts Street when Henry Clarke, the owner, came up to him. "You didn't bring Mrs. Heller with you shopping?" he asked with a big smile on his lips.

"No, she's out in Kansas City today, picking up a load of supplies that came in. I thought I'd surprise her with a new settee, seeing as how she complained about the one that's soiled and ripped."

"How's everything going these days?"

Otto pondered the question as he stroked his beard. "Frankly, I sort of miss the publishing business. I might get back into it someday. Maybe I'll wait until this war is settled and these border invasions stop. Publishing is a dangerous business these days."

"You know," Henry said, tucking his thumbs under his broad suspenders, "just living here is dangerous. I'm a member of the militia, with guns and ammunition at my disposal, and I still don't feel safe."

"You've got to be careful you don't show any fear to your children. I try to relax in the evenings with a good book. That reminds me; I'm going to pay Edward Fitch a visit and buy another copy of *Leaves of Grass*. I gave the only copy I had to Miss Radford."

Henry's eyes twinkled as if he knew a dark secret. "I heard a rumor that Miss Radford dressed like a man and helped push Bragg into Chattanooga. Is that true?"

"Can't believe everything you hear these days, Henry."

Penelope made her way past stacks of merchandise in the back of her store. The early afternoon sunlight streamed through a small window overhead, illuminating Tinker, who was hunched over and playing with his harmonica. His living area, set well aside from a small inventory of store merchandise, was furnished with a cot, a chair, and a table. The square wooden table had on it an oil lamp, a copy of the *Kansas Weekly Tribune,* a Bible, and a dog-eared copy of Longfellow's *Song of Hiawatha.*

"I got some sandwiches for you," Penelope said. "Real bread, too. None of that hardtack you had to eat while in the service."

He looked up at her, his face drawn, tired.

Penelope recalled Tinker telling her how he enjoyed reading *Hiawatha* to Nellie when she was younger. He cried huge bawling tears when he told her how much he missed Nellie, and why did the Lord take her away? Penelope tried to reassure him there was always a hope that maybe she was still alive, but Tinker would not hear of it. Penelope never mentioned the book or Nellie's name after that.

Tinker bowed slightly to her as she walked over to his table with the plate. "Thank yuh kindly, Miz Penelope."

"Tinker, this is rather silly. You can come to the house anytime and live with Otto and me. No sense you flitting between that cellar at night and the back of this store during the day."

"I likes it, Mrs. Heller. It about the same kind o' room I get in the regiment. But I have it all to mahself. Don' worry none about me."

"Lawrence is a pretty liberal town here, Tinker. Always has been. You don't have to be concerned about slave catchers here at all."

Tinker dropped down on his cot and took a sandwich from the plate. "It ain't slave catchers I worry 'bout, Mrs. Heller. It's the military. Yuh gots a recruit camp here, the Kansas Fourteenth. If they see me, they's gonna turn me in."

"You worry too much, Tinker. The Yankees are too busy with the war to worry about one deserter. Besides, you look right smart in those clothes I bought you. I bet you could walk back and forth right in front of that recruit camp, and no one would even suspect you were a soldier."

"I sure glad I know how to read," Tinker said, smiling as if he were coaxing her to change the subject. "If Mr. Heller has more books for me, I sure would 'preciate it."

"Matter of fact," she said, "he's going over to see Edward Fitch about some books that might be coming in. Mr. Heller can get one from him if he doesn't already have it. What book would you like?"

Tinker thought a moment. "Lazarus like *Uncle Tom's Cabin*. Maybe that one."

"Good. That happens to be a book Mr. Heller had already ordered. I'll tell him you want to read it."

Penelope left, shaking her head. What a prison for him this had to be, she thought. During the day he stayed in the back room, and after sunset, he'd hasten to that obscure cellar in the vacant lot on Vermont Street. Penelope regretted having told him about it because she would have rather he slept in a decent room. Tinker refused to sleep in the store at night because he didn't consider it safe. "I knows they say we be forty miles from the border," he once told her, "but I still don' feel safe. The ruffians they can come and can kill everybody they see."

Penelope couldn't persuade him otherwise, but she wouldn't give up trying. It just seemed unfair that she and Otto lived in a comfortable house and he didn't. While Tinker never complained about his living conditions, she wasn't convinced he wanted this kind of life. This certainly could not have been the kind of freedom he had dreamt about.

Tinker relaxed after Penelope left. She be good woman'n he don' deserve such respect. He wolfed down the sandwich and lay on his cot. He put his arms behind him and heaved a sigh.

He done a lot o' thinkin' these days. He ought to be the one who got hung, not Ishmael. He ought to be the one who got shot, not Lazarus. If it not be for him, they be alive. He need to do something in their memory. Something they both be proud of. Maybe something even Mr. Lightfoot, his former mastah, be proud of.

Tinker ran his hand through his hair. If only he be brave... if only he get chance somehow to do something good...

Soon he dozed off to sleep.

"Nice sign, Ed," Otto said after entering Edward Fitch's bookstore."

"Thank you," Ed said. "I had the painter do my store name in red letters to match the awning over my window. The way I see it, if that's what it'll take to get folks out of the liquor store and into my place, it's worth it."

Otto inhaled deeply through his nose. "Ah yes, I can tell you've got some new books in recently."

Fitch laughed. "You still remember the smell of ink, paper, and glue, don't you?"

"I can't seem to get the publishing business out of my blood, Ed."

"I know what you mean. After teaching the first school here at Lawrence, I can't get used to not seeing children sitting at their desks in the morning." He raised his bony finger as a thought struck him. "By the way, those titles you wanted came in just yesterday. *Uncle Tom's Cabin* and *Leaves of Grass*. I'll go in the back and get them."

Watching Ed Fitch disappear to the back room, Otto couldn't help wondering what a great world this would be if everyone was as pleasant as that man. He and Penelope ought to invite him over for dinner sometime.

August 7, 1863
Lawrence, Kansas

Dear Mary,

I suppose you are right in saying that war does strange things to people. Having been a soldier myself confronting the horrors of battle, I know what it is like to face the imminent prospect of death. So I can see how you and Matt may have felt the need for each other before the day of a deadly battle. If I were in your place, I may well have acted similarly. I want you to know we are still the best of friends

You ask me how I feel about Matt, and I don't honestly know. I suppose it depends a lot on where his heart truly is when he returns to Lawrence in August. But my thoughts now are elsewhere. I have other matters weighing heavily on my mind, especially my concern over having almost taken my revenge on such an innocent Christian man like Roger. I am pleased you were successful in helping him find his way safely back to his family in Chattanooga. I want to thank you for giving him that daguerreotype of me so he would have it to give to Nellie. She will be ecstatic knowing I am back here praying for her. I hope Nellie doesn't mind that I now have in my possession her bronze medal. I plan to give it to Tinker as I know he cared dearly for that young lady.

You talked to me last time about forgiveness. I agree with you that, as difficult as it is, I need to force myself to forgive Sam Toby for what he did. I will try, and I hope I can…but I pray that I never have to put it to a test by meeting him face-to-face. I will make an effort to refocus my thoughts on my writing, but frankly, I am going nowhere with it. This war is constantly on my mind, and I find I spend most of my time joining up with other women in such tasks as rolling bandages, making cloth for uniforms, writing letters to soldiers in the field, and raising money for the war effort. I'm even making occasional visits to the recruit camp for the Kansas Fourteenth regiment here in Lawrence to see if I could be of any help with supplies or uniforms. No, Mary, I am not suffering from delirium…I'm beginning to enjoy doing these little things. Let someone else be a hero for a change.

Your loving friend,

Jessica Radford

Chapter 20

August 10
Lawrence, Kansas

If only the walls of this place could listen, James Lane thought as he surveyed the bar at the Eldridge Hotel, what secrets would they hear? A father who just learned his boy's body was found at Gettysburg? A Redleg who turned tail and became a bushwhacker? A man who struggled with his conscience, having just robbed an elderly couple of all their possessions? A lot of deals were made here, a lot of plans sown—some, Lane could only guess, that were quite sinister. A number of folks even regarded the Eldridge Hotel as the citadel for any major undertaking in the state of Kansas.

He sat where he felt safest—at a corner table, his back against the wall, where he could observe anyone coming toward him without worrying about anyone attacking him from the rear. Some of his friends thought he was paranoid, the way he always anticipated being attacked. Tonight, Lane just wanted to relax with a beer before meeting with Captain Banks upstairs. As provost marshal of Kansas, Banks had in his office at the Eldridge the draft enrollment lists for the various Kansas regiments. There were some men in Douglas county who had managed to avoid the draft, and Lane wanted to check those lists with him carefully.

Talk, laughter, and occasional outbursts of surprise buzzed all about him at the various tables as well as from the men seated at the bar. Lane couldn't pick up any useful threads of conversation. People seemed too eerily complacent tonight, with no concerns or fears being expressed over the scanty protection provided for this town, and it bothered him.

Lane noticed a young man in his twenties, sporting a small mustache and neatly trimmed short beard staring at him. The man smiled and jaunted over to Lane, as if making eye contact was an invitation to approach him. "Mr. Lane?" the man said. "Mind if I join you?"

"Not at all," Lane said, moving his beer closer to him. "I don't believe we've met."

The man extended his hand. "Lance Taylor, sir. Pleased to make your acquaintance."

"What can I do for you, Mr. Taylor?"

"Well, Senator, I'm a horse trader who's just moved to Lawrence. I heard about your reputation and wanted to meet you."

"I hope you only heard good things about me," Lane remarked, after taking a sip of beer.

Taylor leaned on the table with both elbows and his eyes darted about as if he were nervous. "I don't know if they're all good things, Senator. I hear talk about how you and your troops burned the town of Osceola and took many wagonloads of spoils with you."

"I resent the implication that I'm a thief," Lane said, his voice rising. "Sympathizers for the border ruffians had to be punished. They're evil, just like those Missouri demons who steal our freed slaves and plunder and kill our citizens."

Taylor took his hat off and fingered its brim. "I mean no such implication, Senator," Taylor said, his voice mellowing. "I'm a free soiler myself and always have been. All I want to do is provide for my family, and so I most humbly ask for your assistance."

Lane relaxed. "I apologize for appearing to be annoyed, but I hope you can understand my station. I'm not particularly well-liked by some folks. How can I be of help?"

Taylor explained that he wanted to know more about the town—who their more prominent citizens were and what they were like. As Lane rattled off a few names, Taylor began asking more specific questions about them: "Wasn't he a Jayhawker at one time?" ..."Whereabouts does he live?"..."Does he travel to Missouri often?"....

Lane glared at him with suspicion after answering some of them. "I don't understand what such information has to do with your establishing your services for the buying, selling, and caring of horses, Mr. Taylor."

Taylor grinned. "I just want to know what sort of neighbors I'm gonna have. That's all." He stroked his chin as if another thought hit him. "I understand you don't have a tele-graph office yet. That true?"

"Unfortunately, it's true. And no bridge and no railroad. We're quite isolated out here."

"Well," Taylor added, "at least you have some protection with a garrison, a recruit camp, and an armory."

"Surely you're joking, Mr. Taylor. A handful of soldiers across the river, a small camp of new recruits, and an armory where citizens are required to turn in their weapons—none of this gives me a great deal of comfort."

"I suppose you're right," Taylor answered, with a circum-spect edge to his voice.

Mid-August
Johnson Country, Missouri

Sam Toby rode his horse as hard as he could, but Kate Clarke King outdistanced him. She waited for him by the creek bed, rearing her horse in victory.

"Where the devil did yah learn to ride like that?" Sam asked, dismounting. "I thought fer sure yah'd stop when yah came to that fence back there, but 'stead you jumped it."

"My pa told me I could ride a horse like I was born in the saddle." She dismounted and led her steed toward Sam. "I suspect some folks are just naturally good with horses."

Sam tied up his mount to an oak tree and waited until Kate did the same. "Did Bill say when he'd be back tonight?"

"Sometime before sunset," she said, her eyes surveying the farmland surrounding them. "Bill and I used to ride a lot to-gether."

He reached for her hand. "Do yah think he suspects any-thing?" Sam Toby asked. "I mean he'd kill me right quick if he knew."

"Don't worry about it none. I don't think he knows." She touched her brown hair, rolled into a chignon. "I've been en-joying our time alone, Sam. She drew her face closer to his and kissed him. "I sure wish my husband was as attentive to me as you."

"Maybe," he said, gripping her shoulders firmly yet gently, "yah'n I could do more than just talk'n kiss. Yah know what I mean?"

She pushed him away gently and smiled. "I do not wish to be unfaithful to him. "But I appreciate all your attention, Sam. Those Morning Glories you gave me yesterday were pretty."

"What 'bout that sapphire ring I gave yah last week? Got it from one of the raids. Yah like that too?"

"Yeah, I sure do. I like gettin' gifts. Shows me you care."

She took his hand and walked with him along the creek bed. The sky was pale blue and cloudless. Somewhere beyond the distant hills, Quantrill's men were probably preparing breakfast. Sam felt fortunate that among all the other men Kate could have befriended, she had chosen him. Maybe the others were just cowards, afraid of messin' with Quantrill's lady.

She stopped and turned towards him. "I wish Bill was the same like he was when we first met. He used to give me gifts too. We'd go on long rides, and we'd talk a lot. But things are different now."

"How're they different?"

"Right now, he's got his mind too chock full of killin' to be thinkin' 'bout me. Don't rightly know if it was that Kansas City jail collapse or rumors about General Ewing's plan to order rebel sympathizers out of Jackson county that did it for Bill, but I never seen him so damn angry before."

"Kate, yah think maybe the Feds fixed it so that the Longhorn Tavern would fall and kill them there lady prisoners?"

She nodded. "I have no doubt about it. You should've seen Bill Anderson. He grieved something severe when he heard his sister Josephine was killed." She closed her eyes for a moment. "The girl was only a year younger than me'n she's dead." Her face flushed as the heat of her resentment erupted. "Those bastards! They killed John McCorkle's sister and Cole's cousin Armenia. Accident, they say? Was no accident! Those blood-thirsty Yankees don't mind killin' women."

A moment of silence passed between them. Sam placed his hand on the revolver in his belt. "Kate, I got no use for those puke scum Yankees mahself," he growled. "I'd kill every one if I had the chance."

"You might get your chance sooner than you think," she said.

Sam stared at her, frowning. "What d'ya mean?"

"You know that meeting he's plannin' to have this Wednesday with Captain Gregg and the others under his command?"

"Yeah. What about it?"

"Well, they're gonna vote on whether or not to attack."

"Attack? Where?"

"Lawrence."

Lawrence, Kansas

After spending the last two days at his cabin near the Delaware Reservation across the Kansas River, Matt Lightfoot took the ferry across to pay Jessica a surprise visit. He got to her home on Indiana Street by noon, intending to invite her to have lunch with him. He hesitated as he came within sight of her white buttonbush shrubs and a giant oak overlooking her front yard. What would he say to her? That they both made mistakes in the heat of battle—he with her friend Mary and she with John Howell? That he was a fool in allowing his military rank to overcome his real ambition: to preach and minister?

Jessica opened the door after he knocked the second time. Her blond hair was cut short, and her face, though pleasant, took on a more serious tone...maybe, he suspected, because any fanciful ideas she had before were replaced by the cruel realities of war.

"Why, Matt! What brings you here?"

He couldn't tell if she seemed more annoyed than surprised. She wasn't smiling, but perhaps she had a lot on her mind at the moment. "I'm back for good, Jessica. I'm fixin' to do some preaching for the Lord."

She gripped the edge of the door firmly, as if intending to prevent him from opening it wider. "I thought that's what you were going to do for the soldiers. Or did you become more soldier than preacher?"

292

Matt's heart sank because he knew she was right. "I'm terribly sorry for the things I've done and the way I've acted. I do hope that you and I can patch things up."

Footsteps and a feminine voice came from within the house. "Who's that, Jessica?" the voice asked. Penelope appeared at the door and broke out into a big smile when she saw him. "Why, Matthew Lightfoot! How good to see you again. Jessica, why don't you let the man in?"

Jessica frowned at the suggestion, but she let him enter the parlor. "Would you care for some tea?" she offered.

"No thank you, Miss Radford," Matt said, feeling awkward at the sight of two pretty ladies staring at him like this. "I don't intend to stay long."

"Please sit," Penelope insisted, pointing to a sofa. "I was about to join my niece here for lunch and to scold her for not telling me earlier about Nellie."

"Nellie?" Matt asked. "I thought she was dead. Has she been found?"

With great hesitation in her voice, Jessica explained that she learned Nellie was still alive and living in Chattanooga.

"Why, that's wonderful." Matt said. "And just how did you manage to learn that?"

"Didn't Jessica tell you?" Penelope said, her voice rising happily. "Why this is a most fascinating story. It seems that she—"

"Penelope!" Jessica said with an edge in her voice. "I don't wish to bore Reverend Lightfoot with those details."

Penelope appeared to be offended by Jessica's sudden outburst as she turned to her niece. "Excuse me, Jessica, but I naturally assumed that you and Matthew were—ah—"

"Friends," Jessica interjected. "We're just good friends, right Reverend Lightfoot?"

"Yes, of course. Good friends." He had thought about asking her out for lunch today, but since that was out of the question, he remembered the concert he had been thinking of attending. "Jessica, I know you happen to enjoy good music. The Lawrence City Band is making its first appearance Thursday evening at the riverfront next to the ferry. Would you care to join me?"

Jessica appeared to be mulling it over, but Penelope rose to the occasion. "Go ahead, Jessica. It'd be fun. As you know, Otto's taking me as well. We could go as a foursome."

"But what about the children? I was going to watch them while you and Otto went yourselves."

"I've changed my mind," Penelope said, smiling, "we'll go as a six-some then. We'll take Emma and Mitzi with us."

"Well, I guess that'll be fine then," Jessica said, forcing a smile in return.

"I'll pick you up here at seven," Matt offered. "I think the City Band is expecting a good turnout."

Matt excused himself, kissing the hand of each lady with the flourish of a gentleman, saying he had other matters to attend. As he walked down New Hampshire Street toward the river, he realized it might take a while to win Jessica's affection. She must think him a fool for the way he treated her when he thought she was Walter Brontë, constantly reminding her about military regulations.

After entering the dining room at the City Hotel, which Matt still thought of as the Whitney House, he ordered a moderate lunch of pork sausages, potatoes, peas, and a glass of ale. War, he thought, does strange things to people. Men who were once teachers and lawyers were suddenly transformed into officers who risked the lives of others in order to gain a small parcel of land for the Union or Confederate side.

He looked about in the dining room and spotted Nathan Stone, a blue-eyed, gray-haired man in his sixties, sitting at a table nearby and working on a set of figures in a ledger. Matt questioned Stone's judgment of character by the way Stone befriended a man named Charlie Hart a few short years ago. By now, everyone knew Charlie Hart had been none other than William Quantrill, the man whose gang pillaged farmhouses and small towns throughout eastern Kansas. Yet, Nathan and his wife Laura were such a good-natured, happy couple, Matt tried to convince himself that the Stones simply didn't know any better when it came to choosing friends.

"You're working much too hard, Nathan," Matt said to him from across the table. "You need to hire someone else to do the books. You ought to be out relaxing."

"I find *this* relaxing," Nathan said, flashing a grin back at him. "Did you hear my daughter Lydia's engaged?"

"Really?"

"Yeah, to some fella from up north. He bought her a nice silver ring, but Lydia still wears the diamond ring Mr. Hart gave her some time ago."

Matt bristled at the mere mention of Quantrill's alias. "Why in blazes would he have given her a ring?"

Nathan shrugged. "Guess he just wanted to show his appreciation for her concern. She nursed him back to health when he was sick here at the hotel. Nice man, that Charlie Hart."

Matt couldn't stomach this discussion any longer. He got up, paid his tab, and departed. Since he wasn't in a hurry to take the ferry back to the reservation, he decided to walk along Massachusetts Street and browse. It was by chance that he happened upon a store called "New Necessities," and he walked in, curious at the wide array of merchandise displayed in the window.

"Well, hello again," a cheery voice called out to him from behind the counter. It was Penelope, who was stacking some merchandise behind the counter. "I wish you would have stayed at Jessica's for lunch. She makes the most incredible chicken sandwich."

"Maybe next time," Matt said. "By the way, I didn't realize this was the store you and Otto ran. I ought to stroll down Massachusetts more often."

"Yes, you really ought to." Penelope came out from behind the counter. "Reverend Lightfoot, I don't know what's become of Jessica with her being so upset. It's not like her."

"She's been through a lot these past several months."

"Yes, she has. But I'm especially happy to hear that Nellie's alive and well. Tinker was overjoyed when Jessica gave him Nellie's medallion and told him the young lady was alive."

"Tinker?" He instantly recalled the conversation he had with Colonel James Martin on the day he officially left his regiment....

"Lightfoot," the colonel had said, "I know all about the fact that you used to own a slave named Tinker. I know you had given him his freedom and that you befriended him when he enlisted in the service."

"Yes sir. He's a good man, sir."

"He *was* a good man, Lightfoot. He's a deserter, and he must be brought to justice. If you find Tinker when you return to Lawrence, it is your sworn duty to this army to report him to us. Do you understand?"

Matt looked away, not wanting to deal with his personal struggle between military justice and Tinker's freedom.

"Do you understand?" the colonel repeated, raising his voice this time.

"Yes, sir. I understand."

"Reverend Lightfoot," Penelope said, with a puzzled look on her face, "you haven't heard a thing I asked, have you?"

"I'm sorry, ma'am. I was lost in thought."

"I said that Tinker's here, in the back room of this store. He made his home here because he's afraid of getting caught as a deserter."

"Tinker's here? In the back room of your store?" The colonel's words blared in his head: *He's a deserter, and he must be brought to justice.*

"Yes, of course," she said, frowning. "You seem upset. Anything wrong?"

Matt bit his lip. "No, nothing wrong," he answered, racing to the back door behind the counter. He swung open the door.

Gone. Tinker was gone. The back door leading to the rear exit of the building was ajar.

Tinker darted like a shot across the open field behind the store as soon as he heard Matt express surprise at his being there. He remembered how Lieutenant Lightfoot had reeled Ishmael back in when that slave was trying to escape. Ishmael might have gotten his freedom instead of being tried and hung had it not been for Matt's insistence on "following procedure."

Tinker, his breathing now getting heavy, had meant to turn left once he got to Vermont Street and head toward Penelope's obscure cellar. But he made the mistake of turning right instead—toward Pinckney Street. His foot got caught in a honeysuckle shrub fronting a garden, and he fell, face forward, cursing at himself. After untangling his foot, he noticed Matt closing in on him. Pushing himself up, he ran again, his heart pumping, sweat gripping his arms and legs like maggots.

He raced westward on Pinckney Street, turning behind only to see Matt gaining on him. "Stop!" Matt yelled. "I want to talk to you, Tinker!"

No way yuh is goin'tah just talk to me, Tinker thought. Yuh wanna get me back in prison or hung. No suh. I sooner be dead now. *Slave they be. Set them free. Slave they be. Set them free.*

The ravine was in sight and Tinker veered off to the right as soon as he passed Kentucky Street and headed straight for it. He thought quickly, trying to decide whether to climb one of the cottonwood trees and hide in the branches or dive into the thick foliage near the creek. He chose the latter and lay on his side, surrounded by weeds, tall grass, and shrubbery. His tears flowed freely as he thought about the fate of Lazarus and Ishmael, two people in his life he had felt close to and who were now gone. He touched Nellie's large medallion hanging from a chain on his neck. *Sissy, if yah have the Lawd's ear, please ask Him to help me. I don' want my mastah tah find me. I wants to be free. I can't go back to jail. Please help me, Sissy!"*

"There you are!" Matt's voice thundered above him. "C'mon, Tinker, get up."

"I can't!" Tinker howled, his chest heaving with grief. "I can't go back to prison. I rather you just kill me, mastah!"

Matt crouched down next to him, smiling. "You keep calling me 'master.' I'm not your master. I set you free, Tinker. I never should have owned you as a slave. I realize that now."

"But I don' be free no more."

"Why?"

"Because you take me in. I no longer free. Never will be."

Matt sat down and clipped off a cattail with his fingers. "You see this here plant, Tinker?" he asked, showing it to him.

Tinker, puzzled, sat up, facing him. "Yeah, I do."

"Well," Matt said, "it grows tall and healthy only when it's near water but would die in an arid climate. It's only free when near water. If I took you in, you'd surely die, maybe not

297

at the end of a rope but inside. You'd die inside, Tinker. And I'd die inside, too, because I would have killed your dream of freedom."

Tinker was stunned. "You not take me in, mastah—I mean, Mr. Lightfoot?"

Matt inhaled deeply. "No, I can't. That's why I was racing to catch up to you. I wanted to ask you to trust me." As he sat, he slowly brought knees up and gripped his legs. His eyes were looking not at Tinker, but beyond him, way beyond him, somewhere in the past. "My father taught me all about discipline and bravery, but it was my mother who taught me something better—tenderness and compassion. I used to think anyone showing tenderness and compassion was a weakling. But after watching Miss Delaney conduct herself so nobly as a nurse, I realize how powerful those qualities are."

"I don' understand, suh. What are yuh sayin'?"

"I'm saying that discipline has its place, Tinker, but sometimes mercy has to take over. I thought it was a generous thing I once did, giving you your freedom. But I had no right to 'give' it to you. Freedom should have been yours all along. And since I've given you what you should have had anyway, who am I to take it away by turning you in?" He paused a moment, a touch of sadness sparkling in his eyes. "I think it's time now that you rejoice in your freedom, Tinker."

Chapter 21

August 19
Columbus, Missouri

The two men rode on horseback on the small hill, surveying a large group of men assembled near the Blackwater River below. One of them was a young man in his twenties with soft blue eyes and the meek, fresh look of a student. "Hear that?" the young man asked, looking up into the branches of a peach tree nearby. "That's a goldfinch. I can tell by the way it sings something like *swe-si-iee* between chirps. Wonder what sound it'd make if you pulled off its wings. I always wanted to do that."

"We got more important things right now, Bill," William Gregg growled. "We've got almost 300 men we've got to organize. They're getting restless, just waitin' for us."

"You're right," William Quantrill said to his second-in-command. "Where's Fletch?"

"Fletch Taylor? He's a-comin.'" Gregg waved on a young man trotting toward them on a tan-colored mare. "Make haste, Fletch!"

Fletch greeted Quantrill and Gregg with a tip of his hat and dismounted. "Good news, colonel," he said, addressing Quantrill. "I've been in Lawrence three weeks, and I've got to tell you we're in excellent position."

"How's that?" Quantrill asked.

"They're like chickens in a coop, ready for slaughter. I even talked to the man himself, James Lane, and he admitted Lawrence is virtually defenseless. Looks like the mayor's gonna be there tomorrow, as well as Lane, Fisher, and most of the men you've got on your death list."

"That's good," Gregg said. "What about the town itself?"

"They rebuilt the place since the raid seven years ago. Got a bigger, nicer Eldridge Hotel, wide, clean streets lined with trees, a lot of shops, and neat and comfortable houses."

"Anything else?" Quantrill asked.

"I rode across Lawrence many times, and I think the best way to attack it is from the large park south of town, where there aren't many houses. We can branch off from there and proceed north. I'm thinkin' if we take the major streets, like Vermont, Massachusetts, and New Hampshire, we can proceed straight to the river and plunder and burn as we go. But we need to do this at the crack of dawn before the folks get up."

Quantrill thanked Fletch for his services and trotted with Gregg down to the throng of men at the riverfront. "We'll assemble into four companies," Quantrill told Gregg. "I'm thinking maybe we'll have Todd, Anderson, Yeager, and Cole take charge."

"I wish we could kill Ewing for issuing those general orders yesterday," Gregg said. "I can't believe the Union's just gonna clear out all them folks living near the western border of Missouri. I'd hang him personally if I had the chance."

Quantrill smiled, just as he always did when he pronounced a death sentence. "The man I'm gonna personally hang is that butcher, James Lane. He'll pay for what he did to Osceola. I swear, he'll pay!"

Late afternoon
August 20
Lawrence, Kansas

"I don't understand why you still want to hide in that cellar," Penelope told Tinker as she was closing up her store. "Matt already told you he was trying to work something out about getting you back into military service. He's thinking about claiming you were caught by the rebels and sent to a Confederate prison camp but escaped. Mary and Jessica will even back him up on that story."

"Yah don' understand," Tinker explained, putting a supply of food into his haversack, "White men gonna come here from Missourah to kill us. I only feel safe in the cellar."

"Well, I can't stop you from thinking that way, Tinker. But it's foolish you livin' like this. You deserve better."

Penelope felt like sharing with him what Jessica had told her about her vision of an angel called Sissy. Maybe Jessica

300

was hallucinating at the time, but the words this so-called angel said to her were comforting: "Love is stronger than fear."

But, Penelope thought, Tinker lived with fear all his life. Maybe for him, love was actually stranger, not stronger, than fear.

5:30 PM
Aubrey, Kansas

"What did you say, lieutenant?" Captain Joshua Pike asked, looking up from his cluttered desk.

"I said, sir, that they're out there and fully armed."

"You sure they're Quantrill's men?" Pike asked, frowning, his eyes wide in disbelief.

"I'm sure. Looks like more than four hundred of them. About a hundred men under Colonel Holt's command may have joined up with them, sir."

Pike drummed his fingers on his desk as he gave the lieutenant a frigid stare. "If I heard you correctly, lieutenant, Quantrill's men are camped on Grand River, about ten miles from the Kansas line."

"Yes sir. Sir, may I make a comment?"

"What is it?"

"Sir, there're a lot of reasons why Quantrill would want to target Lawrence. I believe a good preventative measure would be to warn the town of his presence."

Captain Joshua Pike put a finger to his chin. He could indeed send a courier to Lawrence, but what if that wasn't Quantrill's target? Besides, it'd make more sense to engage Quantrill here. Of course, he'd need reinforcements to do that, reinforcements General Ewing could well provide.

"Sir?" the lieutenant said, drawing the captain's attention.

"That'll be all," Pike said, dismissing him with a salute. After the officer left, Pike sent for a courier, instructing him to report this news to General Ewing in Kansas City. He went to his wall map and put one finger on Quantrill's position and another on Lawrence, Kansas. No, that'd be foolish, he thought. Quantrill wouldn't ride forty miles in utter darkness, risking observation from other patrols, just to attack a town like Lawrence. It just wasn't likely.

Lawrence, Kansas

As Otto brushed Mitzi's hair, he thought about his daughter's interesting question: "Why won't the Yankees let Miss Radford fight like a soldier?" He had no ready answer for Mitzi, other than the fact there was an unnecessary gulf between men and women, just as there was an unnecessary gulf between white and colored people. What was it Walt Whitman had written in *Leaves of Grass?*—

> *"I am the poet of the woman the same as the man,*
> *And I say it is as great to be a woman as to be a man,*
> *And I say there is nothing greater than the mother of*
> *men."*

"It's a good question," Otto told his eight-year-old as she sat on his lap, "and I think you ought to ask Miss Radford that next time you see her."

Mitzi looked up at him, her eyes sparkling with enthusiasm. "Is Miss Radford coming with us to the City Band concert?"

"She and Mr. Lightfoot are going to meet us there." He gently removed her from his lap. "Now run along and have your mother put a ribbon in your hair. And tell her how pretty you look."

Mitzi giggled as she ran to the living room.

"I've got the reddest roses for the nicest lady," Matt said, as she opened her door. Jessica took the roses and smelled their sweet fragrance. "Why, thank you, Matt."

"I've got something else for you as well," he added, presenting her with a red garnet brooch. "This would look wonderful on your dress."

"Oh Matt," she said, giving him a hug. "You need not have done this."

"But I wanted to." He pinned the brooch to her dress. "There, you look marvelous."

302

"So do you," she said, gazing at him, dressed in a butter-nut-colored jacket, boiled shirt, dark brown cravat, black velvet waistcoat, and black bowler. "You resemble a wealthy Southern plantation owner," she remarked, stifling a laugh. "Hope no one thinks you're a rebel and takes a shot at you."

"Not in Lawrence. Everyone's too tolerant over here." He touched the lapel of his jacket. "Got this outfit from a clothier in Tennessee while I was there. He didn't carry anything in Yankee blue colors."

"Well, *I* like it." She disappeared for a moment and returned with a basket filled with cheese, crackers, wine, and wine glasses. "In case we want to dine under the stars tonight."

"And I have two blankets in my chaise for us to sit on. So I guess we're all set."

It was a short ride, but Jessica broke the silence to tell him she appreciated what he had done for Tinker. "I'm sure it must have been difficult for you," she said.

"Yes, but now that I have, I feel much better about myself. I'm sorry I gave Walt Brontë such a difficult time."

"Mr. Brontë has forgiven you," she said, smiling as he drove up to the livery stable on Winthrop Street.

"But the real question is," he said, "have *you* forgiven me?"

She nodded. "I owe you an apology as well. I shouldn't have been upset when you asked me how I knew Nellie was alive and living in Chattanooga. I didn't want to let you know Mary had conspired with me on a certain matter."

Matt smiled. "You are referring to your masquerade as a male soldier, no doubt."

Jessica nodded. She had already decided she wouldn't tell him how she and Mary conspired to save a rebel soldier from prison. At least not until Mary returned home from the war.

"Also, Matt, I didn't want you to lecture me on the horrible thing I almost did."

Matt blinked with surprise. "What horrible thing?"

The memory of that ghastly afternoon burst like a shell in her mind....

"You asked me once what I'll do to you," she had said to the wounded man. "I'll tell you what I'm gonna do to you. I'm gonna tie you up, and then I'm gonna slice you like cheese, one piece at a time. You're gonna suffer before you die, you swine!"

Jessica's stomach churned as she told him how she had almost murdered the wrong man... how the man she might have killed, Roger Toby, had actually saved Nellie from harm. "Then I saw her," she said, her voice quaking. "I saw Sissy, Nellie's Sissy, or—" She stopped, pursing her lips, the shock of that day coming alive. "—or maybe I didn't," she said, exhaling. "But this girl or angel that I saw thank God, she prevented me from making a horrible mistake."

"Have you taken ill, Jessica?"

"No." She looked at him for a moment. "I'm sorry. It's—it's hard for me to talk about this." She thought about the Colt .31 revolver she now carried in her dress pocket. What was the point of her promise to Uncle Adam that she'd always have it with her? She didn't carry that anger with her anymore—or did she? She hoped never to find out.

A few minutes drifted by before Matt asked her if Roger knew where his brother Sam was.

"He has no idea." She felt like adding that she didn't care either. After all, didn't she tell herself she never wanted to see Sam Toby again?

Jessica offered Matt her hand as they walked in silence down Massachusetts Street, following clusters of other people moving in the same direction—toward the City Band concert. When they reached Pinckney Street, Matt stopped. He held her gently by the shoulders and looked deep into her eyes. "Jessica, at the funeral, when I sang 'Amazing Grace,' you swore you'd send Sam Toby straight to hell for what he did."

Jessica nodded. The pain was still there, even after all this time. "Are you asking me if I feel the same way about him to-day?"

Matt studied her but said nothing.

Jessica looked away. The memory refused to leave. Pa's words of revenge still hung in the air...

"Dreams don't mean nothin'. Besides, if them rats are loose in this area, someone is bound to catch 'em. Everyone here hates them rebels. I'd string 'em up myself if I caught 'em."

Jessica looked up at Matt." I honestly don't know," she answered quietly.

August 20
Miami County, Kansas

"We got 'bout half an hour for waterin' the horses," Sam Toby told Kate King while the two of them strolled in the darkness, out of sight from the more than 400 men camped out near a small river inside the Kansas border. "It'd be just enough time for yah'n me to have some fun. Lots o'places to hide. No one would see us."

"No, Sam. I couldn't deceive my husband like that. I think maybe it's best that you and I—"

Clutching her, Sam kissed her hard on the lips. She fought for a moment but soon surrendered to him. As he withdrew his lips from her, he thought he heard a twig snap. His heart jumped. Looking around, he saw nothing. Must have been his imagination. He moved his hands to her waist and pulled her closer.

She'd be such a nice lady to make love to, he thought. Quantrill was foolish to ignore his own lady like that. All she wants is fer someone to love her, to hold her, to kiss her. Quantrill had to be crazy lookin' for something when he had it all right here.

Lawrence, Kansas

There were at least two hundred people on the lawn, clapping after the City Band finished its rendition of "Hail Columbia." Not even the slightest breeze could be felt in the night air. Pinpricks of white stars filled the sky, and a yellow moon hung like a huge lamp. Mitzi and Emma lay on a blanket gazing at the sky, while Otto and Penelope sat behind them. Penelope's eyes were closed as she listened to the City Band playing "Home Sweet Home." She used to sing this when she lived in Toledo with George, miserable at the choice she had made for a husband:

'Mid pleasures and palaces though I may roam,
Be it ever so humble, there's no place like home;
A charm from the sky seems to hallow us there,

Which, seek though the world, is ne'er with me elsewhere.

Jessica, too, closed her eyes as the band played "Home Sweet Home." It was the same song she had heard being played by opposing armies prior to engaging in battle at Shelbyville, Tennessee. A musician from her regiment, a gifted colored man playing a saxhorn brass instrument, took up the refrain while the rest of the band played it. The same melody was taken up by the Confederate band only a mile or two away, as both sides of the conflict shared a common emotion. Maybe music, she thought, not guns, was the way to achieve peace among brothers.

Jessica moaned with pleasure when Matt drew her to him.. She knew it wasn't proper for a woman to unbutton the front of her dress, unfasten her bodice, and allow a man's hand to slip inside, under her chemise. But she liked the gentle way he fondled her bosom. "It's been a long time since I let a man do this," she cooed as she lay next to him on a blanket, far away from the rest of the crowd enjoying the concert.

"I've always been tremendously fond of you," Matt whispered, as he explored her breast. "Even when I was alone with Mary, I thought about you. But I didn't think you cared for me, ever since you and Mr. Howell—"

"Shhh," she interrupted in a soft voice. "I'll promise to forget Mr. Howell if you promise to forget Miss Delaney."

"Agreed."

Jessica missed Mary Delaney. How could her friend stomach all that misery? She hoped Mary would return to Lawrence—as she promised in her letter—after the expected battle in Chattanooga.

While Jessica fingered the brooch Matt had given her, the band began playing "Battle Hymn of the Republic." Things had changed so much so fast since college, she thought. Coming back home had seemed so strange….

"How's Ma?" she had asked Pa on the way back to the farm.

"Oh fine, and fit as a fiddle. She's helpin' out trying to raise money for getting uniforms and supplies and such. She's also

doin' all she can for her church, with bake sales and helpin' out in the sacristy and things like that."

"I assumed both you and Mom would be here today."

"Foolish woman," Pa had grunted. "She plumb thinks she'll go to hell if she misses Sunday Mass. That's why she ain't here."

Jessica began to sob. Matt placed his free hand on her arm. "What's wrong?"

"Just sad, that's all." But the tears wouldn't stop, and Matt offered her his handkerchief.

"I don't want to go back to my empty house tonight," Jessica said, drying her eyes. "I'd just lie in bed with a lot of pain in my heart. I'd rather spend the night with you, under the stars, after the concert is over."

Matt thought a moment. "There's a large grassy field by the river, near the Waverly house. "I saw some boulders there that would make a great shelter and give us some privacy—if you wouldn't be cold, that is."

She pressed his hand against her breast. "I won't be cold tonight. Especially with you by my side."

Spring Hill, Kansas

William Quantrill shook his head with disbelief after Gregg gave him his scouting report. "It's amazing," Quantrill said, "with all those Federal troops guarding the border, none of them seemed the least bit suspicious about all my men being here. I'm especially surprised at Captain Pike."

"Y'mean when he and his hundred men at Aubrey just watched us pass by?

"Yeah. No wonder the Yankees are losin' this war."

Quantrill peered into the semi-darkness and spotted Spring Hill in the distance. He could easily overrun that town, plunder it, and burn it to the ground. But the big prize was Lawrence, he thought. Why risk alerting the few Union soldiers who might be present at Spring Hill?

"Luck's been with us so far," Quantrill told him. "Except for Colonel Sims not being in Squiresville tonight."

"You got a pretty long death list, Bill," Gregg said. "We're doing pretty damn good if Sims is the only one that got away."

"None of the rest on my list are gonna get away," Quantrill added with a deadly smile on his thin lips.

11:00 PM
Lawrence, Kansas

"They're both sound asleep," Penelope whispered to Otto after tucking Emma and Mitzi into their cots in the back of their store. "It didn't make sense taking them all the way home tonight."

Otto shook his head as he watched Mitzi lying on her side, with a protective arm over Emma. "Why do children look like little angels when they sleep?"

Penelope grinned. "That's so we can tolerate them when they're awake. C'mon, you and I can sleep in the store and leave the children in the back room. I've got a lot of blankets. We can spread them on the floor and sleep."

After setting up their sleeping accommodations on the floor in front of the cash register, Otto began to undress his wife.

"Just what do you think you're doing, Mr. Heller?" she teased as he unbuttoned her dress.

"I couldn't wait until they were asleep so you and I could—"

"Could what?" She got the message after she noticed the playful twinkle in his eyes. "Why, you naughty man!"

A half hour later, working up to a volcanic state of excitement, he finally exploded inside of her. "Oh, darling," he gasped, "it's been a long time, hasn't it?"

"Yes," she said, moaning with pleasure. "But it's been worth the wait." She had never felt such ecstasy before with George Radford.

Matt poured the rest of the wine into Jessica's glass and returned the bottle to the basket. She could tell he was upset with himself as he sat facing away from her on the blanket and said nothing.

Over an hour ago, the City Band's first performance had concluded. Everyone else had left, but she and Matt remained behind, moving to the shelter afforded by the huge boulders near the Waverly house, away from prying eyes. Jessica lay on her back, naked from the waist down, waiting for Matt to enter her, telling herself she no longer wanted to save herself for marriage. But it was Matt who couldn't consummate the affair.

They now sat on a blanket, she in her chemise and he in his trousers, staring at the mirror-like, flat and motionless Kansas River. Cottonwood trees across the other side made an interesting pattern against the yellow moon. A campfire from the Delaware reservation still glimmered in the distance. A cricket chirped.

"I'm sorry," Matt finally said, disappointment filtering through his voice. "I wanted you so much tonight, Jessica."

She put her arm around his waist. "I know you did, Matt. I understand."

He turned to her, looking first into her eyes and then gazing out into the distance. "It could be God's way of telling me I'm a minister and what I'm doing is wrong. But how could it be wrong for me to want you when I truly love you?"

"Oh, Matt," she said, kissing him.

"Maybe it's a blessing in disguise. I've always dreamed about marrying a virgin. And if I were to marry a virgin, it would certainly be you."

Jessica laughed as she took his hand and pressed it against her breast. "Even a flat-chested woman like me?"

Matt's face remained serious. "I think I've just proposed marriage to you, Jessica. Maybe I should exchange that brooch of yours for an engagement ring."

She turned her attention to the river. Everything was happening too fast.. She was just getting to know the real Matt Lightfoot—a man who had always been a mystery to her...a former slave owner...a devoted minister...a man who wanted to remember his Cherokee roots...a lieutenant who followed orders...a man who decided to follow his heart and take mercy on Tinker...and a man of passion.

"Darling, you've got to give me more time," she said, kissing his hand.

Matt nodded, his lips forming a straight line as he looked at the river. "My father used to say, 'Even if you do not wait for tomorrow, tomorrow will still come and waiting will not make it come any faster.'" His face brightened into a smile. "Jessica, you're worth waiting for—no matter how many tomorrows there are."

August 21
12:10 AM
Kansas City, Missouri

The courier sent by Captain Pike thanked Pelathé again for accompanying him on his long trip to General Thomas Ewing's office. "I don't know these trails as well as you," he said, "so I am indebted to your service."

The tall Shawnee Indian bowed in appreciation. "May I be of further assistance?"

"I'm not sure," he told Pelathé, "so perhaps you can accompany me when I give my report to General Ewing."

Pelathé followed the courier to a well-furnished office, replete with two walls of bookcases filled with binders containing military documents, books on war strategy, civil codes, and Indian territory charts and maps, as well as several different newspapers and journals. General Ewing, with a hint of annoyance on his face, tapped his fingers on the desk as the courier promptly recited what he knew about the Quantrill sighting.

"Perhaps Quantrill is going on one of his many raids across the border," the general said, looking disinterested and annoyed.

"Excuse me, General Ewing," another man standing near the doorway interrupted, "but it definitely appears that Quantrill is headed for Lawrence."

The general pointed toward the man by the door. "Gentlemen," Ewing said, "this here is Theodore Bartles. As a scout and a Redleg, he probably knows more about Quantrill and his band than anyone else." Ewing returned his attention to Bartles. "So why are you so sure you know where he's headed?"

Bartles went to great lengths to describe the hatred Quantrill and his band had for the people of Lawrence. "Events," he went on, "such as Sheriff Walker's expulsion of Quantrill from Lawrence in 1860, the Kansas City jail collapse, and your Order Number 10, driving guerilla supporters out of their homes,

310

have probably pushed him over the edge." Bartles paused and took a couple of steps toward the courier. "I assume that Lawrence has been warned of an imminent attack."

"No, it hasn't," the courier answered.

"I can't believe it!" Bartles screamed. "What insanity!" He hurried out of the general's office while the courier remained, awaiting any reply Ewing might want him to deliver to Colonel Pike.

Pelathé took a quick glance at the clock and raced after Bartles. "What can we do at this late hour? Can you beat Quantrill there?"

"I don't know," Bartles snapped. "I just don't damn know! If I've got to travel north of the Kansas River to avoid border ruffians, I'll never make it."

Pelathé thought quickly. "I know these westward trails very well. Give me a horse, and I'll do it."

Bartles studied him for a second. "Maybe you can. C'mon with me. I'll let you use my mare."

3:15 AM
One mile west of Hesper, Kansas

Joseph Stone came out in his nightshirt when George Todd and several others with the Quantrill gang forced their way into his house. Stone's face was as white as his thinning hair, and his voice shook as he demanded to know the reason for the intrusion.

Todd glanced at his death list. "Are you Joseph Stone?"

The old man's eyes darted from Todd to the others in the room. "N-n-no," he stammered.

A bedroom window creaked open, and two of Quantrill's men rushed into the room. "Gone!" one of them explained. "I bet it was the Stone's boy."

"Look," Todd said, his voice getting raspy, "I want you to be honest with me. If you tell me you're Joseph Stone, I'll let you go. Otherwise, I'm gonna kill you right here."

The old man wrung his hairless arms and looked back at Todd with pleading eyes. "My name's Joseph Stone."

Todd reached for his revolver and thought a moment. "Please step outside, Mr. Stone. I need to talk to you for a minute." He brushed aside Sam Toby, who was blocking the door.

Once outside, Todd grabbed the man by the shoulders and shook him. "Listen, Stone, I didn't much appreciate you gettin' me arrested in Kansas City."

Stone dropped down to his knees and begged for mercy. Just before Todd pulled out his revolver, Quantrill grabbed his arm. "No, don't do it, Todd!"

Just when Todd felt that perhaps his leader had gone soft, Quantrill added: "I don't want the discharge from the gun to awaken anyone. Can't risk it."

The old man grabbed Todd's leg. "I beg you. Please set me free."

Todd kicked him away. "You sure as hell didn't show me any mercy. Why should I show you any?" Todd took the musket Quantrill handed him. After getting an approving nod from his leader, Todd whacked away at the man's head with the barrel of the musket until it was a bloody ball.

"Pay back," Todd grunted. "Sure feels good."

Mrs. Jennings, a close neighbor of Joseph Stone, was awakened by the guerrillas pounding on her door of her home. She, her children, and her servant girl, all stared in horror as the men ransacked the house.

"Where are they, woman?" one of them demanded.

"Who?" Mrs. Jennings asked, her voice quivering.

"The men! Where are they?"

"I swear to you there are no men in this household."

"You are a liar, old woman," another man snorted.

They continued to search her house, overturning furniture and kicking open doors. Finally convinced she was telling the truth, they decided to leave.

"We wasted too much time here," one of the men said. "We've got to get to Lawrence before daylight."

After they left, Mrs. Jennings was still shaking. She watched in disbelief as one of the men grabbed a neighbor boy, Jacob Rote, off his horse as he rode along the trail leading to the Stone house. Poor Jacob, she thought. After his father moved from Lawrence last year, only to be brutally murdered by bushwhackers, Joseph had schooled him. This summer, the 13-year-old boy, while living at the Stone house, helped Joseph with early morning chores. Now the men have taken the young lad captive!

She ran outside, shouting at the men to return the boy, but they continued on, riding into the darkness of the night. Mrs. Jennings knew there was nothing she could do, but she looked across the way, at the house of William Guest. Surely Mr. Guest would understand. Not only had these monsters kidnapped that poor boy, but they would be attacking innocent people in Lawrence. William Guest would surely help.

Mr. Guest finally answered the door. "No, I am not going to travel to Lawrence," he told her after she pleaded with him. "Do you realize what time it is, woman?"

"But I clearly heard them say they were going to Lawrence. We need to warn the citizens. Their lives are in danger. Please!"

"Mine would be in danger too, Mrs. Jennings. You expect me to get on my horse and outrun them?"

"I'll go," a voice said from the interior of the Guest home. Henry Thompson, a colored servant for Guest, came to the door. "All I need is a horse. I'm a pretty good horseman, ma'am."

"Well, I'm not trustin' you with *my* horse, Henry," Guest snorted. "Now go back to bed, woman, and be sensible about this."

Five miles west of Lenape, Kansas

Pelathé was worried about this mare. She had already stumbled once and was now breathing heavily, and her pace was lumbering. Pelathé had run a considerable distance already, traveling west along the north side of the river. It was still dark out, but there was enough moonlight to illuminate his trail. By his reckoning of where the river bent suddenly from a southward to a westward direction, he probably had about eighteen miles left to go.

"Don't quit on me now," the Shawnee said in his native tongue. "Can't stop to rest."

He saw white foam building up all about the horse's mouth. And the mare was now making loud groaning noises. "Please!" Pelathé shouted. "You must go on. You must!"

Just then the mare stumbled again, and Pelathé jumped off before the animal fell to the ground. Unlike the last time, however, the mare didn't recover and return to a standing position. She kicked and groaned while Pelathé thought quickly. As a Shawnee, he believed there was often enough energy left in a dying animal that, if it can be revived, it could go on further.

Pelathé emptied the gunpowder from his ammunition into his cartridge box. Taking out a long knife, he held the weapon to the sky, asking the Sacred Winds to breathe more life into this dying animal. With a great deal of effort, he brought the animal upright, got back in the saddle, and in one quick motion, stabbed the mare's shoulders, causing the animal to rear. While hanging tightly to the bridle, he poured gunpowder from his pistol charges into the open wound and rubbed it in. The animal let out a horrible screech and took off fiercely down the trail, riding faster than she had before.

"I'm sorry." Pelathé, leaned forward in the saddle, whispering to the crazed horse. "We must get to Lawrence. Please don't die. Please don't die."

Lawrence, Kansas

While Matt slept, Jessica rose and walked a few feet toward the river's edge. Lowering herself, she sighed as she trickled on the stones beneath—glad she was comfortable in her chemise on this fine, warm August evening. But she felt foolish now, having been so willing and eager earlier to give in to Matt's lustful desires. Would Matt now think less of her?

Yet it was that nagging fear tonight that bothered her, that same sense of dread she had when she returned from college fourteen months ago....the same nightmare she had then that had just jerked her from sleep tonight....

"They're all dead, rebels got 'em."

4:25 AM
Just south of Eudora, Kansas

Henry Thompson made it on foot as far as Eudora. Now totally exhausted, he sat on a tree stump near the main road to town to catch his breath. Although it was still yet dark, the moon gave off enough light for him to see a chaise coming toward him. Immediately, the Negro rose to his feet and stood in the center of the road, waving for the driver to halt.

The chaise came to a stop and a man with a white beard and mustache and dressed in a black frock coat, trousers, and top hat peered at Thompson. "What's the problem?"

"Help me," Thompson said, gasping for breath. "Please help me."

"Help you with what? What in tarnation are you talking about?"

"My name's Thompson, sir. Henry Thompson. I'm a servant for Mr. Guest in Hester." He took a deep breath and exhaled. "An hour or so ago, Quantrill'n his men paid a visit to Joseph Stone'n murdered him. Mrs. Jennings, a neighbor, told me she overhead them say that...that...."

"Yes? Go on."

"That they gonna attack Lawrence."

The man drew back at the news. "What? Are you certain?"

"Yes, sir. They on their way there right now."

"It's fortunate that you found me on this road, Henry. My name is Frederick Pila, and I was just returning home late from performing a marriage ceremony. I'm the justice of the peace."

"I got to get to Lawrence," Thompson said. "But I'm dead tired from running all the way here."

"By Jove! You must be exhausted, Henry. Hester's more than eight miles away. Take a seat next to me. We best be getting to Eudora to warn the folks there."

Once Thompson climbed aboard, Pila drove his chaise to the main streets of Eudora, arousing from sleep as many as he could with his shouts and gunfire. A crowd gathered around the chaise. Three men offered to ride to Lawrence to warn the residents there. One of them, the Eudora city marshal, took off immediately, but he had no sooner left the outskirts of town when he was thrown off his horse. The two riders who were following him decided not to stop when they saw that he was not seriously injured.

"Not sure we can make it there, even at a full gallop," one of the two men shouted.

"We've got to try," the other one hollered back

Just then, the first man's horse stumbled and fell, crushing the rider. The other man halted immediately and ran back to his friend's aid. The injured man groaned in pain.

There was a faint white glow coming from the east. The sun would soon be rising. The man left his injured friend on the ground and went back to town to find a doctor.

4:49 AM
Douglas County, Kansas
Six miles southeast of Lawrence

Jacob Rote rode on William Gregg's horse, with Gregg in the saddle behind him. His arm shaking, Jacob pointed to a trail bearing to the right. "Lawrence is there, sir."

"You've been a good guide," Gregg said, squeezing the boy's shoulder. "It would have been hard to find it without your help, boy. Like I promised, once we get there, I'll get you a suit of clothes and a horse. Would you like that?"

"I don't care about that," Jacob sobbed. "Why did they kill him? He was a good man."

"I told you not to talk about your friend Mr. Stone any-more'n you're still doin' it."

"I'm sorry," he said, choking on his tears.

Gregg gave him his handkerchief and another squeeze on the shoulder.

Near north bank of Kansas River
Five miles from Lawrence

After the mare died, Pelathé ran down the trail just as the eastern sky began to lighten. His heart beat frantically as he raced toward the Delaware reservation north of the river. Once he'd get there, he'd sound a war cry to the Delawares about the danger facing Lawrence.

316

His thoughts nagged him. If only he could have gotten a faster horse. If only the mare had not died on him. If only he would have learned of this raid sooner. No, he told himself. He had to deal with reality. His heart told him he had to save Lawrence. His head told him he'd be too late.

He kept running anyway, hoping for the impossible.

Chapter 22

It was beginning to get light just above the horizon when George Maddox and Sam Toby, two of the scouts under Gregg's command, departed from the long Quantrill line. Toby pointed to a man milking a cow inside his yard. A large dog with floppy ears and a coat of black hair chased a squirrel running toward a tree.

"Ain't that Snyder?" Toby asked Maddox, nodding toward the man in the yard.

"Yeah," Maddox said, pairing off with him, as they both raced toward the Snyder house. "That damned fool is Reverend Snyder—a lieutenant with a colored regiment. He's on Bill's death list."

"Let's do it," Toby said. "I hate them nigger-lovers." Without waiting for Maddox's reply, he charged at Snyder, shooting him in the back. Snyder cried out, falling over to one side. The frightened cow lumbered away from the scene, kicking over a bucket of milk.

Maddox caught up with Sam. After shooting Snyder again, Maddox was about to shoot the black dog, racing toward them and snarling. "Don't shoot. Let'im be," Sam shouted.

"Why? It's just a cur."

"No. The dog don't mean no harm. Let 'im be."

"Have it your way, Sam," he said, but he fired yet another shot at Snyder.

"Just want to be sure he's dead. C'mon, let's get back in line." The two of them galloped away to catch up with the others.

Reverend Hugh Fisher, unable to sleep well because of his recent illness, sat by his window. His eyes scanned the small plot of land owned by Reverend Snyder. Then he saw Snyder, who walked out with pail and stool, and sat by his cow. Every morning it'd be the same—Snyder milking his cow, then going back to the chicken coop to pick eggs. Today would be no different, Fisher thought.

Fisher couldn't believe what he was seeing. Two bearded men in broad hats raced through Snyder's yard, firing their pistols at the man. Snyder slumped over and the cow moved away, overturning the bucket.

Fisher blinked in disbelief as the two murderers joined a horde of screaming men racing toward the center of town.

Taking a northwest approach, Quantrill halted his troops when he reached the vicinity of Quincy and Rhode Island Streets. He lowered the stars and stripes, a flag he had used as a ruse to confuse any travelers into thinking they were Yankee cavalrymen.

Behind him was a long, formidable trail of armed men. They were now 448 men strong, thanks to Colonel Holt joining him with 104 of his own and another 50 men merging with them four miles from the Kansas border.

Wanting to be sure he wasn't entering a trap, Quantrill sent his five best horsemen ahead to trot up Massachusetts Street to see if all was quiet. While he waited for their return, some of the men grumbled among themselves about the wisdom of shooting up the town. "We should just rob a few stores."... "Could be armed soldiers out there."... "Maybe they heard we're comin'."... "I don't want no part of any outright killin'."

Quantrill and Gregg paced on horseback up and down the line, telling the men if they were cowards they could leave now and there'd be no repercussions. A few did leave, but most stayed on, waiting for the return of the scouts.

Within minutes, the five horsemen returned to their leader, giving him a signal indicating all was quiet. "Damn it," Quantrill shouted, "I'm going in. Follow me! Rush on to the town!" All at once, the guerillas bounded forward, yelling and screaming their rage. "Kill 'em! No mercy! Damn 'em all! Remember the jail! Remember Osceola! Remember the Redlegs!"

Following Quantrill's prearranged plan, they split into four groups, each taking a street—Vermont, Massachusetts, New Hampshire, and Rhode Island—and riding north up to the river. Quantrill rode ahead of the Massachusetts group, intent on reaching his trophy—the Eldridge Hotel, the stronghold of the town. Expecting his biggest fight there, he ordered his best shooters to accompany him to the hotel.

Sam Toby, charging along with Larkin Skaggs, followed Gregg up Massachusetts Street, shouting obscenities and shooting his pistol at anything that moved. To his right was a camp of recruits for the Kansas Fourteenth regiment. The recruits were getting out of their small tents, obviously bewildered by all the commotion.

"Hell," Toby yelled at Skaggs, "this is just like huntin' rabbits, maybe better." He laughed as he shot at the young recruits who ran about in their underwear. He managed to kill two of them, while Skaggs misfired his revolver three times.

Skaggs pulled out his other revolver and managed to fire a shot into the back of an escaping recruit. "I guess that's why Bill wanted us to carry more'n one gun," he snorted.

The marauders riding behind Toby and Skaggs also fired at the recruits—including three who tried in vain to fire back before being killed. Five others ran across the field toward New Hampshire Street, but Skaggs and Toby took off after them. Skaggs got one of them, but others in Quantrill's band who were also racing down New Hampshire got the other four recruits.

"I got to get me a drink," Skaggs said to Toby. "I fight better when I'm as loaded as my gun," he laughed.

The pounding on the rectory door of St. John the Evangelist Church was incessant. Father Sebastian Favre, roused from sleep, wondered who could be in such distress so early in the morning. He took the watch from his pocket. 5:20 AM. The sun had not quite risen although the eastern sky had turned grayish-white. Bishop John Baptiste Miege and two other priests were probably still asleep, so Favre went to answer the door. What could be so urgent that it would justify such an awful pounding?

A round-faced man with a broad-brimmed black hat excused himself for the interruption. Favre recognized him as Joshua Parkinson, the Quaker minister, who was accompanied

320

by his wife, Ann. Before Favre could say anything, Parkinson pushed his way in, insisting on taking sanctuary in the church because Quantrill and his horde of men were invading the town, murdering its citizens.

Ann was in tears. She grabbed hold of Father Favre Sebastian's black cassock. "Please help us. Quantrill has a particular dislike for ministers. He'll kill my husband! I know he will."

The priest immediately roused Bishop Miege and the two priests from their slumber. "The first thing we need to do," the bishop told Favre after being informed about Quantrill, "is to hide Reverend Parkinson. How about in the basement of this church?"

Miege and the three priests escorted Joshua to the basement. "He'll be found here for sure," the bishop said, surveying the area.

"Not if we roll him up in that carpet in the middle of floor," Favre replied.

"That is an excellent suggestion," the bishop said. "Let's do it."

Fifteen minutes later, Favre joined the bishop, the two priests, and Ann in the chapel for prayer. Favre prayed that Reverend Parkinson would be safe in that rolled-up carpet against the south end of the basement. While Favre knew he had to believe God would save them all, doubts flooded his mind anyway. What if Quantrill's men unrolled the carpet? What if they set fire to the building?

The dreadful knock on the door! It had come sooner than expected.

Bishop Miege, his face a ghostly white, rose up to answer it. Another pounding on the door. Ann began sobbing. The two priests had their eyes shut tight, their lips moving in prayer. Favre's heart hammered inside his chest.

After taking a pony from an enclosure at the Delaware reservation, Pelathé rode toward the Lawrence ferry. The sun had just peeked over the horizon, and by the time he approached his destination, he heard the sound of gunfire from across the Kansas River.

Pelathé dropped off the pony and knelt on the ground, pounding it with his fist, cursing his bad luck. The sounds of firing intensified, resounding over the surface of the river. He looked up at the doomed town, his voice choked with tears. "I tried my best," he whispered hoarsely. "I tried."

Jessica awoke to the sound of gunshots. Matt was already dressed, and his shock was evident in the deep lines of his forehead and the way he gawked in disbelief at his surroundings. "We've got to hide," Matt told her as she put on her petticoat. "Hear those volleys? Border ruffians, no doubt."

"It sounds as if the whole town is under attack." She slipped on her dress and removed her red garnet brooch, putting it in her pocket for safekeeping. "What shall we do, Matt?"

"I don't know. Maybe you ought to wait here while I run ahead and see what's going on."

"Are you insane?" She quickly buttoned her dress. "I'm not going to stay here and wait to see if you get killed. I'm going with you." Her gun was still in her dress pocket. She thought of telling Matt she had it but then decided against it. Maybe Matt would do something rash. Best he didn't know she had a weapon.

Jessica could sense Matt was going to argue with her about her joining him, but she grabbed onto his arm and kept pace with him. They stopped when they got to the corner of New Hampshire and Pinckney Streets. Far down one street were hordes of men on horseback shooting and yelling.

"We can probably make it to the City Hotel," Matt said, his voice wavering, his eyes revealing his fright. "C'mon."

Some people were standing outside with stunned looks. Matt avoided talking to anyone and kept urging Jessica to walk faster, to run if she could. When they got there, the City Hotel owners, Nathan and Laura Stone, looked puzzled as they stood near the entrance. Nathan recognized Matt with a polite nod. "Any idea what's going on, Mr. Lightfoot?"

"Looks like we're being attacked. Maybe it's Quantrill and his bunch. There's been talk he might do something like this."

Nathan scratched his head. "If it's true, I can't believe it. When I knew him as Charlie Hart, he was always well-mannered."

Matt's face soured and he was about to say something in response, but Jessica quickly jumped in: "We need a room. Anything you've got."

Nathan's wife Laura had Matt sign the register and showed them to a room on the third floor. "Normally," she said, trying to make light of the matter, "I wouldn't rent a room to an unmarried couple. Given what's happening this morning, I don't care." She disappeared out the door before Matt or Jessica could thank her.

"Maybe that's a reason we ought to get married," Matt joked.

Jessica wasn't in the mood for lighthearted banter and went to the window. A crowd of men on horseback had gathered outside the Eldridge House. "That's strange," she said.

"What is?"

"No volleys. No yells or whoops. A lot of the men—maybe those ruffians who invaded the town—are just standing quietly outside the Eldridge, looking up. What's going on?"

Otto felt someone shaking him, telling him to get up immediately. At first he thought it was part of his dream where he had knocked on the door of a cabin to inquire if the occupants would accept a slave girl he had just rescued. The physical shaking Otto now felt confused him. But when he opened his eyes, he was surprised to see a look of alarm on Penelope's face. All she had on was a chemise and her wedding ring. She looked beautiful...but frightened.

Otto pushed himself up off the floor where they had made their bed last night. "What's wrong?"

"Just listen. Hear that? It sounds like a band of outlaws have taken over the town." She hurriedly put on her petticoat. "We've got to get the children up and leave."

Otto heard the sound of hooves and intermittent gunfire and yelling. Thoroughly confused as to what was happening and why, he got dressed immediately. After helping Penelope with her hoop skirt and buttoning her dress, he roused the children from sleep. Six-year-old Emma kept pressing her father with questions as he dressed her: "Where're we going?...Why are you scared?...Aren't we gonna eat breakfast?..."

"I'll answer all your questions later, sweetheart," he replied, lifting up the child while Penelope took Mitzi's hand. Otto glanced at Penelope and felt he could read her mind. She was probably thinking if this were Quantrill's band, he might be in mortal danger. But where should he and his family go?

When they stepped outside, a building at the far end of the block was on fire. One man lay dead on the wooden sidewalk four doors away. Marauders on horseback rode back and forth down the street, firing their revolvers.

Penelope grabbed Otto's arm. "Put Emma down and hide down under here," she said, raising the hem of her dress. Otto put the child down but blinked at her suggestion. "You mean under your skirts? I'm sorry, but I refuse to do that!"

"Shush! Do it if you love me. Please!"

Otto felt foolish as he hid under her voluminous dress. "I feel like such an idiot," he said, holding her legs for support while hunched over in the strange darkness of her underclothes.

"I'd much rather have a live idiot," she said, "than a dead martyr."

He heard his daughters giggle, but Penelope shushed them as well.

"Otto, I've got to hide you in that secret cellar of ours on Vermont Street. Tinker probably hid there last night. You and the children will be safe there."

"And how do you suppose I'll get there by hiding here, darling?"

"I'll walk slowly so you can walk on your knees and keep pace with me. We'll get there eventually."

Otto, feeling increasingly foolish and wanting no part of this humiliation, was about to crawl out from under her dress when he heard the gruff voice of a man: "Who yah talkin' to, lady?"

"To my daughters. And it's none of your concern."

"Yah look familiar. You're Mrs. Heller, aren't yah? Where's your husband? I want to see him."

Emma giggled. "You can't. He's playing peek-a-boo."

Otto felt the blood drain from his face. *Please, Emma, be quiet!*

"What does she mean by that?" the man growled.

324

"She's just a child talking nonsense," Penelope said. "Leave her alone. I'm not Mrs. Heller and I don't have a husband, so please quit pestering me."

"I'm wastin' my time with yah, woman," the man said. There was no further conversation, but Otto heard other terrible sounds—gunfire, shouting, and ladies sobbing in soulful desperation to save their husbands. Penelope started walking, one small slow step at a time. Otto, crawling on his knees, his hands on her thighs, tried his best to keep pace with her. He imagined the disgrace that the slave Ishmael must have felt when he had to hide, with trash heaped upon him, in the false bottom of Otto's merchant wagon. Safety, Otto thought, comes with a price, sometimes a humiliating one.

His thoughts evaporated when he heard Penelope shriek, "Otto! It's a good thing you can't see what's going on here. What a horrible sight! I just saw a man thrown into a burning building.

When they heard the gunshots, Hugh and Elizabeth Fisher took their children and headed toward Mount Oread for safety. Two of their older boys, Willie and Charlie, ran ahead of them. Eight-year-old Joey held his father's hand, while Elizabeth carried their six-month-old infant.

Hugh stopped, gasping for breath, as he leaned against a tree. "I won't be able to travel that distance, Elizabeth. Not after my illness."

Elizabeth looked back at their brick house a hundred yards away, at the northwest corner of South Park. She then turned her head toward the west and spotted Willie and Charlie running off with their friend, Bobby Martin. Twelve-year-old Bobby, wearing a suit of clothes made from his father's blue Yankee uniform, was easy to spot.

Elizabeth worried why her two boys were taking off with their friend, not bothering to look behind them to see where their parents were. She'd run after them if only she wasn't carrying the infant and if she didn't have to be concerned about the safety of Joey and her husband.

"Don't worry about the boys," Hugh said. "They're fast runners."

"But I *am* worried. They're just boys and there are insane men out there shooting guns."

Hugh pressed her hand. "Please, Elizabeth. Trust in the Lord."

By the time they arrived at their house, dust from the charging horsemen could be seen billowing in the distance, less than a half mile away. "Quick, hide in the cellar," Elizabeth said, looking around to be sure no one saw him entering the house. "They're not going to find you there."

No sooner had Hugh gone down to hide in their unfinished cellar, when there was a rapid knock on the door. While her son Joseph sat on a chair in the dining room, Elizabeth, holding the infant, answered the door. Four rough-looking guerillas pushed their way in. "Let me speak to Reverend Fisher," one of them demanded.

"He's not here," Elizabeth answered. "He left some time ago."

"I don't believe you, ma'am." He strode in with the three others and started throwing furniture about. Joseph, obviously terrified, ran to his mother and clung to her leg. After going from room to room, one of the men came back, his face flushed with anger. "We've got orders to see him. Now I'm gonna ask you again: where is he?"

"I've already told you he's not here."

"You're a damned liar. Let's search the cellar, men."

Elizabeth said a quick prayer while they went down to the cellar. "It's too dark down there," one of the men said. "Bring me a lamp, woman!"

Elizabeth's mind raced. She wasn't about to give them a lamp to help them find her husband. "It'll take some time for me to find," she answered. "I don't know where it is." She thought about the new kerosene lamp they had bought. It was an invention that perhaps these bushwhackers hadn't seen yet. Holding her infant, she went up to the second floor, but stopped at the top of the stairs.

The men came up from the cellar. Three of them began searching the house again. One of them looked up at her. "Hurry up and find it, woman!" Another began racing up the steps, cussing at her.

Elizabeth knew she couldn't stall any longer. Running into one of the bedrooms, she grabbed the kerosene lamp. "I found one," she shouted, as she turned down the wick into the coal oil before bringing it to the ruffian waiting for her on the stairs.

The man tried repeatedly to light the kerosene lamp, but failed. He passed the lamp around, but no one seemed to know how to light it. The men were furious when Elizabeth insisted she didn't know anything about this type of lamp. All the while, she hoped and prayed the delay would give Hugh sufficient time to somehow escape.

"Get me another lamp!" one man demanded.

"I can't," Elizabeth said. "I need to watch my child."

"Damn you! I'll watch your precious child for yah." He took the baby from her and ordered her upstairs to look for another lamp.

She brought down a lamp, which the man lit and took with him, racing down to the cellar. All kinds of horrible thoughts went through her mind. What could she possibly do if they discovered him? How could she prevent his murder?

"He must have escaped!" the man yelled, returning from the cellar. "Burn this house down, men! If he's here, he'll be a dead man!"

Elizabeth tiptoed downstairs when no one was around. She looked about. No sign of him. But then she heard him whisper, "I'm still down here."

The fire, Elizabeth thought. They're setting the house on fire, and Hugh's still in the cellar!

Willie Fisher ran down Quincy Street with Charlie and Bobby, overwhelmed at seeing a man shot after he answered a knock on the door of his house. "Where do we go?" he asked his friend Bobby, seeing yet another house set ablaze. "They might kill us if we go back home."

"I don't know," Bobby answered, peering about the corner of the building. "I-I-I don't know." He started to cry, but Willie pretended not to notice. Boys weren't supposed to cry.

A bullet whizzed by Willie's neck. Two ruffians on horseback were fast approaching. Willie let go of his brother's hand, yelling at him to run faster. Bobby soon outpaced both of the

Fisher boys, slicing his arms through the wind as he flew by them.

"Get that bastard Yankee!" one of the men shouted. "Damn that blue-boy!"

A bullet roared into Bobby's head and something soft and spongy flew into Willie's face.

Later, Willie realized what that soft and spongy material was—Bobby's young brain, blown out by a man who apparently hated the boy's blue uniform.

Bishop Miege prayed that his life would be spared because he had so many plans for the Catholic Church in Kansas. As the first bishop assigned to the Kansas territory, he'd be needed to oversee all the churches and missions in the state. But who was he to advise God what to do?

Suddenly a bang, several kicks, and a bump. It sounded as if several men were pounding the door at the same time. The bishop looked at the worried faces of Father Sebastian, two other priests, and Ann. Then he opened the door and met the soulless face of Quantrill himself, grinning back at him—as well as six of his men, all holding revolvers pointed at him. Miege closed his eyes for a moment. *Please God, help me!*

"Who are you?" Quantrill snarled, challenging him with a steely gaze.

"Bishop Miege. I'm the Catholic bishop here in Kansas on a tour of the churches to give the Sacrament of Confirmation."

Quantrill peered inside. "Who's the lady?" he barked.

The bishop swallowed hard, glancing at the minister's wife. "A Christian woman in prayer. May I be of assistance to you?"

"Everybody up!" Quantrill ordered. "Put your valuables here where I can see them," he added, pointing to a small table in the entryway. The bishop took the cash out of his pocketbook. Ann removed her ring. The priests emptied their pockets and put the contents on the table.

Quantrill aimed his revolver at the bishop's forehead and smiled. "Any last words you got 'fore I kill you?"

"Just one," Bishop Miege said. He agonized as he took a deep breath. If this didn't work, he thought, he and the priests were all dead men. "Let Lydia Stone know," he answered, "that I won't be present at her marriage ceremony next month."

Quantrill put the revolver down, a questioning stare crossing his face. "What are you talking about?"

"She asked if I would join them together—her and her betrothed next month."

The guerilla leader shot an angry glance at two of his men who began picking up the valuables from the table. "Take your hands off of that!" he yelled. The men immediately dropped what they had.

Quantrill, his face softening a degree, turned his attention back to the bishop. "Nathan Stone's a good friend of mine. If you're doing his daughter Lydia a favor, then you're doing me a favor."

"C'mon, Colonel," one of the guerillas pleaded with Quantrill, "let's take all this loot like you said we'd do."

"No," he snapped, sticking his revolver in his belt. He swept his arm across the room. "Let's leave. Now!"

The sounds of men's voices flooded the hall on the third floor of the City Hotel. Earlier, Jessica and Matt were at their window, watching a stream of men leaving the Eldridge and walking toward this hotel. "You're probably thinking the same thing I am," Jessica told him. "Quantrill, for some odd reason, has evacuated the Eldridge and is bringing those guests here."

There was a knock on their door, and Jessica and Matt faced each other. "If they're here to kill us," Matt said, "there's nothing we can do about it." He opened the door to find Captain Banks, the Provost Marshall, and Nathan Stone staring back at him. Nathan was the first to speak. "Mr. Lightfoot, I realize we rented you this room, but because of circumstances beyond our control, we'll need to house a lot of men in this hotel."

Captain Banks poked his head in the door. "Sorry for the intrusion, ma'am," he said. "I had surrendered the Eldridge Hotel to Quantrill and his band. In return, he promised he wouldn't harm us. His men marched us over here, and even though we're squeezed into this smaller building, we're safe."

"You have me to thank for that," Nathan said, with a haughty smile on his face. "Quantrill said he had once stayed here and our family was kind to him."

Matt didn't know whether to strangle Nathan for his smugness or thank him for influencing Quantrill to save them from harm.

"What's going to happen to the Eldridge?" Jessica asked.

"See for yourself," Captain Banks said, pointing toward the window.

Jessica and Matt went to look. The Eldridge Hotel was on fire, as were several other buildings on Massachusetts Street. Jessica guessed that Otto and Penelope's "New Necessities" store was also being destroyed, although she couldn't see the building from the window.

Banks peered out the window with them. "I fear for someone named Arthur Spicer, whom I met at the Eldridge. He made the mistake of striking up a conversation with Quantrill. Now Quantrill forced him to join his guerillas to serve as a guide to Senator Lane's house."

Jessica, her eyes wide with fear, put her hand to her mouth. "Oh my!"

"If Mr. Spicer fails to produce Lane," Banks said, "Quantrill promised he'd be killed."

Mary Lane was glad her husband James had been prepared for the possibility of an attack. He had told her that in such an event, he would depart immediately to the cornfield in the rear of their Mississippi Street home and hide among the stalks. She knew all too well her husband was a prime target for Quantrill and eventually Quantrill would seek him out.

By the time she awoke to the sound of gunfire and the hooves of charging horses, Jim was already gone. No sooner had she searched the house for him than she heard a terrible pounding on the door.

When she opened it, she recognized Quantrill immediately, although she knew only one of the men behind him—Arthur Spicer, an acquaintance of theirs. Spicer was jabbing his finger at her. "This is the house," he shouted. "And that's Mrs. Lane!"

Mary was convinced that Mr. Spicer, a normally polite and friendly sort, must have been forced to play Judas for this mob.

Quantrill, all smiles, tipped his hat and asked to see the general.

"I'm sorry, Mr. Quantrill, but he's not in," she said, with all the charm she could muster.

"We'll see about that. Men, c'mon in!"

A dozen charged into her home and got to work at once, busting up her furniture and racing from room to room. A couple of the men appeared to be drunk, using foul language, and even fighting with each other over possessions they wanted to keep. Quantrill stood by while members of his band went about their business of destruction. He placed his hand on her newly polished piano. "I bet the general bought this from the loot he got from Osceola," he said, smirking. "Half of this furniture doesn't even belong to him. He's a thief!"

He gave a signal to his men, and they tipped the piano to the carpeted floor. Soon they were jumping on the keys and defacing the wood with their knives. One took out his revolver and shot at it several times. Other men took out matches and lit the curtains.

Mary tried putting out the fire, but the men restrained her. "Why are you doing this!" she screamed.

"I'll ask *you* a question," Quantrill retorted. "Why did your husband send his Redlegs to Missouri to wipe out innocent people?"

Everyone left the house as flames roared through the open windows. Quantrill and his men saddled up to leave, grumbling that they couldn't find Jim Lane. Mary, standing a distance away from the front of her burning home, was more furious than sad that everything precious to her was going up in flames.

Quantrill tipped his hat as he passed her. "Please give Senator Lane my compliments. Tell him I would have been very glad to meet him."

Mary glared back at him. "He would have been glad to have met you under different circumstances, Mr. Quantrill."

"Good day, Mrs. Lane. If we find him, we'll let you know where you can locate his body."

By the time Penelope reached Vermont Street, the children no longer relished the novelty of their father being escorted to safety by hiding under her dress. Both Emma and Mitzi were in tears. When a building on Massachusetts Street collapsed on top of a wounded man and he screamed in agony, Emma dug her fingernails into Penelope's hand. They both cried, and Mitzi turned pale and vomited. Penelope tried to drown out the sights and sounds of this terror by silently reciting the "Our Father."

At one point, she twisted her ankle. There was no way she could sit somewhere with Otto still under her, so she asked if she could rest on his shoulders. Poor Otto! She could only imagine how he must be suffering—probably perspiring from the warmth of her body, gasping for air, his knees throbbing with pain. Now she added to his discomfort by putting all of her weight on him.

She could feel him adjusting his shoulders to accommodate her. "How much further?" he groaned.

"We're very close to the cellar. How are you holding out?"

"Under different circumstances, Penelope, I suppose I'd enjoy being your chair. What are the children doing?"

"I'm worried about them," she said, her voice starting to crack under the emotional strain. "They've already seen too much violence. Emma wants to hold you, but I keep reassuring her to be patient a while longer."

"If I only had a gun," Otto said, his voice muffled by going through multiple layers of clothing, "I'd kill some of those bast—"

"Otto!" she screeched. "The children will hear you!" She stood up, straightened her skirts, and continued on, taking one slow step after another. Finally, she stopped. "It's got to be around here somewhere."

"The cellar?" Otto asked.

"Yes, I can't locate the entrance."

"Here," he said, crawling out from under her dress, "let me help you find it." No sooner had he said that when Emma rushed up to him, giving him a hug. "I love you, daddy." Mitzi joined her sister, holding his leg as if she'd never let it go.

A ruffian on horseback stopped in front of them and looked in their direction. "Oh no!" Penelope exclaimed. "Hide!" It was too late. The man had jumped off his horse and rushed over to them. Although dressed in dirty clothes, he had a clean-shaven face, thin eyebrows, thoughtful blue eyes. He didn't fit in with the way the other guerillas looked. Still, he had two guns tucked under his belt.

"Ma'am," he said, bowing slightly in her direction, "you had better take him and your children away from here. I got a wife and two children in Missouri, and I'd hate to see them without a father."

Penelope glanced quickly at Otto, who was speechless. "Are you with the Quantrill band?" she asked, confused.

He nodded, shame washing over his face. "I thought maybe we was just gonna rob a few stores and leave. Didn't know they was gonna kill innocent people here." He pulled out one of his revolvers and Penelope shuddered. "Here, ma'am," he said, handing her the gun. "You might need this for your protection. I still got one."

He got back on his horse and rode away before Penelope could recover from her shock. She handed Otto the gun, exchanging silent stares over what had just happened. Wasting no time, Otto found the entrance and slid down into it. He then took Emma and Mitzi down with him. Penelope noticed that across the street at the Johnson House, guerillas were marching about a dozen men out of the hotel and down the alley. Maybe, she hoped, Quantrill was moving the guests to a place of refuge.

She saw a man scurrying down the street, being chased by three men on horseback shooting at him. He fled to the Spicer house, already in flames. Apparently realizing his mistake, he ran back out, and one of the horsemen shot him several times.

Penelope, horrified at what she had just seen, looked away. If only she could have directed that man here, to the safety of this hidden cellar...

Just then, she heard the sound of a gunshot, then another, and another coming from behind the alley at the Johnson

House. Oh, no! Please, no! They must have just killed those men at the hotel!

"Hurry," Otto called out to her from behind the tall jimson weeds and dirt mound camouflaging the cellar entrance. "We're waiting for you to come down."

She thought about that man who had fled down the street, being chased by three ruffians on horseback. She should have guided him here to safety.

"I'll be there later, Otto. You just take care of the children. How's Tinker doing?"

"Tinker? He's not here."

That's odd, she thought. Where could he be hiding?

Hearing the confused sounds of yelling and gunfire, Tinker had scrambled out of his hiding place and dashed toward Massachusetts Street. His first inclination was to see if the Hellers and their children were safe. But when he reached Winthrop Street, he was bewildered at the sight of rough-looking men on horseback charging up Massachusetts, firing at men standing in the street, looting stores, and burning them.

A man on horseback took dead aim at Tinker, but his pistol misfired. Tinker didn't give him a chance to reload and took off down Massachusetts. Scurrying into a structure adjoining the *Tribune* building—which was already in flames—Tinker thought he heard a man yelling at someone to come back, a sound from the cellar below. Suddenly, a young man came charging up the steps, bumping into Tinker. "I got tah get to my brother Bob," the man said, his wide shock-filled eyes pleading with Tinker, as if Tinker could do anything for him.

"What happenin'?" Tinker asked, his hands grasping both his arms. "Who are yuh?"

"John Speer Jr.," he answered, lines of panic etched on his young face. "They're burning down my father's *Tribune* building, and Murdock and me, why we've been hiding in a deep pit in the cellar. But I've got to leave to find my brother Robert. Help me!"

Tinker released his grip on John. "I help you? How?"

334

"Run over with me to the *Republican* up the street. That's where he works. C'mon, help me get him!" He rushed outside. Tinker, confused by all of this, followed him out.

At first, John turned right and headed toward the *Republican* offices at the corner of Winthrop and Massachusetts. He stopped sharply and headed back toward Tinker. "Too late, the *Republican's* on fire."

Tinker looked up to see flames gutting the second floor of the Allen Farm Implement and Hardware building, where the *Republican* offices were. He was still staring at it when John grabbed his shoulder. "I've gotta get home," John said. "Find out how my parents are doin.' Maybe both of my brothers are there already."

"Where be yah home?"

John let go of Tinker and was breathing heavily. "Berkeley and Maryland."

"Too far to run," Tinker said. "Maybe I can steal a horse."

"Let's do it," John said. "Follow me!"

Tinker was unable to keep pace with John, who outdistanced him as he raced toward Henry Street and then turned left toward New Hampshire. Tinker could not remember any battle he had been in that was more vicious than this one. A man had just run up to a boy on the street, a lad not older than John, and shot him in the head. A woman was restrained by two ruffians from going to him. One of them stole the hysterical woman's purse.

Tinker, aware now of Nellie's heavy bronze medallion banging against his chest, shouted out for Nellie's angel. "Sissy, help me! Sissy!"

John reached the intersection of Henry and New Hampshire Streets some fifty yards before Tinker. A coarse-looking, middle-aged horseman, wearing a red bandana and displaying an outcropping of scraggly hair, ran toward the young man. "Where are yah goin', boy?" the coarse man said, slurring his words like a drunkard.

Tinker cried out for Nellie's angel again. Just then, he felt a bullet graze the side of his head. He turned to see a horseman waving a revolver at him. "Damn nigger, calling *me* a sissy!" the man said, snorting with laughter. He fired off another round, hitting Tinker in the chest, knocking him backwards.

Darkness settled over Tinker's eyes like a sudden nightfall, but not before he heard the gruff voice of the man in the red bandana who had accosted John, "Is this all the money yah got?"

"Sorry, sir," came the reply.

"Sorry's not good 'nough." The last sound Tinker heard before passing out was that of a gunshot, coming from where John had been.

About forty-five guests from the Eldridge had now spilled over to the City Hotel and four of them shared the room where Jessica and Matt were staying. Sickened by the sight of the burning town through her hotel window, Jessica turned to tell Matt she'd want to go outside to see if she could be of help, but he was nowhere in sight. Jessica hastened from room to room, looking for him. She recalled the last words he had said to her before he disappeared. "I can't just stay here and watch people die."

Thinking perhaps he might be in the restaurant downstairs, she thrust open the door only to find a crowd of strangers talking, some stridently, some in hoarse whispers, about the tragedy occurring outside. "Matt!" she shouted above the din. The crowd stopped talking and all eyes were upon her. Jessica surveyed the room, no sign of him. Nathan Stone tugged at her sleeve. "Mr. Lightfoot said he had to leave. Told him I didn't think he could because Quantrill's men are guarding this hotel."

"The fool!" Jessica snapped. She tried to exit but was stopped by a sentry. "Did you see a man leave from here?" she asked, her heart hammering.

"Yeah, I did. The man looked like he was 'secesh' and he told me he was with Quantrill, so I let him go. Took a horse that didn't seem to belong to nobody and rode off."

Jessica was bewildered. Matt—a secessionist? Must have been those Southern clothes he was wearing. She had to find him. "I'm his lady," she told the sentry. "I need to join him. Can you give me your horse?"

The sentry laughed. "Ma'am, I just can't give you my horse. I mean I—"

"Here," she said, removing her garnet brooch from her pocket. "Can I buy your horse?"

The sentry's eyes expanded into a look of disbelief at the glistening red jewelry. He took her brooch and promptly led her to a side of the building where several horses were tied up. Another sentry looked at her with suspicion but the other man made his lie sound convincing—that she was a close friend of Quantrill himself. "It's dangerous for you to ride alone in the streets, ma'am," the sentry said after she had saddled up.

"Never mind," Jessica answered, feeling the comfort of her Colt .31 in her dress pocket. "I can take care of myself."

She took off, riding down Massachusetts Street, now blackened with smoke from multiple fires. Sounds of hooves, sporadic gunfire, and men pleading for their lives punctured the air. One man on horseback made an obscene suggestion to her, but Jessica paid no attention to him, turning her head from side to side searching, searching. Matt, she thought, what is wrong with you running away like this? Are you trying to get yourself killed?

His parting words haunted her—"I can't just stay here and watch people die." She felt the same way. She couldn't just stand idly by and do nothing. But what could she do? How, she wondered, were other people in town handling this tragedy—people like her good friend, Amelia Read?

After five different sets of guerillas had visited her house, Amelia used water and blankets to once again extinguish all the fires they had set. Her husband Fred, unable to get to his store to retrieve his revolver, was still hiding in the second story of their house. Amelia felt indeed fortunate—so far, her lies had convinced the ruffians Fred wasn't here.

But her house was now a shell of what it used to be. The charred rubble of mementos, paintings, clothing, and other possessions they had set afire remained at the foot of the stairs. In the bedroom, they had ripped open the hair mattress and set fire to the clothes. All the money and jewelry that she and Fred owned were now gone—even those precious memories of her dear little Addie that Amelia had been keeping in her bureau drawer....

Earlier, Amelia had followed one of the ruffians to her bedroom. "No!" she screamed when he opened the back side of her bureau drawer and took out a little box. The man held in his rough hand a pair of gold and coral armlets that were used to loop the dress of her little girl, Addie, who had died only a few months earlier.

"Please," Amelia begged, "that is all that remains of my dead infant! Don't take them!"

The man stuffed them in his pocket. "Damn your dead baby. She'll never need them again."

Amelia was about to go upstairs to check on Fred when there was a brutal pounding on the door, as if the intruders were attempting to bust it open. When she opened it, several men rushed in, all appearing to be quite drunk and insisting on seeing her husband. After she protested that he wasn't home, one of them demanded to know who had put the fire out in this house.

"I did," Amelia said, defiance rising up in her throat, "and I'd do it again."

"Toby," one of the men ordered, "restrain that woman so she don't do a fool thing like that no more."

Sam Toby grabbed Amelia's wrists, squeezing them until she felt like screaming. But she wouldn't give him the satisfaction of letting him see her suffer. She watched helplessly as the others piled up bedding and books against a cotton lounge that they had carried to the window. They then lit a match and shouted in jubilation as the flames feasted hungrily on this new fuel.

Smoke soon filled the room, and the men ran to the porch while Toby dragged Amelia there. "Yah a feisty little tiger, ain't yah?" Toby said as she tried to loosen herself from his vise-like grip.

The curtains and cotton lounge were ablaze, with flames licking up to the window. Toby finally released her, cursing. "Damn yah, lady, yah can have your home now—if yah can put it out!" He ran to his horse and joined the others. Moments later the ruffians were gone.

338

Amelia immediately dashed to her smoke-filled bedroom and grabbed two pillows, one in each hand. Then she flew to the burning window and threw herself against the burning sash and frame, falling into the street. She ran back in, snatched some blankets and put the rest of the fire out. She dropped onto the porch, exhausted and wrenched with pain from burns and cuts on both arms. She inhaled deeply and gagged from the fumes. This was the longest and most painful morning she had ever experienced. But at least she had saved her husband.

Jessica resented the angry stares and catcalls she was getting from women on the street. They assumed she was with the ruffians and perhaps directing them as to what buildings they should pillage and burn. One of the guerillas even rode alongside her, mistaking her for "Sallie Young"—apparently some female traitor who had been riding with Quantrill's band.

Trotting toward her down Henry Street was a horseman in a tattered butternut chesterfield and dirty black waistcoat. He waved a black bowler at her as he came nearer. "Jessica!" he shouted. "Lord, it is so good to see you."

She brought her horse to a stop at Vermont Street. "Matt? What are you doing? Why did you leave me there at the hotel?"

"Had to. One of the guests, a rebel sympathizer, recognized me as a Yankee lieutenant. I decided to leave immediately. Lucky the sentry bought my story about my need to rejoin Quantrill's men." Matt looked around, frowning and biting his lower lip. "By the way, I saw Penelope earlier. Maybe you should be with her."

"Yes, of course. Where is she?"

"Follow me."

Penelope counted seven men and two boys she had saved so far. She had been ushering them into her secret cellar as she stood vigilant at her empty lot some twenty yards from the entrance to her hiding place. The Johnson House across the street was still in flames, as was the Spicer house nearby. But she kept her attention focused on the ruffians riding furiously up and down Vermont Street. She hoped to find men running from these outlaws so she could rescue them.

Here comes one now, she thought, as she saw a boy in tattered clothes rushing toward her. Apparently crazed by events, he kept repeating "I don't want to die. I don't want to die." Penelope looked down both sides of the street to see if any guerillas were in sight, then she grabbed the boy by the shoulders. "Quick, lad. I'll hide you!"

The boy, probably about fifteen, stared blankly at her. "What?"

"Come quick," Penelope said, directing him to the entrance of the cellar. "Get in there," she ordered. Soon, Otto's hands reached up, grabbed the boy's ankles and pulled him down into the cellar.

As Penelope walked back to where she had been, three horsemen riding down the street, reined their horses in front of her. "Men keep disappearing here," one of the men growled, looking down at her with black, contemptuous eyes. "Yeah," said another. "Where're they hiding?"

"I'm not going to tell you," Who did they think she was, she thought, a fool?

The first man drew his horse nearer to her and pulled out his pistol, aiming it at her face. "Tell me, lady, or I'll shoot you!"

No man, Penelope thought, should ever dare tell her to do the wrong thing. She lived her life believing that. And she'd die—if she had to.

She glared back at him. "You may shoot me if you will, but you won't ever find out where the men are." She waited for the explosion of his gun, knowing that at least Otto, her children, and the others down in that cellar would still be safe. *Love is stronger than fear.* Go ahead, she thought, kill me, you Satan!

The man spat on her. 'Whore!" He put his gun back in his holster and ordered the others to move on.

Penelope wiped the man's saliva from her cheek. *If a whore is a woman who saves the lives of others, I'm glad to be in that company.*

Minutes later, Penelope was shocked to see Jessica dismounting and walking toward her. "What in tarnation!" Penelope exclaimed. "How did you—?"

"It's a long story. Matt's riding to the ravine to hide out. But I thought I should be with you. Where's Otto and the children?"

Penelope reminded her about the secret cellar. "Almost got my fool head blown off, Jessica. But you know what?—I don't give a damn. I've got a dozen souls down there, including Mr. Heller and the two girls."

"Weren't you the least bit afraid?" Jessica asked.

Penelope smiled. "You can't focus on love and fear at the same time."

Otto quieted down the nervous boy and escorted him, in the darkness of the damp cellar, to a spot next to the others. Emma wrapped herself around her father's leg. "I'm scared, Daddy."

"Don't worry, Emma," Otto said, fingering the revolver stuck in his belt, the revolver the guerilla had given him for protection. Too bad, Otto thought, he couldn't go outside and take a few of them down.

Otto turned to the boy sitting next to him. "You're Guy Smith, aren't you? The shoemaker's son?"

Guy's body shook and his face was a frightened mask. "Yeah," he answered, his teeth chattering.

Otto recalled John Speer telling him he had planned to take his son William and Guy Smith, the boy's friend, fishing today. For a minute, Otto wondered if fifteen-year-old William had managed to escape harm.

William Speer and his friend, Frank Montgomery, finally made their way home to Maryland Street on the eastern side of town. "Do you think it's safe now?" Frank asked, hiding with William behind a stone fence some thirty yards from the partially-burned Speer house.

"Yeah, I think they're gone now," William answered, looking at the deserted road. There were only a few homes on Maryland, and they were all on fire. William was surprised their home was still standing, although the outside walls were badly scorched. Surely the ruffians had attempted to burn it down, he thought.

William heard sobbing when he cautiously entered the house. The living room was barren and black streaks across the walls as well as an ash heap made everything unreal. Elizabeth Speer sat on the floor in the corner of the room. Her face soaked with tears, she looked up at her son and his friend. Both her arms had dark red splotches of burn marks. A Sharps carbine lay across her lap and her dress was coated with gray ash.

"Oh, William!" she said, attempting to get up. "You're alive! Thank God! Have you seen your brothers? Are they alive?"

William shrugged.

She swept a glance across the empty, filthy room. "They tried to burn the place down and I kept putting the fires out." She peered up at William. "How did you manage to escape?"

William told how he had crawled out from underneath a wooden plank sidewalk and had to lie when a guerilla asked him his name.

"You did the right thing," she said. "Your father was probably on Quantrill's list." She took a deep breath and closed her eyes. "Son, I don't know if he's alive or if any of your brothers are alive." She looked up at William and began crying again.

The boy ran up to console her, but she handed him the weapon on her lap. "Here," she said, her voice low and bitter, "this is your father's carbine. I want you and Frank to go out and kill those demons with it."

"But—" William was shocked. What was his mother saying? He had never heard her talk like this before.

"Go!" she said, almost screaming at him. "Do it!"

The boys ran out of the house. William, holding the single-shot breech loader, turned to his friend. "I was supposed to go fishin,' but I guess I've got to go killin'."

Otto gave Guy a reassuring squeeze of his shoulder. "You're safe now. They won't harm you here."

The boy shivered, his body shaking as if he were freezing. "Sh-Sh-Sh-She told me how they k-k-killed him. They had no reason to, b-b-but they did it anyway."

"Who are you talkin' about?"

"Edward Fitch."

Otto's stomach knotted in disgust. Mr. Fitch was more than Otto's favorite bookseller. He was a kind man who'd never harmed anyone. "What happened?"

"Mrs. Fitch and her three children were s-s-sitting on the grass away from their b-b-burning house. She cried a lot. But then she talked and she said the murderers sh-sh-shot him in the doorway. To make sure he was dead, they kept shooting him. Then they set fire to the house and-and-and poor Mrs. Fitch—"

Otto patted Guy's shoulder and waited for the boy to catch his breath.

"—poor Mrs. Fitch," Guy said, "sh-sh-she wanted to drag her dead husband outside, b-b-but they wouldn't let her."

Otto was about to curse in disgust when he remembered his children were nearby. "Then what happened?"

"She told me she just s-s-stood there in the house while it was burning, w-w-wondering why this was happening. They got her out of that house. B-B-But while Ed's body lay in the d-d-doorway of the burning building, one of the men went back in, t-t-took off the man's boots, put them on, and w-w-walked away."

No more, Otto thought, fuming. No more. Those pigs were not going to get away with this.

The boy slumped on Otto's shoulder. "I just wish I knew."

"Knew what, son?"

"If my f-f-father's still alive. They burned down his store. D-D-Don't know where h-h-he is."

These terrorists had to be stopped, Otto thought. Enough is enough. He reached for the revolver the young raider had given him and hoped it was loaded. Then he went up close to the entrance and listened for the sound of the next intruder that might appear.

Tinker awoke when he felt something licking his cheek. It was an average-size dog, all white except for a black spot around his eye.

"What the—?" Tinker was surprised at finding himself lying on a sidewalk, a burning building towering above him.

The heat was scorching, and he instinctively rose up and started to run. Only then did he realize he had blood on his hands. Was he dead? He looked down at his chest and noticed a large dent in the center of his medallion. His chest had a circular, purplish-blue bruise, right where the medallion was. Nellie's relic had stopped a bullet!

His head was spinning. A sharp pain on the side of his head. He put his hand to it. Bloody. A bullet must have grazed him. He looked up at the roaring flames. The dog that had befriended him barked.

Tinker, coughing from the smoking debris about him, noticed that the dog wouldn't leave. "What d'yah want from me?"

The dog barked again, ran back a few steps, then ran back to him again, still barking.

It dawned on Tinker that the building above him was about to collapse. He got up immediately and rushed through the clouds of black smoke. The white dog would stop every so often and wait for Tinker to catch up with him. "I'm-a comin', doggie, I'm a comin'."

Tinker followed the dog until he got to the middle of Vermont Street, where the animal disappeared. He looked around and saw a guerilla brandishing a pistol at Jessica in front of an empty lot. Penelope was there too, trying to free herself from another man who was restraining her from behind. *I gots to do something, Tinker* thought. *But I ain't got no gun.*

After Sam Toby made Larkin Skaggs bring Penelope under control, he waved his revolver in front of Jessica's face. Jessica saw Tinker, his head already bloodied, standing behind him. She wished Tinker, who appeared astonished at what he saw, would run away. Maybe he could dart over to the brick wall over to his left and hide. He'd certainly be killed by the next horseman riding up the street. "Run, Tinker!" she shouted.

"Who yah talkin' to, nigger-lovin' white trash?" Sam snarled, his stare still fixed on her. "Yah know, yah never did take it all off for me in yah Pa's cornfield."

Jessica, her hand inside her dress pocket, fingered her Colt revolver.

"That nigger girl of yahs," Sam added, slurring his words, "I really enjoyed lettin' her know what a real man felt like. What was that bitch's name—Nellie?"

Jessica wondered what his ugly face would look like with bullet holes in it. *Killing him would be so easy, so quick...forgiveness, more difficult.*

"She was nothin' but a whore," Sam grunted. "That's all she was."

"How dare you, you depraved, vulgar pig!" *I've got to pull this trigger. ...No, Jessica, let him go.*

"Y'know," he continued, "yah Pa done give me a hard time when I shot him..."

I can't forgive him, Sissy. ...No! You must forgive.

"He shot me twice'n missed," Sam laughed. "Then he ran back for a knife'n called me a name I didn't 'preciate."

Three shots into his pig face. ...No, Jessica! Hate begets hate.

"And yah Ma," Toby continued, "well, she done call me names, too. I didn't kill her with mah gun. No suh, I shot both her legs so she don't walk. I made a good fire in the house, and then I threw her in. She scream, tryin' to get out, scream like a sick cat, she did."

Jessica whipped out her gun.

Sam's mouth dropped open.

Claire's young face...*Her scream*...My promise to Sissy. *I forgive you, Sam. There! I said it.* Jessica lowered her gun.

Sam laughed as he pointed his gun at her and cocked it. "Yer gonna die, woman."

Instinctively, Jessica shot him. She surprised herself at her reflexive action.

Sam, his widened eyes protruding through a frozen mask of shock, stumbled and dropped to the ground. His angry mouth remained open, his final words never spoken.

Larkin Skaggs took aim at Jessica. "Damn you, bitch!" he shouted. Just then a shot rang out, knocking off his hat. Otto Heller had just climbed out of the cellar and smoke was rising from a revolver in his hand. "Bastard!" he screamed as he shot a second time, missing Skaggs again.

Skaggs took off, running for his horse. Tinker, his face drenched in sweat, ran toward Jessica. "Are yah all right, Miz Radford?"

345

Jessica nodded, her trembling fingers over her mouth.

Otto looked at Sam's dead body and surveyed the street for any sign of Quantrill's band of raiders. "Maybe they're gone. But I'll make sure Penelope stays below with the children to be safe. How are you doing, Jessica?"

"I've forgiven him," she said quietly.

Otto cupped his ear with his hand. "What? I couldn't hear you."

"Never mind."

Tinker pointed to a white dog with a black mark around its eye. It looked at Tinker for a moment and barked.

Tinker shook his head. "If it not be for him I be dead man."

Jessica was about to ask him what he meant when the sound of approaching horses interrupted her.

Otto looked around. "Hurry!" he shouted. "Behind that brick wall."

Within moments, three horsemen stopped at the very spot where they had just been. Jessica peeked from behind the wall. It was William Quantrill himself, along with two others.

The white dog, unperturbed by the presence of the strangers, sniffed around the entire perimeter of Sam's body.

Quantrill pointed to the corpse. "That's the swine Sam Toby who's been foolin' around with my Kate," Quantrill said. "Nothing but scum."

The dog lifted its leg and peed on the dead man's face. All three men laughed.

"Even the dog agrees!" Quantrill sneered. "I want Sam outa my sight. Hey, Gregg—you and Todd carry his dumb dead ass out of here and dump him in the fire across the street. I want nothing left of him but ashes, y'hear?"

"Yessir, Bill."

Todd and Gregg dismounted and carried out the order. With great effort, they heaved Sam's body into a burning building. When they returned and mounted their horses, Quantrill told them he planned to do the same thing with Larkin Skaggs. "Have either of you seen him?" he asked.

"No sir, Bill," Gregg replied.

Todd nodded. "Same here.

"Well. I'm gonna kill that moron with my own hands when I find him. Can't believe he killed my friend Nathan Stone. Even tried stealin' Lydia's diamond ring. Drunken fool!"

"Might not have time to find him, "Gregg said. "Union troops a-comin'."

"We best going then. Let's round up the others." Giving his horse a swift kick, he took off, with the others following. Soon the sound of horses' hooves faded.

"It might be safe now," Otto said, moving out from behind the wall.

Jessica looked about. Black columns of smoke arose everywhere. Weeping now replaced the sounds of gunfire. Women walked through the wreckage, hoping to find something or somebody important to them. Lawrence was a graveyard. The world had gone insane.

"I guess we've seen man at his worst," she said.

Tinker's face, still bloodied, scanned the smoke-laden sky. "Yeah. Hate come so easy to people."

The white dog, wagging its tail happily, approached Tinker. Tinker, his sour face surveying the destruction, petted the animal.

"We still got lots to learn 'bout gettin' along. Lots to learn."

—the end—

Book Discussion Questions

1. Discuss Jessica Radford's fear of the Colt .31 weapon she owned. Is this compatible with her characterization as a free-thinking, independent woman who was not afraid of doing chores men would normally do?

2. How do you think Jessica felt about Matt Lightfoot when she returned home from college? Did that feeling change later, and if so, how?

3. Did you feel the slave girl Nellie showed signs of unusual insight into human character?

4. Who was Sissy before she became an angel and what lesson did she want to impart to Jessica?

5. What made Jessica finally decide to disguise herself as a man and fight?

6. How did the experience of the war change Jessica? How did it change Matt?

7. What feelings did Jessica have for John Howell? How did those feelings differ from how she felt about Matt Lightfoot?

8. What did you find unusual about the character of Roger Toby? What were the similarities and differences with his twin brother Sam?

9. What event was the singular turning point in Jessica's life? Why?

10. Tinker, Ishmael, Lazarus, and Devin were all black soldiers. Were they essentially the same or quite different from one another? For which of these four did you feel the greatest sympathy? Which one surprised you the most?

11. Which characters did you admire the most, and why?

12. Why do you think Otto made reference to *Hebrews 13, 2-3* near to where he posted the names of the slaves he had rescued? How does it relate to Jessica meeting Sissy on the battlefield?

13. Why did Jessica later try so hard to forgive Sam Toby for what he had done?

14. Where there scenes in the book where you were surprised by the sense of compassion a character emoted?

15. How do you feel about Matt's dilemma about combat during a war and his obedience to the Fifth Commandment?

You Will Certainly Enjoy the Next Novel of the Jessica Radford Trilogy

Tom Mach's intriguing second novel, a well-researched historical novel entitled *All Parts Together*, continues the Jessica Radford saga. You will want to know about what happens to Ms. Radford after the Quantrill and how she ends up meeting Abraham Lincoln.

Hill Song Press
P. O. Box 486
Lawrence, KS 66044
email: hillsong@sunflower.com

You may also obtain additional copies of *SISSY!* by ordering directly from the publisher at:
www.hillsongpress.com